"I MISSED YOU when you went away," I said to Trevor.

I hadn't meant to say that. It had surfaced out of old longing and loneliness. In any case, my words hadn't reached past the guard he seemed to wear. I hated the roughening of his voice as he answered me.

"I'm not that man anymore. No more than you're the young girl I remember from those days."

"Perhaps that's regrettable." I tried to sound light and casual in order to hide the small hurt that stabbed through me. "I wonder what happened to us?"

He paused in the doorway. "I think you know," he said, and went away.

How well I knew. I had married his brother, David.

PHYLLIS A. WHITNEY

The Glass Flame

FAWCETT CREST • NEW YORK

THE GLASS FLAME

THIS BOOK CONTAINS THE COMPLETE TEXT OF THE
ORIGINAL HARDCOVER EDITION.

Published by Fawcett Crest Books, a unit of CBS Publications,
the Consumer Publishing Division of CBS Inc., by arrangement
with Doubleday and Company, Inc.

Excerpt from "Kudzu", Copyright © 1963 by James Dickey.
Reprinted from *Poems 1957–1967*, by permission of Wesleyan
University Press. "Kudzu" first appeared in *The New Yorker.*

ISBN: 0-449-24130-0

Alternate Selection of the Literary Guild
Selection of the Doubleday Book Club

Printed in the United States of America

10   9   8   7   6   5   4   3   2   1

For my very dear friend,
Lee Wyndham

With my affectionate thanks to Bernice A. Stevens and Alice E. Zimmerman, craftsmen, of Skyhigh, near Gatlinburg, Tennessee. Not only for introducing me to the beautiful Great Smoky Mountains, but also for driving me so untiringly around that Tennessee and North Carolina area.

My thanks as well to Marjorie Mortensen, who generously took me back of the scenes in an architect's office.

To my readers: Don't expect to find Trevor's lake or the hotel Greencastle if you visit Gatlinburg. Nor do any of these characters live outside of my imagination. The kudzu vine, however, is very real, and the open-air theater exists, though in a different location. All else is as true to this beautiful area as I could make it.

I was only a few miles from Gatlinburg when the sign pointing right caught my eye: *Belle Isle*. I hadn't intended to stop until I reached Trevor Andrews' house, but the name compelled me. This was the place to which my husband, David Hallam, had come. This was where he had died. His burying still lay ahead of me, with all the problems and questions it would involve.

The car I'd rented at the Knoxville airport carried me a little past the sign before I made up my mind and turned around, found my way back to the side road. Gravel crunched under my wheels and in the growing September dusk tree shadows fell across the way, so that I drove into a tunnel of green gloom. Three miles, the sign had said, and I drove slowly, reluctantly, unable to help myself.

I shouldn't be doing this—I knew I shouldn't! Especially not while I was in this numb and shattered state.

Only ten days ago I'd had a letter from David. A furious letter. He'd even left out the "Dear Karen" of a salutation, spilling out more of the anger he'd felt for me at the time he left New York. I had expected that. David had never let any possession of his go easily—not even when it was something he no longer wanted. When I had told him that I would leave him, his rage had been frightening, and there had been moments when I'd feared that the physical hurt he might do me would be worse than on occasions in the past. I was slight and not very tall—hardly equipped to stand up to as big a man as David. After he left for Tennessee on his new assignment, I could feel only relief for this borrowed time.

However, there had been more in his letter than the usual threats to disturb me. Something seemed to have alarmed him, threatened *him,* for a change. "If anything happens to me down here," he wrote, "don't let it pass as an accident. You owe me that, Karen. You've owed me since the day we were married."

It was dreadful that this should be true. After the first year I had known that the blame for our marrying must be shared, yet at the same time, mine was the greater fault. That was what he meant by the debt I owed him. Now I had my own futile sense of guilt to drive me.

When the phone call had come from the police a few days ago, it seemed the inevitable fulfillment of David's warning, yet it was a shock at the same time. There was a strangeness in the grief I felt. Grief for the wreckage of a marriage that had ended years ago, and that I would have broken off sooner if I hadn't been afraid of his rages. I had never really faced the fact that if I stayed *I* was responsible for what happened to me. There is always a door to be walked through, yet I'd lacked the courage to open it until recently. Now, nevertheless, there was a rather terrible pity in me for the loss of all that dark drive that had characterized David. He had always seemed to me indestructible, though he had been perfectly able to destroy.

Belle Isle and the fires! This was where the ending for David had come. Perhaps the greatest irony lay in the fact that Trevor Andrews had sent for him to come here. Trevor, the older half brother with whom David had grown up, and of whom he had been bitterly jealous all his life.

Fires were David's business. When he had come home wounded from Vietnam, he had gone to work for a company which investigated fires for insurance firms all around the country. And for the first time he had stuck to what he was doing and had become amazingly successful at his work.

I had been surprised when David had responded to Trevor's call for help. The estrangement had never been Trevor's fault—perhaps the blame was mostly mine, though Trevor had never known that. David had seemed amused by the letter from his brother, and after a day or two of consideration he had asked his company to send him down. That he should have died in a fire at Belle Isle was doubly ironic and tragic.

Ahead of me trees opened on either hand and the road divided to circle a jewel of a lake tucked into its pocket of mountains. Here in the valley dusk came early, with the ranges that formed the Great Smokies cutting off the sun. Traces of rose and amber still painted the rippled water, lending light to the scene. Out in the center the island that gave the place its name was a smudge of black, with rosy water lapping its shores. Like a reflection of fire.

I could understand why Trevor Andrews had chosen this lovely spot for his project. Belle Isle was not any standard jerry-built "development," but the dream of a gifted and distinguished architect. Ever since I was a young girl I had followed Trevor's career, taking pride in his successes, remembering the days when he used to come to my parents' home in New York to draw encouragement and wisdom from my father's generous fund. I'd been no more than sixteen at the time and Trevor had been my first love, worshiped from afar—my first fantasy of love. How vital he had seemed with all that dynamic energy and creativity fairly pouring from him.

Of course he had hardly known that I existed, except as a rather shy young girl who crept in to listen and—though he didn't know it—adore. For me it was a time of secret happiness and dreaming. Later, when I was grown, I was to photograph his imaginative and sometimes spectacular houses many times for *Country Home Magazine,* which employed me. Though I doubted that he knew who was behind the uncredited pictures.

There was further irony in the fact that the attack upon Trevor's houses had been due to arson—that heinous and most frightening of crimes—and that it had been this crime that had brought my husband, Trevor's brother, here to his death.

In the growing dusk it was hard to see the houses clearly, but I could make out well-spaced structures fronting the lake shore beneath a great many trees. Trevor was never one to bulldoze a property heedlessly, and I imagined that the average builder would have hated him. No one lived here as yet. The project was still in the course of being created. I chose the left-hand road around the lake and drove slowly. The first fires had done some damage, I understood, but the last one had been complete.

When I came upon what was left of the house it was with a sickening sense of shock. I braked my car and, drawn by a nameless dread, I got out and walked between damaged maple trees that had shaded a still-unpaved path —to what had once been a house. A portion of it rose roofless against the sky like a dark skeleton. One corner of the frame was left, a stone chimney, and a hollow doorway, blackened and lifeless. From that one corner a window shape empty of glass stared at me without soul, and I could smell the acrid stench. The rest had been blown apart by the explosion, destroyed by fire, and lay all around in splintered and burned wood, crumbled plaster and broken stone.

That was the awful thing—that this house had been *set* to explode, and David had been inside when it happened.

I went no closer, but stopped where I was. "David?" I spoke aloud softly, as though his spirit might answer me. It was not to the David of that last letter that I called, but to the almost forgotten man who had wooed me and to whom I had turned in my eagerness for love, never admitting to myself that this was all make-believe. In fact, for a little while it had been real enough, and it was to the memory of that young and tender love that I called. Even though I knew now what a pretense the tenderness had been. A breeze stirred the treetops, coming down from the mountains, but the ruined house gave me back no answer. I could almost hear the crackle and roar of flames, and glimpse the red of fire against a darkening sky.

When a hand touched my arm I stifled a scream and turned about in alarm. The man before me wore a brown jacket above khaki pants, a visored cap shading his eyes. In the growing dusk his expression was disapproving.

"You looking for something, miss?"

Only the past, I thought. Only for answers. But obviously he was a watchman and I explained quickly.

"I'm Mrs. Hallam. I'm on my way to Mr. Andrews' house. I—I just turned off when I saw the sign."

He became solicitous at once. "Maybe you shouldn't have come here so soon, ma'am. Not all by yourself like this. Better go back to your car."

I stood my ground, though I felt ill and shaken. "Tell me about what happened?" This was the question I was to ask so many times, that I *must* ask at every turn—because of David's letter.

He was clearly uneasy. "I wasn't around then, ma'am. They, fired the other fellow. Reckon he went to sleep on the job. But Mr. Andrews came down right after it happened. You better ask him."

I took three wobbly steps and then leaned on his arm as he walked me back to the car.

"You okay?" he asked. "You sure you can drive all right?"

"I'll be fine," I said. "I'll just sit here for a little while. It's been a—a shock."

Once I was in the driver's seat he backed away and disappeared on his watchman's rounds. I put my arms on the wheel and leaned my head against it, while disconnected thoughts flowed through my mind.

David hadn't stayed with Trevor and Lori Andrews when he came down here, though Trevor had invited him to their house. In spite of the fact that they had shared the same mother, all David's old resentment and jealousy of his half brother still possessed him so strongly that I had wondered why he'd come at all. There had never been resentment on Trevor's part, but always an effort to understand and to make peace with his younger half brother. When he came to New York, Trevor sometimes took David to lunch, though David never brought him to our apartment. What motivated my husband wasn't anything Trevor could understand—he was too big and generous for that. Never once, I was sure, had Trevor suspected my own unhappy role in the antagonism David exhibited toward him.

How strange to remember that it was Trevor who had brought David to my father's house in the beginning, proud of his handsome younger brother. My father had been a noted architect in his day. His books were still gospel in the field and he had been a fine teacher and lecturer as well. When a stroke paralyzed him, he continued to give of himself from his bed and armchair to those who came to learn—Trevor among them. And Trevor, eventually, had brought his brother David with him.

David had been nearer my age, and sixteen didn't seem so hopelessly young to him. In those days David resembled Trevor physically far more than he did later. Unfortunately, David, always alert when it came to feeding his jealousy, saw what Trevor never glimpsed at that time— my adoration for the older brother. Perhaps for David that was enough. He kept his eye on me from then on, made his own plans to distract me, win me away—overwhelm me. The most dangerous thing—for me—was that resemblance to his brother. They had the same tall build and the dark hair that swept back in a slight wave from a wide forehead. Their hands, especially, were alike—strong and long-fingered. David had as well certain mannerisms that he had picked up from Trevor. A way of turning his head, a gesture of dismissal when he was impatient, an intent, studying look, though Trevor's eyes were gray, and David's brown. No matter how I tried not to, I kept seeing Trevor in David, and that meant disaster for me. I was all too ready for love, and David had no scruples about taking advantage of that fact. Nevertheless, no one had forced me to marry him. I had done that of my own free will, betraying us both.

Emotionally, I suppose, I was bound to him, even before the outside world intervened and he was the brother who went to Vietnam. Trevor hated the war and was fortunate enough to miss the draft. All the while he was gone David wrote to me fervently, and I wrote back. After all, David had become my "real" love, while Trevor was only a dreamed-of ideal—perhaps superimposed to some extent upon a David I didn't really know—for all that I thought I did.

While David was out of the country, my father died, and Mother went to pieces rather badly. I would never forget Trevor's kindness to me at the funeral and the way he stood beside me attempting to comfort, though grieving himself. Those had been the closest moments I'd ever shared with him.

Afterward, he had come to the house a few times to see Mother and me, and I think that on the last time he came I let him glimpse too much of my adoration. I was growing up, and he was tender and careful with me. But when he left that time, he didn't come back. How I'd despised myself for being hopelessly young and immature, and I had written even more warmly to David.

I was determined to grow up fast and be fully a *femme fatale* by the time *he* came home. In the meantime months passed and I moved into my own place and found my own absorbing work.

David returned wounded—he would walk with a slight limp from then on, though that never hampered him in getting about. I went to see him at the hospital, and such weakness in a man who had been so strong physically broke my heart. He was still terribly like Trevor in appearance—he was the nearest I could get to Trevor, and I had already convinced myself of my love for him. Never once did I face the danger of reality that might lie ahead, and we entered into a sort of taken-for-granted engagement.

When Trevor married Lori Caton and an invitation to their wedding came for David, he had shown it to me and then torn it up. At the birth of their son there had been an announcement, and behind David's back I'd sent a gift. After David and I were married, it was I who sent greetings at Christmas, and presents for Chris, until a year or two ago when David had put a stop to that. Now Chris was ten—and though David and I had been married nearly eight years, we had no children, which was just as well. Once I had longed with all my heart for a son, a daughter. Later that wish was buried, obliterated—because I wanted no child of David's who might inherit his dangerous rages, his closeness at times to a paranoia he would never admit. To say nothing of the fact that he was not cut out for fatherhood.

After he had recovered from his wound, David had gone into the exciting work that he found so much to his taste—the investigating of fires and the tracking down of arsonists. He had a flair for ferreting out arson and I was proud of the way he advanced in his company until he was one of the best men in the country at his job. I tried to give him what support I could in his work—since I knew I had failed him in other ways. As, indeed, he had failed me as well.

Now I had come to Tennessee to bury my husband, and I couldn't ignore the warning in the letter he had written me—that if anything happened to him, I must not let it pass as an accident. His words reached out from death and set an obligation upon me that I couldn't side-step, no matter what our last years together had been.

When at last I raised my head from the wheel of the

car I found Belle Isle nearly dark, with only a little light in the western sky. Something in me seemed to have burned away to ashes as dead as those of the house where David had lost his life. Cold ashes, incapable of ever again quickening to flame. It was better that way and I accepted.

The headlights of my car cut the darkness as I switched them on. I should have gone while there was more daylight and I could better follow Trevor's directions. He had wanted to meet my plane at Knoxville, but I had put off the moment of facing him. I would need a car while I was in Tennessee, I told him, so I would rent one at the airport and be able to move about more freely. He had agreed and sent instructions for finding the house.

I drove slowly away from Belle Isle and back to the highway, watching for signs.

When the authorities had phoned four days ago to tell me what had happened, they had first suggested that not much purpose would be served in my coming down. Because of the violence of the explosion and the fire that had followed, destroying everything in its path, a full-scale investigation was under way. The county sheriff had called again yesterday when they were sure about David. Did I want the remains shipped north? Horrid words, yet kinder in their blunt way than delicate allusions would have been. I said I would come down at once.

By that time Trevor had been on the phone to me several times, and I had been invited to stay with him and his wife, if I wanted to come. I told myself that I was a grown woman now and that first love was years behind me. It was no more than a faint twinge of memory now and then, a distant, nostalgic sadness for something that had never been. In the last few years I had raised a protective barrier against feeling anything. Love had proved a delusion, and I would never again allow my own treacherous emotions to surface. I wonder how many women have told themselves that, while old yearnings go underground, waiting their chance to surface and take over again?

When I heard the sound of Trevor's voice on the phone I was furious at the unguarded leaping of my heart. I knew then that I would surely see him, even though I told myself I didn't want to. But I had to go to Tennessee so I assured the police that I would come, and let Trevor know I would be happy to accept his invitation. There were obligations I wouldn't avoid.

Now I was here, where David was born, where he would have wanted to stay. His mother had been born here and lived in these mountains while she was married to Trevor's father. Trevor had been born here too, and when Trevor's father died and his mother married again, the family had lived on in the area, moving north when David was in his teens. David's roots were here, and it was here that I would bury him.

But David had not died by fire alone, nor by the devastating explosion. I was convinced of that. The question of his death was a legacy he had left me and I understood very well that it was not something I could turn from lightly. Not when it might have been—murder.

My turnoff up the mountain should be near now, and I mustn't miss the sign. All sunset traces had gone as clouds moved in and the rain had started. I turned on my windshield wipers and slowed the car still more, peering ahead. In a moment my brights illuminated the curving arrow and I turned left off the highway onto a rough gravel road that climbed through the woods.

It was very dark and a little misty under the trees and I drove carefully, aware of a drop-off on my left and a road that turned perilously as it climbed. As my beams swung, lighting swathes of tall trees around the turns, I began to feel confused. Trevor had written that his house was on the crest of the mountain—so surely I couldn't miss it. Yet I seemed to have been turning back and forth around the curves for too long a while. There were only trees around me and the rainy mists below, with never a house in view. Not that there were many houses on this mountainside, as Trevor had said—only two of his design, and perhaps three others on the lower slopes.

Suddenly the woods parted ahead of me, and I drove into an open space before a house. The road ended here and in this high place there was a little more light. In relief I switched off the motor, and a moment later I was out of the car on a blacktop expanse. From this spot the trees stopped rising up the mountain, and the earth seemed to drop away into invisibility around the clearing.

Rain was coming down harder than I'd realized. I wore only a light coat, with no covering for my head, and my face and hair were wet by the time I'd dashed for the nearest door of the house. I could just glimpse a low, winged structure cantilevered out over the mountainside.

Ahead of me shone a lighted window, and as I ran a door opened, flinging further warmth and light across my path. Trevor came out beneath the overhang, dressed in jeans and gray turtleneck, and for an instant of shock I thought, "David!" Then he had an arm around me, drawing me into a vast kitchen with polished, wide-board floor, walls of wormy chestnut, and the welcome odor of brewing coffee.

"Get out of that wet coat," he ordered, and helped to pull it from me. There was no time to examine the flood of emotion that swept through me, or even know what it meant. Except that it frightened me. No barrier built with years of effort should go down so suddenly. In chagrin I recalled my thoughts of burned-out ashes of only a little while before. Had there been a remaining spark all along to light a conflagration?

But no—I wouldn't allow that. Not ever.

"I'll get your bags from the car," he said. "Sit here by the fire and get warm. Here's a towel for your hair." His words were peremptory, but not unkind.

A kitchen with an old-fashioned hearth and a welcome fire to warm me! I pulled up a cherry wood chair and bent over so heat would dry my hair as I toweled it, glad for its short straight cut that nothing could muss for long. David had disapproved when I cut my hair—but then, David had disapproved of so much. It was difficult to realize that he was dead and no longer to be fought or resented. I still moved in that limbo which the living experience for a time after a death. Life goes on in an ordinary manner, ordinary things are done, everyday conversation indulged in—because one is marking time, and reality hasn't yet cut through. Perhaps when the funeral was over I could think more clearly, know better what to do. I would then recognize myself in the new role of widow—free to be my own woman. Yet in a sense not free because of the terrible legacy David had left me.

Trevor returned in a few moments, having parked my car out of the way. He set my bags down in the wide hall and came into the kitchen to busy himself setting out mugs on a table of cherry wood rubbed to a dull glow. Now, for the first time, I was able to observe him. His greeting, his arm about me as he rushed me out of the rain, had seemed warm and welcoming, and he had taken charge. But already there had been a withdrawal from old friendship, a coolness I didn't understand. It was better that way—better for me.

He looked the same, only a little older. Thirty-eight to my twenty-eight. And perhaps thinner than I remembered. Tall, with wide shoulders, physically strong, as David had been, his thick, straight hair like David's as darkly brown as my own. My heart was doing a sick thumping that I could feel at the base of my throat, and I was swept by waves of mindless emotion that I didn't want to feel. *I* was not that sixteen-year-old who was imprisoned in the past and trying to assert herself now. All she stood for belonged to long ago, and had no right to seize me now. Yet the senses have a memory of their own, and I had never dreamed that seeing Trevor again would shake me like this. Had I never stopped loving him?

Again I denied. That was a thought I couldn't, wouldn't accept. I must think only of David—dead.

"Lori and Chris are away in Asheville," he told me. "They'll probably be home tomorrow." There was a note in his voice that I didn't remember—something not as clear and strong and joyous as I'd known in the past. Clearly I couldn't help thinking of the living as well as the dead.

Trevor had always been enormously, vitally sure of himself, sure of what he wanted to do. Not with David's arrogant assurance—a front he put up to impress others, but a true certainty, a confidence growing out of his creative talent and his enjoyment of it, out of his own knowledge of who he was and what space in life he meant to occupy. Yet into the voice whose timbre I remembered so well there had crept a note that I didn't like or understand. Something in Trevor had hardened, something had changed him. I'd never met Lori, though I'd often wondered about her. Now I wondered again, fleetingly.

"Coffee?" Trevor asked.

"Thank you. I'll take it black."

He poured two mugs full from the bubbling percolator and brought me mine. I saw that the mug had been hand

turned on a potter's wheel, and was finished in a dull
brown glaze with robin's-egg blue on the inside.

"It's local, isn't it?" I said. "Beautiful."

"Yes. The Highland crafts are good and I've used
them through the house wherever I can."

He stood beside the stone hearth, looking down at me,
the chill in his eyes lessening a little.

"I'd have known you anywhere," he said. "You always
resembled your father. You're slim like your mother, but
you can thrust your chin out the way your father used to,
and you have that same dark, searching look."

I dropped my gaze, unwilling to meet his eyes lest I tell
too much. I was angry with myself because of this betrayal
of my own senses. But at least I had sense enough to know
that I must resist such inner treachery.

"As you always looked like David," I said pointedly.

The chill returned and that was safer for me.

"People used to tell me there was a likeness, though I
could never see it," he said. "What do you do with yourself these days, Karen?"

There was no reason why he should have known. David
certainly wouldn't have told him, since he had always disliked my being successful at what I did. An unwanted
memory flashed through my mind of David smashing a
new and expensive camera because I'd angered him and
he couldn't endure even the small name I was making for
myself. He had been as jealous of my work as he had
always been of his brother's. Until he had gone into fire
insurance and investigation, he had failed at job after job,
always believing that he deserved better. So that the successes of others—especially Trevor's—diminished him.
That was one reason I'd been glad of his expert work in
the past few years, since there would be less tendency to
fling out at me in resentment when I got a raise, or an
especially good assignment.

Trevor was waiting for my answer, and I caught my thoughts back from the past, grateful for small talk that would keep me for a little while from all that lay ahead. Perhaps Trevor understood this—if he was still as sensitive as I remembered.

"I work on *Country Home Magazine*," I said. "I started on layout, but somehow I fell into the photographing of houses."

"Aside from being your father's daughter, why do you photograph houses?"

No one had ever asked me that before, and I couldn't answer him easily. "Both photography and architecture have always fascinated me. Once or twice on the magazine I was sent out to take pictures of a house, and the prints turned out well. After a while, I was doing it as a regular part of my work. Just modern houses—they send someone else to do the old mansions and period pieces. I've photographed a number of yours, as a matter of fact."

"So that's all there was to it? An accident you fell into?"

I shook my head. "I don't think it was altogether accidental. Not after all those hours I spent sitting in a corner of Dad's library listening to him talk with you about architecture. After a while I began to see with my own eyes, and I wanted to record what I saw. I've always felt that houses have a life of their own once they're off the drawing board. They can be beautiful or ugly, imaginative, ordinary. At different times of day, in different lights, they say different things. I suppose I try to get them to talk to me before I take their pictures."

This was the longest speech about houses and picture-taking I'd ever made. But now perhaps I could talk to Trevor—where I had been so terribly young and tongue-tied in the past.

His expression had softened again and I knew he was

remembering those days when he had come to our house. "You sound like your father's daughter. What do houses tell you when they talk?"

I considered that. "The exterior tells me about the designer, of course. Whether he's bold and innovative. Whether he's practical and remembers that people have to live in his houses. Whether he respects the landscape or is a tree killer. Whether he's content to be stodgy and imitate what's been done before. Or perhaps has an inventive flair."

"All that?" he said. "What have my houses told you?"

The direct question made me suddenly self-conscious. Who was I to be talking to Trevor Andrews about houses? Especially about *his* houses.

"Go ahead—tell me," he urged. His heavy dark brows had lifted, not in disapproval, but questioning, as though my opinion interested him.

I picked up my shreds of courage and stared into the fire. It was hard to concentrate on words when I looked directly into Trevor's face.

"Sometimes your houses frighten me a little. I'm not sure I would want to live in one. There's a—a sort of defiance about them. As though you were daring the world to disagree with you. Yet at the same time they can be secret, private houses—hard to understand and photograph. I wonder what my father would have thought of them."

The dark eyebrows raised a fraction more. "Maybe you're right. Though no one has ever put it just that way to me before."

Strangely, I began to feel more comfortable with him, more relaxed, sitting here in this kitchen. He hadn't ridiculed my words, but seemed to respect them. And my idiot heart had stopped its wild thumping. I would be able to get used to Trevor again. After all, I was long accustomed to watching from a distance, and I'd never expected anything closer. I was safe because even if he might have suspected a crush, he'd never dreamed of how deeply I felt. Now he was married and had a son, and I could resist him safely.

Silence grew between us as we sipped coffee, and into that silence the memory of David began to emerge from the shadows where we had been mutely holding him. Once long ago I had thought that David's long-fingered hands were like Trevor's. Now, as Trevor turned the mug in his fingers, I thought how like his hands were to David's, and my resistance grew. This man was David's brother, and that should be enough to put me on guard. I wasn't sixteen now, and I didn't know the man he might have become.

"I want to hear about what happened," I said into the waiting stillness. "I want to know everything about David's death."

There was a change in my voice, and again I sensed withdrawal and a chilling of the atmosphere between us. Trevor had indeed changed. He had always been generous to David, offering friendship and affection, even when David rejected him. But now the mere mention of his brother's name seemed to make him stiffen.

"Let's leave it for tomorrow," he said. "You must be tired from your trip and the drive. Talking will be painful, and if we talk now you may not sleep."

"A little while ago I stopped at Belle Isle," I told him.

The sound his mug made as he thumped it down on the cherry wood table broke the quiet of the room, but he did not speak. In the fireplace charred wood fell into embers and I stared at blackened ashes, shivering, remembering. When Trevor bent above the hearth and poked at the fire, putting on another log, I knew he was waiting for me to continue.

"I saw the Belle Isle sign," I said. "I had to follow that road. I couldn't help myself. When I reached the house I got out of my car and went close enough—to see—" I broke off and closed my eyes.

Behind me Trevor moved restlessly about the room, offering no sympathy, no comforting words.

I made an effort to go on. "Your watchman found me. He spoke to me and helped me back to the car. I don't think what had happened to David really hit me until then. I suppose I've been numb with shock. Now I'm beginning to feel. I'm trying to accept the awful way he died. If you'll tell me about it, perhaps that will help."

"All right," Trevor said abruptly. He pulled a straight chair across the hearth from me. "Perhaps it's better if you know exactly what happened. How much did David tell you about our affairs down here?"

"Not very much. He wasn't very good at writing letters." Not until that last one, I thought. But I didn't want to mention that letter yet.

"Belle Isle was a dream I had," Trevor went on. "It still is. I don't mean to be defeated because of all that has happened. I won't go into the ramifications now, but it was coming along well. Some of the houses were finished and people were interested. I was encouraged by the way everything was shaping up. I've been completely in charge, and there has been some resentment over that—another long story. I have four years to make it work. And two are gone already. A few months ago fires began to be set in the place. One was in a completed house down by the lake, and three were on the near side. The first was only a small fire, and we caught it in time." He appeared to hesitate, as though remembering something disturbing, then went on. "We thought it might have been started by —children. The later fires did more damage, and were expertly set.

"The police couldn't find out anything in the beginning, and I thought of David. We've been in touch now and then over the years, as you may know, and he was the best man in the country for the job. So I asked him to come. I didn't know whether he would agree or not. I was even a little surprised when he turned up."

"He stayed much longer than he usually does on an investigation," I put in.

Trevor too had been staring into the fire as he talked, but now he turned his head and looked at me sharply. His expression startled me, and with sudden clarity I recognized that here was a man in whom a shattering anger was being suppressed. Yet in the time when I had known him, Trevor had never been an angry man.

"Yes, David stayed," he told me shortly, the words clipped, the anger barely hidden.

"Something's wrong, isn't it?" I said. "Something's terribly wrong. Something besides the fires."

He held back whatever rage had seethed to the surface and forced himself to speak quietly. "David stayed. He appeared to be onto something. But he wouldn't tell anyone until he was sure. This last fire wasn't like the others. This time an explosive was used."

"The watchman said you were there soon after it happened."

"I was. David had told me he had a feeling that one particular house would go next. The fires were always set in one that was nearly finished. So he was going down to spend the night there. I offered to come with him, but he said that with two of us it would be harder to hide. And he was fully confident that he could handle anything that came up."

Yes—that was David. How well I remembered his swaggering confidence—a confidence that had not always been justified, until recently.

Trevor continued. "I was uneasy that night, and I kept a watch here at our house. I heard the explosion from our deck and I saw the flames. As soon as I'd called the fire department I drove down. The house was an inferno, with blown-out bits of debris burning all around. David was in there and I knew there was no way to save him. We tried, but the heat was too fierce and we couldn't investigate properly until the flames were out and the smoke had cleared a bit. I was with them when the police and the firemen found—what was left of him."

I listened, sickened, my eyes never leaving Trevor's face. I saw him tighten one fist and ram it hard against the palm of the other hand. After a long silence he seemed to remember me.

"I'm sorry to be brutal. But since you wanted the truth, it had to be told the way it happened. The sheriff has found out nothing except that a trap must have been prepared. The house was probably set to blow up and burn. But what sprang the trap and who was supposed to walk into it, there's no way to tell. Probably David—because he was getting close to something dangerous. Perhaps even me, because there are those who don't like what I'm doing at Belle Isle."

"It was meant for David," I said.

Trevor had started pacing the room and he stopped at my chair looking down at me. "Why do you say that?"

"David wrote me a letter. He said that if anything happened to him here I could be sure it was not an accident."

"I'd like to see that letter."

I shook my head, knowing that I could never show it to anyone, least of all to Trevor. There had been too much spite in David's words against me, even to the point of threatening me if I tried to break up our marriage.

"There was nothing else he wrote me that would help,"

I said. "Only that if something happened to him it would not be an accident."

He let the matter go, seeming to suppress the inner anger that had driven him close to an outburst. I didn't know him anymore, I thought in sad relief. He had become a stranger—stronger, harder, more determined and impatient, just as I was a stranger to him as David's wife. Now I could dispel an old mirage.

"I'll show you your room," he said abruptly. "Dinner will be at eight tonight. Usually we follow local custom and dine earlier, but Lori is away, and this is Lu-Ellen's day off. It's hard to find household help these days, and Lu-Ellen is a recently acquired treasure. So we don't interfere with her plans. But tonight we're on our own."

I stood up, willing enough to be alone for a time. Only the innocuous was safe to talk about now.

"I'm looking forward to seeing your house tomorrow by daylight," I told him. "I couldn't see it very well as I came in, but you're obviously near the very top of the mountain."

"Right," he said. "It's a house everyone can see for miles around."

There was a ring of pride in his voice, and I couldn't help my words. "King of the Castle?"

"There's no king and no castle. But the mountains know the house is here." He sounded curt, putting me in my place.

I regretted my flip remark. It was the sort of thing I had learned to use with David—defensively. But Trevor would never be king of any castle. He was more like a soaring eagle, and only an eyrie high on a cliff would be right for him.

"It has the feeling of a big house," I said, "judging by the spaciousness of this kitchen."

"It's middling, I suppose. Not all that many rooms.

This ground level is the top floor. The house drops down the mountain from here and spreads out."

I carried my mug to the shining stainless-steel sink and ran water into it. Above were countless cabinets built of handsome mountain birch, with double windows in the center that looked out upon a last fading streak of color in the sky.

The sound behind us was hardly more than a whisper. I turned to look toward the doorway at the far end of the room just as a woman in a wheelchair came into view. The hallway down which she had rolled was uncarpeted, so her rubber-tired wheels moved easily onto the bare wood floor of the kitchen. She sat looking at me with a curious, almost challenging stare.

Trevor smiled at her. "Nona," he said, "this is Karen Hallam, David's wife." And to me: "This is my aunt, Miss Nona Andrews."

I had known nothing about an aunt, but there was no reason why I should. In the days when Trevor came as a young man to my father's house he had seemed to exist only within our orbit. I hadn't been curious about what and where he came from. It had been enough to look and listen and adore him in the present.

She held out a hand that was small, with fragile bones, and when I went to take it I found her grip surprisingly strong. Her skin was brown from the sun, so her incapacity, whatever it was, apparently didn't keep her indoors. She was probably in her mid-sixties and her graying hair had been twisted into a long braid that hung over one shoulder with shorter wisps hanging free about her face.

I knew I was staring, but I couldn't help it, and her bright, challenging gaze indicated that she didn't mind, that perhaps she was accustomed to people who stared. A long gown of a rather muddy mustard color encased her small body, and about her neck were hung strands of beads, brown and yellow, green and red—all made of seeds, gathered, I suspected, from local fields. But it was her eyes that were her most arresting—and unsettling—feature. They were totally green and very large, so that when she widened them the whites showed in a disconcerting way. Perhaps she recognized their power and didn't choose to waste it on me, for she swept pale lashes downward as her look narrowed and became a little sly. There had been an enormous curiosity in that first stare, but now she was hiding it.

"David's wife," she said in a voice that sounded brittle, perhaps from age, perhaps because she disapproved of me and had no welcome for me here.

I took back my hand and glanced at Trevor as he moved toward the hall.

"We'll leave everything to you, Nona," he said. "I was just about to show Karen to her room."

The woman in the wheelchair nodded and rolled herself skillfully across the big kitchen. I had a feeling that she was determined not to like me even before she'd seen me, and she dismissed me now with a shrug. Clearly David had not ingratiated himself here.

"Lu-Ellen fixed everything before she left, and the room is ready," she said over her shoulder to Trevor.

Out in the wide hallway he picked up my bags. "Lori hasn't a domestic bone in her body, so it has been up to Nona and Lu-Ellen to keep things running. Nona is a superb cook."

"But—how does she manage?"

"Better than you might think. She's able to do most of the things she used to before the car accident. Mainly because of sheer determination and an unwillingness to face more operations that might not succeed. She can stand and move about quite well with her crutches, or when she holds onto something. Sometimes I think the wheelchair is hardly more than a prop that gives her a power she doesn't hesitate to wield. She can drive a car, and she even gets out in the woods to collect all that stuff she hangs around her neck." His words were uncritical because of the affection in his voice.

Nona might be interesting to know, and I hoped she would like me better, if I had to stay here more than a few days.

As Trevor went ahead and I followed, my photographer's eyes searched out details of the house. This upper floor was bisected by a wide, uncarpeted hallway of handsome marquetry. On my right as I moved along were closed doors, and on the left, separated by open, plant-filled partitions, was a dining room, unlighted now, except for radiance from the hall. Farther on, bookcases lined both sides of the passageway, and at the end I could glimpse a huge living room that stretched the width of the house, fronting on the mountains. Ceiling-to-floor glass panels would allow the view to dominate by day, but we turned off before reaching the big room that must be the heart of the house.

Stairs were always interesting in Trevor's houses, often combining the grace of the old with modern materials. Here the curve that led to the lower floor was eighteenth century, but a Lucite waterfall chandelier hung at the top, and the banisters were a gleaming black above shining metal posts. Trevor led the way down steps carpeted in soft gray-blue. The lower level was not under the upper section of the house, but ran on along the hillside under its own roof. Not, perhaps, an economical way to use space, but far more interesting than the usual contained cube.

Down here the hallway was carpeted in the same blue-gray, and I gathered that the movements of Nona's chair were confined to the upper floor. The hall ran past more closed rooms, ending where a door stood open. Trevor touched a soundless switch just inside and gestured me ahead, following with my bags.

The room was generous in size, though not excessively so, and everything about it invited me to rest and let my worries and weariness go. Pale green wallpaper, sprigged with white, enfolded the space, and a four-poster bed that somehow managed to look modern wore a figured spread in green and gold, with a brief matching flounce around the top. A small, neat dressing table offered numerous intriguing drawers and cabinets, as well as a mirror that folded out. Two armchairs had been pulled before a stone fireplace and a table by the bed held books between carved bookends, with a good lamp for reading. Draperies of pale gold were drawn against what was undoubtedly another view of the mountains.

"It's a lovely room," I said. "Though I'd thought fireplaces in bedrooms went out with the Victorians."

"The chimney is shared by my bedroom on the other side of the wall," Trevor said. "I enjoy a fire on a chilly night. That's Crab Orchard stone, from over on the Tennessee plateau. It's beautiful stone, and wherever I could I've used it for the house."

His tone had warmed as he spoke of the work he had put into the house, and I glimpsed for a moment the Trevor I remembered.

"Of course," he went on, "the woods always offer plenty of fuel in fallen trees. I hope to experiment eventually with solar heat."

"I've been inside so many of your houses," I said, "but this is the first time I've stayed in one. Thank you for putting me up."

He ignored my thanks. "Look at the ceiling," he said.

I obeyed and saw that the beamed ceiling slanted upward toward what must be an outflung peak of roof, and that an oblong of skylight had been set into it just above the bed.

"You can cover it over by pulling that cord on the wall," Trevor said. "If you don't care to have the sky watching you."

"I shan't pull it," I told him. "When it's not raining, I'll lie in bed in the dark and watch the stars."

His smile was slight. He was still holding back. "That's what it's for. I'm glad you understand."

"I've never been able to see the stars from my bed, come to think of it. Certainly not in New York."

He lifted my larger suitcase onto a rack and held up the smaller bag. "Your camera equipment?"

"Yes, I couldn't travel without it."

"Your bath is over there." He gestured. "I think everything's here that you'll need. Come upstairs a little before eight. Earlier if you want to look around." He seemed in a hurry now to get away.

"Perhaps I can help Nona?"

He shook his head. "She wouldn't welcome that."

There was a moment when we stood looking at each other rather strangely. As though questions had suddenly churned up between us and could not be spoken. I didn't know what the questions were that he would have asked me: I didn't even know what questions I might have asked him, yet I knew that certain words must be said quickly unless he was to move even farther away from old friendship. No matter what I'd been telling myself, I knew suddenly that I didn't want that. As always, David had damaged whatever he touched, but once Trevor Andrews had been my friend, and I wanted to hold to that old, harmless relationship. Yet I mustn't speak dangerous, upsetting words. Not words that had to do with David. Something more honest, something that reached back to a more innocent time.

"Trevor, thank you," I said.

A faint surprise crossed his face, and I hurried on.

"Not for now only. For that time I was never able to thank you for, when my father died and Mother went to pieces. Everyone was around trying to comfort her. No one thought of me except you. You helped me get through that awful funeral because I knew you felt about him as I did. We'd both loved him, and you held my hand and stayed by me, and I will always be grateful. I missed you when you went away."

I hadn't meant to say that. It had surfaced out of old longing and loneliness. In any case, my words hadn't reached past the guard he seemed to wear. I hated the roughening of his voice as he answered me.

"I'm not that man anymore. No more than you're the young girl I remember from those days."

"Perhaps that's regrettable." I tried to sound light and casual in order to hide the small hurt that stabbed through me. "I wonder what happened to us?"

He paused in the doorway. "I think you know," he said, and went away.

I closed the door after him and stood looking about a room that I didn't see because my gaze had turned wholly inward. I hated what I had done. I had offered him a tiny bit of my heart out of that long-ago time, and he had not only refused it, but had stung me with those strange words: *I think you know.* But I had no idea what he meant. What was there to know?

I stepped to the light switch and let the room blink into darkness. Then I flung myself down on the bed and lay on my back looking up at a sky of darkest, deepest blue. It had stopped raining and the wind had blown the glass dry.

From a distant part of the house came the sound of someone strumming an instrument I didn't recognize and singing softly. Mountain music, I thought, and caught the tune, "Down in the Valley." This was a mellower, more golden sound than a guitar. Not a beat to dance to, as it slowed and grew more plaintive, more sad. As I lay there listening, the music drifted wistfully into an accompaniment to that old heart-breaker, "Barb'ra Allen."

Far above me stars twinkled into view here and there.

A phrase Trevor had used echoed in my mind. He had said "*my* bedroom," not "ours." Meaningless, of course. In a generously built house husband and wife often had their own retreats. Yet I felt saddened, somehow. I wanted him to be happy.

What I didn't want was to think, to feel. All I wanted was to be cool and calm and far removed from any fire. I lay very still, allowing all that vast universe out there to engulf me. My existence in this tiny speck of space was inconsequential. Tomorrow it would be important again. Perhaps even tonight when I left this room it would once more swell to its painful mortal size. But for now—for this moment—I would shut it all out and listen to the silence of the stars.

I would not think of Trevor. I would not think of David, or of a house that had exploded.

It was terrible that when I closed my eyes I saw only flames.

Two

Since that moment when I'd closed my eyes, only to imagine flames, the climate of the house had changed. The evening and that disturbing dinner were over. I had returned to my room to lie beneath the skylight again, to sleep. Yet now I knew certain terrible facts that I'd been ignorant of before.

A misty shimmer illumined the skylight, erasing the stars. Morning had come and the mountains were out there waiting for me. Painful experiences lay ahead, but for a little while I wanted to be free. I slipped from my bed and went to the long golden draperies that covered one wall, pulling them open by their cord. Sliding glass doors let in a crack of cool air. I stepped out onto the deck that ran across the front of my room and past the master bedroom next door, my flowery robe blowing in the breeze.

Beyond the protective rail a sheer cliff of rock dropped to a stand of pine trees that descended the hillside in graduated heights. To my left and above, where the house rambled along the mountain, stepping up to the higher floor, I could see another great semicircle of deck cantilevered over the mountain. There were lounging chairs up there, where one could lie in the sun far above the world.

But it was the distant view that held me spellbound. The mountains were true to their name this morning, smoking with mists that filtered into overlapping folds, thickening here, blowing away there, to let the great ranges stand free, blue-green against the sky, and very close. Here and there patches of red earth stood out against the green, and where roads were visible the yellow center lines made strips of color.

I returned to my room and dressed hurriedly in warm gray slacks and a yellow pullover sweater. Then I slung my camera bag over one shoulder and opened the door softly. It was only six-thirty and the house was utterly still. The day ahead of me would be a hard one, filled with more horror, more pain, so I would take this small space of time to refresh myself. Again with my camera as a companion.

The stairs, with their soft blue-gray carpeting, made no sound under my feet and the upper hall was empty, the Lucite strands of the chandelier hanging quiet. The only door whose location I knew was the front one, and I unlocked it and went outside to breathe deeply of pine-scented air. Now, by daylight, I could make out something of the structure of the house.

From this area of garage and turnabout, its upper, ground-level section gave an effect of stone walls crouching low, with a wide overhang of shingled roof that sheltered and concealed. Viewed from this side it was one of Trevor's secretive houses. If one moved only a short distance away it might have been taken for part of the mountain. Except in the kitchen, there were no windows overlooking this utilitarian area, and I remembered how Trevor treasured wall space in his houses, using windows generously where there was a view, but allowing for paintings to be hung on walls to warm an interior and give it life.

It was this outer aspect of his houses that had sometimes defeated me as a photographer. Shots that cut up a Trevor Andrews house could never show the freedom and grace of the whole. Nevertheless, I took my 35-mm camera from the bag and set the stops for this misty light. At home I'd have used my view camera, but that was larger and required a tripod, so I hadn't brought it on this trip. My bag contained only extra film, two or three special lenses and filters, and a light meter.

The sun was just beginning to break through behind me, sending straight beams between the branches of trees, so that the shadows were interesting, and I took several shots.

Above the point where the house dropped to its lower level and spread out along the hillside was a low sustaining wall banked with orange chrysanthemums. When I walked over to it I found I could look down upon the roof that pitched upward, with its slanting skylight set into my room. Mine seemed the only room with a skylight, though I could see others that had high clerestory windows set close to the ceiling, to let in light without interfering with inner walls. From here the house seemed formless, though not unshapely in its rambling along the hillside below me. Formless in the sense that an outcropping of rock might stand upon a mountainside, integrated with the earth, yet with a strong character of its own.

As I followed the retaining wall, I saw that an open space had been left below in a pocket between the mountain and the lower house. In this early light the little patch of space was still shadowed, but I could make out the unexpectedly charming picture it formed. The water of an irregular fishpond gave back a gleam of silver light from the sky. Nearby a dwarf pine stood guard beside a stone temple lantern, and a stone bench invited one to tranquil contemplation. It was a lovely spot. Some other time I would take the steps carved into the hillside at a farther point in the wall and go down there. But now I wanted a wider, more distant view of the entire house.

I was well aware of the artful way in which Trevor could lull one into dismissing one of his houses as undistinguished at first glance, and then stun the senses with some new and arresting aspect. This was what I would search for now, and I knew it would lie in the direction of the mountains.

A path led off at an angle from the garage, following the hillside into a gentle slope. I left the house and struck off through the woods, filling my lungs and salving my soul with this heady mountain air, savoring the pungent green restfulness all around. Only occasional sourwood trees offered an accent of red, and there were thickets of rhododendron and laurel along the way. Deep in the woods the trees dripped a little from the mists, but I kept on, knowing instinctively that the path must soon return to the open. Movement, action, prevented me from thinking— about anything.

Sure enough, the trail, with its generous trim of goldenrod and Queen Anne's lace, turned toward the open again, and crossed a driveway that led upward to another house.

I passed it by, interested only in Trevor's house for the moment. The path ended in a trodden space before a great boulder that thrust outward from the hillside, its top offering a vantage point from which to look back at the mountain.

As I walked out upon its rough surface, the clean, soaring beauty of the house struck me with all its power. It seemed to poise on the very crest of the mountain like an eagle with its wings spread, ready to fly out into space. More than ever before I understood what had been my father's thesis—that in the designing of a house, ceilings, floors, walls were not separate elements, but all one thing, and a part of the earth as well. In this high place where it was fitting to soar, this house was a winged entity that belonged to both sky and earth.

Now, even though the eastern lighting was wrong, I used my camera eagerly. I wanted a good shot of the peaked rise of rooftops that thrust into the sky above cantilevered decks. This was the best possible spot for viewing the house, and I could imagine Trevor and Lori bringing their guests here for the magnificent view.

Inevitably, however, I must turn my attention from the house to the vast spread of mountains, where the sun was already burning away the mists. These peaks didn't line themselves up in monotonous ranges, but folded intricately in upon one another, with glimpses of streams and roads and valleys in between.

One spot of water caught my eye—a portion of silver-blue lake, with a green island floating upon it, and reality came crashing back. I knew this was Belle Isle, and not even the beauty of the scene from this height could free my thoughts of horror.

I sat down upon rock that was beginning to warm in the sun, and pulled my knees up to clasp my hands around them. Now nothing could stem the flooding of remembrance.

Last night, dining with Trevor and Nona had been an uncomfortable experience. Nona seemed to like me no better than at our earlier meeting and it troubled me not to know why. Trevor had been remote, almost absent-minded, and in a way I was grateful for that. I had already steeled myself against any betraying emotions that might be dredged up from the past. The young girl who had been so sure she was in love was gone, and an eternity had intervened. Trevor and I no longer knew each other, and he was making it clear that he wanted it to stay that way.

Nona had planned a simple casserole supper, with a salad and home-made brown bread, a custard for dessert. I was permitted to help carry things into the dining room, though even in her wheelchair she had little trouble in steering a cart that she loaded with dishes from the kitchen. She still wore her mustard-colored gown, and it seemed to suit her. When she left her chair, leaning on Trevor's arm to make a few steps to her place at the table, its long folds fell about her slight person, giving her stature, concealing whatever was wrong with her legs.

The dining room had been done in white and gold and green, with a wide mural of ferns painted along one wall. My attention was arrested by the mural at once. Ferns made one think of cool woods where streams might flow —but these ferns were not like that, and once we were seated I couldn't help staring.

The lighter greens had a tendency to be strident, while those that filled the shadows were the near black of mala-chite. The painting seemed alive with giant curling tendrils that wove endlessly in and out of themselves in a purpose-less reaching—for what? At the heart and focus a queen fern seemed to reign—a monstrous plant, with lush fronds filling the frame, while lesser ferns waved about her like handmaidens. I felt almost revolted, my senses assaulted, and yet the whole was stunningly beautiful and had obviously been painted by someone with an original talent.

"Who is the artist?" I asked Nona.

Apparently the woman was local, and Nona warmed for the first time and began to tell me about the painters and craftsmen who had come from all over America to live in this beautiful area.

"That's what Belle Isle is all about," she said earnestly. "Trevor is building interesting, distinguished houses that artists and other creative people will find satisfying to live in, yet which won't be priced out of their reach. There are always places for the very poor and the very rich, but hardly anyone thinks of creative artists, poets, writers, sculptors—they're a neglected minority. It's all due to Trevor that old Vinnie Fromberg decided to turn Belle Isle over to this purpose."

I knew nothing about this and I looked inquiringly at Trevor. "Who is Vinnie Fromberg?"

"Money. Money that Vinnie made himself," Nona said before he could answer, her eyes widening so that their green sparkled with its own rather eerie light, reflecting the ferns. "Scads and scads of money! Vinnie's dead now, but he was pretty smart. He owned most everything in sight. Building companies, hotels—the Greencastle in Gatlinburg—oil wells, aircraft—name it and he was into it. But Belle Isle was his favorite spot in the world. You tell her, Trevor."

Trevor smiled at her vehemence and came back from whatever distant reaches he had lost himself in. "He was my wife's great-grandfather—in his late nineties when he died, though his brain was still sharp and he was active to the end. He'd made his first fortune before he was thirty, and he turned it into more and more wealth. He built a house on the island when he was thirty, and brought his first wife there to live. She was an actress—only seventeen —but she gave up the stage when she married Vinnie. He wouldn't have been one to stand for her having a career in those days. I expect he'd have liked to lock her in a tower and keep her there."

"There are surprises on the island," Nona put in. "Not only that weird octagonal contraption he built, but that other—folly. Where his wife died. His first wife. His second wife hated the island and wouldn't live there. No towers for her. But she died too, though more quietly. And then all these years later Trevor came along and sold his ideas to Vinnie in his old age. Tell her, Trevor. Karen is part of Belle Isle too. Because of David Hallam."

It seemed to me that she spoke David's name with a surprising venom, and I knew his relationship must be the source of her disliking for me.

Trevor glanced at me remotely. "I think not, Nona. Karen will be leaving soon. There's nothing to keep her here. So let's not go into all that meaningless ancient history."

I didn't tell him that there might very well be something to keep me here. "Do go on," I said.

After a moment he shrugged and gave in. "Oh, all right then. I got the idea of building some interesting housing in a beautiful place that might be afforded by the creative people who come here. Not on the island, but on the land along the lake. I went to Vinnie with my ideas and he listened. I warned him that there wasn't much money to be made in the project, but that it might be turned into something distinctive that would make a name for itself. Eventually it might even grow and be productive. He already had enough money, and he liked the idea of prestige, so he gave me four years in which to prove I could make it work."

"Against plenty of opposition," Nona added. "Eric Caton! I get so mad at him, even though he's an old friend. Sometimes I think you should never have built him a house up here on the mountain, Trevor. I know he watches you and waits for you to fail. Sometimes I feel mighty sorry for Maggie." Nona turned to me. "Maggie is Eric's wife. She's the artist you asked about—the one who painted that mess of ferns up there on the wall. Sometimes I think I'd like to take them down and cook them. But I expect she needs the therapy of painting, being married to Eric."

Again I looked at Trevor for enlightenment and he smiled ruefully. "Maggie's all right. She's just been under Eric's thumb for too long. Eric is Lori's uncle. Maybe he's a bit like his grandfather Vinnie at times. Certainly he's been against my plans for Belle Isle from the beginning. He always served his grandfather well and he wanted that property for a project of his own. So he never forgave Vinnie—or me—for what I'm doing there. But the old man was pleased, and everything was going well. The first fire came just before his death. That was a year ago —and you know the rest."

He was silent, lost in his gloomy thoughts, and I tried to find a lighter subject.

"A little while ago in my room I heard someone playing an instrument I couldn't recognize. Something sweeter than a guitar."

"Nona's dulcimer," Trevor said. "They used to be played a lot around here in our mountains. But there aren't too many these days who can play a dulcimer."

"I learned as a child," Nona said. "For me it's comforting music."

We were busy for a time with Nona's good food, and I found myself staring again at those compelling, rather frightening ferns that Maggie Caton had created. Her queen fern seemed to exude an enormous and mysterious power, so that I wondered about the woman who could create such a concept.

It was Nona who spoke first. "In a way, I can understand a firebug. Look at these candles here on the table. The flames hold your eyes, don't they? It's such a mysterious thing—fire. People always run to watch a building that's burning. If someone around here were crazy enough in that direction . . . if someone . . ."

"I don't think there's anything crazy about this," Trevor broke in impatiently. "Someone wants to make sure I don't succeed. It's as simple as that."

"He thinks Eric might be behind what has happened," Nona said. "I don't mean that *he* would set a fire, but if Trevor falls on his face, Eric will inherit Belle Isle—and he'll put up God-knows-what in the way of a cheap development. That's valuable land."

"I *don't* think it was Eric, and neither do you," Trevor contradicted. "I don't suspect anyone. That's why I brought David down here. To find out."

"He sure enough suspected somebody!" Nona was growing excited. "But he wouldn't tell us anything. So he died. He was killed because he got too close, became too dangerous."

"Nona!" Trevor said sharply. "David's death was an accident. No one could have known that he would go into that house."

She gave him a surprisingly sweet smile and went on as though he hadn't spoken. "The first fire was started by kids, you know. But after that what happened was too sophisticated for any child to have planned."

Trevor looked unhappy and said nothing. I had begun to hate all this—the talk about fires, the heat and crackle of real logs burning on the flagstone hearth behind my chair, the hypnotic flickering of the candles. Especially the candles. Opposite my place at the table a wide mirror gave back the room, pinpointing living flames in the glass, and seeming to link motion to the writhing ferns. My eyes followed their eerie movement until I tore my gaze away.

"I'm sorry," I said. "I'm very tired."

Trevor was at once courteous and considerate in his remote way. He came with me down to my room and stood for a moment in the doorway, his eyes even darker than I remembered them. A look to get lost in—as alive and hypnotic as a candle flame. I blinked hard and turned away.

"Don't pay any attention to the things Nona says," he warned. "She's really a very capable and sensible person. You mustn't let any of this get to you, Karen. I know it's painful for you now. But in a few days the worst will be over, and you can go back to your own life." His very tone told me how much he wanted me gone.

I nodded and said good night. When the door was closed I stood with my back against it and looked up at the slanting ceiling and the patch of dark sky over my bed. No comfort came to me now from the stars. Nona had said that my husband had died because someone had planned his death. I believed her more than I did Trevor.

My handbag lay on the dressing table where I'd left it and I went to open it, and took out David's letter. Then I sat in one of the armchairs beside a lamp and spread it upon my knees. I had opened and folded the letter so many times that the pages were ready to tear, and I handled it carefully.

Rejecting the early paragraphs of vituperation against me, I found the passage I must remember:

If something happens to me here, Karen, you can be certain it won't be an accident. I'm close to discovery and I'm not sure anymore which one of us is the hunter, or which the hunted. Our arsonist is getting nervous and I think he'll try to act soon. I will try to be ready for him.

One thing I'm sure of—there's a torch involved in this. That means these are all professional jobs, except maybe the first one. Professional, hired jobs. Usually a torch will skip in, do his thing and get out —fast. But this time there's been a series of fires, and I think he's staying on, well concealed, to set more. That means he has help of some sort. If I can identify him I'll find out who pays him. Then I'll know who is really responsible for what's been happening.

Once more I folded the pages and put them away, this time in a pocket of my suitcase. I didn't want to carry the letter around with me. David's conjectures were all too clear. In the vernacular of arson a "torch" was a skilled professional who set fires for pay. Often this was so the owner of a failing business could recoup through insurance claims. The Belle Isle fires, however, had another motive, if, as Trevor thought, they were intended to stop him from succeeding in his project.

That David had indeed identified the "torch" or gotten too close to him for comfort, seemed clear. And that he had in turn been trapped himself. Whatever anyone might say, his letter hinted at murder. And as was indicated by the use of an explosive, murder by an expert in arson. But I needn't search for him directly, as David must have done. What I needed to discover was who had hired him. In that direction lay the greater guilt.

This was the debt I owed to David. This was the reason why I must stay, no matter how much Trevor and others wanted me gone. I felt cool enough now. Cool and able to meet whatever I must.

When I finally went to bed, it was a long while before I feel asleep.

But the night had passed, as it always does, and in the morning I had come out here to sit on a rock in the sun and take my pictures. Morning at least was a more hopeful time, no matter what difficult problems lay ahead. I knew what the immediate one would be. First a trip to the funeral parlor, where David's remains were being held. Then when the arrangements were made, there would still be the quiet funeral. By that time perhaps I would know what my next steps must be.

"Good morning," said a voice behind me. "I'm Maggie Caton." I turned about, as startled as I'd been yesterday by the watchman at Belle Isle. I hadn't known another soul was anywhere near.

The woman who stood at the foot of the rock was probably in her early forties and clearly made no effort to look any younger. Her straight hair hung in a shaggy mass to her shoulders and was an odd salt-and-pepper red, as though she had grown confused about her rinses. Her eyes were large and rather beautiful, reminding me of the color of rain on a gray day, and her chin had a solid, capable look. She wore jeans pulled tight over plumpish hips, with a worn place at one knee, and there was a middle button missing on her green-checked blouse. I was to learn that Maggie Caton often seemed to be put together with pins and clips and bits of string. Only when Eric took a hand and put down his foot did she fling herself into something that gave her a deceptive air of elegance and fashion. Somehow she didn't seem at all like my conception of the artist who had painted those splendid and terrifying ferns that decorated Trevor's dining room.

"You must be David Hallam's wife," she said into my startled silence. "Eric and I are the Andrews' neighbors—

the only ones this high on the mountain. Trevor designed our house too." She nodded toward the driveway I had seen.

I packed my camera away, scrambled down from the rock and held out my hand. "Yes, I'm Karen Hallam. I'm staying with the Andrews for a little while."

"I know." She gave my hand an oddly nervous grip and dropped it. "Your husband didn't make himself all that popular around here, but I'm sorry about what happened."

"He had an unpleasant job to do," I said shortly, remembering that Eric Caton had set himself in strong opposition to Belle Isle.

"Right. Maybe he did it too well—that job. You're up early—like me. Can I give you some coffee? There's nobody else at the house right now, and I'd enjoy company."

Coffee was probably what I needed, and I also needed to know anyone whose life had touched David's in any way.

"Thanks," I told her. "I'd like that. No one seemed to be up at Trevor's, so I came out for a walk."

We went together along the path to the Caton drive, which rose on an incline to a carport under the house. Maggie chose a shortcut of stone steps and went nimbly up them ahead of me. I paused before I reached the top to look up at the second house that Trevor had built on the mountain. This structure had no intention of flying. It was a low two stories, the upper main floor apparently built on a huge platform that overhung the utility area below and extended toward the view in a wide deck. This entire face of the house seemed to be glassed in with doors and windows, and I knew that Trevor would have used the opposite side against the mountain to offer a blank face. There was less grace in this house, but it presented a confident strength that perhaps spoke for the man who'd had it built.

We went through a glass door into a kitchen of stone and brick, with ample storage and counter space, far more neatly arranged than was Maggie Caton herself.

"My castle," she said with a wave of her hand. "The only thing I'm any good at is cooking. I expect that's why Eric married me. He was tired of beautiful faces." Her grin was self-mocking.

I slung my camera equipment bag to the floor and sat on a high stool at one of the counters. "Last night at dinner I saw your fascinating fern mural," I said. "So I gather you do have another talent."

"Oh, that!" She shrugged off my words. "Cooking takes real talent. Painting is like breathing—just something I do. How did you like my ferns? Squirmy, aren't they?"

I smiled uncertainly. "I'm not sure I'd want to live with them."

"Nor does Trevor. They must be dreadful for the digestion, but they've only been there a short while and Trevor's had his mind on other things. Otherwise he'd have had them off by now, I'm sure. Nona doesn't like them either, but Lori adores the painting and she'll scream when it's removed."

"What made you do it?"

She poured coffee from a pot already plugged in and set a cup before me. "That's the way my imagination works. I don't try to explain it—it just happens. And I do think the effect is beautiful."

I couldn't quarrel with that and I sipped scalding coffee in silence.

"I'm alone at the moment," Maggie went on, "because Eric's off with Giff and Lori and Chris in Asheville."

"Trevor mentioned that Lori and Chris were away," I began, and she nodded her red and gray head at me.

"Maybe you're not up on all the complicated relationships. Gifford Caton is my stepson, Eric's son. Old Vinnie's great-grandson, as Lori is his great-granddaughter. Giff is staying with us for now and works for his father. He's Lori's cousin, of course, and Eric is her uncle. I'm only an outsider around here, without any kin except by marriage. After what happened, Lori was showing signs of falling apart, and Chris has been in a pretty unsettled state. They've taken him out of school for a while. Eric and Giff drove them off to visit more Caton kin in Asheville. I wish they'd all stay away for a while. I miss Eric, but it's more peaceful when they're gone."

Her tone gentled as she mentioned her husband, and I found myself wondering about him even more.

She placed a jug of what looked like real cream on the counter and shoved a sugar bowl toward me. When I continued to drink my coffee black, she nodded her approval.

"Never touch sugar myself. Poison. And cream's too fattening."

I didn't want to sit here and talk about sugar and cream. While I had Maggie Caton alone, I had to ask questions.

"What did you mean about David's doing his job too well?"

Maggie seated herself beside me at the counter and picked up her cup. "Did I say that? I often talk out of turn. You'll get used to it."

"Will you tell me what happened?" I said. "How do *you* think David died?"

This time she gave me a quick glance from rain-cool gray eyes. "I shouldn't think you'd want to talk about that. Hasn't Trevor given you the whole story?"

"He gave me his view of it. I was wondering about yours."

"Playing detective? But that's what got your husband into trouble. And you're an amateur. Were you on good terms with David?"

Her directness startled me. "Isn't that an odd question?"

"So are yours. Except that you have a right to ask, and I haven't. Sorry."

"David and I understood each other," I said.

"Good enough. But I can't tell you anything more about his death. I only know what Trevor told us."

I wondered about that, but her words carried a certain finality, and I didn't dare probe too hard. When my cup was empty, I slipped off the stool.

"Thank you for the coffee. I'd better be getting back now."

"If you'll wait until I get my foot out of my mouth, I'll walk you over to Trevor's," she offered.

I accepted readily, and when we were on the path leading through the woods she began to talk in her low, slightly husky voice.

"Don't mix yourself up in what's happening here," she said. "Get the funeral over with, meet the formalities, and then go home as soon as you can. And don't look back."

"Why?" I asked bluntly.

Her answer was evasive. "I gather that arson is an especially nasty sort of crime to deal with. Only a week or two ago, David came to our house for dinner and I heard him talking to Eric about fires and the people who set them."

"What did he say?"

"He only spoke in generalities. You know—women who start fires are usually angry or frustrated. They're likely to set fire to their own belongings. The pyromaniac has a few screws loose. Sexual, that is. Mostly he acts on impulse and lacks motivation. The fire to raise insurance

money is often done by a professional in the employ of
the owner. But a fire isn't always for monetary gain.
Sometimes it's an effort to hide some other crime."

She had listened well, but she wasn't telling me anything I hadn't already heard David discuss a hundred
times in the course of his work.

"How do you explain the explosives that were used at
Belle Isle?" I asked.

"I'm not trying to explain anything. But maybe that was
only intended for the house. Wasn't it just David's bad
luck to walk in at the wrong time? That's what the police
decided. Maybe it was murder, all right, but not first-
degree, not intentional. It might have been Trevor or Eric
or anyone else who was killed. Could be it was only a
different, more emphatic way of destroying a house."

I thought of David's letter back in my room. "I don't
believe that."

She stopped beside me on the path and I saw the white,
pressed-in look about her mouth, as though some barely
restrained emotion pinched her lips.

"It was an *accident,* Karen. Only an accident! Good-
bye now. I'll see you again." She turned from me and
walked back in the direction of her house, a sturdy, determined figure.

I stood looking after her for a moment in dismay, and
then went onto Trevor's. What had I said to so upset her?
Only that I didn't agree with her.

As I reached the house Nona came out upon the
curving arm of a ramp that ran down to ground level,
moving easily in her chair. This morning she wore a
gown that was the orange-red color of bittersweet berries,
and once more a half-dozen strands of beads looped her
neck. She stopped her chair close to me and raised a
hand in greeting.

"Been for a walk? Good. I'm glad you're not the brooding type. Let the hills heal you. Have you been taking pictures?"

I patted my camera bag. "Yes. I found a rock on the mountainside where I was able to get several pictures of this house."

"Fine. You'll be hungry now. Everyone gets his own breakfast around here, since Lu-Ellen doesn't show up until nine. You'll find what you need in the kitchen, I expect. Trevor's there now."

She waved her hand again and rolled herself expertly toward the garage. As I reached the front door I heard her car start.

Last night I hadn't had a good chance in the dusk and rain to admire the entryway Trevor had designed for this house. Now I could stand still and enjoy it. The doorway was of a generous and inviting width, set well beneath the deep overhang of the roof. Three steps leading up to it were of natural stone, and beside them a crude stone dog with a sly grin on its mouth rested on its hindquarters, one paw outstretched as though in greeting.

I bent to pat the stone head. "Good fellow," I said, and went up the steps, to find Trevor just inside, watching me. The shock of seeing him suddenly was not as great as it had been last night, but the memory of old emotion stirred in me—emotion that I wanted only to forget, that I had to fight at every turn.

"I like your stone dog," I told him lightly.

"He's local. Maggie Caton chopped him out of a chunk of stone in a whimsical moment. She's more gifted than she knows."

"I've just me her," I said, and let it go at that.

"The dog's name is Simon," Trevor told me. "Nona says that's the name he claims. How are you this morning?"

"I've been bracing myself for what's ahead."

He nodded. "Come in and I'll give you breakfast."

I paused in the doorway because now I could look down the full sweep of the hallway, clear to the glass of living-room windows at the far end, with the marvelous vista of mountains and sky forming a backdrop tapestry.

"I've never seen a more beautiful spot than you've found here," I said. "Your house fits the mountain as though it had grown from it."

He led the way into the kitchen without comment. There was no fire needed on the hearth this morning, and now I could savor the spaciousness and light that were always a part of Trevor's rooms. He worked with space as if it were an entity in itself.

While he dropped bread into a toaster and brought me a glass of orange juice from the refrigerator, I sliced a banana over bran flakes. When the toast popped I buttered it and added country marmalade. It felt wonderful to be hungry. I hadn't wanted to eat since David's death. Perhaps by lunchtime my appetite would have fled again, so I'd better take advantage of it now.

"Maggie Caton explained all the relationships to me," I said. "Lori, Eric, Giff and so on. Perhaps I'll meet them before I leave. Though Maggie seems to think I shouldn't stay around here for long."

"She's right, you shouldn't," Trevor said, once more curt and abrupt.

"Why do you feel that way?"

"It must be painful for you here. I shouldn't think you'd want to stay."

I set down my second cup of coffee and looked at him. "There's more than the distress to me that everyone seems to be thinking of. Tell me why you want me gone, Trevor."

For just a moment he regarded me sadly, almost pityingly. Then he shrugged, and the chill I had felt yesterday was there again. "Stay as long as you like, Karen," he said, and I knew he had moved to some remote psychic place where I couldn't go.

We left for Sevierville, the county seat, as soon as I'd finished breakfast, and the trip was made mostly in silence. It was a barrier I had no desire to cross. Trevor had brought down some sort of bar against the possibility of friendship between us, and that was fine with me—and safer than friendship. Much safer, I told myself firmly.

At the funeral parlor I had only to make arrangements for the burial. There was a little cemetery not far from Gatlinburg, where some of David's family had been buried and I chose that for his resting place. In two days' time, I agreed, and we went back to Trevor's car. I knew that I was behaving stiffly, all too matter-of-factly, as though none of this had anything to do with me.

"Are you all right?" Trevor asked as I got into the car.

"I'm all right," I told him numbly. That was the trouble —that I had felt so little in that muted, impersonal place, with its soft lighting and phony background music. Only the place itself made me angry, but there was nothing of David there, and anger for an established custom was a waste of emotion right now. When I had stood before the ruin of the house at Belle Isle where David had died, emotion had shaken me, but now I could find no tears, no pain or regret. The numbness was frightening. More frightening than if I had been grief-stricken. To be cool when it came to Trevor was one thing, but to feel nothing at all now about David was alarming.

We drove out of the city and when we were on the highway again I grew aware of Trevor's uneasiness with me. I wasn't behaving as a proper widow should, and I supposed that he was waiting for me to collapse in grief. I made an effort to reassure him.

"I really am all right," I said. "Don't worry about me."

"It's better to let it out. If you hold everything back it will hit you harder in the long run. It's better to cry, you know."

"Crying is the last thing I feel like doing. But if that time comes, I'll cry."

"All right." He withdrew his momentary sympathy. "In that case, this is as good a time as any to make another stop."

"Stop where?"

"County sheriff's office. They're holding some things of David's. Articles that were retrieved—after the fire. Identification has been made, of course, but they'd like you to confirm these items."

"Naturally," I said, but this time a shiver went along my spine.

Only a deputy sheriff named Keegan was on duty when we arrived. A tall man with sandy hair and a searching look, he gestured me into a chair a bit watchfully, and I suspected that he had dealt with distraught widows before. When he brought a small box and placed it on the desk before me, Trevor stood beside my chair, and I knew that he too was watchful, though still remote.

"You understand, Mrs. Hallam," Keegan said, "that almost everything was either destroyed by the explosion or burned in the fire?"

I nodded, finding that I was tensing now, as I had not done at the funeral parlor.

He took the lid off the box and I avoided looking inside as he reached in a tanned hand and brought out an object that he held toward me in his palm.

"Do you recognize this?"

I knew it very well. What he held was the ruin of a handsome belt buckle of Mexican silver that I had given David one Christmas a few years ago. I didn't touch the bit of twisted metal.

"Yes," I said, and knew that strain sounded in my voice. "That belonged to my husband."

Again searching fingers dipped into the box and again a lump of blackened metal was brought out. This time I took it into my hand, the better to examine what was left of David's expensive and treasured wristwatch. When I turned it over I could just make out the initial "D" on the back. The rest was obliterated.

"This was David's too," I said.

"And this?" He was holding out a ring in his fingers—a carved gold band that had been partly melted, the stone in the setting gone.

I shook my head. "I've never seen that before."

I was aware of a sudden exchange of looks between the two men. Deputy Keegan spoke brusquely.

"It was his, all right. Several people down here identified it because they'd seen him wearing it. Perhaps it was something given to him since he came here, or something he may have purchased."

David had never cared particularly for rings and wouldn't have bought it for himself. So who would have made him such a gift?

The next article was a scorched and battered flashlight and I shook my head. "He always carried a flashlight or two in his car, but I wouldn't know one from another."

"That's okay," Keegan said. "We had a real break there. The batteries came through pretty well inside the case. We were able to get his fingerprints from them. It was his all right."

"It's probably the one he had stuck in his belt when he went down to the house," Trevor said.

I hardly listened because I was still thinking about the ring. Had it been a gift from a woman? I'd had no illusions about David's fidelity for a long while. It didn't matter. I would never even know who she was. Yet perhaps someone here grieved for him more than I was able to.

"Just one more thing," Keegan said. "The explosion tore everything apart, of course, but this scrap of cloth came through. Do you recognize it?"

I could only nod. Staring at it, I felt a little ill, and Keegan went quickly for a cup of water from the cooler.

"She's had enough," Trevor said.

I reached out and touched the remnant of brown suede, torn and blackened, but recognizable as coming from David's favorite jacket. He had always liked expensive clothes, and he had worn them well. I had seen him in that jacket a hundred times and had been wryly amused when he had created his own fire emblem of a conventionalized flame that had been sewed onto a pocket. Traces of the red emblem were still there. The sight brought David before me with sickening clarity, and I could see him as vividly as though he'd been in the room with us, wearing that suede jacket, with his favorite Stetson cocked at a jaunty angle on his head.

"He—he used to wear a hat," I faltered, and heard my voice crack.

Keegan held up some charred scraps. "A Stetson, yes. These, probably."

I sipped cold water and tried to breathe deeply. But Keegan wasn't quite through with me. "Of course the final identification was the teeth. We found enough to—"

"That's it!" Trevor said. "Don't show her anymore. I'll take you home now, Karen."

He put a hand on my arm and I rose obediently. I didn't try to explain that it was not the idea of David's teeth but his jacket and the remnants of his Stetson that had made him real for me again. I already knew about the teeth, of course. I had given the police the name of

David's dentist, and I'd talked to him afterward on the phone.

Keegan was putting the blackened objects back into the box. The bit of suede—all that remained of David Hallam—last. I could cry now, helplessly, silently. In a way, I think Trevor was relieved. He hadn't understood my blank passivity.

He put an impersonal arm about me as we walked to the door, while the deputy stood helplessly by with the box of David's things in his hands.

"I'll take that," Trevor said, and put the box under his arm.

We walked to his car together and I slumped into the front seat weeping. He sat beside me silently, letting me cry.

"I'll be all right in a minute," I said.

If only I could have clung to him and been comforted, but he did not touch me again, and I permitted myself no such weakening gesture.

"It's going to be rough for a few days," he told me when I sat up and wiped my eyes. "But this will be over soon and you can get back to your work, Karen. If you can keep busy things will get better a lot faster."

He was saying the things one had to say in the face of loss—the old things that were always said, when nothing at all can really comfort in the immediate and empty present. Only he didn't know that none of the clichés applied to me. I wasn't weeping for my own loss, but for David's —tears for the ending of a life, but not in the way Trevor meant. I had wanted to be free—but not this way.

When I'd managed to swallow my tears I tried to speak in a voice that wouldn't break. It was necessary, somehow, to make him understand.

"I'm not crying because I loved David, but perhaps because I cheated him. We cheated each other."

He nodded, sitting stiffly beside me. "Yes, he told us a little about that. But you always went back to him, didn't you? He knew he could count on you for that, at least."

My tears were gone in an instant, and I stared at him, shocked. What had David said? What lies about me had he told?

"I don't know what you're talking about," I managed, and realized as I spoke that it was useless to defend myself. Now I was beginning to understand the prejudice against me. "Never mind. I don't suppose it matters now what he may have said. I wasn't crying because I loved him any longer, but because he was so full of raging life. And now it's all wiped out. Now I do owe him a debt. Someone caused that fire. Someone caused his death. And I'm going to stay here until I know who it was. That's all that matters now."

Trevor started the car with an explosive burst of speed, and I could tell by his carved-in-stone profile how much I had shocked him. He had shocked me just as much, but there was nothing to be done about that.

On the drive back to his house he didn't speak to me at all, and there seemed nothing left that I could say to him. He couldn't possibly understand. Not ever.

Three

When we reached the house a red Ferrari stood in the space before the garage.

"Lori and Chris are back," Trevor said. "You'd better come inside and meet them."

In spite of everything I had told myself about his never understanding, I found that I couldn't let him go until I at least tried to explain. "Wait, please. I've told you badly. There's so much more."

"Knowing my brother, I don't doubt it," Trevor said. He got out of the car and came around to my door, the box Keegan had given him under one arm. "In any case, it doesn't matter, does it?"

I had spoken those same words a little while ago, and I already knew they were false. "It matters to me. It does matter!"

Clearly he wasn't interested in what mattered to me. "Let's skip it," he said, and I sensed that something had pushed him close to the exploding point. Perhaps something that had little to do with me.

I let him help me from the car, feeling more hopeless than ever. As we approached the house a girl appeared in the doorway. She was generously built, with a shining fall of blond hair caught by a ribbon at the nape of her neck. Her young, sober face was turned worriedly toward Trevor.

"This is Lu-Ellen, who helps to keep us running," Trevor said. "Lu-Ellen, this is Mrs. Hallam."

She gave me a sympathetic look, said, "Hi," and went on urgently to Trevor. "Mrs. Andrews and Chris are back. You saw the car? Mr. Giff is staying for lunch, but Mr. Eric's having a big go-round in there with all of them right now. I don't think he'll stay."

"Thank you," Trevor said.

The girl went on, clearly feeling herself one of the family. "I don't reckon Mrs. Andrews is feeling much better."

Trevor nodded, and Lu-Ellen disappeared in the direction of the kitchen. He turned back to me. "You'd better come in and meet the rest of the family. Lori's inclined to be—emotional these days. I don't know—" He stared at me for a moment and then gestured toward the door.

Before we could go through it, however, a large, rather burly man came toward us down the hall in an angry rush, pulling himself to a halt when he saw Trevor.

"I thought getting Lori away to Asheville would help!" he burst out. "But I can't do anything with her. Maybe you'd better take over."

"I'll manage," Trevor said. "Karen, this is Eric Caton, Lori's uncle, and our nearest neighbor. Eric, this is—"

"Yes, I know. David's wife." He regarded me from beneath bushy gray eyebrows—a penetrating look that probed disconcertingly. "You've popped into a hornet's nest, young lady. I hope you're not allergic to bee venom."

Maggie's husband was a bit overwhelming and I had no answer for his remark.

He seemed to expect none, and I suspected that he rather enjoyed taking people by surprise.

"I'll leave Lori to you, Trevor. The family has done all they can for now. We understand, all right, but we don't approve. If you need help, I can send Maggie down. Sometimes she listens to Maggie. Right now she's upsetting Chris badly."

Trevor said nothing, and glancing at him, I once more had the impression of a powerful anger held in check.

Eric threw me a wry look and strode off in the direction of the path through the woods.

"If you like," I offered, "I can go to my room and stay out of sight for a while. I'm sure you don't want me intruding in the middle of family problems."

"You are already in the middle. Come along, and we'll get it over with."

There was no escape. He opened the door for me, and then went ahead down the hall. Before we reached the living room a boy of about ten came hurtling toward us. I had a quick impression that he was tall for his age, and thin, with very fair hair. He would have run straight by, but Trevor reached out with one hand and caught him.

"Chris!" he said. "Chris—what's the matter?"

The boy struggled in his father's grasp, broke away and ran out of the house. For just an instant I glimpsed the look of pain on Trevor's face, and then his guard was up again, rigid and controlled.

"Come along, Karen."

There was nothing I wanted less than to "come along." I felt as though I were marching into a battle line when I didn't know what the war was about. But there was no help for it and I went with him. When we reached the wide door of the living room I could look through glass to the big semicircle of deck beyond, reaching out over the side of the mountain. Two people stood at the rail, with their backs to us. The man was tall and slender, with ash-blond hair as pale as that of the slight woman who stood beside him, leaning against his arm. Her cousin, Giff Caton, undoubtedly, and the woman—Lori. She was crying bitterly, weeping aloud like a child, and he was doing his best to quiet and comfort her.

"Stay here," Trevor said. "And hold this, please." He thrust the box the deputy had given him into my hands and went to the deck.

I stood helplessly in the living room, bewildered by unleashed emotions that seemed to be flying in all directions, and wanting only to escape. In order to distract myself, I looked about the big room that made a pool of calm and quiet in the center of what seemed a serious storm.

Colors of bark and beige and rust had been used in the furniture. The beautiful, shaggy rugs were undoubtedly mountain crafted—handwoven from natural dyed yarns in browns and tans. The walls were a light neutral color that added to the sense of stillness. Both ends of the room were solid background, with only clerestory windows set high at one end, lending a translucence to the room. In just one place a full window, tall and narrow, had been set into an end wall. It stood alone, perfectly framing a long-needled pine tree. A lovely touch. All the rest of the glass was across the front, opening out upon the mountains, decorating the room with the magnificent view. It needed to be a quiet, unemphatic room, with the mountains out there running to the horizon in every direction, and the sky painting the ceiling.

"It is beautiful, isn't it?" said a voice from an opposite

corner. I turned to see Nona Andrews sitting quietly in her wheelchair watching me. "Come over here," she said. "My chair doesn't move easily on the rugs."

From the open doors the sound of sobbing had lessened, and I kept my eyes away from the deck, not wanting to stare. Obediently, I went to sit upon a leather hassock beside Nona's chair.

"It's a good thing Trevor got home," she said. "Sometimes Lori listens to him when she won't to anyone else. Giff is fine when she wants to go on a spree, but not for this sort of thing. And her Uncle Eric can't do much but roar around when she really goes to pieces. *If* she's gone to pieces. That's quite a performance she's putting on out there."

Nona had changed to another long gown, this time of rusty red, and had clipped on dangling ruby earrings. Her graying hair that I had last seen in a heavy braid over one shoulder had been wound into a thick coil on top of her head, giving her a look of dignity no wheelchair could lessen. Her bright green eyes were ashine with lively malice as she watched the scene on the deck.

"Why is she crying like that?" I asked.

"Because she thinks Chris is behind the fires and she's blaming everyone in sight for not controlling him. Or at least this is what she is claiming this time. We all know better. Even Chris knows better."

I started to ask a further question, but she leaned forward and tapped the box I had rested on my knees.

"What's that?"

I hesitated for just a moment and then opened it to show her.

She looked inside and recoiled. "Close it, close it! I don't like dead things." Then as I was replacing the lid, she stopped me. "Wait!" One small, bony hand darted in, clasped the ring in her fingers and drew it out. With a macabre playfulness, she dropped it over the tip of a fore-finger and let it slide loosely down to the knuckle. "I see the sapphire stone is gone."

Sapphire, I thought. So the ring had contained David's birthstone.

"I never saw that ring before," I said. "He must have bought it since he came here."

She shook her head, her small, firm mouth stretching into a cat's grin. "He didn't buy it. Lori gave it to him. She found it in one of the craft shops in Gatlinburg."

I sat very still, returning her look, hardly blinking. This, I knew, was the edge of real trouble, the rim of disaster. Or perhaps not the rim of anything, but the eye of a hurricane.

"You might as well know," Nona said. "I don't suppose anyone else will tell you. I went up to see Maggie in my car this morning and she said she hadn't said a word to you about it. Trevor's hoping you'll just go away before someone speaks out. But Maggie told me you're planning to stay awhile. So you'd better know. Probably it wasn't altogether Lori's fault, though God knows she can be im-pulsive. And often a little cruel. Her mistake was to take David seriously, and not know he was just trying to spite his brother. She still hasn't realized that. So his death has hit her hard."

I wanted to put my hands over my ears, to stop her words from penetrating. But I had heard them all. Trevor's wife and my husband. Now a number of small pieces began to fall into place. Nona had understood David very well, as poor Lori might not have done.

"David was really a stinker," she went on. "I don't think I need to tell you that. And Lori was ripe for the picking. Maybe that was partly Trevor's own fault. It didn't take much effort on David's part to have Lori adoring him. She's smart in some ways, pretty silly in others. But I expect you know what David could do. You must have been there too, once upon a time. Though I doubt you are anymore. Not from what David told us."

"I hope you're not being as cruel as this to Lori," I said.

She blinked at me, veiling her green look as the wisps of hair danced about her face. "So? You're not as meek as you seem? Good—I like a little spirit. And you needn't think I took everything David said as gospel truth. Maybe we haven't been too welcoming, Karen, but we had to expect David's wife to be a poor sort. Maybe we were wrong. Anyway, if you need help, come to me. I make it my business to know what's going on, and sometimes I have more influence than you might expect."

Now she was talking in riddles. I set the box on a table and left my hassock to move about the room. I had to think of something else quickly. Anger with David was futile now. I looked at the paintings on the walls and saw that they were good. No more ferns. Here a little drama of color and execution had been permitted in the quiet room. I admired what looked like a De Kooning abstraction, and a Bermuda impression by Charles Demuth. Both comparatively old and good. Trevor's taste or Lori's? But I thought I knew. Nona had given me an all too betraying glimpse of Lori, and Maggie had spoken of Lori's liking for the mural of ferns.

All this art appreciation was playing games, I knew, to keep me from thinking of David.

Behind me I heard movement and I turned to see Giff Caton coming through the glass doors from the deck, with Trevor and Lori moving slowly behind him, Trevor's arm supporting his wife.

Lori's cousin came toward me, moving with no great animation. His blue eyes had a rather sleepy look that made me wonder if it was real or assumed. His mouth seemed sensitive and mobile, though thin-lipped, his nose a little too classically carved. He missed being extraordinarily handsome.

"I'm Gifford Caton," he said, "and of course you are Karen. I'm sorry about what happened to David. Useless words, but perhaps there's a little comfort in hearing them spoken."

I put my hand into the one he held out and thanked him. Oddly enough, he was the first one who had uttered any real regret over David's death. Maggie hadn't sounded too sincere in her offhand words.

There was no time for anything else because Trevor was drawing Lori toward me. She looked at me with brimming eyes, her soft mouth trembling as she made an effort to speak. Then she gave up and fled from the room. Trevor followed, but in a few minutes he rejoined us and I could sense the mingling in him of pain, deep resentment and that smoldering anger he couldn't release.

I hated what David had done. I could understand better now Trevor's coldness toward me, but I had no way of lessening it in my own defense.

Nona moved a hand, as though she dismissed Lori. "I've set things out for Lu-Ellen to get us a light lunch. She can make a passable omelet, though I've never convinced her to do anything but wave at us when a meal is ready."

I turned to see the shining, well-scrubbed Lu-Ellen gesturing hospitably from the doorway to the dining room.

"Lori's gone to lie down," Trevor said. "Lu-Ellen will take her something later. Chris often likes to eat lunch in the kitchen and escape the grownups."

Oddly enough, after the glimpse I'd had of storm, this was a pleasanter meal than we'd enjoyed at this table last night. Giff Caton could take credit for smoothing troubled waters. He had the southern man's natural charm, and a gift for easy conversation. He could talk rather lazily and well on almost any subject, and he and Nona carried on a good-natured sparring, in which he lost to her gracefully. With Trevor he seemed slightly less comfortable, and I sensed some core of contention between them—perhaps because Giff was Lori's cousin and Eric Caton's son?

During the course of the meal I tried to tell Trevor how much I liked his house, inside and out, but he only listened remotely and I began to run down very quickly.

"I took some pictures this morning," I wound up feebly. "I'm not sure the lighting was right and I want to go back to that rock out there for more."

"Lover's Leap," Nona said.

I glanced at her and saw that the ring with the missing stone was gone from her finger and wondered what she had done with it. Not that it mattered. It was nothing I wanted to keep. Indeed, I wanted to keep nothing in that box. All its horror should be buried with David.

"I don't know of anyone who has leaped off that rock," Trevor said.

Nona grinned at him. "I'll wager we could find somebody if we dug back far enough. There are always lover's leaps."

Trevor seemed annoyed, but Giff picked up the subject. "Of course the real Lover's Leap is down on the island— Belle Isle. There's a spooky place for you to photograph, Karen. I can show it to you sometime, if you like."

"I've already been to Belle Isle, and I don't specialize in spooky places," I said. "I like to photograph houses. Modern houses."

Trevor's remote look focused a little. "Doesn't that become pretty limiting after a while?"

From him such a remark was unexpected, and I wondered if he was baiting me. "Limiting? You're an architect. You keep on designing houses."

"People live in my houses. Haven't you wanted to broaden your field—take pictures of people, animals—anything alive?"

That was a large and rather sore subject, as Trevor couldn't know. I *had* wanted to branch out more ambitiously. There had been times when I grew tired of even the finest and most handsome of houses. Human expression—faces and the lives behind those faces—had always drawn me, and I had talked to David about trying my hand in a new field. Not studio portraits—more an action type of picture. The sort of thing that might flash a story at the beholder and leave him with better understanding. David had been against my experimenting from the first, and I could remember his very words: *You've got a good thing going that you're paid for well. Why dilute your efforts?*

I hadn't felt that it would be dilution, but perhaps a step into a more challenging and interesting skill. I'd thought about it a lot, but I'd lacked the confidence to persist in the face of David's discouragement. He had become a master at putting me down, and though I knew that in an odd way he had been jealous of what I did, I'd given up and let him stop me. Now Trevor had opened the door a crack with his question, and something in me, too long suppressed, responded.

I smiled at him so warmly that he looked surprised. "That's something I've always wanted to do. Photograph people, I mean. Not just faces—but human beings in real situations. Perhaps even in stress situations."

Nona shook her head in disapproval. "That's the very thing that ought to be stopped. News photographers poking their cameras into the faces of the bereaved, the suffering. Horrible!"

"Yet we all watch, don't we—when it comes on television?" I said. "Though I do agree. I've seen the callousness displayed, and I suppose I'm thinking in different terms. Not just the news story that has to be caught right now. I like to think of some of the great pictures that have been taken without any special pressure, simply because the photographer had a perceptive eye. There's something else, too. I wonder if it's ever possible to photograph good and evil? So they can be recognized, I mean."

Trevor was listening with more interest now. "At least the effects of either can be caught on film."

"Yes, there's that," I said eagerly. "But I wonder if there's something in a face—something caught in some one frozen moment that tells you everything?"

Giff laughed, but the sound carried no ridicule. It was soft and easygoing. "Sure—but what's caught is usually false. Take almost any candid shot of the great and famous and it can be made to look like something from a police line-up."

"Some of that is deliberate trickery," I said. "Downward shots can be flattering and ones from below devastating."

Trevor said, "Why don't you try it out, Karen?"

For just an instant his eyes held mine, and the old warmth and affection for his friend's daughter looked out at me. Though now there was something more—as though he had recognized me as an individual and a woman. With his own intuition he had cut through—for the moment, at least—whatever lies had clouded his memory of me. In surprise I recognized that perhaps no explanations, no contradictions of David's lies would be necessary with him. In the long run he would trust his own judgment.

Without warning tears rose in my eyes, and I blinked hard and turned my attention to eating. Such foolish weakness wasn't for display.

Not until an odd silence fell upon the table did I look

up again, aware of tension. They were all staring toward the door, where Lori stood looking in.

Dressed now in white pants and a blue flowered blouse, her fair hair floating to her shoulders, she looked almost as slight and delicate as the flowered print she wore, and hardly older than her son. Hysteria was past, and her wide blue eyes, still a little red from weeping, regarded me with a fixed look that was unsettling.

"Come on in, honey," Giff called to her, and Trevor pushed back his chair.

"Would you like to join us, Lori?" he asked.

She shook her head. "No, thanks. I was just wondering when you'd be through." She gave me another long, oddly questioning look and vanished from the doorway. We could hear her light steps as she ran down the uncarpeted hall, and I could only wonder why she had come back, and why she had stared at me in that strange, intent way, as though she wanted something of me.

"She's got to come out of this!" Nona snapped. "She can't always shy away from you, Trevor."

"Give her time. She'll recover. She mustn't go on thinking—" Trevor broke off, and Nona finished the words for him:

"Thinking that you planned David's death? Of course she mustn't! It's the most idiotic thing I've ever heard. Maybe what happened was planned—who knows? But not by you."

I must have drawn in my breath sharply because Trevor looked at me down the table—a strange, bleak look that asked nothing, revealed nothing. The moment of warmth was gone as though it had never been.

Once more Giff began to talk in his light, cheerful way, filling in with a change of subject that drew us all to safer ground. For the rest of the meal, however, I found that I didn't want to look at any of them. I fixed my gaze instead upon the giant ferns writhing about their evil queen in Maggie's mural. They were nightmare ferns, really—not pretty plants one would want to share a lifetime with.

Nona saw my fixed attention. "Sometimes that beastly vegetation gets into my dreams at night. Don't misunderstand—I'm very fond of Maggie, and she has real talent. But her imagination can go off the deep end. Maybe it's therapeutic, but sometimes I wonder. . . ."

I hardly listened to her words because once more I had a sense of some current running beneath the surface. Not only here at the table, but through the entire house. Though I couldn't tell from which one of them it emanated. Someone disliked me fervently and wanted me gone. Of that I was sure.

I couldn't shake off this feeling, and when we had finished our fruit and cheese, I excused myself the moment I could leave and hurried to put them all behind me. I was driven now by the new and frightening thought that Nona had stated so bluntly—Lori's belief that Trevor was behind David's death. I could see the trend of her thoughts clearly enough. Trevor discovering his wife's infidelity, yet perhaps blaming David more than he did Lori; perhaps quarreling with his brother so fiercely that others had observed the quarrel. It could easily have happened that way. Whatever had occurred had clearly left him with a furious resentment—yet still he seemed to be protecting Lori, who was clearly in deep need of his help.

All this I could see, and I could imagine him striking out against David in the hot anger of the moment. But to plot against him, to murder by calculated plan—never!

Nevertheless, there had been plotting. Otherwise why the use of an explosive, when only fire had been needed before? No matter—this would never be Trevor's way, and I knew that my instincts were right and that he could never have changed that much in the years since I had known him. I would never believe anything else.

I had reached the lower hallway on my way to my room, and now, for the first time, I noticed something that I'd hurried past before. Halfway along the hall a glass door, leading outdoors, had been set into the passageway. With the bright sun of early afternoon shining down, the exterior was brightly lighted and I saw that the door slid open upon the little grotto I had glimpsed earlier from above.

Under the sky the fishpond shone blue-gold, and I could see goldfish darting in its shallows. But what arrested my attention was the sight of Trevor's son standing beside the stone lantern that was a little taller than the boy. He seemed to be reaching up beneath the curved top, probing into openings cut into the stone, where candles might be placed. As I stood watching, he reached into his pocket and drew out something thin and a few inches in length. He rose on tiptoe to thrust this object into a hollow in the stone.

Having hidden whatever it was, he stepped back and looked around, his eyes searching the high rail on the cliff above, where I had stood early this morning. I barely had time to step back out of sight before his eyes turned my way. When I looked out again cautiously, Chris was kneeling beside the pond, feeding scraps of fish food from a paper packet.

I opened the glass door and went out to stand beside him, watching the reflected face that looked up at me. This boy was Trevor's son, and an unexpected feeling of tenderness toward him touched me.

Under golden bangs the face in the water scowled and Chris rose to his feet. As he stepped back from me, I experienced a swift flash of recognition that marked the resemblance to his father. Not feature by feature, but in the grave, remote expression that withheld and concealed. Then the resemblance disappeared as such things sometimes do and I could see only Lori in his face.

"Hello," I said. "I've been wanting to meet you."

"Why?" He could speak as bluntly as his father.

I answered him quietly. "Because your father was a friend of my father's a long time ago. I was only a little older then than you are, and he was kind to me. I'd like to know his son."

The blue eyes seemed dark and stormy, as his father's could be, and his chin had Trevor's firm set.

"You're *his* wife," he said.

The rejection of me was complete—a rejection of me as David's wife—and I couldn't allow that to remain.

"I wish you'd help me," I said, snatching at the only idea I could think of.

His backward movement halted with the dawning of curiosity. "How do you mean—help you?"

"Just now at lunch I was talking to your father and the others about wanting to photograph people as well as houses. People doing interesting, natural things. The sort of things they do in real life. This would be a good place to start if you could help me think up something. Not just a pose, but something you could be doing. Will you wait until I get my camera, so we can try?"

He gave me neither agreement nor dissent, but stood where he was, staring at me with those wide dark eyes that were so much like Trevor's.

"Just wait there a moment," I said and ran into the house and down the hall to my room.

Its door was ajar, though I seemed to remember closing it. When I pushed it open and stepped inside, I found her waiting for me—Lori Andrews, in one of the armchairs beside the cold hearth.

"Hello, Lori," I said in uneasy surprise. But I couldn't

stay now to find out what she wanted. "Back in a moment," I told her, caught up my camera and returned to the grotto.

Chris was already in retreat, climbing the steps that had been built into the rock. "That's a good idea!" I shouted, setting the stops in a hurry, looking for him in the finder. He was halfway up the cliff when I caught him just as he paused to look angrily down at me. When I'd snapped the shutter twice I waved to him.

"Thanks, Chris! I'll give you prints when I have them made."

He stood for a moment longer, staring down at me, and unexpectedly his mouth spread into a lightning smile that vanished almost as quickly as it had come.

"You sure are fast," he said.

I returned the grin as jauntily as I dared. "Photographers learn to work fast. Sometime I'll show you my camera, if you like."

He didn't answer that but disappeared behind the guard wall above. I gave a last curious look at the stone lantern and then returned to my room. I wanted to know what Chris had hidden there. Not out of idle curiosity, but because this was a troubled boy and he was Trevor's son. Also because I sensed that whatever worried him might be part of my search for the truth. However, this was not the time to investigate, while his mother waited for me.

She was still there when I returned. "Your son was posing for me," I said and dropped my camera on the bed.

She looked a bit surprised, regarding me with those deeply blue, dark-fringed eyes, and I returned her look with frank interest. This was the first time I had seen her long enough to note the details that made up the whole.

Her mouth was small, with a bee-stung look, and I thought of Eric Caton's odd remark about bee venom. Her hair fell to her shoulders, not in a shining sheath like

Lu-Ellen's, but in a curly mass that badly needed brushing.

"You're not a bit like David said you were," she told me, indulging in her own appraisal.

I tried not to sound grim. "Sometimes David liked to fantasize."

"He said you were terribly dull and serious, and not very pretty," she went on, speculating almost as if she spoke to herself.

"I expect I can be all those things."

"It's true you're not pretty. I'm pretty. But people look at you, don't they? Because something reaches out of you toward them?"

Her words surprised me, and I sat down in the chair opposite her, waiting. I didn't think she had come here to analyze me.

"I liked what you said about photography," she went on after a moment. "I was listening to that from the hall. I'll pose for you, if you want. I'd make a good model."

I could only watch her in growing amazement. Where were the tears I had seen, the evident despair?

"You'd make a lovely model," I said, "but posed pictures aren't exactly what I'm looking for."

"You want something unexpected and dramatic, don't you? Do you think I can't be those things?"

"I think you can probably be very dramatic and unexpected." Oddly enough, talking with her was a little like talking to a child. Or was that only the role she played?

Her smile was faintly sly, and again I felt uneasiness. "Okay, then—come along and we'll take some pictures now. I know exactly the right place."

I sat where I was, not trusting her, not wanting to follow her lead. Besides, I had come to my room to be alone, to think about the new and terrible idea that had been put into my mind concerning Trevor. I had to think about it quietly and sanely, in order to dismiss it fully.

She must have seen that I wouldn't be easily moved, for she leaned toward me, not touching me, but very close. "Please, Karen. If I sit around and do nothing for another moment I'll go absolutely mad. And I think you will too. It's all too horrible to think about. We have to push it away until we can get used to it."

But I had no time to push anything away, I thought. Horrible it was, and it might become more so, but I had to face what was there because I owed that at least to David Hallam. I wondered what Lori might know. If what Nona said was true and Lori thought that Trevor . . .

"All right," I agreed, and once more slung my camera bag over my shoulder. Oddly enough, as I lifted it from the bed I had a feeling of being watched. Lori had gone to the door to wait, paying me no attention. Remembering the skylight, I looked up, and caught what might have been movement as something up there slipped out of sight. For a moment I stood still, listening, but there was no sound from the slanting roof and I decided that I must have been mistaken. Drifting clouds overhead, a change of light and shadow could give an effect of something moving. On the other hand, Chris might be up there. It didn't matter.

"I'm ready," I said.

Lori led the way into the hall. "We can go through the door down here. We needn't take the inside stairs."

Following her, I stepped into the little pocket of garden and pond. Lori crossed the patch of grass, hurrying ahead to climb the steps up which Chris had disappeared. Moss grew upon the uneven face of rock, and there were bits of clinging lichen, but the steps had been kept clear and I went up after her, holding onto the iron railing. Once, when I stopped for breath, I looked back. I was well above the lower wing of the house and I could see that it too was bordered by the pocket of rock, with the overhang of the roof extending sufficiently so that no one without a ladder could climb above my skylight. A boy might know a way.

"Come on!" Lori called down to me impatiently, and I mounted the remaining steps and followed her toward the red Ferrari. When I got into the low bucket seat she had already turned the key in the ignition, and a moment later we were rolling out of the drive and down the mountain.

"Where are we going?" I asked.

"You'll see." Her words were curt, and I could tell by her hands clasped tightly on the wheel that she was tense and trying not to snap at me.

We said nothing more on the way down the mountain and I saw that we were taking the road by which I had come only last night. It wasn't until we turned off at the Belle Isle sign, however, that I knew with dismay where we were going. When I glanced at Lori, questioning, she spoke for the first time since we'd left Trevor's mountain.

"Even if you've been to Belle Isle, I don't think you've seen everything I can show you. Of course we're just going to take a few pictures. Remember that—it's only for the pictures."

I nodded, understanding. "Not for questions?" I said. "Not for trying to find out what really happened?"

"I don't want to know what happened!" Tension crackled in her voice and I touched her arm lightly.

"I do. I think David would want me—want *us*—to find out."

"Yes—I'm sure he would. An eye-for-eye and all that! But not right now. Now it's only for the pictures."

"All right," I agreed. "But just for now."

"Nona told you, didn't she? About David and me?"

There was no point in pretending anything else. "Yes."

"And you don't really care?"

"It's happened before. I got over caring a long time ago."

"If you ever did care," she said.

I had no answer for that. I no longer knew what the answer was.

The car was moving more slowly now along the narrower road to the lake and Lori eased her foot on the gas still more.

"You don't really care," she repeated and I heard the break in her voice, and could only pity her. David had left so much damage behind in his philandering.

I tried to be honest with her, to an extent at least. "Perhaps not in the way you mean. But I do care—about David's death. And about people being hurt."

The sound she made was probably laughter—a strange little gurgle of mirth, when nothing was funny.

We reached the branching road that wound around the lake and I saw something that I'd missed last night. A small building—hardly more than a hut—guarded the entrance to Belle Isle, with a sign marked PRIVATE. A different watchman came out, recognized Lori and waved us through. As I had done last night, she chose the way to the left, slowing the car as we neared that dreadful, burned-out ruin. A shiver ran from the back of my neck down along my arms.

"Hurry past," I said, unable to help myself. "I don't want to see that place again."

Instead, she put her foot on the brake and stopped where the broken path led between scarred trees. Before I knew what she intended, Lori was out of the car.

"Come with me," she ordered. "This is your first picture."

Watching her run toward the house, her white trousers

brushing indifferently past a charred bush, picking up a smudging of black, I felt a little ill.

"Not here!" I managed to call after her. "Please come back, Lori."

She turned and I saw her face—blank as though she were sleepwalking. "Come!" she directed. "Bring your camera. Now!"

_____

Four

Something about Lori's look, her voice—no longer light and childlike and feckless—commanded me. I took the camera from my bag and got out of the car.

By daylight I could see that the walk to the house was littered with ash and cinders. Leaves on the nearest trees hung scorched, withered, telling me of the intensity of the heat. Ahead stood the roofless shell of what had been a house, and I walked toward it, aware once more of the terrible burned-out smell—symbolically, for me, an odor of death.

Last night I had spoken David's name aloud in this place, questioning, seeking. Now I promised him silently that his death would not go unchallenged. Whatever he might have done, this was not deserved. Whatever I could do, I would do. This I owed him. I looked up at blue sky framed by blackened ruins and saw a speck that was a plane sailing over far above. An awareness stabbed through me because of this contrast between life in the sky and death on the earth, and I felt doubly shaken.

Ahead, Lori had paused with one foot upon a littered step. "Get your camera ready, Karen. You're looking for unusual pictures, aren't you? Pictures that come out of life—and death."

I tried to stop her. "You said you wanted to push all of this away. But this isn't the way to do it."

She flung me a look that was both agonized and oddly excited, and ducked beneath the fallen timbers of what had been a door. Cinders and char crunched under her feet, and the stench grew even more sickening. Once inside the ruin, she turned about and rested an arm along the slanting beam that blocked the door opening, looking out at me.

"This is the picture," she said. "Take me here, Karen."

Sunlight fell across fair hair that lifted at her shoulders in a slight breeze. Her blue and white blouse and slacks made a screaming exclamation of life against the dead, blackened wreckage behind her.

"Don't do this, Lori," I pleaded. "Don't torture yourself."

Her eyes were wide and staring, as though she looked at something terrible that I couldn't see, and I knew that she wouldn't move from where she stood until I took the picture she demanded. Reluctantly, feeling more sickened by the moment, I set the stops, looked for her in the finder and clicked the shutter. But when I turned away she called after me.

"Wait, Karen! Come in here. Come inside. You were his wife, as I couldn't be. Let me show you where he died."

I wanted to cry out to her to stop tormenting us both,

but already she had moved among the fallen timbers and broken walls of the interior.

"Come!" she repeated. "Come here, Karen," and I heard the rising hysteria in her voice.

It was better to humor her for the moment, and then try to coax her away. I bent to crawl beneath the beam as she had done and felt the crunching beneath my shoes as I moved toward her. The terrible smell stirred afresh as Lori went on ahead of me like a sleepwalker, her white shoes blackening, her slacks smudged with charcoal. I closed my eyes and tried to breathe shallowly, choking back the sickness that rose in me. In my ears I could almost hear the roaring of flames, feel heat singeing my very skin. A man I had married, a man I once thought I'd loved, had died here. Terribly.

"Look!" Lori commanded.

It was almost a shock to open my eyes, not to the scarlet of flames that had seemed all too real, but to the ruin around me. Plaster and lath had been knocked outward by the explosion, but the roof had caved in and burned, and beams had fallen every which way, blocking and barring. I climbed over and under until I was as blackened by smudges as Lori. When I reached the place where she knelt poking with a sooty hand among the cinders, she looked up at me, still like a sleepwalker who had not yet awakened. I was suddenly afraid of what might happen if she realized too abruptly what she was doing.

"It was somewhere about here that he died," she said. "He was alive—so excitingly alive. He held me in his arms. He loved me! And now he's nothing—scattered bones and ashes. He held you too, didn't he, Karen? Can you remember that?"

Her words rang in my ears. Yet they didn't evoke the memory of love and loss she meant to stir in me. Without volition, memory presented me with a scene that had only been one of many. David flinging my schoolgirl love for Trevor scornfully in my face because *he* would teach me what love was all about. I could almost hear the cloth of my nightgown rip, feel the rough pressure of his mouth as he took pleasure in bruising me. Pain was something I'd learned to accept as almost commonplace. Yet I had never wanted pain in my loving. I had always yearned for tenderness.

"You think Trevor is different, don't you?" he'd taunted me. "But he's not. Karen, we're brothers—we're alike! So love me now as you wanted to love him!"

Why had I stayed with David? I wasn't weak, I wasn't without resources of my own. Perhaps it was partly because he always seemed so sorry afterward, when he'd hurt me. Perhaps because I sensed a weakness in him, a need, even a fear of himself that he would never admit. Perhaps because I kept him—to some extent—on a saner road than he might have followed alone. Yet in the end it had been too much and I'd taken the step I should have taken long before. No one—man or woman—should accept so self-punishing a responsibility for another life.

"Karen, what's the matter?" Lori demanded. "Is it getting to you, Karen?"

I came back to my surroundings, and it was almost as though I could see David again, standing here where he had died, arrogant in his suede jacket with the embroidered flame on the pocket, and that broad-brimmed hat that he'd affected set jauntily on his head. In memory his eyes seemed to mock me from under its brim. How did *I* think I was going to help solve the riddle of his death, he seemed to be asking. My incompetence had always been a favorite theme of his, no matter what I might accomplish out in the world.

"Take a picture of me now!" Lori demanded. "This is

the picture I want—here where he must have stood when the explosion came and everything went up in flames. At least he died quickly. At least there was no time for him to suffer."

I knew that in a moment she would break. I was taller than she was and perhaps a little stronger, so I hung my camera by its strap around my neck and took hold of her arm, pulling her up. Somehow I managed to thrust her toward the side of the ruin, where there was no obstruction and only a brief drop to the ground. She took the step blindly and stumbled, and I jumped after her, steadying her as best I could.

"Let's get back to the car," I said.

Her tears held off until she was in the driver's seat and then she did what I had done last night. She put her head on her arms against the wheel. Only I hadn't wept as Lori did. I let her cry for a time, recognizing release, while my thoughts whirled on. Doggedly now, I had only one answer to offer David. Incompetent or not, I had to stay in the vicinity until I *knew*. And that might mean the exposure of a murderer. What David might have done to bring this on himself, I dared not question. I wouldn't judge him now. Memory must be rejected. The blame was not all his, and a debt must be paid.

However, I couldn't make that promise to David and know that I would be heard. I could only promise Lori, and I did so in words that must have spilled out with little coherence. At least I startled her enough to stop her tears, for she raised her head and stared at me.

"What good will that do—finding out who it was? It won't bring him back!"

"David wrote me a letter before he died," I told her. "He said that if anything happened to him it wouldn't be an accident. He said I owed him something. I don't know if that's altogether true, but I think I'll never rest until I pay. If you loved him, you can help me."

"No! Leave it alone, Karen. There's such wickedness here. I don't want to know who's behind it. David had begun to stir it up—so he had to die. I don't want to die, Karen. And nothing will bring him back. What's ahead for us now? That's the only thing that matters. What do *you* want of life?"

The sudden questions surprised me. There was nothing childlike about her now, and once more the hysteria had passed. Now, however, I was learning caution, growing adept at raising barriers. I had already said too much, trusted her too far.

"I want my work, of course," I told her. "It's satisfying, and—"

"Safe?" she put in. "Is that all you want out of life, Karen—to be safe?"

"I thought *you* were making a plea for safety?"

She answered me airily. "Oh, I like high places, but only when I can see the edge." She switched on the engine and smiled with astonishing sweetness. "I have more pictures for you, Karen."

Pictures were the last thing I wanted at the moment. More than anything else I wanted to escape from Lori's company. I wanted to wash the stains and the odor from my hands and face. I wanted to bathe and change my clothes. We were both soot-streaked and carried the smell of stale smoke about us. But already she was driving on around the lake, and I knew it would do no good to protest.

We passed houses in various stages of construction, each one individual, though each faced upon the lake and the green island that floated near the far shore. I tried to shut everything else out of my mind and think only of this creation of Trevor's.

These would be livable houses, using the land well, visually pleasing on the outside, as I knew they would be inside. I could imagine families sitting peacefully on their high decks for an evening meal in the summer and I tried not to remember the color of fire.

Most of the construction appeared to be along the road in the other direction from the way we were taking, and I could hear voices and hammering and the slamming of planks beside the water. But Lori was avoiding the work area.

The road curved toward the far shore as we neared the island. It was a good-sized island, I realized—a hundred acres or more. Most of it seemed heavily wooded, but in one place a strange-looking brown structure thrust above the treetop. Its roof was formed by shingled wedges that rose to a central tower with a balcony running around it.

"What on earth is that?" I asked.

Lori appeared to have recovered, her tears and unsettling words behind her. "It looks like an especially ugly water tower, doesn't it? That's my great-grandfather's octagonal house. That's where old Vinnie took both his brides. Only the second one wouldn't live there."

As we approached along the shore road, I saw that a narrow causeway reached out to the island.

"Great-grandfather Vinnie built that," Lori said. "He wanted access without using boats—since he was going to live there with my great-grandmother. Cecily was his first wife—the one who died so tragically. I'll show you where. Even with the causeway, though, she must have felt imprisoned—the way he wanted her to live. Their daughter was my grandmother—the one who married a Caton."

"Did you know your great-grandfather well?"

"Well enough. By that time he didn't like children. And when I grew up he was awfully old. An old lion. He outlived both his wives and moved back to the island for part of each year. But he let it grow wild and go to pieces. If Trevor takes that part over he'll have a big job on his hands. Though with these fires he'll probably never get that far." She spoke Trevor's name bitterly, as though she had little patience with his objectives.

We drove carefully along the narrow causeway, where the paving had crumbled and potholes prevailed, and she went on telling me about Belle Isle.

"The only time it's really an island is when there are heavy rains and the streams feed the lake, so its level rises and the causeway gets washed over. But mostly you can drive across. The wonder is that Great-grandpa Vinnie didn't put in a drawbridge to pull up after him in his last years."

"Yet he let Trevor come in and start building houses?"

"Oh, he didn't mind that, so long as Trevor didn't touch the island. He used to sit up in that tower and watch everything through his binoculars. Nobody came across the causeway without his permission. My mother and I visited him a few times, but he didn't really like me much until I married Trevor. Trevor was always his darling boy —like the son he never had. Oh, of course there was his grandson Eric, Giff's father, and believe me Vinnie used him. But he didn't like him the way he did Trevor. I don't think Uncle Eric ever got over that."

She braked the car near a grove of shaggy hemlocks that had been planted too close and were crowding each other in a dark thicket.

"It always made Uncle Eric wild," she went on. "But what could he do? Vinnie was in charge. And Trevor is still the fair-haired boy according to the will, unless his Belle Isle project fails. The old man could never stand failure. So there are penalties written into the contracts. Come on. This is where we get out and walk. The driveway to the house isn't impassable, but it's not comfortable."

We picked our way over thick vines that pried up the pavement in spots, stepped over cracks where weeds grew rampant, and eventually reached wooden steps that led to the octagonal veranda running around the house. Old Vinnie had built in wood, not stone or brick, and even though the rest of the island had not been cared for, the house obviously had. It had weathered to an ancient dark brown, but repairs had been made. The first-floor veranda that followed the octagonal structure around boasted a carved railing that was still intact, and there was intricate gingerbread around the supports of the veranda roof. Windows with drawn blinds looked out at us from seven of the wedges, and in the eighth a massive front door with a brass lion's head knocker barred our way.

"It's a creepy place, isn't it?" Lori said. "As he grew old, Great-grandfather Vinnie came to look like that lion on the knocker. The house has always fascinated me, but it still gives me the shivers."

"This I must have a picture of," I told her. "It's a change from my modern houses. Will you be part of it, Lori?"

This intrigued her and while I set my camera she flitted from one pose to another, enjoying herself as simply as though there had been no tears and near hysteria only a little while before. She was a creature of contrasts whose moods couldn't be counted on from one moment to the next.

"There," I said, "that's the one! Hold it."

She stood beside a tall window to the right of the door, looking through the glass.

"But my face won't show," she objected.

"It's not your face I want. It's an attitude. Something

you see through that window terrifies you. Make your body show it."

She caught the idea at once. With one hand she shaded her eyes from outside light as she peered through the glass. The other arm was stretched behind her, palm raised, as though she stopped someone who had followed. The very tensing of her shoulders, the frantic warning of the upraised hand gave an impression of alarm. She turned her head just as I clicked the picture.

"I think someone's in there," she said softly. "Something moved and then was still."

So her sudden tension and the hand warning had been real.

For a moment we stared at each other, perhaps each questioning the other's courage. I was suddenly and intensely aware of the small forest of hemlocks and oak trees that crowded around the house, undoubtedly darkening the windows when the sun was at a slant, cutting off daylight and any view of the lake. Only now, when it was late morning, did the sun reach down to the house.

Lori began to search her bag for a key, and I knew we were going in. That was what I wanted, wasn't it? No more vague questions, but a direct course of action whenever it was possible. An assault upon anything that needed to be answered about Belle Isle. Yet I was uneasy.

"I must have left the key in my other bag," Lori said. "It doesn't matter. Chris has shown me the way he gets in. In fact, it may be Chris who is in there now. My son's an explorer!"

She started toward the steps to join me below, and then, on second thought, reached for the brass doorknob. It turned easily so that the great door swung open ahead of us, the lion's head giving way.

"That's funny," Lori said. "Trevor sends Lu-Ellen over

to clean once in a while, but she's always supposed to lock up when she leaves."

She pushed the door back and stepped across the threshold. I followed on her heels, and we stood together in a foyer shaped like a blunt pie wedge. A somewhat shabby red carpet covered the floor, and there were several pieces of dark, overly carved furniture that might have come out of medieval Germany. The room was empty and dust free.

Across the narrow part of the wedge another door stood ajar and Lori pushed it open upon a vast central room built around the steep flight of stairs that zigzagged back and forth. Sunlight from the high tower at the top flooded down upon the central room, but the outer rooms beyond the balcony rails that circled the stairs were lost in gloom. There was an airless odor of mustiness and disuse.

"Chris?" Lori called. "Chris, are you there?"

Her voice echoed and returned to us from the stairs, but there was no other sound. And no movement until I caught something from the corner of my eye and turned sharply.

"Look!" I said.

The largest and most commanding white cat I had ever seen was stepping toward us out of the shadows.

"Commodore!" Lori cried. "I might have known. Come here and meet Karen. Karen, this is Commodore Vanderbilt. Great-grandpa Vinnie was fond of cats, so long as they weren't thoroughbreds. Not being one himself, he didn't hold much with pure breeding. Aunt Maggie gave him this cat as a foundling when it was a kitten. She said its queer eyes and that black patch over one of them made him look like a pirate. He does look like one, don't you think?"

Commodore came toward us, at first challenging and

defiant, though he deigned to recognize Lori. Then he mewed with an unexpectedly plaintive sound. I wouldn't have expected such a cat to plead. I saw that he had one blue eye and one yellow one, and that he carried this oddity off with confidence and dignity. He was not ready to accept me, and I made no quick overtures, even though I liked cats. David had liked them too, and we'd had one in the early years of our marriage. That was one of the few things we'd been in accord about.

"Why is he here in an empty house?" I asked.

"Because he lives here. It's his ship, I suppose, and he's unhappy anywhere else. Someone from the project brings over milk and food for him nearly every day and leaves it on the veranda, but he forages for himself pretty well, I imagine. He was reasonably fond of Vinnie—since they were two of a kind—but he's never cared much for any-one else. Usually he stays outside, not in the house. I sup-pose, like Chris, he knows various ways in if he chooses to use them."

I moved about the big room, exploring. Apparently it had been used as a conservatory at one time and there were a few pieces of wicker furniture remaining, along with several potted plants. Though some of the latter had died and showed only brown stalks in their large pots.

"Not very cozy, is it?" Lori said. "When I was little I used to think it was like a lighthouse."

"How many stories are there?"

"Five, if you count the tower. There are dozens of these high-ceilinged, pie-wedge rooms running around the outer edge. With the doors always closed. Spooky. Can you imagine my poor little great-grandmother rattling around in a place like this? Vinnie could go out to all his business enterprises in places like San Francisco and Chicago and Dallas and Philadelphia. Not New York because he hated New York. But little old Cecily had to stay here waiting for him until he chose to pop back. No wonder she couldn't take it. Look—here's what I suppose was called the drawing room." She went to a door and pushed it open.

Three of the pie slices had been expanded into one high-ceilinged space, and all the original furniture seemed intact, some of it very fine. There were rosewood and walnut pieces, with authentic Victorian touches in moldering tasseled draperies, their red velvet darkened by the years. There was even a horsehair sofa, only a little the worse for wear.

"Vinnie was still young, but already very rich when he built this house just before the turn of the century. He was thirty and Cecily seventeen when they married and came here to live. But she never liked it. While I was little this room always smelled of Great-grandpa's cigars, but now it just smells stuffy and dead. I wouldn't dare struggle with those old windows."

"Has any of the vandalism touched the island?" I asked.

"Vandalism?" she widened her eyes at me.

"I mean the fires."

"No. Strangely enough, no one has ever bothered this place. I think kids have gotten in a few times, but the damage was small. Of course Trevor keeps a guard at the entrance to Belle Isle, but the whole place can't be walled in and protected."

"What will Trevor do with the house?"

"Nothing, for now. It still belongs to Uncle Eric, since Vinnie never let it go with the project. Trevor says it's getting to be an antiquity and ought to be preserved. He cares more about taking care of it than Uncle Eric does. Maybe he'll work out something so he can open up the ground floor at least, and make a sort of museum out of it. Me—I think I'd just burn the whole thing down."

"Oh, no!" I cried.

She looked at me sharply. "I didn't mean that. We don't speak lightly of burning things down anymore. Come along and I'll take you upstairs. That's where you can get more pictures."

The zigzagging steps made steep climbing, but Commodore chose to come with us, still nimble, for all his years. Near the second floor he hopped up a step just ahead of me, again with that plaintive mew, and in the light that fell from the sunny tower, I noticed a stain on his thick white fur. Near his shoulder a wound shone wet.

"I think Commodore has been hurt," I said.

Lori came down the stairs at once and sat on a step to part the cat's fur. The wound looked open and raw, with some of the hair about it worn away, where he had probably been licking at the sore place.

"Someone must have thrown a rock at him," Lori said, stroking him gently. "How perfectly horrid! Stay around, Commodore, and when we leave I'll get you to a vet." She walked on along the second-floor corridor that circled the stairs, beckoning to me. "There's something I want to show you here. A real curiosity. Pretty sybaritic for old Vinnie, I must say. Who'd ever have suspected him of this!"

The door she stopped before opened upon a bathroom that had seen better days. Many of the floor tiles were loose, or missing, and several of the many mirrors were cracked. But the Roman splendor of the room was its sunken tub of pale, rose-mottled marble. The tub was circular, deep enough to sit in with water up to one's chin, and with marble steps leading to its wide rim. There were even marble handholds to help one down into the bath, and golden faucets on the far side indicating the luxury of running water.

"He had it put in when the house was built," Lori said, "and he brought that rose-garnet marble here from Mexico. He used to invite guests straight upstairs to see this bathroom, he was so proud of it. But I expect he also enjoyed more private moments in it with Cecily. She would have looked beautiful reflected in all those mirrors."

I wasn't sure why the bathroom with its glass and enormous marble tub made me a little uneasy.

"It's not exactly Victorian," I said.

"Oh, but it is—from what I've read about the Victorians. Only Vinnie must have been more open about his predilections."

Perhaps Cecily really had enjoyed herself in this hard glass and marble setting. At least I hoped so as we walked back along the circular corridor.

Lori stopped before another brown door that seemed like all the rest, until she pointed to a brass bolt that had been set on the panel, to close it from the outside.

"He used to lock her in sometimes," she said. "Whenever she got especially rebellious. Cecily was his greatest treasure, you know, and he had a phobia about someone stealing her from him."

"Or of her running away, I should think." I was beginning to sympathize with poor Cecily and the life she must have led.

"Probably. He got over all that with his second wife. Maybe Cecily scared him so badly by what she did that he stopped trying to be a jailer."

Lori pulled the door open and drew me into the dim interior of the room. I was immediately conscious of an odor that was different from that of the rest of the house. This one room was not damp and musty like the others, but carried a familiar scent that I couldn't quite place.

Lori sniffed the air. "Smells like Nona's sandalwood candles. Someone's been over here. There's no electricity in the house now, so it's dark. But this is where our little ghost lives."

She tittered nervously, and I looked about the shadowy,

wedge-shaped room. A couch stood against one wall, and various easy chairs, footstools, tables and taborets were set here and there in a rather haphazard manner. Pictures still crowded one inner wall that slanted toward the center of the pie.

"This was Cecily's sitting room," Lori told me. "The bedroom she shared with Vinnie is through that door over there. And of course people say she still comes here and that she'll haunt these rooms forever. Though I can't see why, since she always hated the house. Anyway, this is the one part that Lu-Ellen won't clean. Sometimes I come over and do it—just for Cecily. Because, after all, I can't have my poor little great-grandmother living here in dust and cobwebs."

Lori went ahead of me into the room and opened a window that moved up easily enough upon fresh air and sunshine, as though it had been recently used. The shadows fled and dust motes danced in a gilded beam as Lori moved on about the room, opening a cabinet here, touching a finger to a marble tabletop there, pausing beside the couch.

"You can see that Cecily's been sleeping here," she said.

Startled, I glanced at the green coverlet on the one piece of furniture that was a modern anachronism. An indentation showed where a head might have lain on the pillow.

"Ghosts hardly ever leave imprints like that," I objected. "Perhaps it was Commodore."

Lori gave her odd little gurgle of a laugh. "No, I suppose it's not very ghostly to dent pillows. It was probably Giff. He could have used the candles too, to freshen the air and give him light. I expect that's why the front door was unlocked. Sometimes, since the fires began, Giff has stayed here overnight. Aside from the drawing room and library, there are only two rooms still furnished—this one and Great-grandpa Vinnie's bedroom. Giff would certainly prefer Cecily's company. He thought he could roam out from here and see who was starting the fires. You can view all of Belle Isle from the tower. I thought it was pretty enterprising of him since he doesn't usually make that much effort."

"Has he learned anything?"

"I'm not sure. If he's onto something he isn't talking. I shouldn't think he'd really want to know, since Uncle Eric, his father, will profit if Belle Isle reverts into his hands."

I asked my question quickly, to take her off guard. "Which side are you on—Trevor's or your uncle's?"

She shrugged a careless response. "Maybe I'm not sure. Anyway, it doesn't matter anymore because it's over now. Whoever set that last fire must have taken off pretty fast. He wouldn't stay around for a murder charge."

"You said there was wickedness," I reminded her. "What did David tell you?"

Moving away from me on another circuit of the room, she touched an article absently here and there. Then she seemed to make up her mind and turned to face me.

"He said that someone had been hired to damage Belle Isle houses. He said the man was a pro who had been brought in. Somebody named Bruen. Joe Bruen, I think."

"How could he know? Had he seen the man?"

"He didn't tell me that."

"Have you told this to Trevor?"

"Trevor hasn't asked me. He's not interested in my conversations with David."

"But who hired this man? Did David tell you that?"

"That's the trouble—he didn't. I think he knew, but he didn't have enough proof. Maybe he found the proof. Maybe that's why he was killed."

"That's what I think," I agreed. "But until we know who was behind this man—or find this Joe Bruen—"

Lori gave me a quick, frightened look. "Leave it alone, Karen. David's been killed, and whoever caused his death could be twice as dangerous now. I don't think there will be any more fires, so just leave it alone. It would have been better if David had never come here. Though of course there are other possibilities. Trevor—"

"You know Trevor wouldn't harm Belle Isle!"

"Oh, not at first. But he might if he could get rid of David. They always hated each other."

"I don't believe that, and you don't either. It was Trevor who asked him to come down here."

"How do you know what I believe?" She began to back away from me toward the door. "Just because you were in love with Trevor a long time ago doesn't mean that you know him now. Oh, yes you were! David told me about that too. David told me a lot of things. About Trevor. And about you."

"There was nothing to tell. I was barely sixteen when he used to come to see my father. He didn't know I was alive."

She fumbled for the gold chain she wore at her throat and pulled out the ornament that dangled on it—concealed until now. "Do you see this?"

As she held it up, I recognized the gold circlet. Not an ornament, but a ring with an empty setting. So Nona must have returned it to Lori.

"I gave this to David!" she cried, and there was a kindling of excitement in her eyes that I didn't like. "It came out of the ashes of that house, and now it's all I have of him. You never really knew anything about either of them. Not about David—or about Trevor."

She was moving into excitement again and I could find no words to quiet her.

Still backing toward the door, she made a quick, astounding move. She sprang through the opening, banged the door upon me and shot the bolt. I was locked in as Cecily had been, and I could hear Lori's light gurgle of laughter beyond the heavy wooden panel.

I wasn't immediately frightened—only astonished and annoyed. This was a child's trick, irresponsible, and I would not give Lori the satisfaction of rattling the door or commanding her to open it. When she found that I wasn't going to respond in a satisfactory way, she would open it again, and I would ask her to take me back to the house. I'd had enough of Lori Andrews' company, and I was beginning to realize that she hadn't brought me here merely to take pictures.

Out in the hall the silence was complete and I fancied that she must be standing close to the door, listening for any outcry from me. I swung my camera bag from my shoulder and set it on a small table. Then I went to the door of the adjoining bedroom and tried the knob. The door was locked, of course. Two wide windows looked out into the dark branches of hemlocks, and I knew that it was only now when the sun was high that light was able to fall into this room at all. It would be dark with shadow later on—and without electricity.

Even from this second floor the ground seemed far away—much too far for climbing or jumping, had I been so inclined. But there was no need. This was a waiting game, and after a while Lori would tire of it. In the meantime I might as well amuse myself by examining Cecily's hideaway. Or prison.

As I moved about I made no effort to be quiet. Let Lori deduce what she could from any sounds I made. Near the couch where Giff might have slept, I found that a bedroom item had been brought into the sitting room. On a low commode had been set an old-fashioned washbasin and pitcher—white with large blue flowers. Beside it rested a clean towel and a used cake of soap. Undoubtedly water had been turned off in the house as well as light, but there was water in the pitcher, so Giff must indeed have been using this room. Here, at least, was something I could do.

I poured water into the basin and washed my face as well as I could manage without a mirror, and scrubbed my hands thoroughly. The odor still clung to my smudged clothes, but at least I felt cleaner.

Now I could continue my examination of the room. The spread of photographs on one wall drew me and I crossed the faded Aubusson carpet to look at them. There were several pictures of a young man, probably in his late twenties, dressed in the mode of the well-to-do of his day—frock coat, watch chain, gold fob and all. Vincent Fromberg undoubtedly, in the early days of his burgeoning business ventures. That must have been shortly before he had married the girl who appeared in several of the pictures.

Cecily at seventeen, when she had come to this house, was a gentle beauty with dark hair and lustrous dark eyes that not even the photography of that day could quench. In one picture she looked up adoringly at her taller husband, but mostly she was pictured alone in rather artificial poses. Theatrical poses. I was especially fascinated by a profile portrait in which she sat in a carved chair, with a garland of flowers across her knees, her gaze upon a very artificial crescent moon, her costume in the Grecian style of Isadora Duncan.

I bent to look at the printing across the lower corner of one picture and saw that it had been taken by a theatrical photographer. As a young and beautiful girl, Cecily had been on the stage. Poor young thing. Even if she had married for love and not wealth, to be brought like a captive to this island and buried alive in such a mausoleum was hardly a happy fate.

The turn of my own thoughts was unfortunate. Being

buried alive was not something I wanted to think about right now. Time was passing, and apprehension began to grow in me. Surely Lori wouldn't carry this small trick too far. Moving more nervously now, I returned to the window, but I could see nothing except trees and a space of ground immediately below. Lori's car was out of sight on the other side of the house and we had walked quite a distance from it.

At least there were sounds from far away that told me that I was not wholly isolated. Across the lake that I couldn't see, workmen were making the sounds of their craft as the building of Belle Isle houses continued. If I became desperate I could at least shout for help and someone would surely hear.

A sound reached me that was closer than the noise of construction—the sound of a car starting, moving away over the rough road that led to the causeway. So Lori had abandoned me. This was carrying her joke too far! Or *was* it merely a childish prank? Was Lori driven by something more spiteful, more dangerous and unpredictable than I had been willing to face?

Now I had no hesitation about rattling the door. I even flung my body against the bolted panel that shut me in, and only a bruised shoulder jarred a little sense into me. Losing my head wasn't going to help.

Was there any tool to be found in the room? Any instrument that I might use to break through the panel? I was no wilting Cecily to take my imprisonment without fighting back, but I must do it sensibly. Of course Cecily had fought too, in her own sad way—eventually. I wondered where she had died. Had she flung herself from the high tower at the top of this house? How old had her daughter been at that time? How old had Cecily been? Lori had said she would show me where it had happened, but a more intriguing form of amusement had offered itself, obviously.

I wondered if Lori had planned from the first to bring me here and shut me in. Somehow I didn't think so. More likely, it had been a spur-of-the-moment impulse.

Nothing offered itself immediately as a means of attacking the door, and I returned to my exploration. The double doors of a wardrobe pulled open easily, revealing only a storm lantern on the floor inside, a box of kitchen matches and several candles. I sniffed at one and wrinkled my nose at the scent of sandalwood. I hoped I would need none of these.

Near the double windows stood a small desk, where Cecily might once have sat writing notes to her friends—if she had been allowed to keep any friends.

I sat down in the small chair with its faded upholstery, and began to open drawers idly. All were empty. Not even a scrap of notepaper remained that might be of interest.

As I studied the cubbyholes above, equally unrewarding, I rested my hands on the old-fashioned blotting pad. Its corners were tucked into a leather holder and the green blotter under my fingers bore faded traces of brownish ink. For want of anything else to do, I examined them. The script was in reverse, of course, and most of the blottings I couldn't make out. Spelling backward, one word seemed to be "lonesome," and another looked as though it might be "desperate."

How strange and pitiful that only these shadows of words remained of a desperately lonely wife. Perhaps this was the blotting of a last note she had written before she died.

Tracing the faint script, my fingers found an unevenness beneath the blotter, as though something might have been tucked under it. I pulled out two corners and bent the blotting paper back to reveal a folded sheet of ruled paper. When I picked it up the sheet fell open and I read the few words scrawled with a black felt pen.

Tomorow it will be done. Dont worry.

The misspelling of "tomorrow," the omission of the apostrophe in "don't" showed near illiteracy. But whose illiteracy? For all I knew, some cleaning woman who couldn't spell had left her promise to do as directed.

Only I didn't believe that. The skin on my arms crept a little as I stared at those scrawled words. This note was something that mattered—I was sure of it. I folded the paper again gingerly and covered it once more with the green blotting paper. It could stay hidden until I could do something about it.

I left the desk and returned to my search for a weapon that would help me with the door. Now, more than ever, I wanted to reach Trevor. I must show him what lay under the blotter and I must tell him about the name Lori had mentioned—Joe Bruen.

Continuing to circle the room, I came to the inner chimney, with its fireplace. It must not have been used for years, but an iron poker still stood in its stand by the hearth, and I picked it up in triumph. This would get me out of Cecily's room.

The panel did not break easily in that stout old door, though cracks appeared in the varnish after a blow or two. I continued to strike at the panel until the satisfactory sound of splintering rewarded me, and the poker went through. I'd drawn it back for another furious blow, when suddenly the outside bolt was slid back, and the door pulled open. My blow was already descending as Trevor caught my upraised hand. I gaped at him for a moment and then went limp, dropping the poker.

"Thank goodness!" I said and fell into a chair. "I—I was locked in."

"I know," he said. "I'm sorry. I was down at one of the houses talking to the builder when you and Lori went by in her red car. I supposed she was bringing you here, since it's one of her favorite places. But when she drove back a while later without you, I decided to investigate. Judging by all those smudges, you must have stopped along the way."

I nodded, not wanting to go into that. "Is Lori often given to this sort of trick?"

He looked down at me grimly and I found myself remembering what a joyous person he had once been—a man with a zest for life and a brimming vitality that had carried him far. Had it been Lori who had quenched all that—Lori and his brother?

"I'm sorry it happened," he said, not answering my question.

I couldn't explain the rest—not the details about Lori's behavior in the ruined house.

"I thought she was near hysteria once or twice," I told him.

He looked away, not meeting my eyes, and I sensed his torment, sensed an anguish that went deeper than he wanted anyone to see.

"Never mind," I said quickly. "And I am sorry about damaging the door. I was getting a bit desperate and I had to get out. Though I don't suppose she'd have left me here forever. She brought me over to show me the island. We were supposed to climb to the tower, where I could take some pictures."

He made an effort to rouse himself. "Then why not finish the tour, now that you're here? If you're not too upset."

"I'm fine. But first I want to show you something." I

went to the desk and slipped the paper from under the blotter, held it out to him. "I found this by chance. Do you think it means anything?"

He studied the black scrawl for a moment. "I don't know. It might."

"Lori said David had told her he believed a man named Joe Bruen was behind the fires. A hired pro, Lori said."

"Yes. David told me there was a torch involved. He was sure of that. But he didn't give me his name. Perhaps this furnishes something more to work with."

Trevor took an envelope from his pocket and slipped the folded sheet into it carefully.

"Can you really find out something from that?" I asked.

"Maybe. I'll send it to David's company in New York and see what they can track down."

"Fingerprints?"

"It's possible. Though they won't be just Joe Bruen's prints, of course. We've both handled it. And we can't know if the person it was intended for ever saw it. It would be good to come up with his fingerprints too."

"Lori says that Giff Caton has been using the house lately. Sometimes sleeping here, so he could watch for what was happening."

Trevor shrugged. "I didn't know that, but don't let's leap to conclusions. After all, the island still belongs to his family."

"The house would be a good place to work from if you were going to set fires, wouldn't it?"

He let that go. "At least there haven't been any since David's death. Now if you're ready, we can climb to the tower." He sounded impatient, perhaps eager to be rid of any duty to me.

Once more I picked up my bag, and when we were out in the hall I looked about for the cat.

"I hope Lori has taken Commodore away," I said. "He

had a shoulder wound that looked bad. As though someone had struck him with a rock."

"I didn't see him when I came in, so we'll hope she's
picked him up. Lori is fond of animals, and Chris dotes
on that cantankerous old pirate of a cat."

We started up the stairs together, and I was no more
comfortable in Trevor's company than I'd been in Lori's,
though for a very different reason. It would be easy to let
myself go if he would let me, and enjoy being with him. I
found that I still liked to be near him, and I was all too
aware when our arms touched casually as we mounted the
stairs. But that was a road I dared not travel, and his indifference to me was a protection against myself. He
wouldn't quickly forget that I had been David's wife, and
therefore suspect. Nor did I forget for a moment that he
belonged to Lori, and that he was far from indifferent to
her, no matter what she had done.

I climbed the stairs beside him, feeling torn and far
more tense than I wanted to be.

From above, the glass panes around the tower room
flung light down upon us, though the circling floors were
dark and shadowy with their closed doors.

"What is in all those rooms?" I asked.

"They're mostly empty now. A lot of the furniture has
been taken away. Some of it was old enough to be rated
antique, and what hasn't been moved to Asheville for the
use of the family has been sold. There seems to have been
a tacit agreement, however, to leave Vinnie's library and
bedroom, and Cecily's sitting room, as they were. Maggie
says the family doesn't like to upset Vinnie, even now that
he's dead."

"Lori spoke of your turning the house into a museum
that people could visit. It's certainly distinctive enough to
be worth preserving."

"The Catons would have to give their permission. Vinnie never intended his seclusion to be invaded. But I'd like to see the island opened up and made available. With a little success, I think Eric would give in. However, with all the troubles we've had—"

"Don't you think the fires are over now?"

"I hope so. I only wish that David had told us more."

Trevor turned away and climbed ahead of me to the top of the house—the tower. When I reached the last steep step, he extended a hand to pull me up, and I found myself in a small, glass-enclosed room, with a balcony circling outside. A door led us out into the wind.

The tower was higher than the four chimneys which the house boasted, and which grew from four wedges of roof below us. Once more the view was marvelous—reaching across treetops toward the Great Smokies, where for once the mountains stood up blue and clear from their many folds. In the other direction we could look over the lake to Trevor's houses and follow bits of the road that eventually wound its way up the mountain. I found his own house almost at once. What drama he had created up there! The house seemed poised to take flight from its eyrie, the roofs pointing outward like wings that would carry it away.

"Did you know it would look like that?" I asked softly. "Before it was built, I mean?"

"It was down on paper," he said, "and I'd built a model. But even more it was a vision in my mind. Of course nothing ever quite matches the vision. Practical matters hold you down. Human limitations. But I think it comes close to what I imagined. I used to stand at this very rail and see in imagination what it would look like up there against the rock."

"It's the finest of all your houses. Those I've seen. The most brilliant."

He said nothing, and to break a moment that was, for

me, close to tears, I took out my camera and attached a telescopic lens. I wanted to catch the sweep of the mountain rising to the house at the very crest and bring it all nearer. When I went home I would be able to look and recall this moment of standing beside Trevor, looking at the faraway house he had built.

While I was about it, I tried a shot or two of the nearer Belle Isle project, all too aware of the loss of joy, the loss of creative satisfaction in the man beside me.

"There are closer views of the island and the houses," he said. "Since you're here you should see something more of Vinnie Fromberg's beautiful isle."

I hung my camera strap around my neck and studied the nearer view—woods and winding paths, and a beach that had been put in, where ripples touched the sand. Beyond, centrally located on the island, was something else —a low white structure that sloped down a hillside and disappeared behind more trees.

"What's that?" I asked, pointing.

"It's been called Vinnie's Folly for years. He built it for Cecily. He was so wise and clever and shrewd—and so foolish when it came to his wife. He thought he could hold her here and keep her happy by giving her toys to play with. He belonged to a generation that still patterned itself after the Victorians and never seemed to learn very much about women. It's an open-air theater, with which she was supposed to amuse herself."

"I saw some of her stage pictures in her room. But didn't having a baby make up for losing the stage?"

"I gather that her daughter's care was mostly taken out of her hands by nurses and governesses. And later a suitable boarding school. Would you like to come and see her theater? It's only a short walk."

For this small moment I wanted nothing more than to prolong my time alone with Trevor. The terrible question that I had gone to my room to think about had been resolved, dismissed. He had changed, but not in that way. There was a great deal to trouble, to haunt me, but I knew that Trevor Andrews would never have harmed his brother.

Five

We didn't follow the original carriage road, but took a path that led through deep woods of oak and hickory, with here and there lovely tulip trees that would bloom in the spring. There were stands of hemlock and pine, and where the woods thinned, patches of sunlight crossed our way and September wild flowers bloomed on every hand.

Trevor identified some of them for me. Those clusters of pink over there were joe-pye weed, and the yellow was wild artichoke. In a low damp place bright cardinal flowers grew, and there were stands of wild purple asters everywhere. The devil's walking stick fascinated me—thorny, like a small tree with purple-red berries—and I loved the little heart's-a-bustin'-with-love flowers. Always, of course, there was the surprise of the sourwood trees splashing their early autumn red among the green of other foliage not yet ready to turn.

"Now we come to trouble," Trevor said. "Look what's happening here."

The path had turned away from the water and a large area of sunlight opened on our left. The sun, however, lighted the strangest of scenes. Running toward the opposite side of the island, a heavy broad-leafed vine had swallowed the landscape. It had grown over bushes and trees and run along the ground unchecked, covering everything in its path. The shape of trees and shrubbery showed beneath the vines in rounded forms—almost like waves running across the island in undulating greenery.

"I've never seen anything like it!" I said. "What on earth is it?"

"Around here they call it mile-a-minute. It's kudzu, a Japanese plant that was mistakenly introduced into the South before World War II. It was supposed to be good for fodder. And it was good for shade and ground cover, and rather beautiful—before it became terrifying. Only once it took hold it couldn't be stopped. So far they figure it has swallowed at least a million acres of the South. King Kong Kudzu!"

I left the path to touch a broad, three-pointed leaf in wonder. "What does it do—seed itself in?"

"No. The American plants don't produce seeds, but every twelve inches of the vine there's a joint capable of producing new plants. That's the way it moves. It can grow a foot in a night and there are jokes about closing your windows at dusk so the kudzu won't climb in. James Dickey even wrote a poem about it and called the vines 'green, mindless, unkillable ghosts!' "

A marvelous description, I thought, regarding the monstrous jungle landscape with misgiving. It looked so—unnatural.

"How did it get started here on the island?"

"I suppose someone brought over a pretty plant—and this is the result. If it isn't stopped it will bury trees, house, everything. Kudzu doesn't strangle trees the way some vines do. It just covers them over and shuts out the sunlight so they die. Everything under there is dead or dying. The stuff's hard to kill, because if you dig it up it will grow wherever it's discarded. And it's difficult to burn. There are chemicals that will kill it and I'll start with them over here the minute Eric gives me a green light. We can't have it swallowing Cecily's theater, among other things."

At least the main thrust of the vine was toward the other side of the island, and the path had been left free, so we were able to walk on until our way met the carriage road again. We followed its broken surface through the woods to a tall hedge, where a gate barred our way. Here the drive ended in an open space where vehicles could be parked.

"There used to be a stable here," Trevor said, "but it rotted away long ago."

He opened the rickety gate and set it back on loose hinges. As I went through, the sight of the theater burst upon me in one breathless vision. It was a little Greek amphitheater, still a dazzling white as it ran down the hillside in circling stone steps to the wide spread of a stage below. Crowding hemlocks formed the wings and made a perfect backdrop to the stage. An effort had clearly been made to create a theater that was professional in every respect. High at the top, above the concrete tiers, were roofed sheds and a small building where piles of wooden chairs were still housed. On either hand towers built of open metal piping that would not hide the view held lighting equipment, with ladders climbing to the platforms at the top.

"Did it give Cecily any pleasure at all?" I asked.

"I think it must have at first. I've heard Vinnie talk about those days. He even brought in a company of players to act with her, and she had costumes made for the productions. Apparently she had a nice little voice and the acoustics here are good. She could dance a bit too, and Vinnie encouraged her and probably made her think she was better than she was. He told me once that she could never have made it outside on her own. Perhaps that was only what he wanted to think."

"But to lock her into her room, as Lori said he did!"

"I think that was later, when she must have become a little unbalanced."

"What happened to her?"

"He never liked to talk about that. I only know that she got away and came down here one moonlit night. She climbed that ladder over there to a lighting platform and threw herself off, down on the concrete. They say she died right away. She was only thirty-seven."

So this too was a haunted spot, I thought, and found myself sighing. Poor young Cecily, dancing and singing her heart out down on that small stage. Then climbing to the lighting tower and flinging herself off to die on these very stones beneath our feet.

"It's a sad place," I said. "Perhaps you should let the kudzu have it."

Trevor shook his head. "It's better to build something useful on the old and wipe out painful memories. This is a little jewel of a theater and it could be easily restored. When Belle Isle is finished, and when the people I've built it for are living there, they could use a place like this. Then it would be for the living—as it should be."

"I think Cecily would like that," I told him, marveling again at his tenacity. Despite all that had happened, he hadn't given up. I felt far more clearly convinced of his attitude toward Belle Isle than I did about how he felt concerning Lori and David. Now and then I'd glimpsed an inner rage, but the volcano was kept well underground and if he harbored anger against Lori, he wasn't letting it show. Which might in itself be dangerous.

At least, since the moment when he had found me locked into Cecily's room, his antagonism toward me seemed to have lessened a little. Indifferent he might be much of the time, but he was no longer blaming me because I was David's wife.

He smiled at me now as we walked down the steps, and I found that my hand was in his. He held my fingers lightly, casually, as he drew me along, steadying me on the descent.

On the stage below us something moved, then slipped away into the hemlocks at one side. Trevor saw it too and stopped beside me on the concrete steps.

"Who's there?" he called.

For a moment there was no response. Then a man stepped out from the dark shelter of branches and stood looking up at us from the left side of the stage. It was Gifford Caton—Eric's son, Maggie's stepson.

"Hello up there!" He raised an arm in languid greeting and his voice carried to us clearly. "Are you showing Karen our haunted theater?"

"That's right," Trevor said, and as we went down the remaining tiers together he did not drop my hand. "What are you doing out here, Giff?" he asked, as we reached the edge of the stage.

Giff stood just above us now, his ash-blond hair shining palely in the sun, and when he smiled I lost the sense that he wasn't really handsome. It was a beautiful smile that flashed down at us, yet I had a strong feeling that it wasn't entirely real. Giff, I suspected, would have been more pleased if we hadn't discovered him here, and I wondered why. Nevertheless, he answered Trevor's question without hesitation.

"Dad wanted me to have a look at this place, Trev. He wants a report on its condition."

"Why?"

The smile flashed off like a light extinguished. "Belle Isle is never going to work out the way you planned. You must know that by now. It will revert back to Dad and he'll put it all to more practical use."

"Not for another two years," Trevor said.

"You'll give up before then."

"No," Trevor told him quietly, "I won't. The fires are over now and we'll move ahead. No one would stay around to set another and possibly get caught. Even charged with murder."

Giff turned and waved an arm again. "Come on out, Maggie. Our secret has been discovered."

Again there was movement from the hemlock wings and Maggie Caton sauntered out upon the stage to join her stepson. She wore a man's white shirt over her jeans, and her plump person still had a look of being put together with pins and bits of string. The pepper-and-salt mass of red hair turned dingy in the sun as she came to stand beside Giff, staring down at us from the edge of the stage.

"My secrets are still secret," she said and grinned at me. "Hello, Karen. What do you make of Belle Isle? Have you met Cecily yet?" Her look traveled over me rather oddly, and I remembered the smudged state of my clothes.

"I'd like to," I said. "Lori tells me that she's still around. That is, she told me before she locked me into Cecily's sitting room."

I was being deliberately provocative. Trevor dropped

my hand and I moved a few steps away from him, sensing his disapproval but feeling that small attacks on every front were the only weapons I could use. And I meant to use them. Only with surprise could I catch anyone off guard.

Giff shook his head at the thought of Lori locking me into Cecily's room, while Maggie looked down at me from the stage, owl-solemn.

"Do you remember what I told you this morning?"

She had told me a lot of things, but I knew what she meant—that I should go away as soon as the funeral was over, and never look back.

"I don't remember."

Trevor spoke brusquely. "There's not much else to see, Karen. A few dressing rooms are around in back, but they were built of wood and they're falling down. Shall I take you home now?"

There was no further point in staying with him. I had probably misread that moment of friendship, and I disliked his cold courtesy.

"You've taken enough time from your work on my account," I said. "Perhaps Giff and Maggie will let me go back with them. When they're ready."

Maggie gave her stepson a quick look, and I suspected that I was not entirely welcome. But that was where I must be—where I was least wanted. Trevor couldn't tell me anything more for now, but perhaps Giff and Maggie could. An increasing sense of tension was rising in me. Almost without my being aware of it, I was being driven by a race with time. As though some hidden clock were ticking away toward—toward what? Were the fires really over? But even if the man who had set them had fled, the influence behind him remained and was all the more dangerous because of the guilt of David's death. It was the man who gave the orders who must be found and exposed. I must think only of this. Doggedly.

Trevor left us and went up the tiers in long strides to the side entrance by which we had come in, disappearing through it.

"Have you seen all you want, Giff?" Maggie asked.

"Enough for now. My car's around on the service road, Karen. Shall we walk over there now?"

Once more I was aware of his charm—aware but not susceptible. I trusted Gifford Caton no more than I did anyone else.

We went through an opening in trees that edged the stage and down steps leading to ground level. Here I saw that a semicircle of connecting wooden dressing rooms had been built. Several were in a state of near collapse, but there was one with an open door that showed a partially furnished interior. Curious, I went to look in.

Giff spoke at my shoulder. "That's where Great-grand-mamma used to dress. Some of her things are still there. As you can see, Lori has been fixing it up."

"It's her own private museum," Maggie said.

"Do you mean the theater has never been used since Cecily's death?"

"Vinnie wouldn't allow it," Giff explained. "But of course if Dad takes the place over after Trevor he'll turn it into a real theater. There could be money in a place like this if it was opened to seasonal visitors. We'd tear all this stuff down, naturally, and rebuild."

The vultures waiting, I thought, still strongly on Trevor's side.

I went up the single step and through the door. One wall of the small room was still a mirror and I saw my soot-streaked yellow sweater and gray slacks reflected in its wavery surface. A wooden chair had been drawn before the make-up shelf, where a single scarlet and black jappened box rested. Where I'd have expected a damp and musty smell, there again seemed to be a faint aroma of sandalwood. When I sniffed, wrinkling my nose, Maggie laughed.

"Nona's ubiquitous candles. Eric brought some home from his last trip to Hong Kong and Nona dotes on them. I wouldn't have them around, but Lori's been bringing them over to the island to counteract must and mildew. To make things pleasanter for Cecily, she says. Lori enjoys whimsical games, as you're already discovering."

Whimsical was not exactly the word I would have used, but I let it go.

The decorated black tin box coaxed my curiosity, and with one finger I flipped up the lid. Inside was a rouge-stained rabbit's foot, a soiled powder puff, a round box of cake rouge with an old-fashioned label on the lid, sticks of dried-out grease paint, eyebrow pencils and brushes. Surely a turn-of-the-century theatrical kit. I let the box lid fall with a clank. These must have been things Cecily Fromberg had used in her pretense that she was an actress on the stage, and the sympathy I'd felt for her in that room at the octagonal house and out in the theater returned. Somehow, leaving these pitiful remnants of her life here seemed almost indecent.

"Why haven't these things been put away?" I asked Maggie, who had stepped into the room behind me. "It's a little macabre, isn't it?"

She looked at me in the distorting mirror. "Vinnie gave an order to leave her dressing room alone, and he never countermanded it. He didn't want anyone coming here to touch her things. Except himself. Since he hasn't been gone all that long, nothing has been done."

"Sometimes," Giff said from the doorway, "he used to come here at night when he was staying on the island. I remember once when my parents brought me here with them, looking for him because he'd disappeared from the house. I remember walking out from the wings with my father and seeing him out there—sitting on a step watching the stage, as though he might see her again. That was after he was old and his second wife had died."

"It's terribly Victorian and sad," Maggie said. "Nobody goes around haunted anymore."

Oddly, a memory of the weird ferns of Maggie's mural returned to my mind, and I wondered. Wasn't *that* a haunted painting?

I moved on about the small room. Again there was a wardrobe cabinet that belonged to the days before closets were in use, and I looked inside to see two or three moldering costumes hanging there, their sequins long since dulled. An age-shredded wrapper that Cecily must have worn when making up clung to a hook, and I closed the door quickly, shutting out my own intrusion. Out in the room stood what might once have been a fine Recamier sofa, straight out of a French painting. Now its satin was frayed and torn, and mice had made a nest at its foot.

"Look at this!" Suddenly Maggie pounced and drew out something from beneath the sofa, holding it up.

The object was an empty tomato juice can, its bright red and white label intact, and the top gone.

"Our ghosts have a thirst," Maggie said dryly.

Giff came into the room, crowding it with his tall presence, and took the can from her. "Sorry, I must have left that behind. I've camped out a few times, both here and up at the house, trying to find out what was happening."

So Lori had been right. "What have you found out?" I asked.

"Only that there's been someone around. Before the last fire, that is. But I wasn't lucky enough to catch him, and I haven't been over here since."

"Did you ever hear of anyone named Joe Bruen?"

Giff shook his head. "I don't think so. Why?"

I was never sure whether Giff was telling the truth or not, and I glanced at Maggie. Her usually direct and open look had turned oddly blank. Yet the expression was gone in an instant, leaving me unsure of what I had seen, and increasingly distrustful of both of them. Why had Maggie and her stepson really come to the island? What were they searching for if the danger of fire was over?

"Let's not stand here talking," Maggie said impatiently. "This place gives me the creeps. It's not all that Victorian anymore. Arson's as modern as that tomato juice can, regardless of its history."

"And sometimes as useful," Giff said. There was irony in his words, but his eyes were bright and watchful, his look fixed on me.

Maggie was right, I thought, and Cecily's long-ago tragedy had nothing to do with what was happening now. Today there was only fire to be reckoned with—and David's death.

"Let's go home," Maggie said.

Again I was aware of how tall Giff was, and of how intent his eyes could be, how watchful behind his often careless manner. He didn't immediately follow Maggie through the door.

"Did David write you anything in those last weeks, Karen? Anything revealing, that is?"

"As a matter of fact, he did," I admitted, and walked past him into bright sunlight.

Giff stepped down beside me. "Is it a secret, Karen? What was it he wrote you?"

"It's no secret. I've told Trevor."

"And you told me," Maggie said. "I mean that David wrote you that if anything happened to him it wouldn't be an accident."

Had I told her that? I wondered. I had told Trevor, yes, and Nona. And a little while ago I'd told Lori. But Maggie? I couldn't remember and I felt confused, unsure.

"And that was all?" Giff questioned.

"Of course," I said. "If I had any real information, Trevor would have taken it to the police."

"Maybe he would, maybe he wouldn't," Giff said, and I knew he believed I'd held something back.

However, he let the matter go, and we left the row of crumbling dressing rooms, walking toward a path that dropped steeply down an embankment. Following Giff, with Maggie behind me, I reached the sandy beach that I had seen when I'd stood beside Trevor on the tower balcony.

"Dad asked me to check on this," Giff said. "We'll need to bring in a few new loads of sand. This inlet is especially good for swimming. Fairly shallow until you get out into the lake." He sounded assured, as though Trevor's plans were already in the past.

A green arm of land lined with pines reached its half-moon around one end of the beach, protecting it and forming a tiny bay. Directly across the water was the Belle Isle project in its beautiful setting, with the hills rising beyond.

But it was not the houses we watched now. A rowboat was coming toward us, already halfway across the lake to the island. Chris Andrews pulled stoutly at the oars, his back toward us as he rowed, clearly unaware of our presence. He didn't see us until he neared the beach and turned around, his fair bangs ruffled in the wind. Then he rested his oars uncertainly, staring at us over one shoulder, his expression as grave as ever.

My camera was ready and I snapped a couple of shots of him in the boat, not sure what prompted the impulse, but again obeying it. Perhaps I wanted a means of coming closer to Trevor's son.

"Come ashore," Giff called to him, and after a moment's further hesitation and a glowering look at me, Chris pulled again on the oars, and the prow of the boat grounded in the sand. Giff pulled it up on the beach and Chris got out reluctantly, standing tall and poised as if for flight.

"You here on some special mission?" Giff asked. "Or just rowing for the fun of it?"

The look on the boy's face was not a normal reaction to so simple a question. He looked so alarmed that I thought he might have run again if Giff hadn't taken him by the arm and led him up the sand.

"What's wrong, Chris? Maybe you'd better tell us."

The boy twisted in his grasp and found an excuse as his eyes fell on me. "It's *her!* She's Uncle David's wife and he was no good. Aunt Nona says he was *evil.* So *she* is too and she has no right to take pictures of me!"

I sensed that he was fabricating on the spur of the moment, blowing up a smoke screen of protest and excitement to cover his real reason for rowing to the island. Nevertheless, his words stung.

"You're right about one thing, Chris," I told him. "I shouldn't have taken pictures of you without your permission. But since I have, I'll give you the prints, and the negatives too when I get the film developed. And I promise not to do it again."

Maggie smiled at us both warmly. "There—Karen has made you a handsome apology and everything's fine. But I'm jealous. She hasn't taken a single picture of me. I'd have thought I'd make a nice plump ghost back in Cecily's dressing room."

Giff, however, was taking no side roads. "You've been over here a lot lately, Chris. What's going on? Were you around when that last fire was set?"

Chris's eyes were agonizingly wide and he looked a very frightened boy.

"No—I wasn't there! I wasn't! I didn't have anything to do with it!"

"But you did light the first fire," Giff said. "So you can't blame people for wondering about the others."

If Chris could have escaped Giff's grasp I knew he would have, but the hold on his arm was too tight.

"Now then," Giff went on, "while I've got you away from your mother, for once, and from your father, suppose you tell us a few things."

Maggie seemed about to protest, but Giff gave her a quick look, and she was silent. This aspect of Gifford Caton was certainly in contrast to the friendly, easygoing guise he usually wore.

"Talk," he said to Chris.

The boy wriggled, trying to get away, and then gave in. "I did set that first fire. You know all that. I was mad at my father and I was trying to get even. But I was sorry afterwards. I've told him so, and I've told my mother. And the sheriff too. I didn't have anything to do with the other fires. Honestly, I didn't."

"So why are you sneaking around Belle Isle at odd hours? Suppose you tell me right here and now what you're up to."

"If I catch him," Chris said, his voice rising, "—if I find out who it is—then I can prove I didn't have anything to do with the other fires."

"*If* there's anyone to catch," Giff said. "And if there should be, what if he turns out to be somebody you like?"

Chris lowered his eyes. "He's *not* anybody I like. He's not anybody I know."

"How can you be sure of that?"

"Because I've seen him. I've seen him sneaking around

the island. Only he was never close enough so I could catch him."

Giff let go of the boy's arm so suddenly that Chris lost his balance and sat down on the sand. "You're making this up, aren't you? This is just another one of your stories."

"I did see him! He's got gray curly hair and he wears lumberjack clothes—a green plaid jacket. Once he caught me watching him from up a tree. I wasn't close, but he went straight under the kudzu."

"When did you last see this phantom?" Giff asked lightly.

The boy hesitated for a moment, as though unsure of how much he wanted to tell. "Yesterday," he said. "Yesterday when—"

Giff cut him off impatiently. "That's nonsense. Whoever started that last fire and set the explosion could be wanted for murder, and he'd be far away by this time."

Chris whirled around and stared at me. "I've got a camera at home. Maybe I'll bring it over and take a picture of him. The way you take pictures all the time. I never thought of that before."

"No dice!" Giff told him. "I'm going to have a talk with your father about this, and you're going to stay off the island. I've been over it thoroughly and I haven't flushed anybody into view. But if anyone's hidden over here it could be dangerous."

Giff glanced at Maggie—a quick, meaningful look— and she came to his aid. "That's right, Chris. You mustn't come here while the island isn't safe. This is something for the sheriff's office to handle."

"Only nobody has!" Chris flung at her. "Nobody's found out anything. They just think it's me."

"Of course they don't. If there was anything to find out,

they'd have found it," Maggie said gently. "But now we'd better start back. You can come with us, Chris."

Coming with us was clearly not his choice. "I've left my bike over by the entrance gate—" he began.

"Then we'll pick it up on the way out and take it back in my station wagon," Giff said, settling the matter.

"If you'll wait a moment," I put in, "I'll use up the rest of my film, and then I can get it developed and give Chris his pictures."

They waited while I shot one picture across the lake to the houses, snapped another of Maggie in the doorway of Cecily's dressing room and finished up with the empty amphitheater. I wasn't attempting to get anything special —just using up the film and making a quick personal record of Belle Isle.

We didn't drive straight back to the house, however, but went on into Gatlinburg, where Maggie had an errand. On the way I was aware, as I hadn't been before, of the kudzu that had enveloped stretches of the countryside, rolling along beside the road, and even attempting to climb a telephone pole here and there. Something that must keep the telephone company busy tearing it down.

I found Gatlinburg an attractive little town, in spite of the fact that tourists were its main business and it abounded in shops and motels. The Little Pigeon River ran along its rocky bed beside the main street, the Parkway, and again I had a feeling of being in a pocket of mountains. David's mountains, I thought again. He had grown up near Gatlinburg.

We parked off the main street near one of the many handcraft shops, and Maggie invited me to come in with her.

"This place is special," she said. "A handful of us run it as a cooperative and I think we're pretty good."

There was a spaciousness and lack of clutter inside that

set it apart from cheaper shops, with unobtrusive lighting and glass windows along two sides. While Maggie talked to the manager, I wandered among the tables and counters, looking at carvings and pottery and jewelry displays, until I came upon Maggie's section in one corner. Her name had been printed on a card, and several of her framed paintings were hung on the wall. Here was more of her strange, oversized vegetation, though not as huge as the mural Lori favored in her dining room. I paused before a lush painting of what was anything but a shrinking violet.

A single blossom splashed its purple-blue at the beholder—not a timid flower to hide along a woodsy path, but bursting with sensual color, its fleshy petals bearing little resemblance to nature. In the next painting a cluster of wild tiger lilies looked as though they might be on the prowl—if such plants could be predators.

Maggie had brought a new picture to hang in an empty space, where something had been sold. When she carried it over I saw that it was a deep red opium poppy with a black center—somehow sensuous with its own intoxication.

"What do you think?" Maggie asked cheerfully.

"Frightening," I said. "Those ferns in the dining room at Trevor's terrify me. And these paintings do too."

"Good! I like to have an impact."

I looked from a leprous tiger lily to Maggie's open, eager expression and shook my head. "But why? Do you really see the world like this?"

"Not the world. Just certain members of the garden variety. Don't try to figure it out. I wouldn't think of analyzing myself and scaring it away. This is the contrary sort of thing that wants to come out when I paint—so I let it come. If there are snaky, horrible things underneath in my nature, I don't want to know about them."

"What does your husband say?"

"Eric? He doesn't look at them. He thinks it's dyspepsia and I ought to take a pill." Her look warmed and softened as she spoke and I sensed again her affection for her husband.

"Do people really buy these pictures?" I asked.

"Of course. Almost as fast as I can paint them. Who wants to hang ordinary flower prints after seeing mine? I've done a lot of tiger lilies, for instance. People are always telling me they're just right for the entry hall at home."

"To scare away burglars?"

"They might, at that. But I can see you're a nonbeliever. Here—I'd like you to have one. Perhaps if you look at it long enough you'll be converted to my wicked ways."

On a table before the framed paintings was a rack that displayed smaller efforts, and she made a selection quickly.

"Here you are. And don't deny me my generosity."

The painting was a soft and glowing pink—the petals of a rose, oversized, but truly beautiful. Then I looked closer and saw that the rose burned out into a deeper fire-red at the farthest point from the heart, swirling into a hint of flame that would consume the blossom itself.

I wanted to tell her that this was a picture I couldn't bear to look at, but she pressed my arm lightly. "It's only the fire of the sunset, Karen. I love the fire colors of sunset. Wait, and I'll have it wrapped for you."

I felt shaken, yet unable to oppose her. In any case, even if I took the painting home, I need never unwrap it, and I would certainly not hang it on a wall where it would be allowed to haunt me. She must know what fire meant to me at this particular time, and I wondered at her motive in forcing this picture upon me. Or was Maggie Caton merely a woman moved by casual impulse and seldom given to penetrating judgment? Her paintings had a primitive quality, and perhaps that was all there was to it.

In a few moments she came back and held out the package so that I had to take it, however reluctantly.

When we left the shop there were one or two more errands to be done in town, and I left my film to be developed while Chris bought a roll for his camera. Then Giff turned the car once more in the direction of the mountains, heading for Trevor's and whatever awaited us there.

One thing I knew lay ahead of me—a confrontation with Lori over the trick she had played by locking me in Cecily's room. I found, a little to my surprise, that I was looking forward to that next encounter. There were a number of things I wanted to say to Lori Andrews.

_____

Six

There had been no immediate confrontation with Lori when Giff brought us home. He left Chris and me at the door, and then drove off with Maggie to the Caton house on along the hill. I'd hoped for a chance to talk to Chris, but he had taken his bicycle and gone off on some enterprise of his own. I could only hope that he hadn't returned to Belle Isle.

Only the stone dog, Simon, was about to greet me and I saw no one when I went downstairs. As I passed the door in the lower hall on the way to my room, I stopped and looked out. By now the sun was dipping toward the west and the shadows of the house fell across the fishpond, the bench and the lantern beside it. I made my decision quickly, set Maggie's picture down in the hall and stepped outside.

For a moment I stood looking around. This lower wing of the house sheltered the grotto in a right angle of walls. Two rooms opened off one side, both with sliding glass doors, but no one stood behind them looking out. Nor was there anyone at the chrysanthemum-banked wall up by the garage area. All seemed safely secluded and I could be unobserved in my actions.

Nevertheless, I moved casually, as though I had no particular purpose. I stood for a moment watching the goldfish and through the clear water I saw that a large stone turtle occupied the floor of the shallow pond. It was as crudely executed as Maggie's stone dog, and I suspected that it was her work too. Apparently when she wasn't painting her monstrous flowers, she enjoyed attacking chunks of stone and hewing them into rough but reasonably innocuous shapes. Under the water goldfish nudged the turtle, nosing the stone and darting away.

I went on to stand beside the lantern that was not quite as tall as I was, touching the mossy stone top, admiring its grace. Then quickly, in hardly more than a single motion, I thrust my hand into the opening in the lantern, found something there, whisked it out and up the sleeve of my sweater. Still sauntering, I walked around the pond, went inside to pick up Maggie's picture and down the hall to my room.

No Lori waited for me this time, and I set the wrapped picture against the wall in a corner where I hoped to forget it. Then I sat on the edge of the bed to examine my find. Blue sky without a tracing of cloud made a color screen over my head, casting bright daylight down upon the object in my hands.

It appeared to be a thin strip of metal, perhaps five or six inches long, and not immediately identifiable. I saw with a qualm that it had been through fire. The metal had resisted, but it had been twisted and blackened, so that soot came off on my fingers.

Why, I wondered, had Chris hidden such an object in the lantern in so secretive a fashion? It was likely that the lantern was one of those special hiding places that children enjoy, but why this particular object? Even if it had come from that last awful fire, what significance could it have? Had it belonged to David?

I turned it about in my fingers, suddenly recognizing what it was—or had been. What I held had once been a mechanical pencil made of some silvered metal that had not been completely destroyed by fire. The discovery told me nothing. Later perhaps I would talk to Chris about it, but for now I hid it beneath lingerie in a drawer. There was a puzzle here that worried me.

When I had showered thoroughly, washing away the last traces of smoke odor and ashes that had clung to me since Lori had led me into the ruin, I changed into a dress of celery green, tied a coral scarf about my neck and went upstairs.

By this time I was beginning to make out the pattern of the house. Kitchen and dining room lay along one side, bordering the hall that ran to the main door. Across the front at the other end stretched the wide living room, with its open deck beyond. The rooms across the hall from dining room and kitchen must be Nona's apartment, with its easy exit ramp to the driveway area. There were two doors here, both closed, and I passed them, walking toward the front of the house, idly exploring.

Now I could see that the living room didn't occupy the entire front as I had first thought. There was space on the right for another large room along a turn in the hallway. Its double doors stood open and I saw that this was Trevor's workroom and office. It too had a wide view of the mountains beyond, and it too opened on the deck. No one was there, and I stepped to the door and looked in.

The colors were muted tans and beige, with a carpet like pale green moss. A huge desk stood at right angles to the sweep of glass at the front of the room, and there were two drawing boards on stands, with work in progress. On a table was an architect's model of Belle Isle, with every tiny house intact. I turned to a wall where several framed pictures of Trevor's houses hung and from where I stood I recognized two of mine.

In delight I went in to look at them more closely, remembering when I'd taken them. One was a beach house made of cypress and built with a simple design that offered both privacy and a view at the same time. The other belonged to the hills of northwestern New Jersey—a handsome two-level house with a sweeping view of the Delaware Water Gap and the Kittatinny Mountains.

I remembered how lovingly I'd photographed those houses, trying to do justice to Trevor's creativity, yet each time feeling that I'd failed. Nevertheless, he had liked these pictures well enough to hang them in his workroom.

Not until he stood beside me did I hear him come in, and I turned eagerly. "I took those two pictures! The one on the beach in Long Island, and the other in New Jersey."

"Did you?" he said, and looked closer. "Yes, I remember those two. You played light and shadow effectively to show depth as well as line. And there's a sense of composition that many architectural photos lack."

I felt ridiculously pleased and my own pleasure was briefly reflected in his face.

"You're very good, Karen," he said gently. "I'm glad you have this work to do. It will keep you busy when you go home. So you won't brood too much."

I found myself stiffening. "You know I'm not going home right away. If I'm a bother here—if Lori doesn't want me to stay—I'll move to a hotel. But I have to stay for a while. Nothing has been settled. Someone is to blame for David's death. If I go away it may all fade into the past, and what really happened will never be known."

"It *has* to be known," he said sharply. "I'm not going to let it go."

"Because of Belle Isle—not because of David. Though I can understand why you hated your brother."

"I didn't always hate him. And you must have loved him in the beginning."

I was silent, unable to explain.

His expression had changed, guarded, yet puzzled. "Why do you feel this—this loyalty?"

"It's not loyalty in the way you mean. In that letter he sent me David set an obligation upon me. I can't put that aside easily. I failed him as much as he failed me. Now I owe him this, or I can't live with myself. Someone caused that fire."

With a sudden movement he took my hands in his, forcing me to face him, holding me so I couldn't turn away. "Karen, listen to me. There was arson—yes. And it's still being investigated, believe me. But David's death was accidental. There's been no first-degree murder charge."

"You forget—he wrote me a letter."

"I knew David very well. That letter might have been written out of a moment's anger, or from some passing notion. You can't let it rule your life."

"I have to stay," I told him stubbornly.

"Then you must stay here." He spoke curtly, concluding the subject.

I hated to have him angry with me, and I made a tentative gesture toward peace between us. "You have a handsome office. May I look around?"

He stepped aside stiffly, and I moved about the room, pausing beside the model of Belle Isle that I'd noted earlier. The tiny houses and painted trees ranging along the bank of a silver-blue lake were all constructed in accurate proportions. The walks were there and a portion of entry road, but the model did not include the island. All was perfection, as it would be when completed, and there were no burned-out houses.

"You're planning to rebuild?" I asked.

"Of course." The words had a grim, unyielding sound, and I wondered if he would rebuild forever—as long as time was allowed him.

"They have to be stopped," I said. "The burnings," and heard the futility in my own words.

"Just how do you propose to find out what no one else has been able to?" he challenged.

I turned from the model to face him. "Isn't it possible that a fresh viewpoint—someone who hasn't been involved from the beginning—might discover something? Something that's been missed. After all, I turned up that note today. And now you know Joe Bruen's name as well."

His stand against me was not entirely adamant, for his look softened a little. "I'm sorry, Karen. I'm not trying to put you down. I just want you gone from here."

"I know about Lori and David," I said. "If that's what concerns you."

He turned away and walked to his desk. He had nothing to offer me on the subject, nor had I any comfort for him. Yet still I didn't want to leave him—not like this.

"How did you happen to get into Belle Isle?" I asked. "I mean the idea of the place, aside from knowing Vinnie Fromberg and the location?"

He accepted the offer of safer ground.

"I've never wanted to be merely an architect for the elite—the rich. Along with my building of private homes,

I've done my share of community centers and housing for the elderly—that sort of thing. And I've done it rather well, I think. But this was my first chance at something for a group that interests me—my own group, in a sense. Also it's a change from private houses, which can be a headache at times."

"How do you mean?"

His smile was wry. "Owners have strong personal feelings about every detail—which is natural. But what they want isn't always practical, or even possible. So there can be a continuous wrangle. A husband and wife can take off in completely opposite directions. You can't imagine what hassles can take place over a doorknob. What builders and contractors do can drive you up the wall, and unions step in to limit you to an advisory role once a house starts going up. At Belle Isle, the whole project is in my hands. I'm in full charge and can make all the decisions. Whatever the result it will be to my satisfaction and perhaps credit—or to my blame."

He broke off, picked up a glass paperweight from his desk and tossed it from hand to hand. I knew he was thinking of how much blame was now likely to come his way.

Once more I moved about the room. A large sheet of drawing paper with plans forming on it was tacked to a tilted stand. And there were the utensils of Trevor's trade in rolls of blueprints, rulers and measuring gauges, pencils and pens and erasers. A large can of liquid glue for filling smaller containers stood on a shelf. But I registered details absently because my thoughts were elsewhere.

"Chris thinks he has seen someone over on the island," I said. "An older man with gray hair."

He turned from his desk to stare at me. "Since the last fire?"

"Yes. After you left us at the theater today, we all went

down to that little beach and found Chris rowing over to the island. He told us he'd seen this man yesterday. Giff didn't believe him. He thinks Chris is making it up."

"The island has always been Chris's favorite playground, but maybe we'd better keep him away from it now."

"Giff and Maggie both told him he should stay away from now on. Chris believes that you still suspect him of starting the fires. He wanted to prove his innocence. Did he really start the first one?"

"I'm afraid he did." Trevor had relaxed a little. "He'd been running a bit wild and there was trouble at school. I gave him one hell of a lecture, as well as lifting a few privileges, and he reacted badly. I think he wanted to hurt me, and the best way to get at me was through the houses. The damage from the fire he set was minor. He even turned in the alarm himself, and he admitted what he had done to me and to the sheriff. He was let off this time, in our care. He's a pretty good kid, really, and a smart one."

There was love and pride and pain beneath the words.

"But he had nothing to do with the new fires?"

"It doesn't seem possible. They started a few weeks later, as though someone had picked up the idea. We never blamed him for them, though maybe he thinks we did. They were more professional jobs than Chris could have handled. David pointed that out as soon as he got here. He found traces of accelerants that had been used, and the paths of fuses that were supposed to spread the fire."

I knew what Trevor meant because David had often talked about his investigative work. Where accelerants or fuses were used there could be areas more heavily burned than the rest. Ashes could be tested chemically. There were dozens of flammatory materials that could be used, but mostly the arsonist chose what came easily to hand.

"I don't think David knew much about explosives," he went on, "and of course there's no telling what he might have found before that house blew up."

"Why does Chris think he's still under suspicion?"

Trevor hesitated. "Maybe we haven't been too wise in handling this. Lori—" He broke off. "Anyway, David's death has upset Chris badly, though I don't think Chris really liked him. Lori took him away for a few days, but that did very little good. Since they got back today, I've had no chance to talk with Chris. He runs from me on sight. Nor have I talked to Lori, for that matter."

I felt bitterly sorry for them both—for Chris and his father.

Trevor stood beside his desk, frowning and lost in thought. Idly he picked up a pencil and tapped it against one forefinger—a silver-colored mechanical pencil. I glanced at the desk and saw several of the same rather distinctive type standing upright in a holder. But of course this meant nothing. Deliberately, I turned my eyes away, as though by not looking I hadn't seen.

"Karen," Trevor said, "I've been meaning to tell you that those belongings of David's that were found at the motel where he stayed have been delivered here. Perhaps you'll want to go through them and dispose of anything you don't care to keep. They've been set out in the downstairs utility room for you, when you're ready. Of course the police have examined everything before releasing them."

"I'll take care of it soon," I said. "Have you done anything yet about that note I found in Cecily's room today?"

"Yes, I've already mailed it to David's company in New York. We'll see what they can find out. In the meantime, I'd better have another look at the island. The police went over it, of course, after the last fire, but I don't think anyone's searched it lately."

"Giff said he'd been over it carefully and there's no one there."

"Giff?" Trevor's frown deepened. "I still think I'll have a look for myself."

"A look for what, Trevor?" Lori asked from the doorway.

Now, lying in my bed in another room, with all the lights burning and the doors locked, I wished that I could erase from my memory that unpleasant scene in Trevor's workroom when Lori walked in. But it wouldn't fade, and it wouldn't let me be.

There had been something almost electric about her as she stood watching us with her eyes bright and taunting.

"A look for what?" she repeated.

Trevor answered her shortly. "Chris thinks someone is hiding on the island. Has he said anything to you?"

"He doesn't talk to me much these days," she said. "He seems to disapprove of us both." Her look shifted slyly to me. "Perhaps you're lucky not to be a mother, Karen. Children can be so difficult at times."

I said nothing and she came a little way into the room, her gaze still fixed on me, some inner current driving her.

"So Cecily let you go?" she asked lightly. "This time."

Until that moment I had thought ahead to my confrontation with her and of the angry things I meant to say to Lori Andrews. But I no longer wanted to say them, and I started toward the door without answering her, only to have her block my way.

"You must tell me how you got out," she ran on, and I saw the flush of excitement in her cheeks and knew that she was prodding, not only me, but Trevor as well. As though she wanted to goad us into anger. "Those are heavy doors in Great-grandpa Vinnie's house. And you couldn't drop to the ground. Not with those high ceilings.

Of course I would have come to let you out after a while. Perhaps after dark. That can be such a spooky old place that I'd have liked you to experience it at night. I have. I love the house when everything's black and you can hear it talking to itself. Or perhaps talking to Cecily."

"Lori," Trevor said sharply, "that's enough!"

"I got out by breaking the door panel with a poker," I told her.

She laughed and I remembered the sound. "How enterprising of you, Karen! Though a shame to damage such a beautiful door. Were you very frightened, locked in that room?"

I stood my ground. "Why did you want to frighten me, Lori?"

Abruptly she shed her taunting, her mischievous game-playing, and answered me with a directness and simplicity that was unexpected. "Because we both want you to go away—Trevor and I. We don't want you to stay here and dredge up the past. We want you to go away as soon as the funeral is over and forget everything that happened here. Perhaps I'll never be able to forgive what happened, but that's none of your business, is it, Karen?"

"David is my business."

"Not anymore. There's nothing you can do for David now."

"Nevertheless, I've just told Trevor that I mean to stay until I know more about David's death. If you'd rather I moved to a hotel—"

She turned her head away with a graceful movement, so that a wing of pale hair fell across her face. "Stay here, by all means. Though I'd have thought you'd want what's best for Trevor now. You may not like whatever it is you discover—if you discover anything."

"I'll stay if you'll let me," I said, and changed the subject abruptly. "What happened to the cat?"

"Commodore? I took him to the vet. He thinks a thrown rock did the damage. Some child, probably. The wound was infected, but he'll be all right. I'll run along now and leave you to your reminiscences."

She gave us another venomously sweet smile and went away.

The silence grew until Trevor broke it. "I'm sorry, Karen. There's nothing I can say."

"I understand." I went quickly out of the room, more shaken than I wanted him to see. I didn't understand at all. I didn't understand how Lori, who was so grievously at fault, could stand there and taunt the husband she had injured. And how could he be patient and tolerant of her behavior? Or was it that whatever burned inside him must be restrained, controlled, lest he strike out at her with devastating results?

I mustn't let it all matter to me—I mustn't! The only thing I really wanted now was to escape from this house and never return. Except that there was still David's death, and I was no more free to do as I pleased than Trevor was.

By the time I reached the top of the stairs I was running, but before I could start down, Nona came out of her rooms in her wheelchair and called to me.

"What is it, Karen? What was all that loud talking about?"

I didn't want to stop, but she wheeled toward me with remarkable speed and reached out to catch me by the hand. Once more her hair was coiled on top of her head in a style that became her, and she wore a long, rose-flowered gown.

"Come along to my rooms. You mustn't go off by yourself when you're as upset as this. It's Lori, isn't it? Come and tell me what's been happening. Maybe I can help."

There seemed to be no way to refuse, so I gave in and

followed her rolling chair down the hall. For the first time I stepped into Nona Andrews' sanctuary.

Her sitting room was long and uncluttered, the floor covered by some neutral synthetic material that enabled her chair to move easily. At the far end it opened into a narrow hall, with a bedroom on one side, and the ramp leading past it that would take her outdoors.

The moment I stepped into the room I caught the too pervasive scent of sandalwood, and found its source at once. On a small table a brass dragon coiled its scales to offer a candle holder, and from the tip of a chunky candle drifted a wisp of scented smoke.

This was a room of delicate rose and gray—a little surprising for Nona. Wide glass picture windows looked out over the lower roofs of the house to the woods beyond, and before one of these windows stood Eric Caton. He turned as we came in, to regard me with a penetrating look from beneath bushy gray brows. At least this time he was not rushing away, and I could observe him more carefully—all the more interested now because of Maggie and Giff.

"You've met Karen Hallam, haven't you, Eric?" Nona asked, and he came toward me, a hand outstretched.

"Yes, we've met. But not under the best of circumstances. I'd like to apologize."

"You don't need to," Nona assured him before I could speak. "Karen knows what it is to run away from Lori. Do get her something to drink, Eric."

He took my hand first—a handsome man, probably in his late fifties, his hair still thick and silver-gray, his eyes shrewd but not unkindly. This, I reminded myself, was not only Vinnie Fromberg's grandson, but he had also been his right-hand man and was now managing the Fromberg empire. He was also very much in opposition to Trevor's plan for Belle Isle. That reminder was necessary because it was easy to be beguiled by his charm and the magnetism he undoubtedly had for women. I had found Giff attractive, but Eric made a far more powerful impression.

"What can I get you to drink?" he asked.

I told him scotch and water would be fine, and sat down at one end of the gray sofa that faced the windows. On a table at my elbow I noticed an odd-looking stringed instrument, made with a narrow waist between two wider bulges. Three strings wound into keys on the short, curved neck.

"Is that what I heard someone playing last night?" I asked.

Nona had left her chair and was propelling herself with the help of forearm crutches. Apparently her legs would carry her weight to some extent, and she came to sit beside me, picking up her own drink and chinking the ice against the glass.

"That's my dulcimer," she said. "Made right here in our highlands by a man who specializes in them. There aren't many such craftsmen left. He taught me to play it, and I've even played and sung at some of our craft fairs that feature Mountain Music."

"The sound is lovely," I said.

She nodded, but her interest lay elsewhere. "Now then, tell us what was going on with Lori and Trevor."

"There isn't much to tell," I offered lamely. "Lori seems to have taken a disliking to me."

Nona brushed this aside. "But what did Lori *do?*"

I dropped my evasion. "She persuaded me to go with her to the island to see the octagonal house. Then she locked me into Cecily's sitting room and left me there. I was breaking open the door with a poker when Trevor rescued me."

Eric's laughter was hearty and it drowned out Nona's

pleased little chortles. Both seemed amused by Lori's antics and my response, and their reaction jarred me. It hadn't been a funny experience.

"Good for you!" Eric said. "I like women to be enterprising."

"He doesn't mean too enterprising," Nona said cheerfully. "I've known Eric for a long time. He used to be an old beau of mine—before all this happened." She waved a careless hand at her legs.

"You know you threw me over," Eric countered and winked at me. "She broke my heart when I was in my twenties. I've never gotten over it."

This sort of persiflage was clearly habitual with them and they beamed at each other in pleased understanding. I sipped my drink, content to be forgotten. But Nona's next words brought me back, startled.

"Just why do you want to stay here, Karen? I should think you would prefer to get back to your own life. It can't be anything but depressing for you here."

"Murder is always depressing," I said.

The room's silence was intense, and without looking at either of them I was aware of their focused interest.

"Murder is an ominous word," Eric remarked. "Though of course since that house was set to explode and burn, I suppose it's appropriate in the sense of being second degree."

It was time to speak of David's letter again.

"Before he died," I said, "David warned me in a letter that an attempt might be made on his life. He had discovered too much and was nearly ready to close in. He was stopped before he could finish what he must have started. I'd like to stay until we know the whole truth."

"I'd like to see that letter," Eric said.

I shook my head. "No—I'm sorry. Some of it is personal. I don't want to show it to anyone."

"Then we shan't urge you," Nona said firmly. "Just before you came we were talking about the man on the island. Perhaps that's pertinent now. Do go on with what you were saying, Eric."

The charm and geniality had vanished, and I could glimpse the cold calculation that Eric Caton might bring to a business matter. I had the feeling that if it had been up to him, he wouldn't have let me off so easily on the matter of David's letter. He answered Nona mildly, however.

"No one is sure there is a man on the island."

"Chris has seen him. Though from a distance," Nona said. "And you told me yourself—"

"What I said, dear lady, was that the island would make an ideal hideout for the arsonist. If he's still around. Which seems unlikely after David's unfortunate death."

I wanted to keep them talking. "Chris says he saw someone there yesterday. A man with gray hair."

Eric dismissed Chris's words with a shrug. "He's an imaginative boy. You can't always count on the truth from him. For instance, he has the notion that his father caused David's death. Ridiculous, of course. We all know Trevor better than that. Besides he'd hardly destroy those houses he's put so much into."

Eric was watching me, challenging me in some way, and I tried not to twirl my glass in nervous fingers, tried to ask my questions carefully.

"Why would Chris think a thing like that about his father? And how do you know that he does?"

Nona said, "The boy is upset because of David and Lori. He's confused, bewildered. He'll come out of it."

Eric had raised an eyebrow at Nona, and she rushed on.

"Oh, we needn't pussyfoot around Karen. She knows all about that nasty little affair between David and Lori."

"Probably because you told her," Eric said wryly, and

she grinned at him. "Anyway," he went on, "I must be going. Maggie said dinner would be early tonight. She has to attend a meeting somewhere."

"Then you'd better be there. She's been edgy lately."

"Aren't we all?" Eric's casual manner had returned and he said good-bye as though he hated to leave us and couldn't wait to be with us again.

When he'd gone, Nona almost pounced on me. "Now then—I know you didn't want to talk in front of Eric. But you must tell me everything that has happened. Not for the sake of gossip, though I enjoy that too. But I need to know what's going on. I'm especially worried about Chris, and I can't always get around where things are happening. If I can be *aware,* I can manage better."

Manage what? I wondered. She could probably get around almost anywhere she wished to go. However, there was no reason to hold anything back. I gave her further details of my experience with Lori in the octagonal house. I even told her about the note I had found under the blotter on Cecily's desk, and she heard me out, nodding now and then.

"Yes, it's exactly the sort of thing Lori would do. You'd better understand what she's like if you're to stay on for a while in this house. Lori loves danger for itself. She only feels alive when she's frightening herself by following the edge of the cliff. But you're to pay no mind to talk about Trevor and that fire. Lori asks for trouble sometimes. That's her way of dancing on the edge of the precipice. But while Trevor has a temper, just the way David did, he wouldn't *plan* murder."

I felt unexpectedly grateful to Nona. Her sharp tongue often cut through to the truth, and I was beginning to like her better—as perhaps she was me.

"Do you think Lori really cared about David?" I asked.

"Of course. She wanted him the minute she clapped

eyes on him. He was a source of that very danger she loves. She could torment Trevor with him. But she didn't love him any more deeply than he did her, if that's what you mean. They were two of a kind. Anyway, Lori won't waste tears on a dead man for long, though she'll milk the situation for whatever advantage it's worth. Mainly to get back at Trevor, I think. For seeing through her! I've never liked David. I detested him from the first time I met him as Trevor's brother years ago. Half brother. We weren't kin, you know. Trevor's father was *my* brother. David always hankered after anything Trevor had. He resented him, you know, because Trevor's talents are real and he deserves all the things David could never win for himself. I'm sure David didn't give a damn about Lori. She was just someone to take away from Trevor. Only when he touched Lori he was playing with danger too, and I wonder if he ever took time to understand that."

I was lost in my own memories of the past. "I *wanted* to love David. In the beginning I thought I did," I told her.

"He'd make a poor substitute for Trevor," Nona said shrewdly. "But I can see how perhaps you weren't altogether fair to David, any more than he was to you."

"I know that," I admitted.

"So now you can't forgive yourself. Irrational, but human."

I sipped the last of my scotch and set the glass down carefully because my hand had a tendency to tremble. It had helped a little to talk all this out with Nona and have her cut shrewdly through to the truth. But it left me shaken.

"That's why you're staying, isn't it?" she went on. "Because of this silly thing called guilt that you've lived with all through your marriage. All because you once had a young crush on David's brother."

"I owe David something," I said for the hundredth time. "It doesn't have to be rational. I just feel that way."

"You owe yourself something too. We all have to forgive ourselves the best we can. Trevor hasn't learned that yet. He still thinks he owes something to Lori. Ridiculous. Chris matters. She doesn't. Trash! I'm concerned because Trevor and Chris are the only two people I'm truly fond of. I would do anything—and I don't care if it kills me— to keep them from harm. Yet I haven't been able to lift a finger to help when it comes to these fires and the destruction of Trevor's dream. It was a good dream, Karen. A big dream. And there's one piece of forgiving that I will never do. I'll never forgive the one who hired this to be done."

She reached for her crutches and began to move about the room, muttering to herself.

"If only I could get around better I know I could do something about what's going on! I've tried—God knows I've tried. But nothing has turned out right. Only now there's you, Karen. Even if it's only a foolish guilt that drives you, perhaps it will help Trevor if you try."

She turned toward me and I stood up. "Yes—I'm here! I'll do anything I can, if you'll tell me what—"

"I'll have to think about it. I'm holding Eric off for the time being. About Belle Isle, I mean. Eric's fond of me, but that's not to be counted on. There's something there I don't understand. I know him pretty well, and I don't thing he's the one we're looking for, in spite of motive. Yet Maggie is living in some sort of fear. That's what worries me. Of what, I don't know because she hasn't talked to me.

"Run along now, Karen. Give me time to think. I'm needed out in the kitchen anyway. Dinner's in the oven, but Lu-Ellen can't be left on her own as yet."

Moved by an unexpected impulse, I kissed Nona lightly

on the cheek. "Thank you," I said. "Thank you for accepting me."

She gave me rather a strange look as I went out of the door.

All these things I thought about later when I lay in my different bed and let the pictures flow through my mind. After all that had happened, I wasn't going to sleep easily, and my thoughts went on like a record player, replaying my life. I must think about and face the frightening attack that had caused the change in my room. I must come to it chronologically in my mind so that I might find any clue that might have led up to it.

Among other things, I wasn't at all sure that Nona was right in dismissing Eric as the man who had hired the arsonist. Nona liked Eric, and she was quite capable of being devious herself. I had experienced a warming toward her, but I wasn't sure where her efforts might take me. I must move very cautiously where she led.

More than anything else, however, the thought of Trevor stayed with me. I could almost recapture the memory of what I'd felt toward him as a young girl. Feelings that were adoring, but not altogether admitted. The nebulous dreamings of sixteen. The restless seeking and growing, the uncertainties—all having to do with the budding of sexual awareness, yet at the same time as innocent as moonlight touching the ocean, and as turbulent as that ocean could be. Into that sentient, waiting state, David had walked. David, who was no dream, but darkly vibrant and alive, a man, strongly sexual—and completely beyond my understanding. I couldn't have known. As Nona had said, I must forgive myself.

Only now could I even begin to understand. The old, unsatisfied longings of youth had turned into those of a woman. If there were ashes, a spark had indeed remained, waiting to be fanned into life. Yet if my longings were adult now, and not the dreams of a young girl, they were still as futile as ever, and I could be angry with myself for harboring them.

Dinner that night had been uneventful. Surprisingly, both Lori and Chris came to the table. Mostly Chris glowered at his plate, or at his father, or sometimes his mother. Once or twice I caught that same black look turned upon me. But he ate his dinner quietly and there was no immediate revolution.

Lori, playing her own game, set herself to be sweet, and readily picked up the harmless subjects Nona made it her business to throw out.

Trevor too made some effort, though his real attention was elsewhere, and now and then he seemed to be studying me oddly. Whenever I could, I backed up Nona's efforts and we all managed to get through the meal, with only Chris completely silent unless spoken to directly. I couldn't help wondering how many such dinners we could endure before someone broke through the polite barriers. How long could Trevor hold back his growing anger with Lori? And why did he hold it back at all?

By the time we took our coffee out on the deck, the mountains were turning the valleys dark with green shadow, and the roads curled through the gaps like white ribbon. The evening was pleasantly cool, and I stood at the rail with my coffee cup in hand, feasting my eyes once more on the tremendous sweep of view. The solace of the mountains! Just to look at them was calming. This I would miss. I was here now and near Trevor. Yet soon it would all be gone and I would never return.

Trevor came to stand beside me. "If there's time I'll drive you up there before you leave. Into the mountains. Perhaps to the Dome, where we can climb the footpath to the top. And there are longer hikes and drives. The National Park out there opened the Smokies to the world less than forty years ago, and some of it is still virgin country."

Wishful thinking, I told myself—that everything was normal and I was here on a vacation trip, to be taken sight-seeing. It seemed unlikely that I would ever get farther away than Belle Isle.

"Some of the mountains used to have appropriate Indian names," he went on. "Others bear the names of early explorers like Mount LeConte."

"Isn't that Belle Isle we can see from here?" I asked.

"Yes. Out there where the water is still catching light from the sky. When the houses are finished and being lived in, the lights will look like wreaths of fireflies from here."

"There's a light there now," I said. "Is that the watchman's hut?"

Trevor seemed to freeze beside me. Then Lori came running to stand at the rail.

"It looks like fire!" she cried.

"It is!" He was rushing into the house even as he spoke the words.

The others were at the rail with me now—Nona in her chair, Lori with Chris at her side. Far down in the dusky reaches of the valley a crimson light glowed and grew stronger, and in a moment flames were rising above the roof of the house, cutting the dusk with spears of fire.

Inside, Trevor had finished phoning and we heard his car start, heard the screeching of tires as he turned to go down the mountain. Moments later came the sound of a fire truck in the valley, speeding toward Belle Isle.

I glanced at Lori. Western light shone full on her face, catching the bright excitement in her eyes. When I looked at Nona I saw an angry grimace twist her mouth.

"Oh, no!" she cried. "Not again! Not when we all thought it was over."

"It will never be over," Lori said softly. "Not as long as there's a house to be burned down there. He ought to know that. He ought to give up."

Without warning, Chris flung himself upon her and began to beat at her with his fists. She was a little thing and he was a strong boy. Nona could do nothing, and I had to help by pulling him off.

"Don't," I said. "Don't, Chris. Your father wouldn't want you to behave like this."

He had torn the neck of his mother's dress and when she could pull away from him she slapped him hard across one cheek and then ran inside. Chris leaned against the rail, his face white, his lips trembling, and I dared not touch him, however much I wanted to.

"It will be all right," I said. "They'll stop it in time."

"At least there's been no explosion," Nona said from behind us. "There'll be no one dead in the ruins this time."

Chris whirled to stare at her. For a moment I thought he meant to answer furiously, but instead he turned his back and fixed his attention on flickering red light that stained the waters of the lake.

As flames rose higher I fancied I could hear the distant crackle. Who had started this fire? And who was to find the arsonist, now that David was gone?

But the boy beside me needed distracting. "At least no one can blame you this time," I said. "You've been up here since before dinner."

He threw me a look of scorn. "You know better than that. Anybody could set it to start—with a cigarette in a matchbox, or a candle, if it was to take longer. There are lots of ways. Then whoever it was could be far away by the time it really got started."

As I knew very well, he was right, and I tried another direction. "Chris, I'd like to show you something, ask you something. Will you come down to my room with me?"

But of course it was futile to talk about anything but fire just then. Chris didn't move, and I doubt if he heard me, all his attention focused upon the burning house. Not until we knew that the engines were there, not until smoke rose, smothering the flames so they began to die down, did he seem to hear an echo of my words.

"What?" he said. "What do you want to show me?"

"It's in my room," I told him. "Will you come there with me now? The fire seems to be under control. They've got it stopped, but your father won't be back for a while, I think."

After a moment of indecision he gave in. "Okay. I'll come."

Nona watched us leave, but she said nothing. Together we started downstairs, brought together in a strange collaboration.

Seven

Chris stared at the twisted bit of metal I held out to him.
"What's that?"

"I'm not sure," I said, "but I think it's a pencil. Perhaps a pencil from your father's desk? Will you tell me why you hid it in the Japanese lantern near the fishpond?"

Now that I had confronted him, he didn't try to deny his actions, but made a fierce counterattack. "Why did you take it? You had no business spying on me! Sneaking around and taking my things!"

"I know. And under ordinary circumstances, I wouldn't have done it. But another fire has just been set at Belle Isle. And the last one killed your Uncle David. I think this pencil came through one of those other fires. Will you tell me what it means, Chris?"

His mouth twisted, almost as Nona's had done, and for

a moment I thought he was going to cry. If he had cried it might have been better because then I might have held him and offered comfort. But his look told me I was an enemy. He snatched the bit of metal from my hand and rushed out of the room.

The exchange left me feeling limp, and I dropped into a chair. Over my head the skylight was darkening, and soon I would be able to see the stars through the glass. They held no consolation for me tonight, no sense of peace, and I couldn't know then that I would not spend another full night beneath that window to the sky.

I thought of Chris again. That he knew something—or thought he knew something, and it was tearing him apart. So far, I was sure, he had confided in no one, and perhaps that made it all the worse. I wondered if I should tell Nona about the pencil, since she was the most likely one for him to go to. And yet—somehow I didn't want to tell her, though I wasn't sure why.

Or was I? How much was I fooling myself?

All of Chris's actions pointed to the protection of someone, and who else would he want to protect but his father? Had he any reason to think that Trevor had been in the house where David had died, and had dropped the pencil there? But the pencil could have come there at any earlier time. Chris, poking through the ashes later, could have found it, made a misinterpretation and held back from telling anyone. Yet it was hard to believe that such very slight "evidence" would be tearing him up to this degree. So there must be something else. Some other "proof" against his father.

Perhaps I had made a mistake in letting him know that I had taken the pencil from the lantern. Now, more than ever, he would place me on the side of the enemy. He couldn't know that I, less than almost anyone, would want to hurt Trevor. If only Chris and I could talk it might be possible to dispel his doubts. Of facts I had very few, but of faith and trust—of love!—I had a great deal.

Now, at least, I could admit that truth to myself.

First love ought always to take its course. It should be allowed to develop or die of its own accord. First love, suppressed, cut off, could go underground and hide behind other guises, only to surface when least expected. The heart didn't forget.

How still the house seemed, how quiet this lower wing. Perhaps Nona and Lori were on the higher deck watching what remained of the fire, waiting for Trevor to come home. This was an utterly dreadful time for him. All his new hopes that the burning was over were now dashed. I supposed I should go upstairs, but I had no heart for anyone's company. Grief over Trevor's defeat held me away.

Against the wall behind my chair the wrapped picture rested—the one Maggie had given me. For lack of anything else to take my attention, I drew it out and tore off the paper.

The great painted rose seemed to burn against the gray background, softly pink at the heart where it had opened fully, but flaring into flame at the outer edges, the petals curling as though almost ready to fall from flame to blackened ash. Now that I looked closely, I could even see a thin wisp of smoke drifting away from the tip of one glowing petal. For all those who had any connection with Belle Isle there was an obsession with fire, I thought, and Maggie had given pictorial life to it in her painting.

Was this a catharsis for her—these strange paintings of giant vegetation? But if so, were they really working? I'd sensed the tension that lay beneath her easy manner. Like Chris, she was afraid of something. They all knew more than they were willing to tell me, including Nona.

I set the painting with its face to the wall. Perhaps the

day would come when I could appreciate its rather dreadful beauty, but that time wasn't now. I only hoped it wouldn't cause a conflagration where it stood. For a long while I sat where I was, with a single lamp burning, waiting for some sound from outside.

The intense, driving purpose that had begun to move me earlier toward the answer I had to find had dissolved into a state of hopelessness. There was nothing *I* could do. It might very well be better to give up and go home, begin a new life, for which at the moment I had little taste. Nona had helped me to feel less guilty, at least. What could I do for David by staying here? Everything lay in other, stronger hands than mine.

I didn't rouse myself from this new lethargy until I heard the sound of a car and knew it must be Trevor coming home. At least I could learn what had happened at Belle Isle. I ran out of the room and up the stairs in time to meet Trevor in the hallway.

There was soot on his clothes, and his face and hands were streaked. He looked weary to the bone. When he saw me he stopped and shook his head.

"It wasn't as bad as it might have been. Only one corner of the roof went. We can rebuild. But what's the use? If this is to go on and on, with never a clue to our phantom arsonist, there can be no fighting it. As usual, the guard saw nothing, for all that he had patrolled the area a half hour earlier."

I might give up myself, but I couldn't bear to see this in Trevor. Yet there was nothing I could say, no comfort I could offer.

"We can't go through the ashes until tomorrow," he went on, "but I don't think they'll tell us anymore than they have in the past. David moved farthest along when he was investigating, but it was like him to want the credit of handling the final exposure. Karen, will you show me that letter he wrote you? I know you've told me what it says, but I'd like to read it for myself, in case there's something you might have overlooked."

"I'll bring it to you," I said.

"I'll be in my office. First, I want to tell Nona and Lori what little I know. And Chris, if I can find him."

Perhaps my notion of a debt to David had lessened, but now something new was beginning to take its place. Not a *debt*. Just the knowledge that a terrible crime had been committed, and that whoever was guilty could not be allowed to go on injuring the living. In any small way I could, I must help toward that end. David's letter, perhaps useless, was at least a step in that direction, no matter how I felt about showing it to Trevor.

I hurried down to my room and took the letter from its place in my suitcase. When I climbed the stairs I could hear Trevor's voice from the living room, so I went past the door and into his darkened office. I found my way to his desk and turned on the lamp.

Chris sat curled in his father's big chair, his head on his arms, worn out and sound asleep. His face was half hidden in the crook of one arm and on the rounded, exposed cheek tear traces shone wet in the lamplight. Long lashes hid the blue of his eyes and his fair bangs were damp and flyaway. A wounding I had no guard against struck through me—forgotten pain like the thrust of a knife. The old need to hold a child hadn't died after all, in spite of my suppression.

As I smoothed errant bangs and felt the dewy skin beneath them, Chris opened his eyes to look up at me.

"The fire is out," I told him gently. "Your father has just come home."

He was still a little dazed, his lids heavy with sleep. I bent toward him across the desk, not daring to touch him, now that he was awake.

"Chris, you know your father had nothing to do with your Uncle David's death. If that's what is worrying you, it needn't. As I've told you, I knew your father long ago when I was very young, and I knew even then how good he was and how honest. He'd never hurt anyone."

"Have you ever seen him mad?"

I was silent. I never had, but I had seen David angry a great many times, and David was Trevor's brother.

"They had a terrible fight," Chris told me. "The day of the fire. Uncle David and Dad. Dad told him to get out. He told him to go away and never see my mother again. They were shouting at each other right here in this room. Nobody knew I was on the deck outside that door where I could hear. Uncle David just laughed at him, and my father said he'd kill him if he didn't go away. So he laughed again and went straight out of the house. And after a while my father went out too."

I ached with pity for the needless burden he was too young to carry.

"Oh, Chris! Those were only words shouted in anger. That quarrel must have been hours before David died. Your father would never have—"

"What would I never have?" Trevor asked from the doorway.

I flung out my hands, entreating him. "Please talk to your son. Talk to him now and make him understand. I'll leave you together. Here's the letter you wanted."

I dropped it on the desk and almost ran from the room, shaken by this new and unexpected emotion that had seized me. It was difficult enough to love the father, but to be stricken so suddenly with this new-old need and have it focus on Chris left me unable to face either of them. At least now they might be able to work this out together.

Before I reached the stairs, however, I knew it was no

use. Chris dashed past me and out of the house into the evening dusk. I continued down to my room because I couldn't bear to see Trevor's face. Nor did I want to be there when he read David's letter. What my husband had said about the Belle Isle fires was combined with his abuse of me, and I was too upset just then to stand up to those written lies.

Back in my room I undressed and went to bed—to lie awake thinking and unable to sleep. How was I to face Trevor tomorrow after he had read that letter? The fact that none of it was true didn't matter, since Trevor really knew so little about me. It was no wonder that I lay awake thinking back over the years. Thinking of Trevor as I felt about him now—with added pain because of his son—was almost more than I could bear.

In the distant house along the hillside upstairs, Nona was playing her dulcimer again, and again I knew the tune she was singing. How strange that now, of all times, she should choose "Amazing Grace." Or was the music, in a way, a prayer she offered to the night—a prayer for Trevor, for the rest of us? And for herself?

The gentle music, so softly golden as she plucked the strings, brought a wetness to my eyes. I could weep now, and the tears eased me, since they were quiet tears, not the stormy ones I'd shed in the past.

I fell asleep to the sweet sound of the dulcimer.

It was after midnight when the terrible thing happened. One moment I was asleep, and the next moment there was a loud crash, a shower of glass, and then a second crash as something hurtled through the skylight and fell painfully on my legs. Only thick quilts saved me from serious hurt. Showers of glass continued to fall as I lay there, stunned with shock. Fortunately, the quilt had protected most of my body.

I suppose I must have screamed, for I heard movement

in the other section of the house, upstairs, and Nona's voice called out to me.

"What is it? What has happened, Karen?"

I shouted to her that I didn't know, but I was all right. No one else came, and Nona couldn't descend the stairs. Gingerly, I reached out from under the quilt and turned on the bed lamp. A continuous tinkling and rattling of glass slivers from overhead accompanied my every movement as I drew my knees to my chin and regarded the large black lump that rested on the quilt. The smell of charred wood was strong—and all too familiar. I knew with a horror that crept along every nerve that the block of wood that lay on my bed had been taken from one of the Belle Isle fires.

Carefully, I pushed the quilt away, trying to avoid the slivers, and put my feet to the floor, seeking a clear spot before I stood up. More glass brushed from my gown and my hair as I reached for my robe and slipped into it. Then, barefoot, because my slippers were filled with splinters, I went into the hall, where I could see Nona leaning on her crutches near the upper curve of the stairs.

"I'm all right," I assured her again, and went to knock on Trevor's door. There was no answer, and I knew that if he had been there he would have come out at the sound of the crash and my scream.

I called to Nona. "Where is Chris's room? And Lori's?"

"You're bleeding," she said. "Your face. Come up here at once and tell me what has happened."

I touched a place on my cheek that stung, and saw blood stain my fingers. But that was a small matter and I repeated my question about the rooms.

"Lori has a room up here," Nona said crossly. "She doesn't share Trevor's anymore. Chris is down there, around the corner from you. But I want to know—"

I ran to the door she indicated and opened it softly,

turned on the switch near the door. Chris appeared to be breathing deeply, unaware, and again I felt that stabbing response to a sleeping child. I switched off the light and closed the door, then ran upstairs to join Nona.

"Someone dropped a block of burned wood through my skylight," I told her. "No one could have done that without being on the roof. So a ladder must have been used."

"Not necessarily," Nona said. "There's a tree near the roof at the front of the house, and I've seen Chris go up it any number of times. But I don't think he—"

"Neither do I," I broke in. "He's sound asleep. But the chunk of wood that came through was brought here from Belle Isle. I'm sure of it."

Nona still wore her rose-sprinkled gown, so she hadn't been to bed as yet. She watched with concern as I moved down the hallway.

"Come to my bathroom and let me treat those cuts," she said.

"Lori first." I went to her door and tapped upon it. There was no answer and I opened it wide, with Nona balanced on her crutches beside me.

The bed had been slept in, but it was empty now, and as we stood watching, Lori herself came running through the hall from the front door and stopped to stare at us in astonishment. She wore slacks, a pink pullover and sneakers on her feet.

"What is it? What's happened? What's the matter with your face, Karen?"

I was calculating how long it might take to climb down that tree, run through the little grotto, mount the long flight of steps to the driveway area and come into the house. The time worked out about right in my mind.

"Show me your hands," Nona commanded, and Lori held out her hands, obedient, but apparently puzzled.

They were free of soot, but that meant nothing. Nor could I tell if there was any odor of char about her. As always she wore a flowery scent.

Nona made no attempt to question, but motioned me with one crutch toward her rooms. Lori came with me, chattering, as I went back to Nona's bathroom.

"What has happened, Karen? How did you hurt your face? What on earth is wrong?"

"Where have you been?" I asked.

Something in my tone made her look at me sharply. "What are you blaming me for now?"

Nona explained as she took a first-aid kit from a cabinet, and Lori listened with an air of disbelief.

"And you're blaming *me*? You think I went out in the middle of the night and climbed up on the roof and—"

"You are out in the middle of the night," I reminded her.

"We can talk later." Nona thrust her kit into Lori's hands and led the way back to her own sitting room.

"Sit here on the couch, Karen," she directed. "And hold still."

She dabbed at my face with wet cotton. The cut proved deeper than she'd thought, and the disinfectant stung. Lori watched with interest, but when I stared at her she went glibly into her story.

"I've been down at Belle Isle. I wanted to see what had happened, and I drove there. That's all."

And perhaps, I thought, you brought back with you a chunk of freshly burned wood.

"Has Trevor gone down again?" Nona asked.

"Yes. He couldn't stay away. He was walking along the shore road in front of the houses. Just walking up and down with the watchman."

"What good is a watchman?" I said. "They need a police force to stop this."

"The place is too big for policing regularly," Nona said. "Anyone could go in behind a patrol. Trevor hates fences, and anyway they wouldn't keep out anyone as crazily determined as this fellow. Do hold still, Karen. I just want to put a spot bandage on your cheek."

Lori sat watching as though entranced. "It must have been Chris," she speculated. "I don't know why, Karen, but he seems to have taken a disliking to you. I think I'll go down and talk to him now."

Anger surged up in me, but Nona answered before I could.

"No!" She spoke sharply. "If he's really asleep, then let him sleep. We can talk to him tomorrow. You can help me now, Lori. Get out some fresh sheets and make up the bed in the room next to Chris's. Karen can't finish the night under that open skylight in a nest of glass. Lu-Ellen can clean the room up tomorrow, but Karen will probably want to be somewhere else after this."

"I can help—" I began, but Nona waved my offer aside.

"You've had a shock, and you're still pale. Just sit there and collect yourself."

Moving with skill on her crutches, she took Lori off to the linen room, while I remained on the same sofa where I'd sat earlier. Now that I was quiet and alone, I found that I'd begun to shake. The scratch on my face was nothing, but the crash of the block of wood falling through the skylight still rang in my ears, and I still felt shocked and not a little frightened. Malice and an intention to injure or alarm—such motives frightened me.

The dulcimer rested on the table beside me and I picked it up idly and set it across my knees. Once ages ago I'd played a guitar, and I plucked at the strings, trying to find a tune, trying to quiet the fear that had shaken me.

Trevor found me there when he came back from Belle

Isle. It was past one o'clock and I looked up into his face that was gray with weariness, hopelessness.

"Oh, Trevor!" I said. "I'm so bitterly sorry. What can you do? What can any of us do?"

He came to sit beside me, leaning back against the cushions. "What is there left for me to do?"

I twanged the strings angrily, so that they gave off a sound that was anything but sweet. "You'll find some way —you must!"

"What happened to you?" he asked. "Your cheek. Why are you up?"

I touched the bandage, hating to tell him. "Someone climbed up on the roof and dropped a block of charred wood through the skylight over my bed. I wasn't hurt, but a lot of glass flew around and my cheek was cut. It's nothing."

He bent forward and covered his face with his hands.

"Don't," I pleaded. "You can't give up, Trevor. There are answers somewhere. The skylight doesn't matter. It probably hasn't any connection." I touched his shoulder. "You've got to keep trying—even if you have to put a watchman in every building down there!"

He sat up, stilling my words. "Don't worry, Karen. I'm not ready to quit yet. I'm not beaten. It's just that—right now I'm tired."

"I know," I said. "If only I could help."

He turned to look at me and there was an unexpected tenderness in his eyes. "You help by being here, Karen. I'm sorry so much of this—ugliness—is touching you as well. You could have been hurt tonight."

"But I wasn't. It doesn't matter."

"It matters—to me." Almost tentatively, wonderingly, he touched my cheek, turned my head toward him. "I read David's letter. There was nothing in it to help—you were right about that. But there was plenty in it to make me angry. Those accusations."

"They weren't true. But I didn't know what you'd think when you read them."

"I thought that David was holding true to form. Neither did I want to believe the things he said about you earlier. And after you came, I knew they were lies."

"I was wrong for marrying him."

"You were too young. You couldn't know—you couldn't dream—once I was fond of him too."

We were both silent for a moment and then Trevor went on, his voice roughening.

"If he hadn't died when he did, I think it's likely I'd have killed him. Or he'd have killed me."

"No!" The sound burst from me in something like terror. "You mustn't say that. You must never say that!"

"Why shouldn't he say it, when it may be true?" Lori asked from the doorway behind us.

She stood with her armload of sheets and blankets and stared at us mockingly.

"I hate to interrupt, but if Karen has recovered from her terrible ordeal, she might as well come downstairs and help me make up a fresh bed."

I rose at once, and Trevor let me go. Not daring to look back at him, I followed Lori. We had come very close in those few moments, and this, I knew, was what Lori sensed.

Downstairs, however, when she switched on a light in another guest room, she chatted amiably, calmly, falsely.

"You'll be comfortable enough in here. There's no skylight. Of course there are windows to the fishpond court, but they lock and you can pull the draperies across for privacy."

She whisked off the bedspread that had been used for a

covering, and flicked open a sheet. Moving automatically, I picked up the opposite hem and we made the bed together as matter-of-factly as though no angry emotions stirred between us. My hands still had a tendency to shake, but I took hold of the bedclothes firmly to control their betrayal. I wanted this to be done quickly, so Lori would go away.

But when we were finished, she stood looking at me for a moment longer, her eyes bright, and her cheeks as warmly pink as her sweater.

"You can move your things in here tomorrow, Karen. Just get what you need for tonight. And, Karen—while I don't really mind you being in love with Trevor, you might as well know that I won't have him falling in love with you. I really think you'd better leave as soon as the funeral is over. I'll call the airline this morning and make your reservation for New York."

She gave me no time to answer, but went quickly out of the room. I stood looking after her for a moment, feeling sick. I hated it that she had read me so well and so quickly. When I'd slipped out of my robe I got into bed, leaving the light burning on the bed table, and pulling the blanket up to my chin. I wanted no more of darkness tonight.

Beneath the covers I lay waiting for the shivering to stop. I waited for a long time, replaying all my records of that terrible day, yet remembering last of all the look in Trevor's eyes when he had turned my face toward his.

Eight

The next morning a tentative friendship began between Chris and me. Or if "friendship" was too strong a word, there was at least something of an alliance. My own feelings were more strongly involved than before, and perhaps he sensed that. Also there was the knowledge of the secret we shared concerning a pencil. That I would miss Trevor when I went away did not bear thinking about, but now I knew how much I would also miss Chris. Oddly enough, it was Lori who brought about the closer relationship between Chris and me.

All of us except Chris met at the breakfast table in the big kitchen at about the same time that morning. The disasters of the previous night had taken their toll and I think we all looked weary and discouraged.

Trevor had gone up on the roof early and had found a

hammer from the tool box in the garage. It had been left near the skylight, and was obviously the instrument used to break the heavy glass before the block of wood was dropped through. Anyone could have picked up that hammer.

Our talk was mostly desultory. Thoughts of the new fire, as well as the smashing of the skylight, hung over us, dampening the atmosphere thoroughly. At least for Nona, Trevor and me.

Chris appeared when we were nearly through eating, and I noted with relief that he looked much better than he had last night. The touching courage that seemed characteristic had returned.

Nona said, "I'll fix you something, Chris. Would you like bacon and eggs?"

He shook his head. "No, thanks. Just milk and some toast. I'll get what I want."

Lori watched him until he had pulled up a chair next to Trevor, and when she spoke there was that sly note in her voice that I disliked. "Maybe before you eat anything, Chris, you'd better tell us about your escapade last night."

He blinked at her, not understanding.

"Go easy, Lori," Nona began. "We don't know—"

Trevor was watching with a question in his eyes, but he said nothing, and Lori ran on.

"You needn't pretend to be so innocent! We all know you dropped that block of wood through Karen's skylight last night. Now suppose you tell us why."

I'd had enough of Lori in a good many ways, and I burst in with more indignation than I'd meant to show. "How can he possibly tell you why when he doesn't know what you're talking about? I looked in on Chris immediately after it happened and he was sound asleep. He certainly wasn't up on the roof. What are you trying to do, Lori?"

Chris gave me a look of surprise, as though for the first time he had really noticed me as a person. Then he scowled at his mother.

"I don't know what anybody is talking about. What do you mean—somebody broke the skylight?"

Lori started to speak, but this time Trevor cut in. "That's enough. Karen's right and Chris couldn't possibly have been up on the roof last night. So don't torment him."

"Sorry, Chris." Lori shrugged. "I didn't realize everyone was so sure you were innocent."

Chris continued to scowl at her. "I still don't know what happened."

I began to explain, and after a few words he dropped his gaze to the toast he was buttering and didn't look up again.

"So that's what happened," I finished a bit lamely, "and none of us really thinks you were to blame."

The faint smile he gave me erased the scowl, but its uncertainty went to my heart.

"Is that how you cut your face?" he asked.

I had removed the bit of bandage and I touched the rough mark on my cheek. "Yes, but it's nothing. I was lucky it wasn't any worse."

"Very lucky." Nona sounded ominous.

I glanced at Lori and saw in surprise that she was crying. Chris saw too and reached across the table to touch her.

"Hey," he said. "It's okay."

She looked at him with swimming eyes. "I'm sorry. I was being mean. I know you didn't do it, Chris. It's just that—that everyone always blames me!" With a quick movement she shoved her chair back and ran out of the room.

Trevor said wearily, "I'll talk to her," and followed her from the kitchen.

Nona made a sound like a snort and began to stack plates before her on the table, while Chris sat at his place, finishing his breakfast in silence. There was, after all, nothing to be said. Lori's rational balance seemed more precarious than ever. Yet she seemed to reject with scorn whatever might be offered to help her and to go her own way.

"I wish Trevor were free of her," Nona muttered.

Chris looked up, but said nothing.

When I'd finished helping Nona, and Chris had risen from his place, I spoke to him.

"Can you show me where the utility rooms are? Your father put David's things down there and I must look through them."

Suddenly he was eager to do anything he could for me. His mother's attack and my defense had moved him in my direction as nothing else had done.

He showed me the door to the basement stairs and ran down ahead. When he'd led the way into the storage room, he perched on a trunk, watching me.

The room was neatly antiseptic, with pale gray walls and a minimum of disorder. Apparently Nona's generalship reached everywhere, even into rooms it would be difficult for her to visit.

Two suitcases had been placed upon a long table and I stopped before them, hesitating because there was a reluctance in me to touch what had belonged to David. Something must have shown in my face—something that reached Chris.

"Do you want me to go away?" he asked.

"No—please stay. Perhaps it will help if you'll keep me company."

Long lashes came down over intensely blue eyes and

he spoke so softly I could barely hear him. "You aren't like Uncle David at all, Karen."

It was an offering of friendship, the words spoken with more conviction this time than when he'd first said them to me.

I managed my own uncertain smile and spoke over a lump in my throat. "I understand, Chris. I don't blame you for the way you felt. But David wasn't always the way you think. Not when I knew him at first before he went away to war. Not in the beginning." I needed to believe that myself.

"When he wanted something a lot he knew how to pretend," Chris said with surprising wisdom. "Sometimes he could be nice, if it suited him. But he hurt my mother. He made her—different. Dad talked to me about it once. He wanted Uncle David to go away—so my mother could be like she was before."

"I know," I said.

But I didn't know, because Chris's expression had changed, as though his own words had alarmed him.

"I mean Dad wanted him to *go away*. Just to go away."

"Of course," I said. "He must have wanted him to leave."

My calm, accepting tone seemed to reassure him, and I turned to my task, wishing there were some way to help him let down his guard and pour out whatever was troubling him. As something of an outsider, I might offer a less concerned, listening presence, should he ever be able to accept it.

Now, however, the suitcases waited for me and reluctantly I raised the lid of the larger one. Shirts and slacks and jackets had been carelessly folded after many hands must have examined them. They hadn't been repacked with the slightly foppish care David gave to his possessions. I lifted out one familiar garment after another, shook them out, examined the pockets and placed them on the table beside me. In a strange sense what I was doing seemed an invasion of David's privacy. As though I had no right to touch these things that had belonged to him.

As he watched me, Chris seemed to be tightening up again. The same fierce tension was rising in him that I'd seen before—clearly evident in his expressive young face. I guessed that he was still thinking of David's death and its possible connection with his father.

I spoke to him gently. "Sometime I wish you'd tell me what is worrying you, Chris. Maybe if we could talk about it, it would help to clear things up. Whatever it is you're thinking, you may be wrong. There may not be anything to worry about."

He shook his head, his eyes fixed in unhappy fascination upon David's clothing as I unpacked the case.

"What will you do with all that stuff?" he asked at last.

"Your Aunt Nona will know of some charity it can be given to. I just want to go through it first, in case—"

In case what? What could I hope to find among David's possessions that the police hadn't already noted and dismissed? Certainly nothing in this first suitcase. I lifted out the last pair of slacks, and felt through the side pockets of the case, where handkerchiefs and other small articles had been packed. There was nothing of interest, and I turned my attention to the second bag.

It was smaller than the first and it contained underwear, shoes and ties, toilet articles, his zippered shaving kit. I opened the leather case and took out an electric razor and a few other small objects, my reluctance growing. These things seemed even more personally a part of David than his clothes had been. Objects that he had handled every day. Among them was something small and lumpy wrapped in a wad of white paper that crackled open in my fingers.

"What's that?" Chris asked.

What I held in my hand was some sort of small metal figure. A seated figure—perhaps a Buddha, though I wasn't sure because the metal had been blackened and twisted beyond clear recognition. Chris reached out to take it from my hand and turned it about in his own slim fingers.

"You can still see the face," Chris said. "It's sitting in a sort of lotus position—like a Chinese god."

"I think that's what it is," I agreed and took it back from him.

Once more there was soot on my fingers, though the smell of fire had long been dissipated from the metal. This wasn't like a chunk of wood that would smell of char until it crumbled to ashes.

"Why would he have it in his shaving case?" Chris asked.

"I don't know. Perhaps for safekeeping. David had a weird sort of collection at home—souvenirs from some of the fires he worked on."

"A collection of what?"

"Oh—rather sad things, I always thought. A burned book, a baby's shoe, a broken china doll—things that had been only partly destroyed. He must have had a dozen or more objects that he'd picked out of ruins after a fire —things nobody would want. This could be something he meant to add to that collection."

"Down here? But there wouldn't be any furnishings or ornaments in the houses at Belle Isle."

"You're probably right. I remember there was a bad fire in an Oriental import house in New York a few months before David came to Tennessee. It was a store that carried all sorts of really fine objects from the Orient."

"Was it an arson fire?"

I tried to think back. "No, I don't believe so. I remember David talking about it because a great many expensive articles were lost and the fire cost the insurance company a lot of money."

"Uncle David said that sometimes owners burned down their stores so as to collect the insurance."

"That's true. But he said there wasn't any evidence of arson in this case. He was called in pretty quickly when it happened."

"Anyway," Chris said, "that thing doesn't look like what would come out of an expensive store, does it?"

I had to agree. The figure wasn't even brass, or it would have come through fire in better condition. It seemed more like one of the cheap tourist items that I'd sometimes seen in Chinatown.

"I wonder what the police here made of this?" I said. "Perhaps they didn't take everything out of his shaving kit."

Chris prodded the figure with one finger. "I'll bet it does mean something. Uncle David could have brought it with him from home, couldn't he?"

"I haven't any idea."

I put the oddly incongruous little figure back in the case without rewrapping it, and set the open kit aside as I continued my inventory.

When I was nearly through Chris spoke again, hesitantly. "I really didn't go up on the roof last night and drop anything through your skylight, Karen."

"Of course you didn't. I've already said that you were sleeping. You couldn't possibly have been up there."

"I know. I—I'm glad you stood up for me. My mother's been mixed up some lately."

His eyes beseeched me to understand. Even though he was angry with her at times, Chris, like his father, seemed to be ruled by a need to protect Lori from her own follies.

"The trouble is," he went on, "I did go up on that roof once when you first came. I—I just wanted to scare you that time."

"I remember. I thought something moved up there, but I wasn't sure. Anyway, it doesn't matter now."

"Mother knew I was there and she scolded me. So maybe that's why she thought it was me up there again. But I don't feel like scaring you anymore."

"I'm glad of that, Chris. Thank you for telling me."

Once more he gave me his rare, beautiful smile and for the instant of its appearance he ceased to look fiercely determined beyond his years.

"Are you really going away right after the funeral?" he asked. "Mom says your reservations will be for day after tomorrow."

So Lori was carrying out her promise and urging me on my way. Nor had I an excuse to remain any longer. My naïve conviction that *I* could learn what no one else had about David's death had gradually weakened. Too much had happened that was beyond my poor efforts. I must get back to New York quickly and begin to make a new life for myself. I had meant to do that even before David had left, so now I would merely continue what I'd already intended.

Or was that only another futile hope? It was easy enough to tell myself that I had only to go back to the way things were, as though nothing had happened. But everything had happened—everything. And my life was already changed. There were two men in it now—father and son.

"Don't go away," Chris said.

I came out of my inner searching and looked at him in

surprise. He was no longer smiling, and he stood beside me, tall and thin and once more fiercely intent. His eyes seemed huge in his small face and they never wavered as he returned my own questioning look.

"But, Chris—" I spoke gently, feeling the tug of his appeal, hating to disappoint him, torn because I knew I must.

"Don't go away," he repeated.

I managed to smile. "That's the nicest thing you've ever said to me, Chris. But I don't belong here now, and—"

"There's nobody else who can help me. There's nobody else I can tell."

Suddenly the room seemed very quiet. What I might want, what I feared, ceased to matter at that moment. Only Chris's need was important, and I knew I mustn't fail him.

"Tell me what it is, Chris. I'll help you if I can."

Perhaps he would have spoken, but we heard a clatter of someone coming down the basement stairs, and the moment was lost as Lori burst into the room. In her arms she carried the big white cat, Commodore, and she came to stand beside the table where David's possessions were spread.

Clearly her mood had changed again. She flicked a quick, nervous glance over the articles I had unpacked. "I'm glad you're getting things wound up, Karen. What are you going to do with David's clothes?"

"Give them away, I suppose," I said. "Can someone here handle that for me?"

"Yes, of course." She held the cat out to Chris. "Take him, will you please—he's getting heavy. The wound is healing just fine and I'll return him to Belle Isle as soon as I can. Will you carry him upstairs, Chris? I don't think he likes it down here."

The big cat gazed at us with his one blue and one yellow eye, the black pirate patch giving him an arrogant look as he squirmed indignantly in Lori's arms. Chris threw me a quick glance that carried a plea, and I nodded reassurance before he went off, the cat on his shoulder. He knew Lori was getting rid of him, but there was nothing he could do about it.

"Commodore can't stand it away from Belle Isle," Lori said idly. She glanced again at the articles of clothing I had spread out on the table. "David always wore good clothes, didn't he? Of course we'll find some place to send them. Hey—look at this!"

She pounced and drew the lump of metal that might have been a Buddha from David's open shaving case.

"Do you know what it is?" I asked.

"I remember he showed it to me once. He got to laughing over it for some reason as though it had a connection with something funny. And yet when I think about it, I don't know that it was an amused laugh. It was more as though he wanted to get even with somebody."

"Did he say where it came from?"

"No. Just that it reminded him of something that made him laugh." Lori dropped the charred figure back in its nest. "Are you ready to leave day after tomorrow, Karen?"

"I'm not sure," I said. "There are a few more things I'd like to do while I'm here."

"Then let me help so you can get them out of the way," she offered sweetly.

I shook my head. I'd had a taste of her help before, and I wanted none of it. The important thing at the moment was to find Chris and persuade him to talk to me. That, at least, must be done before I took any plane to New York.

"Did Nona tell you she's planning a little dinner for tomorrow night after the funeral?" Lori asked.

"A dinner?"

"Yes. She said there'd been enough of gloom and we ought to cheer you up before you leave. There'll just be the Catons and us. And we'll dress up for a change."

I could only regard her in astonishment. Did Lori Andrews possess the slightest depth of feeling about anything? She lived in this house as though her affair with David had been inconsequential to anyone else, and David's death—after her first tears and depression— hardly more than an inconvenience. She seemed unaware of Trevor's tight control over his own feelings, or of his protection of her—as he must always have protected her.

"I shouldn't think this was the time for a party," I told her. "I shouldn't think Trevor—"

"Oh, he'll hate it, of course. But that's part of why Nona wants to do it. He needs people in to talk to. Then he'll have to come out of his office and stop looking like a large thunderstorm about to break."

"If you don't mind," I said, "I'll stay in my room tomorrow night. I won't feel like seeing people and trying to keep up a cheerful conversation. Not after everything that's happened. Don't you feel the horror, Lori? When you took me down to that burned-out house you were feeling it. Don't you remember?"

"I don't want to remember," she said. "I want to be free of all that. I wish I didn't ever have to feel anything awful again. Here—I have something for you."

She reached into her jacket pocket and took out a yellow packet. "I picked up your pictures this morning," she said, tossing the envelope on the table. She was angry now, and in a whirl of furious movement she hurried out of the room. I had clearly touched some chord in her— even if it was to move her to no more than annoyance with me. Did her seeming frivolity hide something else? I wondered—something more disturbing and dangerous?

Now I too hurried, finishing my task in the storeroom, returning everything to the two bags, except for the blackened figure of the little Buddha. I would show that to Trevor. As I picked it up, the wad of paper I'd discarded as wrapping for the figure crumpled open in my fingers, and words written in ink on one sheet caught my eye. I spread it open.

This was not written by the same semi-illiterate hand that had scrawled the note I had found in Cecily's room at the octagonal house, but this too was unaddressed and unsigned.

Here's a present for you. Just a reminder. So you won't get absent-minded. $40,000 will be okay for now. Joe's in touch with us. Don't forget that. If you try anything funny he has his orders. So you better get on the ball.

The storeroom was all too quiet and empty and the note in my hand seemed to shout its threat. Here, perhaps, was the answer to David's death.

I ran upstairs looking for Trevor, and found him in his office. He saw my face and drew me into a chair, closing the door. I handed him the battered figure and the crumpled wrapping as I'd found them, with the writing displayed.

"The police must have missed this in David's shaving case. The paper was wrapped around this lump of something taken from a fire. Not a fire down here, I think. I only discovered the note by chance."

He sat at his desk, reading the words, and when he looked up his expression was grim. "Do you know anything about this, Karen? I mean what might lie behind it?"

"I know that lately David was deeply in debt. But he would never explain why. Oh, Trevor—no matter what he did, he was good at his job. He was respected all around the country. He was an expert."

"Maybe he was too much of an expert. I can also remember, Karen, that he never hesitated to cheat when he found himself on the losing end. David couldn't bear to be beaten at any sort of game. Only it looks now as though this is one game that he lost. I'm sorry, Karen, but this will have to be turned over to the sheriff right away. He may want to talk to you again."

"If David knew Joe Bruen—? Trevor, it may only mean that he'd found the arsonist. Not that he was working with him in any way."

"I don't know." Trevor sounded grave and not very hopeful. "This puts a whole new light on what has happened. Anyway, I'll have something else now for the police. I had a phone call from David's company in New York today and they've found fingerprints on that note you discovered. Bruen's prints. He's been arrested for arson in the past and there was even suspicion in some killing that was never proved. He has served a term in prison. It looks as though he may have carried out orders from whoever's been giving them."

"But then why would he stay here? Why would he take the risk of starting another fire?"

"Maybe someone's been paying him very well for the fires, as David may have discovered, or suspected. My brother could even have been playing both sides of the game, Karen. I'll have to get going on this right away."

I felt stunned, bewildered, and Trevor stopped beside me on his way to the door. When his hand touched my shoulder I looked up at him.

"Would you feel any better if you came with me now?"

I shook my head. "No—I'd rather not. You can tell me later what develops."

His hand touched my cheek for an instant and then he

was gone from the room. I rose listlessly and walked through the glass doors that opened on the deck. No one was there and I sat down in a chair, looking out toward Belle Isle. How peaceful the lake looked in morning sunlight. Trees hid most of the new houses, but I could glimpse the tower of Vinnie Fromberg's octagonal house poking up through foliage, and on the island's small hill a portion of the open-air theater could be seen. All was calm and the view told me nothing.

I remembered the packet of pictures in my lap and opened it, taking out the prints. The one I'd shot of the house where David had died made me shiver. There was Lori, looking out over a fallen beam across what had once been a door, her expression a grimace. A camera could catch an instant that otherwise passed so swiftly it was hardly noted. I didn't remember that she had looked like that while she was tormenting me about the house.

Then there was the other view of her when she had posed looking in a window of the octagonal house. She had objected to my not photographing her face, and in the instant before the shutter clicked she had looked around, her expression startled. That had been when Commodore moved inside, surprising her.

The other pictures were mostly routine. The one I'd done of Trevor's house from the island, using my telescopic lens, was quite good, as were the closer shots I'd taken from the rock. Maggie and Giff were caught in various poses around the crumbling dressing rooms. And of course there was Chris. Chris climbing the rocky steps above the fishpond and looking down at me angrily. Chris in the rowboat. And, last of all, the empty view of Cecily's theater, shallow steps grass-grown, mounting the amphitheater curve as seen from the stage. The legs of one lighting tower visible—the one from which Cecily had jumped. And still higher the roofed section at the top, where folding seats had been stacked. Above the roof, treetops burgeoned on the hill behind the theater.

Something odd in the picture caught my eye. A light-colored spot showed above a row of stacked seats, and seemed out of place—something small and round. Perhaps a face? If only I'd used the telescopic lens here. I studied the spot intently and could believe that it was nothing else but a face, a head, possibly topped with light hair. At home I might have made an enlargement, but here I must trust my eyes and my instinct.

It was quite possible that someone had stood up there at the back of the theater and watched as we walked upon the stage. Not Lori, who had driven off the island in her car. Not Trevor, who had been with us until he'd left the theater. Someone else. Someone interested enough to follow our movements from his hiding place. I began to wonder if what I had caught was indeed Joe Bruen himself, watching us from the top of the theater.

Not that it really mattered. Even if the picture was enlarged, a spot so tiny would turn to rough grain and tell us nothing.

As I sat with the snapshot in my hand, staring blankly out toward Belle Isle and the high mountains beyond, a slight movement far to my right caught my attention. When I turned my head I could see the big boulder that thrust out from the hillside—that rock where I had climbed to view the house on my first morning here. Chris was standing on its crest looking toward me. I waved to him and went to the railing that protected the deck from the steep drop below.

"Chris!" I called. "I've got the pictures I took. Wait there and I'll bring them to you."

He didn't respond one way or the other—as though he might already have withdrawn from that moment of near confidence with me. I called to him again and then hurried through the house and out the door. By the time I reached the woods leading in the direction of Maggie's house, I was running. In only a few moments I came out on the hillside near the rock. Chris still sat here, cross-legged on the stone, waiting for me.

Quickly I climbed to the top and sat down beside him. His manner, less friendly than before, was far more cautious—as though he had indeed retreated from any wish to talk to me.

"Here you are," I said. "I promised you the pictures I snapped of you."

He accepted the envelope and took out the prints. "They're only black and white," he said scornfully.

"Sometimes I like that better for my purpose. There's good contrast and shadow quality. Color film can be tricky. You can get orange shadows in the late afternoon, and a bluish tinge in early morning."

Chris sorted through the pictures. The one with Lori in the burned-out house he put aside quickly. Those I had taken of Chris himself seemed to interest him more.

"I didn't know I looked like that." He held up the one where he was climbing the rock steps behind the house.

"That's what a picture can do—catch a second in time the way it really was. Of course these weren't carefully taken. Part of the time I was just using up film so I could get yours printed quickly and give them to you. But sometimes a quick shot can show more than we knew was there in a scene. Like the expression on faces, and like that one of the theater."

He looked again at the theater picture, puzzled by my words. When he put it down I knew he had seen what must be a face.

I nodded. "Yes. I think that's the man you were talking about, Chris. We never knew he was there, but the camera saw him."

"Will you show this to Dad?" he asked. "So he'll know I was telling the truth."

"Of course. And I'll show it to Maggie and Giff too."

His mouth tightened as though he was making some inner effort. Then he blurted out the words. "Karen—will you go over there with me?"

"To the island, you mean?" His words had startled me.

"Yes. I want to show you something. Something nobody else knows about."

I tried to stall for time because his request alarmed me. "When do you want to go?"

"Not till after the funeral. Maybe the morning before you go away."

So that I wouldn't have time to talk to anyone after he'd shown me whatever it was?

"I'm not sure we should go there alone," I said doubtfully.

"Okay." He sounded almost relieved as he picked out the snapshots I had taken of him and handed the rest back to me. When he stood up I knew I had failed him, and I knew it was important not to.

"Wait, Chris. I haven't said I wouldn't go. I just wondered if you ought to tell your father whatever it is—perhaps show him?"

His expression went blank. "I don't want to do that. I just thought you—you might be the one I could talk to. You're outside my family, but you're still connected. With Uncle David, I mean."

"What has this to do with Uncle David?"

There was a hint of remembered shock in his eyes. "That's what I want to show you. Karen, I've got to show somebody. But not Dad. Not any of the others."

I made up my mind. "I'll go with you, of course, Chris."

He reacted cautiously, verbalizing plans. "Then we'll

go early in the morning day after tomorrow. But don't tell anyone, Karen. If you tell anyone, it's all off."

I nodded, but I gave him no promise, because I knew it was not one I could keep. Whatever was troubling Chris had to be brought into the open. Yet at the same time I didn't for a moment intend that the two of us should go wandering about the island alone. No matter how Chris felt, I would have to talk to Trevor.

Once more he flashed me his bright smile. "You're okay, Karen. So I'll meet you in your car around nine that morning."

"Fine," I said, and he started down from the rock. Near the bottom he turned to look up at me. "Before you go away, will you show me some more about taking pictures?"

"Of course," I promised, and watched unhappily as he ran off to the woods.

Before you go away, he had said. And time was racing all too fast. Of course I could cancel my flight at the last minute if it seemed wise. Right now I didn't know whether I would be on that plane or not. It might depend on what news Trevor brought back from his visit to the sheriff's office. And on whatever it was on the island that Chris wanted to show me.

I had a sense of tension building in me, of a new and frightening dread. David had been involved in something far more grim and desperate than I'd ever guessed. I had less doubt than before that his death had been deliberately caused, but could I bear to face the truth about him when it really came out? I'd had few illusions about my husband, but I had believed in the integrity of his work.

I climbed down from the rock and wandered idly along the path and across the driveway that led to Maggie's house. She must have seen me from a window because she came running outside through a lower door.

"Karen, wait!"

I had no wish to spend more time with Maggie Caton. Or with any of them, I thought. Not even with Nona, who had promised to give me some help that had so far not been forthcoming. Nevertheless, Maggie was beside me in her usual disarray, with her mottled red hair blowing and a green smudge on her nose, and I couldn't turn away.

"Come talk to me," she said. "I'll go batty if I sit around alone much longer. I don't know what's happening, but something is. That awful fire again last night, and that block of wood dropped through your skylight!"

"Who told you about that?"

"Why—I think it was Giff. He was talking to Trevor about the fire this morning, and Trevor told him. Now he and Eric have gone in to Eric's office in the Greencastle in Gatlinburg. That's the hotel Vinnie built. And I don't feel like staying alone. If you'll come up to the house I'll fix a salad for our lunch. Besides, you haven't seen my studio yet. And you can't leave without viewing that spectacle."

I wasn't sure I could take any more of Maggie's artistic efforts, but neither could I refuse without hurting her feelings, so I followed her up to the house. This time she led me into a glass-enclosed lower room—an enormous room that had obviously been built as her studio.

It was not as tidy as her kitchen, since various works in progress were standing about, with brushes in peanut butter glasses, and jars of assorted acrylic colors. Several large canvases stood about on easels, and there was an unmistakable odor of turpentine and paint.

Here and there, blocking the way, chunks of stone had been piled—stone that she must have collected for her crude animal creations. She kicked one of these with her toe.

"Eric says I should buy some proper stone to work

with. The sort of stuff that I dig out of the mountain has weathered and it's tough to work on. Sometimes it cracks in the wrong places, and it's grown a protective skin. But I like odd shapes that hint at what's inside, and I'm not doing anything in great detail when it comes to chopping out my animals. It's a change from the plants and flowers when they get too poisonous."

More of her monstrous vegetation stood on easels, or was stacked against a wall. Always they were handsome and meticulously done, but always they suggested inner horror. I didn't want to look at any of them too carefully, for fear of what I'd find.

"Don't you ever paint figures?" I asked. "I mean human figures?"

She stared at me brightly, as though I had said something surprising. "As a matter of fact, I'm doing that right now. I'm painting something I haven't shown anyone yet. I suppose I might as well show you. Especially since you'll be going away soon."

Her words were puzzling, but I was curious now, and I followed as she beckoned me across the room. A large painting on an easel had been placed with its face hidden and she turned it so I could see the picture.

"It's nearly finished," she said. "Believe me, I've worked on this one. All those leaves!"

What she had painted was kudzu. The vine ran rampant all over the huge canvas, its big leaves making patterns of sunlight and shadow, with only a touch of clouds and blue sky in one corner to indicate that an outside world existed. At first glance the painting seemed cheerful and open and free of Maggie's usual distortion of nature. Indeed, it was rather beautiful, if you could overlook the destructive power of the vine.

"It would make a nice wallpaper pattern," I said. "But there aren't any human figures. I thought you said—"

"No?" The one word challenged me and I looked closer.

Now I saw what was there. In the center of the canvas, almost lost in vines that had crawled over him, stood a man. Or at least the shape of a man. He stood like a scarecrow in the sea of green, his body straight, his arms held out at shoulder height with tendrils of kudzu dripping from them. Creeping over almost every inch of this human figure were the vines, enveloping, smothering his humanity, denying him life. Only his eyes were still free of the devouring blight, still unhidden as they stared wide and terror-filled from the foliage that covered his face and head as well as his body. White showed around the iris as the eyes had widened in shock, and even their color had taken on a tinge of green.

Maggie was waiting and I sensed anxiety in her, as though whatever I said about this painting mattered in some way that I didn't understand.

"It—it's quite awful," was all I could manage.

Behind the leaf-covered figure, defining him, the vines slipped into deep shadow, sometimes gray-green, often fading into black. Indeed, the painting of shadow was as important as the creation of the leaves, giving definition to the whole. The man figure stood out in brightest sunlight, and the foliage that covered him seemed to tremble with a life of its own.

I added to my verdict. "The vines seem almost alive."

Maggie stood close to me. "Yes. It's both those things, isn't it? Awful and alive. Sometimes I'm almost afraid of it. As though by painting it I gave the vine its own life right here in this room. As though it might move off the canvas and reach out for me at any moment. The way it did for *him*."

She stepped past me to turn the easel about and I was prompted to ask a question.

"Who is he, Maggie—the man in your painting?"

She turned back to me slowly. "Don't you know? Can't you guess?"

"You don't mean—David?"

"You named him—I didn't."

"But David died by fire."

"Of course," she said. "Of course he did. Forget it. I wasn't painting David."

But I had the feeling that my guess had been right, and that for some reason she had been thinking of David all the while as she painted smothering, man-eating leaves over the scarecrow figure.

All I wanted now was to escape her company, to get out of this house and into the reality of mountains and clear sunlight.

"I'll fix us some lunch now," Maggie said.

I shook my head. "Thanks, but I'd really better get back. I've some things to do. I'm taking a plane for New York day after tomorrow."

"Oh, dear. I've spoiled your appetite, haven't I? I'm sorry, Karen." She walked with me to the door and I turned back for a moment.

"What made you paint it? Tell me why!"

Her look shifted away from me and she twisted at a strand of her harlequin hair. "I don't know. It all comes out of something inside me. It just happens. Eric says my motivations are beyond anyone's figuring out. Maybe I'd better destroy that picture before they decide to put me away."

"Don't make jokes," I said. "I think you know perfectly well why you painted it."

"Maybe I do," she said after a moment. "Maybe I painted it because I was scared. Catharsis, I suppose. The way Nona says? I had to come to grips with something so it would stop frightening me."

"And has it?"

"Only while I was painting. Don't ask any more questions, Karen. Just go away and forget about all of this. Go back to New York and forget about Trevor and Lori —and all of us. If you stay, you'll be caught in the trap too. The trap of your own fears, the way I am."

She began pushing me toward the door, almost roughly, though I was willing enough to hurry.

"I'll see you at the funeral, and at dinner tomorrow night," she said as I went out on the lower terrace.

I paused. "I'm not in the mood for a dinner party. I plan to stay in my room."

As I turned away she caught my arm in one strong hand and held me there. "No, Karen. You mustn't stay away. I won't be able to stand that dinner if you aren't there. We can be—allies, in a way. So please come. Help me, Karen. I'm so frightened I could die. But you're from outside. You're healthy and young and David never corrupted you, as he did poor Lori. Just *be* there, Karen."

Her entreaty had a wild note to it, and I tried to humor her. "I'll come if you want me there, Maggie," I promised. Gently I drew my arm from her grasp, and this time she let me go. I didn't look back as I walked down the driveway and plunged into the woods.

Only once did I stop on that hurried trip back to Trevor's and that was because of something I saw at the base of a maple tree. Something with large green leaves had begun to grow up the trunk of the tree. When I bent close, however, I saw with relief that it was only some other, less voracious wild vine, and not kudzu.

All the way back to the house the words from Dickey's poem haunted me: "Green, mindless, unkillable ghosts." If I dreamed tonight it would be Maggie's painting that would haunt me.

But what had kudzu to do with David Hallam?

Nine

David's funeral had been kept as simple and private as possible, by my wish and Trevor's. There was no eulogy. It would have been inappropriate and false under such circumstances. Nona persuaded Lori not to come, and it was better that way. Whatever Lori might feel, it was best not displayed in public. As Nona said, there was no telling what she might do when the pressure was on, and Trevor had been submitted to enough. Nona came, of course, and Chris was there, standing close beside her wheelchair, never looking at his father. He showed no grief for his uncle's death, but stared out at the world with his own fierce air of defiance.

As I stood beside the open grave my emotion was one of a deep, enveloping sorrow, mingled with a terror that I was still trying to suppress. What I felt in sadness had to do with the past, not the present. The man I mourned was the man David Hallam might have been—and perhaps the woman I might have been. I mourned too my own inability to have changed him or changed myself.

Eric, Maggie and Giff Caton were all there. Not one of them had liked David, but they were fond of Trevor, in spite of the disagreement over Belle Isle, and David was Trevor's brother. Convention, I supposed, required that they stand beside him. Both Giff and Eric were stiffly correct, revealing nothing of what they might be feeling, but I sensed that Maggie had come close to the breaking point. She clung to Eric's arm and never looked at either the coffin or the grave. Once I saw Giff watching her uneasily, though Eric seemed not to notice her state. Those rain-gray eyes that I had noted as her one beauty looked more haunted than ever, and I could only wish that we might just once have talked with complete honesty together.

When we left the cemetery Trevor drove Nona and Chris and me to the house, with Nona in the front seat, her wheelchair folded into the trunk, and Chris beside me in the back.

With the funeral behind me, a period had been set to the entire phase of my marriage. This was a time of beginning again, yet I could feel only a deep and enervating depression. The years that lay ahead didn't bear thinking of, though when my plane left tomorrow they would have begun.

Chris was silent during the drive. The defiance I had sensed in him at the funeral had fallen away, and he had retreated into his own thoughts, holding me off, so that I could find no way to reach him. We sat close together, Trevor's son and I, and I dared not touch him. Not until we were nearly home did he rouse himself to whisper a reminder of my promise to go with him to the island on the following day. I repeated my assurance that I would be ready, and the moment Trevor pulled up before the house he got out and ran off about his own concerns.

It was nearly lunchtime, and when I'd changed into slacks I came upstairs, to find Nona at the refrigerator in the kitchen. She took one look at my dispirited expression and nodded at me.

"Food will help. Let's take this potato salad out on the deck and lunch together. Lori has taken the cat back to the island. She said she had an errand in Gatlinburg and would have lunch at the Greencastle. Trevor's gone off to talk to the police again and I don't know when he'll be home. Chris goes and comes as he pleases and it's better to ease up on the rules with him for now. Lu-Ellen's coming in late so she can stay for our dinner tonight."

I helped wheel the loaded cart through the house and outside, where we set a small table and I pulled up a chair for Nona. I was glad enough to have these moments alone with her. I'd had no chance to talk to her since Maggie had shown me her terrible kudzu painting yesterday. Now I told her the whole story, including my feeling that Maggie was coming close to flying apart completely.

"I know," Nona said, her green eyes bright, and as always a little malicious. "I noticed her too this morning. Eric may have trouble on his hands."

"But why would she think of David when she painted that awful picture?" I asked.

"Who knows? I expect it's all very symbolic and beyond understanding unless your mind works like Maggie's. I think she's been scared stiff ever since we had that glimpse of Joe Bruen."

I stared at her. "You mean on the island? You mean—"

"No, not on the island. Maggie and I saw him in town one morning a few weeks ago. He was talking to Eric Caton."

Astonishment left me with nothing to say, and I waited for her to go on.

Nona buttered a hot roll and helped herself to more potato salad, obviously enjoying my surprise. I knew by this time that she would milk every ounce of drama from any story she had to tell. When she was satisfied with the quality of my impatience, she grinned at me and went on with her story.

"I suppose you've seen those mini shopping malls they've built in Gatlinburg? They're filled with turns and corners, and fascinating small shops. On the morning I'm talking about, Maggie and I went into town to visit a cheese shop in one of those places. Maggie was pushing my wheelchair. We'd just stopped to look in a shop window when I noticed Eric Caton down the alley a little way. He was standing in a secluded corner talking to a big man in jeans and a green plaid shirt. He was a burly, tough-looking fellow. Not very young—his hair was a lot grayer than mine."

She paused thinking back, forgetting to eat, as though evoking the memory of that meeting disturbed her more than she wanted to admit.

"So what happened?" I asked.

"Nothing much, really. I don't think the conversation between the two of them was altogether friendly, and a minute or so after Maggie and I saw them, the man in the green shirt went off by himself. Maggie waved and called to Eric and he came to join us. Of course Maggie asked who the man was. Eric told us his name was Bruen —Joe Bruen—and he was an unsavory character from New York. A man with whom Eric had had a run-in once before. Unsavory because he'd done a prison term for arson, and Eric wondered what he was up to around here. Bruen claimed that he was on vacation with his wife —merely visiting—and how could he help it if there had been some fires in the area? Fires happened anywhere. Eric said he told him it would be a good idea to get out of town and stay away."

"And did he leave?"

"At least he disappeared. Maggie said Eric looked into the matter and found that he really was staying at a motel with his wife, Gwen. Which doesn't mean that Chris isn't right about glimpsing him on the island. Of course we don't know how much of this was fabrication on Eric's part."

"It sounds as though he was telling the truth."

"Of course. That's the way he meant it to sound. I've known Eric for a long time and I'm fond of him. But when there's something at stake he can put on a masterful performance that may have very little to do with basic truth. He was useful to old Vinnie that way—more useful than Trevor could ever be."

"Did Eric tell David and Trevor about this?"

"Maggie said he did—so he was open enough on that score. But when they tried to find Bruen, the man was already gone, checked out with his wife. Either out of the state, or underground."

"And Maggie still thinks there's something behind this?"

"I don't believe she's thinking, really. She's reacting with all those strung-out emotions of hers. Eric is more important than anything else in her life, and she'd never injure him in any way. But I wonder sometimes if she's bottling up so much that she's injuring herself. Or do those weird paintings keep her sane?"

"I don't know," I said. "I had an awful feeling while I was looking at the kudzu painting that it was insane.

Those eyes staring out of the vines in such dreadful tor-ment—because the man in the picture knew he was being killed by them. Why did Maggie think of David while she painted that?"

"I suppose because David is dead. Don't take on so, Karen." Nona pushed the bowl of salad toward me. "You're not eating enough lately."

I didn't want to eat. "But then why didn't Maggie paint a fire devouring David? Why kudzu?"

"Green fire, perhaps, and more indirect? Anyway, I'm glad to know about this before our dinner tonight."

I looked at her sharply. "Just why are you having this dinner, Nona? It seems an inappropriate time, and—"

"It couldn't be more appropriate! Remember, Karen, I said I'd try to think up a way to help you. To help all of us and bring the truth out where we can stop this damage to Trevor. That's *why* the dinner, and that's why you must come. I know it's painful for you now, but that makes no difference. I'll be lighting a small fuse and if things go as I expect, perhaps there will be a useful ex-plosion."

"Tell me what you're planning."

"And spoil the effect? Never! Lu-Ellen's going to stay on tonight and help me, and she'll serve in the dining room. Her first effort at a company dinner, so it may be interesting."

After that, no matter how I prodded her, Nona would talk about nothing serious. I tried to eat, and before we had entirely finished Trevor came into the house and joined us out on the deck. Nona filled a plate for him and I brought more hot rolls from the oven.

He looked weary and not at all satisfied with the results of his visits with the police. The sheriff's office had agreed to call in the state police and open a further investigation. After the latest fire this seemed even more justified. But no further searches of the island—another one had been made an hour ago—had turned up anything except Lori sitting on the steps of the octagonal house with Commodore in her lap. They had even gone through the entire house again, and it was not a structure built with concealed rooms or hidden walls. The house plans were perfectly simple and clear, and the construction matched in every detail. Only one room had shown any sign of being used, and Giff Caton had already admitted to sleeping there on occasion—though his efforts to discover an answer had been futile. Nor did the theater or the moldering dressing rooms, open and obvious, offer hiding places that couldn't be immediately betraying. The island wasn't all that big, and such places didn't exist.

As Trevor talked, I remembered the pictures in my handbag and brought them out, singling out the one of the theater, which I handed him silently.

He found the face above the stacked chairs at the top of the theater at once, and when Nona held out her hand, he passed it along to her.

"I suppose it could have been anyone, any straggler on the island watching us," I said. "We ourselves were nearly all accounted for at the time I took that picture. Except perhaps Eric Caton, and he would have been in his office. So Chris's island ghost may be perfectly real, and he could be Joe Bruen still up to his old profession."

Trevor had finished what food he cared to eat and he pushed back from the table. "There's nothing to be done for now. Would you like to go for a drive, Karen? You'll be gone tomorrow, and you may not have another chance to see our mountains."

Nona made some small movement, but when I glanced at her she was still, not looking at either Trevor or me. I understood Trevor's need to put Belle Isle out of his life for a little while. Perhaps a change would give his tired mind and body some respite. I would help if I could—and because I wanted to.

"I'd like that," I told him. "I hate to leave without having seen anything but Belle Isle."

"Bring a sweater," he instructed. "It will be cool up there."

Nona waved aside my offer to carry dishes to the kitchen and said everything could stay right there and await Lu-Ellen. When she rolled her chair to the door and watched us on our way, her manner didn't seem altogether friendly, but I couldn't tell what was going on in her mind. If she was worried about anything developing between Trevor and me, she really needn't, I thought a bit grimly.

The mountains seemed more beautiful than ever as our road wound and began to climb above fields of goldenrod, winding into the great park. The sun of early afternoon had burned away the mists, and the crests above us stood clear. The stream that tumbled beside our road frothed white over wet black stones, carving its way between banks where wild grapevines grew to enormous size, thicker than a man's fist. Everywhere the ubiquitous rhododendron and laurel crowded down the hills and clustered along the streams.

"The mountain people call rhododendron laurel, and laurel, ivy," Trevor said. "They always have. And they call them 'hells' too, because you can't find your way out if you get lost in them."

As we began to climb we passed huge exposed rocks that Trevor said the highlanders called graybacks. Moss and lichen grew on every surface, and sometimes little pine trees sprouted out of seemingly barren rock. An occasional jagged black stump stood up alone, left where a tree had been struck by lightning. Still higher grew the spruce, the fir, the giant hemlocks, and the air was fragrant with the spicy scent of the trees. Sometimes on far hillsides we could see bare slashes of red earth, where rocks and trees had gone down in slides after a storm.

I loved it all, and once when Trevor glanced at my face, he reached out to touch my hand. "It's good for us to do this. For this little while we needn't think of Belle Isle. There's only the present moment, Karen."

I smiled with a feeling of contentment that had little to do with reality, and Trevor began to whistle as the road curved back and forth in its winding climb. Words hummed through my mind—"On top of Old Smokey . . ."

"There isn't any one mountain called Old Smokey," he said, "but the song fits. So we'll take our mountain sentiments with us. I want you to remember."

I would remember.

The parking place for Clingman's Dome was nearly empty, for all its size. Later, when the trees put on their autumn colors, visitors would pour in, but now we had the place almost to ourselves. We left the car and stood where we could look out over range upon range of mountains folding in steeply upon one another, with the road to Cherokee threading between them. In the past, before the Scotch-Irish, the English and a few German and Huguenot settlers had come in the early 1800s, all this had been Cherokee land.

"Come," Trevor said. "Let's make the climb to the top. The road is steep, but there are benches along the way."

We used the benches once or twice on the way up because I was a city girl and more used to elevators than to mountain trails. The air was clear and thin in this high place and I found myself breathing more rapidly.

The "top" was like some huge modern sculpture set down in the midst of fir and spruce, the white column of the observation tower rising above a circular foot ramp that looped under and over itself until it reached the high point of the platform. I was puffing a bit by that time, but I climbed the ramp eagerly at Trevor's side.

We'd met only a few people coming down, smugly cheerful, since they were going the easy way, and the circular platform was empty when we reached it. We could stand alone at the rail and look out over the tallest treetops, well above any mists that drifted in the valleys, the mountains themselves reaching up into sunlight and bright sky—blue-green, gentle mountains, lacking the high ruggedness of the west. A light breeze stirred my hair and the sun warmed my upraised face.

"I'd like to bring you here at moonrise," Trevor said. "Though it's always different, whatever the hour."

His arm was around me and I was intensely aware of the moment. This was here and now. This was happening to *me*. Trevor was beside me, his arm around me as it would never be again. In only a little while this lovely, precious moment would be gone forever. Never had I wanted so desperately to make time stand still. All the worry and pain and threat out there in the valleys was nothing while we stood together in the clean, clear air of the heights. This was bliss, perfection, and I tried to hold it close to me with all my consciousness.

Trevor bent his head and kissed me. It was not a gentle, loving kiss, but hard and a little despairing. It took me by surprise and there was no time to return the pressure of his mouth. He took his arm from about me at once, and I saw his hands fasten tightly on the rail before him.

"I can't even tell you how I feel," he said. "I can't ask how you feel, because in the present there's no way out. Do you understand, Karen?"

"I love you," I said. "And I'm trying to understand."

"Chris needs me right now more than he may ever need me again. I can neither leave him in Lori's hands nor take him away from her."

"David has damaged everyone."

"Lori especially. David—" He broke off, since I knew David as well as he did.

The moment of "now" was already gone.

"We'd better go back," I said.

But when we had left the ramp and were walking down the steep trail that dropped between the firs, he paused and drew me more gently into his arms. There were no words, just closeness. Our longing went unspoken, but I knew how real it was. If I stayed . . . But Trevor would never be happy with his loyalties split and we would both be hurt.

There was one more thing I had to arrange. As we walked down the steep trail I told Trevor of my promise to go with Chris to Belle Isle tomorrow morning. His first reaction was to forbid the trip entirely, but I had to resist that.

"I must go," I insisted. "He mustn't be let down on this. There's something tormenting him that must come into the open. He won't tell you and he must tell someone. Since he's chosen me, I have to do as he asks. If you follow us, keeping out of sight, nothing can happen. Trevor, it must be done."

In the end he had to agree, and we made our plans.

At least I was not wholly unhappy as we drove back to the house. I had cared about Trevor for so long that to have something of that feeling returned healed me just a little. I knew the loneliness that lay ahead, but I could face that with more courage for having had this little time between us.

Let it go now. Let it fade and be forgotten.

That afternoon I packed my bags and stayed in my room. Already I was beginning to cut the strands that held me here. I didn't want to think about David's death or the fires. I didn't want to think about Chris's fears. Or about

Maggie and her possible tormenting. I wanted to wipe
from my mind the memory of eyes staring out at me from
smothering green leaves. When it came to Maggie's picture of the flaming rose, I decided that it was better to
leave it behind. I would ask Nona to dispose of it in some
way that wouldn't hurt Maggie's feelings. No need to let
her know that it was something I could never bear to have
in my apartment.

To some extent I was successful in cutting myself free.
It would have been better, I knew, if I could leave at once
and avoid the dinner tonight—no matter what Nona was
planning. I no longer wanted to pursue the road on which
I'd first set my feet. I knew now that freedom lay in another direction and I no longer owed David anything.
Whatever had happened was something he had brought
upon himself, and the truth might be so unsavory that
perhaps it was better not to know.

Only the trip I must make with Chris to the island the
following morning held me here. This was a promise I
couldn't escape. I vowed to myself that I would have it
over as soon as possible. There was nothing Chris could
show me that would make any real difference now.
Though perhaps it was something his father should know
about. All in due course. One step at a time, until I could
be aboard that plane, with Tennessee left behind me.

Through the glass doors of my room I watched sunlight vanish from the fishpond grotto outside and the shadows of the trees above grow long. Nona had set seven
o'clock for dinner tonight and I was glad when time
enough had passed and I could get ready. I put on a long
white silk dress, strewn with red poppies—to give me
courage—and clasped a little strand of pearls about my
throat. David had given them to me on our first anni-
versary—one more reminder. There would be reminders
everywhere for a long time—few of them pleasant. Even

those early years together had gone quickly awry. Strange that a strand of pearls was all that remained of whatever feeling we had once had for each other.

As I went upstairs Maggie came drifting through the front door with her tall husband beside her, and Giff just behind. Strange to think of Maggie gracefully drifting, but apparently there were occasions when she could pull herself together and present an illusion of elegance that was astonishing. She wore a sheath of black jersey, with a chiffon cape over it, edged in narrow bands of blue and green and red. The cape floated when she moved and she no longer seemed pudgy and ungraceful. Even her lipstick was unsmudged, and there was a penciled line of silver on her eyelids.

At the sight of my expression of surprise, she laughed. "Aren't I gorgeous? You didn't know I could turn myself out like this, did you? Nona said to dress up—so I did. We're supposed to counteract gloom." Yet her eyes moved quickly from meeting mine, and I knew her haunting was not yet over.

The men were dressed more casually, yet with a bit of plumage, Giff in a white turtleneck and well-cut navy blazer, Eric in a gray business suit, neat and conventional, with a striking red vest.

"We're sorry you're leaving, Karen," Eric said. "You've added something bright and young to our mountains."

Nona waited for us in the living room, ensconced on a sofa, her crutches beside her. The robe she had chosen for tonight was long and saffron-colored, with a wide boat neck, and she wore a dozen long strands of orange and brown beads that clattered when she moved. Lori and Trevor came in the from the deck as we entered, her arm linked confidently in his, and she was more beautiful than I'd ever seen her—in pale green, with a slender chain of golden links at her throat. Trevor looked distinguished in a white jacket, but there was no joy in him when his eyes met mine.

We were all there, obediently dressed up and festive, because Nona had so commanded. We were to forget mourning and all that was sad, and move on—that was what she intended. Yet I knew that not one of us would ever forget the sight of flames against a darkening sky.

Chris was not present. Lori said he had gone off to dinner at a friend's house, having announced that parties bored him. I could feel only relief. Tomorrow Chris and I would face whatever must be faced, but I didn't want to watch his torment tonight.

To this day I can't remember what we ate that night, though I'm sure Nona outdid herself, and even Lu-Ellen was sufficiently impressed by our handsome company so that she tried hard not to be too cheery and informal.

For a time, I suppose, the conversation was bright and on the light side, though like the food I remember none of it. All through the meal I waited for Nona to speak or act, but she said nothing startling until our fruit compote had been served, and she was pouring coffee from the silver pot. I know something was coming by the subtle change in her voice as she handed Eric his cup.

"You've never told me," she said, "how you came to be acquainted with Joe Bruen."

The silence around the table had a stunned quality. I looked quickly at Maggie and saw that her eyes were almost like the tortured eyes in her painting. Trevor was very still, waiting and alert, while Eric, undisturbed, poured cream in his coffee and sugared it generously. It was Giff who broke the silence.

"What do you mean, Nona? How could Dad know this Bruen fellow?"

"That's what I'm asking him. Don't you think you might tell us, Eric?"

He stirred his coffee attentively, but while his faintly sensual lips smiled, there was something watchful about his eyes. "There's no great secret about it. I'd have told you sooner, Nona, if you'd asked. There was a building Vinnie owned with a partner in Atlanta that burned down some years ago. With suspicion of arson. Suspicion, in fact, of a professional job that might have involved Vinnie's partner in that deal. A man who was losing money in other ventures. I went down to look into the matter and found that Bruen happened to be vacationing there at the time. He was great on fortuitous vacations. I knew about him, and the police picked him up for questioning. He was in the clear, however, and nothing was ever proved. But I talked with him a few times on that occasion."

"And then you met again in Gatlinburg," Nona said.

Maggie started to protest, but Giff put his hand on her arm. "Wait, Maggie. Let Dad tell us. This is all pretty interesting."

Once before I'd had the sense that Gifford Caton was not as fond of his father as a loving son might be. Now I heard veiled derision in his voice.

Eric nodded affectionately at Nona, ignoring his son. "My dear and respected friend—you continue to astonish me! But I'm afraid the meeting you and Maggie happened upon that day in Gatlinburg was completely accidental. I didn't know that Bruen was in town, and I doubt that he knew I lived here. Certainly I didn't feel good about discovering him in the vicinity after our fires, but I couldn't very well have him arrested because he was present. I did tell him that he'd be better off out of town if he wanted to stay clear of trouble. And I haven't seen him since."

"Because he went underground?" Giff said.

"We don't know that, do we?" Eric continued blandly. "Anyway, it was no secret that he was here. David was pretty sure that this man had a hand in the early fires, but

I believe he told Trevor he wasn't ready to act as yet. Isn't that right, Trevor?"

"What he told me," Trevor said, "was that he didn't care nearly as much about whoever was setting the fires as he did about who had hired him. He didn't mention Bruen by name at the time, but I think he expected him to lead to the real cause of the fires. And that's about where everything still stands. We're no nearer than before to finding out who is behind what has happened here."

"Perhaps we are," Nona said lightly. "Lori, what's the matter?"

For the first time since Nona had launched her rocket, I glanced at Lori and saw how white she looked.

Trevor saw it too. "You'd better tell us, Lori—whatever it is."

"I don't want to talk about it. It's just that all this is so—so horrible. It makes me feel ill. I can't bear it when everyone goes on like this. With David dead!" She flung a look of defiance around the table, and let it linger on me.

Eric sat next to his niece, and he put a hand on her arm. "We don't want to upset you, honey. I agree that we'd better talk about something else."

"I don't agree," Nona went on calmly. "You've been wandering around the island, Lori. What do you know that you haven't told us?"

She pulled her arm from Eric's touch. "I *can't* tell you —I can't! I don't know anything to tell. I've only gone down to the island to fix up Cecily's dressing room. So just leave me alone!" She jumped up and ran away from the table, and no one made any move to stop her or go after her.

Giff said, "I'll talk to her when she quiets down. I know what's the matter. She has a crazy idea that she's going to be next on Joe Bruen's list. She's always been scared of shadows. You know that, Trev. She trots along the edge of the cliff as though she had nine lives, and worries all the time about being pushed. Lori likes to flirt with danger, it's true—but that doesn't mean that she's very brave. Just hypnotized."

Perhaps her cousin understood her better than Trevor did, I thought—perhaps better than anyone else ever had. They'd grown up together and they knew each other like brother and sister.

"Why should she have this notion about Bruen?" Trevor asked. "Has she ever seen him?"

"She hasn't said so. But she believes what Chris says—that he's hiding on the island."

"Impossible!" Eric put in. "The police have searched the place thoroughly, and so have Trevor and I."

"I have too," Giff said. "But perhaps there's still something we're missing."

I thought uneasily of tomorrow morning and my promise to go with Chris to the island. To see something he had told no one else about. Once more I was thankful I'd told Trevor and that he would be following us all the way.

"Let's take our coffee out on the deck," Nona said. "If someone will carry mine for me—"

Eric hurried to help her, and as I picked up my own cup and walked outside with the others I thought how pleased with herself Nona looked. She had promised an explosion, and she must be more than gratified over the reaction she'd managed to evoke. Yet I wondered what had really come to light, and I wondered too why I should feel more sorry for Lori now than I'd felt before. If I hadn't known I would be rebuffed, I might have tried to find her, talk to her, but I knew that was best left in her cousin Giff's hands.

Dusk was moving into the valleys, though the high

mountains still stood with their backs in bright sunlight. The lake at Belle Isle still caught a tinting of blue from the sky, a shading of rose, but there were no fire colors.

All was quiet on the island. For a little while longer all was quiet.

Ten

It was time to leave for Belle Isle with Chris. No one was around when I went outside, but I found him waiting for me, ducked down in the front seat of my car. Trevor's car wasn't out on the apron, but I knew he wouldn't be far behind us.

"Let's go," Chris said the moment I got in, and as we turned out of the driveway he looked about anxiously. "I don't want anybody to know what we're doing," he added.

The sky was cloudy this morning, and the mountains smoky with mists. Only the pinkish-red sourwood trees wore color today. Sky and mountains were gray or misty white, and all the fading summer greens had turned drab. The air smelled like rain.

As I drove I was sharply aware of the boy sitting straight and tense on the seat beside me.

"Hadn't you better explain what it is you're going to show me?" I asked. "It might be better for me to be prepared, so I can understand."

He shook his fair head and stared straight ahead through the windshield. "I have to *show* you. Or else you won't believe me. Karen—" He turned his head to look at me. "Karen, you like my father a lot, don't you?"

"Of course," I said. "I've liked him for a long time."

"I know. That's why I can tell you about this—show you. Maybe you'll know what to do."

I reached out and touched his arm gently. "Whatever it is, Chris, we'll try to work it out together."

He seemed to relax just a little in the seat beside me. Now and then I glanced in the rearview mirror as a matter of course, but so far I'd caught no glimpse of Trevor's car. Which was just as well, since Chris too looked around through the rear window at times. It was just as well that his father was staying out of sight. He could catch up with us quickly enough when he wanted to, since he knew where we were going.

The guard at the entrance to Belle Isle knew me by now and waved us through. Everything was quiet and no workmen seemed to be around.

"Where is everybody?" I asked.

"Didn't you know?" Chris asked. "Dad has ordered things stopped since that last fire. I don't know if he'll try again, or if he'll just turn the whole project back to Uncle Eric."

"I'm sure he won't do that until his time is up," I said. But now I wondered whether Trevor's own courage had faltered at last, or if this was only a temporary pause while the police did their work.

"We can leave the car here," Chris said when we reached the causeway. "You don't care if we walk across, do you?"

I'd worn a raincoat against possible showers, so I didn't mind, and we followed the causeway over on foot—a narrow road with gray water on either side. Now it was Chris who went ahead. He ignored the uneven driveway to the house and chose the path that led in the direction of the theater.

"I just want to check something first," he said.

I still hadn't seen anything of Trevor and I hoped he would be able to track us. If we needed him there wouldn't be time to hunt for us on the island.

When we reached the area that was being taken over by kudzu, Chris paused for a moment. I had the feeling that something about the vines disturbed him, but he turned away and hurried on.

As we neared the place where carriages had once been drawn up for the theater entrance, Chris pointed. "There —there it is! I knew she'd come here."

Ahead of us, parked carelessly across the way, was Lori's red Ferrari.

"I saw her go out a while before we did. I thought she might be coming here. My mother comes here a lot, you know. And I'll bet I know what she's doing."

We walked around the car and over to the side entrance, where Trevor had brought me that day when I had first seen the theater. As we stepped through the door he touched my arm.

"Look!" he said softly.

She was there—his mother. Dreamily, Lori moved about the big stage that dwarfed her small figure in its green jumpsuit, her arms outstretched as though she followed the steps of some slow-motion dance.

"What's she doing?" I whispered.

"She likes to pretend that she's Cecily. Sometimes she lets me watch. Sometimes she brings a costume and puts it on in Cecily's dressing room. Then she does a show for me. She used to dance and sing a little, you know, and she's pretty good."

As I watched the woman on the stage, she began to sing, and I felt again a surge of alarm. There was something wrong about this. Something unnatural and weird about her dancing alone on the empty stage. She wore no costume today, but moved gracefully, freely in her jumpsuit. Her voice had no great carrying quality, but the acoustics of the theater brought it to us as we listened—a recent song about being left alone, about all lost loves.

At my side Chris nudged me gently. When I looked in the direction he indicated, I saw something that made my heart thud into my throat. Below us, but far to one side, a man slumped on a concrete step near the outer aisle. His gray-white curly hair grew long over the collar of his green plaid shirt, and he sat bent over, unmoving, his full attention upon the stage.

I took a step into the theater, meaning to call an impulsive warning to Lori, but Chris jerked me back with one strong young hand and almost pushed me out the door.

"Come away," he whispered, and grasped my hand. "Now's the time—while they're busy in there."

I looked frantically around, hoping to see Trevor, and managed to pull Chris to a stop. "Wait—we mustn't run away. Your mother may need us. She may not know that man's in there watching."

"She knows," Chris said. "She's come here to talk to him before. I don't know what about because I can't go close enough to listen and watch. But I think she *wants* him to burn Dad's houses."

A spatter of rain struck my face, and I still held back, not really believing or absorbing his words.

"Chris, Giff said your mother was afraid she might be the next one to be—harmed by Bruen. After all, he's already killed once."

Chris jerked away from me and walked purposefully ahead on the path. "You don't know if he's killed anybody," he told me over his shoulder. "You don't know anything. So maybe he hasn't. Anyway, I don't think he's going to hurt *her*. But he might try to hurt us if he knew we were watching. I stay a long way off, but now I have to show you something while we have the chance."

I was torn between uncertainty about Lori and the need to see whatever Chris wanted to show me. If only Trevor would come!

Chris paused on the path, waiting. "She knows, Karen. My mother knows everything, and she's all right."

This was too new and devastating an idea for me to accept at once, but I made my choice and followed Chris back toward the octagonal house. *Where was Trevor?* Had he been so clever about hiding himself that not even I, who expected him, had caught a single glimpse of him? More and more I was beginning to feel that he hadn't come. But what could have happened to stop him? I was beginning to feel that he really hadn't followed us after all. And if that was true, all I wanted was to get away from this frightening place as quickly as possible, and take Chris with me. If he was right and Lori was in no danger from someone she knew, we might only hurt her and ourselves if I tried to intrude.

Once more we came opposite the thriving expanse of kudzu and this time Chris stopped.

"We have to go in there, Karen."

My sense of alarm increased. "What do you mean—*in?* There's no way into those vines."

But Chris seemed to know a way. He plunged through a patch that grew ankle deep not far from the path and stopped before a large green mound. Then, tugging, he lifted the corner of a heavy blanket of kudzu. It came up with a whoosh and he disappeared under it. His voice came back to me, muffled by the monstrous green foliage that had swallowed him.

"Come under the leaves, Karen. Come in here. It's all right."

I took hold of the thick covering of vines with both hands and lifted. Dust stirred in the air, and the leaves were heavy and resistant in my grasp. Yet they lay like a loose covering, attached to nothing at this point—as though they had been pulled up often. Now I could drop to my knees and crawl beneath the green coverlet into a tunnel formed by small bushes that kept the vine off the ground. The smell of wild vegetation was pungent and stifling, and I had a horrid feeling that the vines might press down to smother me at any moment.

Ahead, Chris had risen and was standing upright. Beneath my hands I felt something like a doorsill, and when I crawled over it I found I was in the small, square room of a log cabin. Kudzu had hidden it completely from view, covering the roof, shrouding the two glass windows, turning interior darkness to an eerie green. I stood beside Chris and looked about fearfully.

"I used to play here when I was little," Chris said, his voice echoing in the cave of the cabin. "Nobody's used it for a long time, and when the kudzu came everybody forgot that the cabin was underneath. *Most* everybody forgot."

He crossed rotting boards to a table, where I saw that a candle had been stuck to a cracked saucer, with a box of matches beside it. The sound as Chris struck a match was loud in the smothering quiet, but the small flame lessened the gloom. I looked about, my sense of dread increasing, as though some disaster might occur at any moment—something awful that I would never be able to stop. And if it did, who would ever know that we were buried here under these monstrous vines?

The smell of rank vegetation pervaded the little cabin, combining with the musty smell of a long-closed room, and now a new, cloying scent of sandalwood that rose on the air—a nauseating scent I knew all too well by this time.

"It's one of Nona's candles?" I asked.

Chris nodded. "I brought some here a while ago. Someone else has been using them. And those matches are new. There's food too, all wrapped up in foil, and some cans and a few dishes in the cupboard over there. There's even a big jug of water."

I could see now that the cabin was crudely furnished with a cot and a single chair, beside the table and cupboard. Tumbled blankets were piled on the cot, and there was a soiled pillow. Now I knew why the police had found no one on the island. No one had remembered the derelict cabin that had long ago been swallowed by kudzu. Only a small boy who had played here knew, and perhaps his mother. Perhaps one other person, as well.

"Why haven't you told your father about this?" I asked.

"Because he already knows."

"What do you mean—he knows?"

Chris's voice was harsh beyond his years. "Just that he does. I don't want to talk about it."

"Does your mother know, Chris? About the cabin, I mean?"

He stared at me, his eyes wide and bright in the candlelight. "Maybe. Maybe not."

Wind rustled through vines overhead and old timbers creaked. I looked uneasily up at the hand-hewn beams. "I should think the weight of the vines would crush the whole roof in."

"They built these old cabins pretty strong. But you can see where the kudzu has broken through, over there in the corner."

I looked in the direction Chris pointed and saw that the green scourge had crept through, with tendrils like the antennae of some horrible insect reaching between the logs, prying them apart.

"Let's get out of here," I said, trying to keep panic from my voice. "That man may come back at any moment, Chris. We'd be trapped if he found us here."

"There's a back door out of that other room," Chris said. "We'll go in a minute. I didn't show you yet. I didn't show you what I want you to see."

As I watched in new dread, he dropped to one knee and placed the candle saucer on the floor. "Look, Karen. Look here!"

Reluctantly, I knelt beside him, but there seemed nothing noticeable about the dirty floor. Perhaps it was a little darker in this area. Perhaps those were stains against the wood.

"That's where the blood was, Karen. This is the place where he died."

"Who died?" My lips barely formed the words.

"It's where Uncle David died. Whoever killed him brought him here and hid him in this cabin. I found him when he was lying there with blood everywhere. From his head, I guess. I didn't want to look, but it was all over his suede jacket and on his Stetson hat."

Horror could be utterly weakening. My knees seemed to dissolve and I stumbled to the single chair and sat down.

"He was dead when I found him," Chris went on, his voice strangely unemotional—perhaps because he had lived so long with his terrible secret. "I felt his hand. It was ice cold and there wasn't any pulse. He was still wearing that ring my mother gave him. The one with the sapphire. I've never touched anything so—so cold before."

His words choked into silence and I closed my eyes

futilely against the images in my brain. David lying on this rotting floor where I now stood, bleeding to death while that dreadful green vine closed in overhead, crushing everything with its weight, obliterating life. Suddenly I understood why Maggie Caton had painted her terrible picture—with David's eyes looking out from those man-eating vines. Maggie *knew.* That was why she had painted the picture. Maggie too had *seen,* and had been terror-stricken ever since.

Now I could understand something else as well. I knew why an explosive had been used when David's body was hidden in the house that had been destroyed. A murder had been committed—a deliberate murder, and fire alone was no longer enough to conceal the fact. The plan had succeeded. It had been possible to identify David, but evidence of murder had been destroyed. Two people other than the murderer had known he was dead before he was put into that house. Two frightened people—a small boy and a neurotic, terrified woman.

Chris recovered his voice. "I was scared when I found him. I ran away and rode my bike way out into the park. I didn't go home until it was dark. I didn't know about the explosion and the fire until it was all over. Next day when they found what they thought was somebody killed in that house, I knew what had happened. Whoever did it carried Uncle David inside after it was dark and set the house to blow up and burn. Maybe so people would think it was an accident, and nobody would ever know that he'd been murdered here on the island."

"Oh, Chris! Why didn't you go to your father about this?"

He stared at me without speaking—and I knew why he hadn't.

"But it *wasn't* your father, Chris. You have to believe that. He could never do a thing like this."

"Maybe he could. He had an awful fight with Uncle David that morning. Because of my mother. And Dad was over here on the island. I saw him before—before I found what was here in the cabin. And I found that pencil too—in the ashes of the house. One that belonged to Dad."

"It doesn't matter," I said. "The pencil could have been dropped there anytime. None of it matters because he couldn't do a thing like this."

Chris's face seemed to crumple. He was no longer old beyond his years and holding back a terrible secret. He was a frightened small boy who needed to be comforted. I put my arms about him and he clung to me, letting go at last to weep stormy tears.

"We'll leave now," I told him gently. "We'll go home and find your father. The man who did this is over there in the theater right now. When we can we must tell your mother too what he has done. If she's trusting him for some reason, she has to know."

"What if she already knows?"

"That's not possible," I said, and hoped my words were true.

Over our heads the rain came with a sudden rattling sound upon leaves and ancient roof. Quickly it dripped through into the cabin from numerous cracks where the insidious vine had pried the shingles apart.

"We'll run for it," I said. "We mustn't stay here. It's not safe."

"Wait," Chris said. "Let me look first. I can hide quicker than you can. I know the places. We'd better not run into him on the way out."

At the thought of that possibility I was willing to wait a few minutes longer in the cabin. I stood in the doorway, with its opening framed in vines, and watched Chris crawl away out of sight. The leaves nearest the cabin quickly ceased to stir, and I waited, listening intently while minutes passed.

Chris should have come back almost at once—but he did not. Now I could hear only the rain beating upon vines and cabin. Then suddenly, from farther away than I expected, I heard Chris's voice, raised in a curious shout.

"Catch me if you can! Come on—chase me!"

I froze in new terror there in the doorway. The unsavory Bruen had indeed been coming this way, and Trevor's son was playing mother bird, trying to lure him away from the nest where I was hiding. I blessed him for warning me, but I was frightened for him as well as for myself. Yet if there was flight and pursuit, I couldn't hear it above the rain.

In any case, I must escape from the cabin while I had the chance. I dropped to my knees, but even as I started to crawl out beneath the vines the sound reached me of someone on the road close by, coming this way. Apparently Chris's challenge had not been accepted.

I rose quickly and went back to the cabin. Chris had said there was a back door, and I ran into the next room to find it. When I grasped the iron handle and worked the latch, the door pushed outward easily, and I looked into a pocket of space that had been cut through the vines beyond the rear of the cabin. Perhaps whoever had used this place for a hideout had also wanted another exit. I stepped quickly from the cabin and pushed the door softly shut after me. There was no sky to be seen overhead, since thick green vegetation crawled above me from cabin roof to nearby bushes, closing in thickly as I moved away from the cabin.

I could hear him inside now, and desperation seized me. No real passage seemed to have been cut into the vines back here, but I struggled with the resisting chains, fighting my way through tendrils that clung and around the shelter of a buried and dying bush. The blanket of vines fell behind me, shutting me in. But I couldn't stay here so close to the cabin. That rear door might open at any moment, and he would find me easily. Chris, at least, was safely away.

I found that it was better if I crawled, pushing my way into the thicket, lifting a blanket patch wherever it would lift, thrusting my way through and under until my hands were torn, my knees sore. It seemed that the vines were fighting me back and they were unbelievably heavy when I tried to lift them. At least I had escaped the cabin.

Rain began to fall more heavily, drowning out the rustling sounds of my passage, turning the leafy earth under my hands to slime. Not until my strength was gone did I pause, huddled and muddy, with rain dripping down the collar of my raincoat, my face wet where giant leaves had slapped across my cheeks, my hair wild from tugging tendrils. Surely by now I had tunneled far enough. The strength of panic was fading and my hands and arms had gone weak and useless. I must stay here until I dared to crawl out.

But when would I dare? How would I know when it was safe to come out of this trap of kudzu? What if that man stayed in the cabin all night?

These were panicky thoughts and I must not harbor them. There might be acres of vines, but they didn't cover the whole island. I had only to struggle in one direction and I would come out—somewhere. First I must rest. I was safe enough. Even if the man in the cabin opened that rear door he couldn't see me now, and he was unlikely to make the desperate struggle through the kudzu that I had just made. He knew Chris was about, but not me.

As I sat huddled on the ground, protected only a little

from rain by the leafy roof, I began to realize that not even I could tell from which direction I had come. The vines had closed in behind me securely, scarcely disturbed by my passing, their smothering presence pressing upon me from all sides—all looking alike. I might easily go straight back to the cabin. Or I might go in circles, fighting the enemy vines and never finding a way out. I remembered Trevor telling me that the highlanders called the rhododendron and laurel thickets "hells," because once you were lost in them there was no way out. Was that what I had come to now?

But this was nonsense, of course. Chris knew where I was, and Chris would never abandon me. Yet fear has little to do with reason and I knew an almost paralyzing terror. A terror as much of these wicked vines as of anything that lay outside them. Did I fancy that movement at my wrist? I looked down and saw that a tendril thick as a man's finger circled my hand. But I had done that—not the creeping vine. Yet if I stayed here long enough it would really happen.

What if Chris hadn't escaped after all? What if the man's return to the cabin only meant that he had the boy with him—silenced perhaps? Who would ever know I was here? All that overpowering greenness would envelop me, bury me here, where no one would ever know I had come.

I jerked my hand free of kudzu fingers. Stop it! I told myself. Stop it! Helpless I was not, and when the time came I would fight my way out. For this little while I would rest and think of other things.

At once I thought of those stains on the floor of the cabin, of David dying there, and of the man who had killed him and was running free. He had to be stopped, exposed. We could do that now, because I knew his hiding place. I would find Trevor as quickly as I could and I would tell him all that Chris had told me. Chris and Maggie might have kept silent for their own mistaken and emotional reasons. Chris protecting his father, Maggie protecting—Eric? But I would tell what I knew as quickly as it was possible, and the truth would come out.

As quickly as I could get away from here.

The rain seemed to be easing a little at the moment, but I was wet and cold, wrapped in my blanket of green shade. If the sun came out I would hardly know it was there. This part of the island had offered bushes and small trees aplenty for the vine to grow over, so that it didn't crawl along the ground, but heaved itself upward into those mounds that seemed to undulate like green waves when seen from afar. But this also meant that I must fight my way not only through the vines but through all the thick undergrowth it had clambered over and between as it smothered the landscape in its terrifying course.

There was a smell too—a dusty, choking odor of wet, green vegetation, pungent and horrid to breathe. It was a smell I would never forget.

Where was Chris? Why hadn't he come to find me?

Had my thought of his being captured been right? Surely no one would harm a child. But if Chris was kept from going home, the vines could close me in, cover me like a green shroud. I could die here and turn to bones— and it might be years before whatever was left of me was found in my green grave!

Again I fought my own fears. Chris might need help. It would be better to struggle back to the cabin, if I could find it. Then I could make sure that Chris had escaped. I could at least peer through a window, spy upon this man who was a murderer.

I struggled up from my place on the wet ground, unable to stand completely because of the weight of vines above me, but able once more to crawl. My earlier passage must surely be marked by bruised leaves, tendrils that had torn away from whatever they grasped. If I looked carefully enough I would surely find my own tracks. Once I located the cabin and made sure Chris wasn't there, I could find my way around it and back to the road.

Once more I gathered my strength to fight my living, grasping, enemy and chose a direction where the leaves seemed to have been slightly disturbed by my passing. Once more I crawled and fought and crawled again.

"Karen!" The sound was only a whisper but it reached me. I answered softly, "Chris?"

"I'm here, Karen—I'm coming. I'll get you out."

I had never heard a sound sweeter than the rustling of the vines as he tunneled his way to me, knowing a path of his own where the vegetation was weakest, perhaps from his own previous attacks. In moments he was beside me, kneeling to look into my face. I held my hands out to him, too choked to speak, and he saw how wet and muddy and torn they were. Quickly he snatched a handful of leaves and wiped my palms with their wetness.

"Your hands will be all right, Karen. They're only scratched." But he must have seen something in my face, in my eyes, for he put an arm gently about my shoulders. "He scared you, didn't he? But he's gone now. He never tried to catch me. He just went back for something in the cabin. I got a glimpse of him afterwards, running off toward the theater, carrying a box. So we're all right now. Let's go back to the cabin and get out that way."

There was kindness in his expression, tenderness and sympathy, and my tears spilled over. He put both arms about me as though he were the adult protector and I the child, and for a moment we held each other. I held his young body in arms that had never held a child so close and lovingly before. He let me cry and patted me kindly. Then he gave me a small, parental shake.

"We'd better go now, Karen."

He knew the way, somehow, through what to me was only a green labyrinth, and I was able to follow him back to the cabin with a minimum of effort. We slipped in through the back door, and went out the open front way. It took only minutes to return to the road, so I hadn't been all that far into the vines, after all.

When we stood up at last in the lessening shower I felt only a sense of enormous relief. That was all I could absorb at the moment. Relief and a deep and loving gratitude to Chris.

Together we ran through the clean light rain that washed away the mingling odors of vines and dust and sandalwood. All those odors of death.

"We'll go to Vinnie's house first," Chris decided. "Then you can dry off a bit and rest. You look real tuckered out. It will be all right. I don't think he comes there anymore. It's down this way."

The octagonal house loomed quickly ahead of us, tall and brown and shining-wet. Now that we were soaked, we might just as well have run across the causeway to my car, but for Chris I sensed that this was a postponement of something he dreaded. He knew now that he had to face his father, and gradually our reversed roles swung back to normal. Once more I was the adult, and he the troubled child. The ordeal of talking to his father thoroughly frightened him.

I could understand this. His own mistaken notion of the truth terrified him and somehow I must ease his concern. Perhaps a pause at the house would give me the opportunity to reassure and comfort him. Besides, I needed a rest. I needed to regain something of my own courage that I had lost back there among the vines.

When we reached the broken driveway I looked about again for Trevor's car, hoping against hope. But it was nowhere in sight. Something serious must have happened to keep him from the island, and I could only wish desperately that he would still come. What I knew must be shared quickly—while there was still time.

While there was still time? Why had those words run so invidiously through my mind?

We climbed the steps of the house to the shelter of the veranda just as thunder rolled down from the mountains and a flash of lightning turned the world pale green. The front door was locked, the lion's-head knocker snarling, but Chris said he knew a window where the lock never worked. We ran around to the rear and I helped him lift the sash. He climbed through first, pulling me after him, and we hurried through a big kitchen that I hadn't seen before. Chris led the way through to the central stairs and, as we started up, Commodore came out upon the landing above and stared down at us haughtily with his blue and yellow eyes. The pirate captain challenging boarders?

Chris ran up the stairs and around the cat, and I ran after him. "Giff has some towels in Cecily's room," he called back to me.

No one had repaired the damage I had done to the door of Cecily's sitting room, but I left it wide open as we went inside. Chris found towels in a cabinet and held one out to me, so that I could wipe my face and blot my wet hair. At least I had a raincoat, while Chris had only a jacket. As he toweled himself I could see that he appeared to have recovered a little. The sharing of so terrible a burden could not help but be a relief. Now I carried it with him.

When I was dry I went to look out the window, remembering how I had considered an escape that day when I had come here with Lori. I tugged the window up and leaned out to see that the rain was over.

"I think we can leave pretty soon," I said over my shoulder to Chris. "But first maybe we could talk a little more about your father."

He held up a hand in warning. "Listen!"

The sound of a car reached us through the open window. The driveway was on the other side of the house, but I knew Trevor must have come at last, and I rushed across the room to the door.

Chris, however, didn't expect him, as I did, and he blocked my way. "Wait, Karen! Don't go out there. We don't know who it is. Nobody drives a car that close to this house anymore. The road's too bad."

His fear reached me, and I remembered that there were others on the island. I waited in the doorway beside Chris while we both listened.

From the far side of the house came the sound of voices, followed by unidentifiable noises from the doorway below. Then a car door slammed and we heard the car moving slowly away over uneven ground. But why should there be voices—in the plural? And why was the driver leaving?

This time I pushed past Chris and walked softly toward the stairs. From the bare boards of the floor below came again the sounds I couldn't immediately identify. Someone was down there, brought here by the car, left here when it went away.

"It's okay," Chris said. "It's only Aunt Nona. Let's go downstairs and find her."

Eleven

Chris had identified the sound of Nona's crutches more quickly than I, but I still felt uncertain as I followed him downstairs. I had no idea why she had come, or even if it had been Trevor who had brought her.

"She's in the library," Chris whispered to me. "That's one of the rooms they've left almost the way it used to be. Except that the best books have all been taken somewhere else."

The door stood open and Nona was inside, propped on her crutches, idly studying a row of partly empty shelves. For once she wore slacks of brown corduroy with a zippered jacket, instead of her usual long gown.

As we came into the room she looked around. "So there you are! Trevor has gone hunting you in the theater."

Chris and I looked at each other.

"I'm sorry he got here late," Nona ran on. "It was my fault. When I found out he was coming over here, I asked him to bring me along. But he was in a terrible hurry and said he couldn't. I wasn't dressed and he didn't want to wait."

"Did you tell my father we were coming here, Karen?" Chris challenged.

"I had to, Chris. It might have been dangerous for us to come alone. He promised to stay back and not try to listen to anything you said. How did you get him to wait for you, Nona?"

"I invented," she told us, her eyes brightly green. "When he was about to leave, I hurried down the ramp in my wheelchair and said that Lori had just had a bad fall on the hillside below the house and needed help. I told him I'd seen her from the deck. So he ran down the hill— it's a long way around and a steep climb back—to have a look. That gave me time to change. He was pretty mad when he knew what I'd done, but I was already in his car by that time, and he couldn't very well turn me out. What's going on, Karen? What did you mean by 'dangerous'?"

There was no time for further explanations. Chris had apparently decided to forgive my betrayal for the moment, and he was looking at me, entreating.

"If Dad's gone to the theater—"

"We can see it from the tower," I said. "Let's go up there."

We left Nona gaping and tore up the flights of stairs to the top. The shower was over by the time we stepped out on the wet balcony, and wind was ripping away the clouds. We looked across the washed green world of the island toward the theater, but trees concealed both Trevor's car and Lori's, if they were there. Nothing moved, and that portion of the amphitheater we could see lay white and empty against the hillside.

"It's no use," I said. "We can't see anything."

Chris was quiet, studying the scene. Across the lake no houses were being worked on today, and there were none of the usual sounds. Nearby foliage dripped steadily, and wind rushed across the island, stirring the trees.

"Look!" he cried, pointing.

From somewhere near the theater, smoke plumed into the air, to be bent and carried away by the wind. Fire! A sick fear went through me, and even as I watched, the gray thickened and spread. Surely after the heavy rain there couldn't be a fire. But something was burning out there.

"Let's go!" Chris was already on the stairs and I knew there would be no stopping him.

As we rushed down, Nona hobbled into the hallway, and I called out to her. "There's a fire near the theater!"

Chris and I ran out the front door and I wished vainly that I'd left my car near the house. But it would take as long to cross the causeway to reach it as to follow the shortcut path to the theater on foot.

Chris was fleeter than I, but I kept up with him pretty well. As we tore past the mound of kudzu I gave it no more than a fearful glance. Where the path we followed ended near the side door to the theater, I saw the two cars —Lori's and Trevor's. Inside the theater there was no sign of fire, but only that rising plume of smoke beyond the stage area. Trevor stood near the stage, not looking at the sky, clearly unaware.

We cut along the tiers of steps, running.

"Dad, there's a fire!" Chris shouted. "It's out in back by the dressing rooms! Maybe Mom is there."

Trevor stared up at us for a startled instant. Then he climbed to the stage, ran across it and disappeared into the greenery beyond. Chris rushed ahead, and by the time I had taken the same route across the stage and come down to the space of ground before the dressing rooms, I could see the source of the fire.

It was burning inside Cecily's room. The door was closed, but glass had broken in the one window and flames were already licking upward, hissing and turning to smoke as they reached the wet wood outside. Trevor battered at the closed door—apparently jammed—and when it gave before his shoulder he disappeared inside. We could see flames back in the room and hear their crackle and roar, but they hadn't reached the door as yet. I was just in time to catch Chris by the arm so that he wouldn't follow his father.

Above the window flames licked the edge of the roof, drying wood that was only surface-wet, catching along the rim. Trevor stumbled into the open, carrying Lori in his arms. He bore her to a grassy space a little way off and laid her on the ground. Her green jumpsuit was burning and he tore off his jacket to smother the flames. Yet her face seemed unmarked, the eyes closed as if she were sleeping, and the fire hadn't touched her pale hair. Chris cried out and fell to his knees beside his father.

Lori opened her eyes and looked up at Trevor. At once there was terror. "The flame!" she gasped. "In the glass! I couldn't put it out!" She choked and coughed and Trevor held her.

From inside the dressing room came the sound of a splintering crash as Cecily's mirror shattered. I could catch again the sickening smell of sandalwood. Nona's candles once more. I had seen them there in the dressing room that time I had visited it.

For me sandalwood would always be the odor of death.

From far off we heard a siren. Someone in a hillside house must have seen the telltale rise of smoke from Belle Isle.

"The engine can't make it onto the island," Trevor said. "Not over these roads. But I've got my car here. We must get her to the county hospital over near Sevierville."

He picked Lori up and carried her toward the car, while Chris ran anxiously at his side. I followed, looking back only once to see that all of Cecily's dressing room was now ablaze. With old, dry wood beneath the wet surface there would soon be a coronet of fire around the entire half circle. At least the theater was safe, being built mostly of stone.

Trevor placed Lori gently on the back seat, and Chris knelt on the floor beside her to keep her steady. I rode in front and we drove back through the island, bumping along as fast as Trevor dared push the car.

We could hear Lori's ragged breathing in a choking effort to get air into her lungs, and when I looked over into the back seat I saw Chris holding her with both arms, his face white and strained. I longed to help him, but there was nothing I could do.

As we drove, I tried to tell Trevor what little I could about her being there—that Chris and I had seen Lori dancing on the stage, and that the man, Bruen, had been watching her from the side. Whether she knew he was there or not, I wasn't sure. The realization came to me only now that she hadn't seemed to be dancing *for* anyone. It had been as though she danced only for her own release and pleasure.

"Did you find out what Chris wanted to show you on the island?" Trevor asked softly, so the boy couldn't hear.

I couldn't possibly tell him all that now, urgent as it was. "Later," I said.

"I don't think she's badly burned," Trevor told me as we drove across the causeway. "But the room was thick with smoke and she was unconscious when I found her.

One of those sandalwood candles was burning and the smell of it was almost stronger than the fire. She may have started the blaze herself in that dry interior."

I had a horrible feeling that she hadn't. A lighted candle could be set with an accelerant around it, and by the time the candle burned down and started the fire, an arsonist could be far away. But a candle, depending on its length and thickness, could take hours to burn, and not that much time had passed. Something else must have helped to start this fire.

I wondered aloud to Trevor, and Lori heard me from the back seat and tried to speak, her voice hoarse and tortured. "A match. In a box. The candle too. I saw."

"Who put you in there?" Trevor asked again urgently. "Tell us who it was, Lori!"

But she broke into a fit of coughing, and Chris said brokenly, "She can't talk now."

When we were over the causeway Trevor stopped to let me pick up my own car.

"I'll follow you," I told him, and he drove on.

When I reached the side road that led away from Belle Isle, I saw the fire truck and the chief's car stopped on ahead, with Trevor halted beside them. He was explaining that the fire was on the island and the roads would never take the big truck. Several men got into the chief's car and they headed for the lake, while we went past the parked engine. Trevor drove at top speed now, and I followed, keeping close behind.

At the hospital Lori was rushed into emergency, and Trevor went at once to the phone to call the police. In the waiting room Chris and I sat helpless, able to do nothing but wait. Once or twice I tried to speak to him, but his face still had a white, empty look, and I doubted that he heard me. His state worried me. He had endured more in these last weeks than any ten-year-old should have to bear.

When Trevor returned, he seemed to look at me closely for the first time and he saw the mud stains and the stains of green on my coat, my scratched hands.

"What happened to you?" he asked.

"It doesn't matter," I told him, and right then it didn't. He had to be told, but not now, when Lori was fighting for her life. Suddenly I remembered Nona. "She's still in the house on the island," I reminded Trevor.

"I didn't want her along." He sounded grim. "It was because of one of her tall tales that I was delayed so long. Now she'll have to wait until someone can pick her up."

Nevertheless, the thought of Nona alone in the octagonal house worried me. Trevor didn't know everything that had happened on the island.

"I'll phone Giff at Eric's office," I offered. "Maybe he can pick her up. I don't think she should be left alone with whoever's roaming that island now."

"He'll be away and gone," Trevor said. "This time he won't dare to stay around, because Lori knows who he is. I've already told the police there was someone there."

"He can't hide in that cabin under the kudzu anymore," Chris put in.

"Cabin?" Trevor stared at his son.

In spite of Lori, a way had opened. This was our chance.

"Tell your father the whole thing, Chris," I said. "I'll go and phone."

A little color had returned to Chris's face, and I saw that he had rallied. He didn't falter as he faced his father.

When I found a telephone and dialed Eric's office, the switchboard answered, but neither Giff nor Eric had come in that morning. Nor did I get an answer when I called Maggie at home.

Back in the waiting room, I found Trevor with an arm about his son, and saw that Chris's cheeks were streaked with tears. For this reconciliation, at least, I could be glad. Chris would be free of torment about his father from now on.

An intern in a white coat came out to speak to Trevor. "You'd better come. She wants to talk, but she's very weak."

They let Chris and me accompany him. Lori reached out weakly and he took her hand, leaning to catch her words.

"Joe set the explosive." She spoke in a hoarse whisper, but her words were clear. "He hid in the cabin on the island. David knew. But Joe never meant to kill anyone in that house. He just—" Her voice faded into silence and she closed her eyes.

The nurse waved us all away. Just as we were leaving the room, Lori tried again to speak, faintly. "The flame—the flame in the glass—"

There was no more and we returned to the waiting room, frustrated and helpless.

"Why didn't she try to get out of the room when the fire started?" I asked Trevor. "Surely she could have escaped easily enough."

"The door was jammed." Trevor's tone was deadly. "Purposely, I think. She smashed the window glass but the smoke got to her before she could get out. I had to break through the door."

After that I sat in silent horror. We had only a little while longer to wait, however, before a doctor came to tell us that it was over. The smoke and gases had done their deadly poisoning and it had been impossible to save her.

"Take Chris home with you," Trevor told me numbly. "And pick Nona up on the way."

His son came with me in silence and there was no comfort I could offer him other than my hand on his arm now and then as I drove.

This time I went straight to the island house, regardless of the bad road, and we found Nona sitting on the veranda steps, with Commodore on her lap, the lion door knocker behind her staring arrogantly. Lori's words came back to me—that the lion always reminded her of Vinnie Fromberg.

Nona's temper had reached the boiling point. "What's happened?" she called the moment we stopped. "I've heard the cars and the fire engine across the lake. You said there was a fire, and I could smell the smoke. But nobody came here and I've been trapped. Did you forget me? What burned—tell me!"

The acrid smell was on the wind, but everything seemed quiet now, with no smoke rising above the trees. Perhaps wet wood hadn't burned for long after all.

Chris spoke first. "My mother is dead."

Nona pushed the cat aside and took him into her arms. She sat on the steps and held him, while I leaned against the rail and Commodore stared at us with his strange eyes, looking wise and superior, as though he could answer all our questions if he chose.

While Nona held Chris, comforting him, I told her everything I knew—even to the part about the cabin hidden under the vines, and Chris's finding of David's body.

She rocked the boy in her arms as though he'd been the baby she remembered, and he clung to her as I'd never seen him cling to Lori. I envied her a little sadly.

After a time she released him and reached for her crutches. "We'd better go home now. We'll need to be there when Trevor comes."

Thus appealed to, Chris helped her to stand, then assisted her down the steps and into the front seat of my car. I sat beside her to drive, with Chris between us.

We had little to say on the way up the mountain. When we arrived, the house seemed strangely empty of Lori's presence, and I found it hard to believe that she wouldn't walk in at any moment, bright and provocative, her moods never to be counted on ahead of time. That she should be gone so suddenly and so terribly—once more through the horror of fire—was impossible to accept.

Lu-Ellen had to be told the worst of what had happened, and Nona managed this crisply, with the fewest possible words, and she dealt with Lu-Ellen's tears gently. We all waited for Trevor's return.

During the next few days Nona was busier than ever, taking as much as possible off Trevor's hands. The brief closeness between father and son had somehow lessened and each had retreated into his own defensive silence.

I grieved for both of them, but I suspected that Chris had never told his father about the suspicion that tormented him, and I had a feeling that it had not died out entirely. If they could have continued to talk openly it might have helped.

In his loneliness and desperation, Chris began to follow me about, and I accepted his company gratefully. He couldn't understand, of course, but he was giving me more than I had ever known in a life that had been empty of children. We had shared experiences that drew us comfortingly together, and perhaps I was the only one just then who could offer him activity, a certain quiet assurance and a loving, undemonstrative presence. It was an assurance that concealed my own inner torment. Chris was interested in my camera and in picture-taking, and a tenuous new relationship began to evolve between us though we said nothing of those terrible moments we had shared on the island.

Inevitably we began to accept, to accustom ourselves, as one does after loss. I hadn't liked Lori, but I'd never wished her ill, and there were still stabs of horror that met us on every hand in the reminder that she was gone—so dreadfully.

There could be no immediate flying home to New York, even if I'd been able to. Nona asked me to stay on for a little while, even before the police mentioned that I would be needed for a few days for further questioning.

"Chris seems to have accepted you," Nona said. "And you're more mobile than I am. So be with him when you can. We must get him back to school soon. Trevor can't manage everything. Too much has happened." She broke off, moving her hands in a gesture more helpless than she usually displayed, and I understood her deep concern for Trevor and Chris. A concern I shared, aching helplessly with love for both of them.

Trevor was, I suspected, blaming himself for Lori's death, wondering what he could have done differently that might have prevented it. Once or twice I tried to talk with him, to at least offer a listening presence, but he couldn't let go of his demons and in his own way he was as tormented as his son.

The police decided this time that no crime had been committed. Lori, as we knew, had been fixing up Cecily's dressing room to amuse herself. He had tacked a large piece of plasterboard to one wall and had been fastening various pictures to it. Chris had seen this, and could describe it in detail. The photos were old ones that Lori had collected over the years. Family pictures, with several of Vinnie, and one or two of Cecily that she had found in old albums. To accomplish the mounting she had apparently brought down a quart container of liquid glue from Trevor's office. True, that was a much larger quantity than she needed, but such glue was commonly used by architects and was plentiful in Trevor's supplies. It was extremely flammable stuff. With the glue in use, Lori must have lighted one of those incense candles that Nona enjoyed, and obviously the whole place had gone up in a blaze. Foolish and needless and tragic—but not criminal. An accident. So the police seemed to think. And at first I was baffled, disturbed by their lack of suspicion, not realizing how little they had been told.

There were a number of questions they seemed content to leave hanging, and no one pushed hard enough for answers that were not easily forthcoming. Who was the man Chris and I had seen in the theater with Lori? The police were interested enough in his identity, but since he was no more to be found now than in the past, nothing could be done about him. The men from the sheriff's office were local, and they could hardly be blamed for making their own judgment of Lori, though they offered no expression of this to Trevor. It was evident behind their questions, but they didn't probe too deeply, knowing Trevor's temper.

His insistence that the door to the dressing room had been somehow jammed, which would have prevented Lori's escape, was discounted. Old wood often swelled, and Lori could easily have jammed it herself. If some small wedge had been forced into it from outside, Trevor had been in too desperate a hurry to get into the room to have been aware of that. So he could offer no proof. The single small, high window in the room had offered no easy way to escape in her weakened state.

The police knew by now about the cabin under the kudzu, and that someone had been hiding there. But neither Chris nor Trevor had mentioned the finding of David's body, and when I asked why this hadn't been told to the police, Trevor turned distant and told me it was better not to mention it. Not now. In deference to his wishes, we said nothing. What he was thinking, what he might be planning, I didn't know, and his silence frightened me.

There was also the curious matter of the container that had held the liquid glue—easily identified as coming from Trevor's office. It had been found empty, not in the dressing room where the glue had ignited, but a little way off in the woods. The explanation that was finally agreed upon was that Lori must have brought down only a small quantity in the can, and then discarded it, empty, perhaps using it from some smaller, more convenient container. When Chris said he thought that the can had been full, the comment was disregarded. There was no immediate dealing with all these small, puzzling matters.

In the end it was decided that this fire was not like the others, in that no connection with arson had been found.

"They don't want to believe it was murder!" Nona said indignantly to Trevor.

"Do *you?*" he challenged, and she turned silent.

But I think we all believed in what was left unspoken and kept our feelings to ourselves. I could only hope that Trevor had his own plans, and, as he pointed out, the investigation wasn't over by any means.

Twelve

The week that followed Lori's death was painful for all of us. The funeral was far more impressive than David's had been, since Lori's family wanted it that way, and it was well attended.

There was, however, one encounter for me during the week that remained clear in my mind for a long time afterward.

I had been wondering how to catch Maggie alone and ask her the questions that were troubling me. Then two days after the funeral she played into my hands. One morning early she turned up at the house with a picnic hamper on her arm, looking as disheveled as usual, her shirt half in, half out of patched jeans, and her pepper-and-salt red hair caught hastily back with a frayed green ribbon. Her gray eyes still looked haunted, but her manner was determinedly cheerful.

"I've packed a lunch," she announced, "and you and Chris are coming with me. I can't sit around the house a minute longer wondering if I am going to be next. And I'm sure you and Chris can use a change. If you've got any extra fruit around, you can dump it in my basket."

When I stared at her in surprise, she grimaced. "Oh, I know what happened to Lori was an accident. They say. But after a while one gets superstitious."

I invited her in, wondering if that was all it was—mere superstition. I had little heart for what she proposed, but I'd wanted an opportunity to talk with her, so I thanked her and went to find Chris. He was always nervously ready for action these days, and willing enough to come. Inaction gave us all too much time to think and grieve. We picked up our cameras and some fruit, and went outside to my car, since Maggie's was in for a tune-up.

After recent rain, this was another beautiful morning, and mists were wreathing the mountains and the little "coves." The latter was the term that always sounded odd to me (born near the sea) for small enclosed pockets of land. Maggie gave directions as I drove, and we turned off the highway into the park. The side road followed a rushing stream, and Chris stirred between us, approving our destination.

"You haven't been here, have you, Karen?" he asked. "It's real pretty and quiet, and there won't be many visitors now."

There were none. Trees arched greenly overhead, hiding the mountains from view as we entered the woods. Only here and there could be seen a hint of coming autumn, with a few maples beginning to turn, and always the pinky-red surprise of the sourwood trees showing. It would be a beautiful autumn. An autumn that neither David nor Lori would ever see.

As the woods thickened and the narrow road ran closer to the stream, a bridge came into view ahead.

"We might as well stop here," Maggie said. "A little way back there are picnic tables when we want them."

The moment I stopped the car, Chris was out and off on his own explorations, his camera ready around his neck. I left mine in the car and walked beside Maggie toward the bridge. Picture-taking had no interest for me at the moment.

"This is one of my favorite spots," Maggie said. "We used to be able to drive over the bridge and up the mountain a little way, but they don't allow vehicles across anymore."

I saw the sign forbidding passage and went with her on foot to midway across the rustic bridge. The water fascinated me in its rush and tumble, and I leaned on the rail, watching the furious stream below me plunging along, varicolored on its downward course. In the shallows where trees overhung the banks, the water shone like green glass, only to turn frothy-white farther on in rapids that tumbled over the rocks. In sheltered pools it swirled like watered silk, turning golden when the sun broke through overhanging branches, spilling like black ink where the shadows grew deep. Always in movement, while all along its course huge tumbled boulders stood up wet and shiny-gray above the heedless path of the stream. Almost like a pattern of our lives, I thought, with rocky obstacles tossed in our paths and the promise of calm only an illusion.

Beside me, Maggie had closed her eyes and raised her face to the sun, breathing deeply as she let tension flow out of her body. I was sorry to spoil her hard-won peace, but I had to begin. Because of Lori, because of David,

I had to begin, but most of all because of the living who were still threatened and unsafe.

"Chris showed me the cabin under the kudzu, Maggie. How did you know it was there?"

Her eyes flew open and she looked at me, startled. "What are you talking about?"

"I *know*," I said. "I know why you painted a man being swallowed by those vines."

She moved away from me at the rail. "I don't know what you mean. Would you like to walk a little way up the mountain, Karen?"

"I'm fine here. You may as well tell me. Chris showed me the cabin. He told me he found David's body there, where he was killed—or where he was brought to die. He's told me everything. Did he tell you, too, or did you see it for yourself?"

"Oh, God," Maggie whispered. "I knew it would come out sometime. I've been terrified thinking about it. That's why I painted that picture—to try to get it out of my mind. But the painting is as bad as the reality, and now I'm doubly haunted."

"That's why you said the eyes of the man in the picture were David's, didn't you? Because you saw his body there too?"

She nodded mutely, her hands clenched on the railing before her.

"There's a big rock over there in the woods," I said. "Let's go and sit in the shade. Then you can tell me."

Telling me was the last thing she wanted to do, but she knew by now that I would never let her off. "All right," she agreed, and followed me to the big stone. I took off my jacket and spread it out to sit on, but Maggie didn't seem to notice the hard surface. She perched beside me, her hands clasped about her knees.

"I don't know where to start," she said, postponing.

"Then start at the beginning." My words sounded harsh and abrupt in my own ears, but there was no way to soften what had to be said. "How did you know about the cabin? How did you happen to go into it at that particular time?"

She thought about that for a few moments with every evidence of distress, as though I had startled her—or frightened her?—so badly that she couldn't collect her wits. When she finally started to speak, her voice was without expression, as though she held back feelings she dared not release. Once more I recognized strong mettle in Maggie Caton.

"I'd been curious for months about what was going on at Belle Isle," she began. "I knew Giff was following events there, under Eric's orders, since the family owns the island, so I decided to have a look for myself. I really wasn't scared then. Kudzu has always fascinated me and I thought I'd go over there to make sketches, do a little painting of that big patch of it on the island. So that's what I was doing that day. I wasn't planning a particular painting at that point. I was just making color sketches and getting down the shape of the leaves, the veining and all that. Or at least that's what I told myself. But all the while I think I was waiting for something to happen. Waiting for someone to pop out of the shrubbery and surprise me."

"Weren't you at all afraid to be over there alone?"

A jay mocked us from a branch overhead and Maggie looked up. "I was afraid *not* to be there. I wanted to *know* —and no one was going to tell me. I'd realized that. So I painted, and while my brush was working I remembered that Chris had told me once that there used to be an old cabin on the island, and that the kudzu had buried it completely. I began to wonder if it was hidden under the mound I was painting, and after a while I began to investigate."

The jays taunted her again, and she said, "Oh, hush up." And suddenly hid her face against her drawn-up knees.

"Go on," I said. "You have to tell me." I couldn't let her off now.

A little of her control had cracked as she continued and I heard the edge of fright in her voice. "It wasn't hard to get under the vines. Somebody had been there before me—Chris, I supposed—and they came up easily. So I crawled beneath them and found the cabin. At first I felt like a kid who'd just discovered a secret cave. It was dark inside and I couldn't make anything out until my eyes got used to the dimness. I knew someone had been there though because the smells weren't just those of heavy vegetation and old, damp cabin." She paused and raised her head, breathing deeply again of pine-scented air, as though to free herself of remembered odors.

"Sandalwood?" I asked softly.

"Yes. Mostly that. And another, awful smell. I knew what it was when I saw him—the smell of blood and death. He was lying on the floor, half under a table, and there were ants crawling around that ring Lori gave him. David was a big man—it must have taken a terrible blow to wound him like that. I got out of there as fast as I could and ran back to where I'd left my car near the causeway."

I had begun to feel almost as sick as Maggie looked and I had to hold on to my own emotions.

"But you didn't tell anyone?"

She looked at me with terror glazing her eyes. "No! I didn't dare to until I'd thought about it for a while. I—I had to figure something out."

"Who had killed David, you mean?"

She didn't answer me directly. "Later on there didn't seem to be any reason to tell what I'd seen—because when the house exploded that seemed to account for his death. So what was the use?"

"The use is the exposure of murder. What happened to the house was arson, but by itself it wasn't necessarily murder. David's being there could have been unintentional. But his being dead with his body hidden in that cabin under the kudzu—that was murder, and the explosion was intended to hide it. Just as Lori's death was murder too. So why didn't you tell?"

She ran both hands through her tangled mass of hair, turning her head from side to side. When she spoke it was with a visible effort.

"I didn't tell for the same reason you haven't told. And Chris hasn't told."

"But I have told," I said. "I've told Trevor and Nona, and now you."

"But no one has told the police—isn't that right?"

"Yes," I admitted reluctantly. "And I don't know why." Or was it that I didn't want to know why. "I suppose we all think we're protecting someone. Or at least Chris thinks he's protecting his father. And that's foolish, of course."

"But *you* haven't said anything to the police?"

"For Chris's sake. Not because I think Trevor had anything to do with it. What Trevor's purpose is in holding back, I don't know, but I think he could be on the trail of something. Someone. This Bruen, who keeps popping up and disappearing, and who is an expert at starting fires."

Maggie jumped to her feet as though she couldn't sit still a moment longer. "Yes—of course that's it. We don't really need to worry, do we?"

"Anyway, not about Trevor," I said.

"Naturally not about Trevor! Come on, Karen. Let's find Chris and take some pictures before we eat lunch."

Her change of mood was a screen, and I didn't think she had stopped worrying. Her concern, I knew, wasn't for Trevor.

After that we joined Chris determinedly in whatever he wanted to do. We took pictures and hiked through the woods, returning hungry to eat Maggie's sumptuous lunch. In a sense this was a respite for the three of us—if it's ever possible to take a respite from evil. I'd begun to feel that I could almost sense it in the air around me from day to day, yet without knowing from what direction the sensation emanated. It certainly couldn't be photographed —not yet.

During the next few days there was a lull that could only seem ominous to me. Too much that was figuratively explosive lay beneath the surface. The police withdrew again and I could go home if I wished. Nona said, "Don't go. Stay. You'll never forgive yourself if you run away now. Chris needs you. Trevor needs you."

Much as I wanted to, I couldn't agree. Trevor didn't need anyone. He moved in his own world of inner torment —where no one could reach him. I made no real attempt to do so until one afternoon when I saw him go off alone on the woods path that led away from the house. This time I dared to follow. There was so much soreness, so much that was hurtful now, yet we both needed to touch someone else—if only in sympathy.

When he heard me coming he stopped and waited for me, and we walked together in silence for a little while. Not a companionable silence, I thought sorrowfully, for he had gone far away from me since Lori's death, and I hardly knew him anymore. We passed the driveway to the Caton house, and he didn't look up toward the overhang of the wide deck. I did, but saw no one there, though there were cars parked in the carport.

We went on together along the rim of the mountain, where it steepened into a rocky cliff that went straight down below us. There was a fallen tree near the edge and Trevor motioned me toward it. Now, for the first time in many days, we began to talk.

"What are you going to do when you go back to New York, Karen?" he asked.

I hadn't thought about that. I hadn't wanted to think. It had taken little persuasion on Nona's part to get me to stay where I wanted to be, but now Trevor's words brought me face to face with reality. All that frightened longing inside me that urged me to stay as close to Trevor as I could was sheer foolishness. To wait, to merely breathe and exist—until someday he would turn his head and notice me—was humiliating and useless. But now that he had done just that—it was with an impersonal question about what I meant to do back in New York.

"I don't know if I even have a job anymore," I said.

"Then you'll find another one. You're good. Someone will want you. But that's for earning a living. Can you move ahead on plans to do something more with your talent? As a free lance, I mean? Photographing people the way you spoke of when you first came here?"

"Houses are safer," I said, and wondered if they were. Not burned-out houses.

He smiled at me and his look was kind. "You're still afraid of being yourself, of tackling living subjects, aren't you, Karen?"

Ever since I had come to Tennessee I had been furiously involved with life—and death. Peace and safety were all I wanted now. Or were they? If that was true, why did I stay on? Why didn't I go home where there was nothing to involve me in turmoil of any kind—except my memories?

When I didn't answer, he asked me another question. "Don't you miss working, Karen? I do. I get restless when I'm not at my drawing board, or conferring on the building of—something. Yet I haven't been able to do anything for weeks."

"I don't know whether work matters all that much to me anymore," I said.

"Maybe not to me either right now," he agreed. "Other things have become more important. Nevertheless, not working disturbs me, both physically and mentally."

I could understand that in his case. But all that seemed to matter to me now was the intense moment in which I was living. This was what I had felt before. It was the *now* that mattered most—while I sat beside Trevor on a fallen log, with all that magnificent view spread out before us. With my love nearby. How could anyone be more foolish than I? Once, while Lori was still alive there had been a moment of closeness between Trevor and me. As though for a little while he had really seen me, perhaps even needed me momentarily. But now she was gone as David was—and I had a feeling that I had lost Trevor completely, even that in some strange way he was a little afraid of me.

"You have to stop blaming yourself," I said.

He turned his head sharply to look at me. "What else can I do? I wasn't able to help her, to stop what was happening, and two lives have been lost. Not by accident, either."

"I don't think they were accidents," I said. "But you weren't to blame."

"Of course I was to blame. I should never have given Lori her head. I should have stopped her in the course she was taking and stopped David."

"How could you? You couldn't lock her up, and no one could control David."

"I knew my brother. I knew everything he was and I knew he hated me. So I should have realized how susceptible Lori would be in his hands."

His words were spoken almost matter-of-factly—as though he judged himself objectively, condemning his own actions. This was no surface self-pity. It went far deeper and it was something I didn't altogether understand.

"It's Chris who matters most now," I said. "You've been busy with the police and with all that had to be done. Now perhaps you can make time for what's troubling him."

"I've tried. I can't seem to break through whatever it is he holds against me. Blame for everything that's happened, I suppose. And how do I explain any of it away?"

I drew a deep breath, bolstering my own courage, trying to state bluntly what couldn't be glossed over. "Chris thinks you went off in a rage after your quarrel with David and followed him to the island. He thinks you killed him and dragged his body into that cabin under the kudzu. He thinks you set the house to explode and burn and put his body into it so that what you'd done would be concealed."

Trevor sat staring at me in shock.

"Don't look like that!" I cried. "No one else thinks it's true. I've tried to talk to Chris, but you're the only one who can convince him. So you've got to start working at it. He listens to me a little and I'll help in any way I can. But you must convince him."

"I didn't know. I never dreamed—" He spoke softly, helplessly. "Why Chris would believe anything like that—"

While my courage still held, I had to ask a question. "Trevor, why haven't you told the police about Chris finding David's body?"

I could feel him moving away from me. Everything in

him was shrinking from me, as though I had suggested something appalling.

"It's not over," he said at last, and ended matters abruptly by standing up. "I'll see if I can talk to Chris now. Thank you for telling me, Karen."

He was being almost coldly polite and his eyes didn't meet mine. Without another word he turned away from me, obviously not wanting to stay longer in my company. I sat on where I was, staring out at mountains where a sunset sky was beginning to fade—though I had hardly noticed. I felt limp and hopeless—and sore as well, as though I had been physically beaten. Trevor was gone from me more completely than ever before. He had looked at me with seeming distaste, repudiating the very small friendship I had been able to offer him. And I didn't understand. I didn't understand at all. Had he changed so much from the young man I had known? Changed even from the older, unhappy man I had found when I came to this place? What I had seen in his face just now was something that truly frightened me.

As though the words I had spoken so bluntly in order to make him understand what Chris was thinking might have carried something of the truth in them. And that consequently he was afraid of me.

But this was a thought I couldn't harbor. It was false and I knew it.

Gradually I came back to my surroundings, aware of them as I hadn't been for some time. Aware of something changed—of something new that had been introduced. The sensation of someone watching me made me turn—to find Giff Caton standing a little way off at the edge of the woods.

He gave me his quick, always ready smile. "I didn't mean to startle you. Do you mind if I join you?"

He waited for no invitation, easing his tall person down

on the log beside me. There he sat quietly, admiring the splendor in the sky. I didn't trust him, yet he was the one person who might have been in his cousin Lori's confidence.

"How long were you standing there?" I asked.

"Listening, you mean? Long enough. I heard what you told Trevor about Chris. Poor kid. He's devoted to his father, and this makes everything a lot rougher—more than he can handle. Maggie thinks it's a good thing you've been spending time with him lately."

"I suppose Maggie has talked about everything by now?"

"Indeed she has. She's been spilling the beans in quart measures all over the place. Eric has a hard time shutting her up."

"Then why haven't you—one of you, at least—told the police about David's body being found on the island?"

His smile had a slight edge to it and he cocked one blond eyebrow mockingly. "For a very bright girl, you ought to be able to figure that out. It's the same reason that's keeping Trevor silent. Though I must say I think he has more cause to worry than the rest of us."

"I don't know what you're talking about."

"Of course you do. Trevor is the wronged husband and the two who wronged him are dead. We can still take this sort of thing a bit hard in the South. Unfaithful wives, I mean. But as long as David's death seems to have occurred under circumstances Trevor had nothing to do with, they won't be picking him up. The minute Chris talks, however, what the boy fears will come through. The police are already puzzling over that door that Trevor claims was jammed. But since everything was burned there's no way of checking."

Giff's expression had sobered, but only for a moment

or two. Then he went on in the light, careless tone he so often adopted.

"Once the police know about David's murder, they'll begin to add things up pretty fast, and Trevor may not stay out of jail for long. Of course we're not going to talk to them ourselves and get him into that sort of spot. We stick by our kin, you know. Even kin by marriage."

His words left me shaken. How basically callous he was, I thought. That two people had died—one of them a cousin with whom he'd grown up and always been close —seemed to have made so little emotional impact that he could talk about these matters as though he were an outsider. Or was that perhaps what Giff Caton really was—an emotional outsider? An observer who never permitted himself to become seriously involved?

"You're not much of a participant, are you?" I said.

He blinked involuntarily, as though I had touched a nerve, and then his easy smile was back in place. "You're probably right. Most of the time I find it more amusing to stand on the sidelines."

"Amusing? At a time like this?"

"Sorry—wrong word," he said, and at least had the grace to look uncomfortable.

I returned to what he had been saying about suspicion against Trevor. "Besides, I'm sure you don't want anyone asking Eric all the same questions they might ask Trevor. You'd like to avoid that, wouldn't you?"

"Oh, I don't know." He was almost jaunty now. "It could be that my father has a few things to explain himself, so of course he and Maggie will keep still. But I hardly think he'd go so far as to harm Lori—now would he?"

"Not unless she became a serious threat to him," I said.

Giff laughed as though my words were funny. He rose

from the log, pulling me to my feet, and for the first time I sensed in him a barely suppressed excitement—the sort of excitement I remembered seeing at times in Lori.

"Enough of all this gloom! You need a change, Karen, and so do I. Let's go into town for dinner. I'll take you back to the house so you can change and let Nona know you'll be out. Then I'll pick you up in half an hour and we'll go to the hotel old Vinnie built on the edge of town. You haven't been to the Greencastle, have you?"

His behavior astonished me. "I really don't want—" I began, but he put one long finger against my lips.

"Hush now. No arguments. Doc Gifford has prescribed and you're coming with me. I promise you'll enjoy every minute. I can be better company than you might expect. Besides, I might have a surprise or two along the way. Maybe I'm more of a participant than you think."

He seemed to be promising me something. I had never seen his eyes so bright, never before sensed this electric charge flowing through him, moving him to some purpose I couldn't guess. It was disturbing to see something so unfamiliar surface in him, and I found it puzzling that the current should be directed toward me.

"Why?" I asked him bluntly. "Why do you want to take me out to dinner at a time like this?"

For an instant the bright look turned to annoyance. "How direct you can be, Karen. Do you really need to ask that? Just look in your mirror sometime, honey. If you hadn't been so single-minded about Trevor, you might have noticed me watching you. I know a lot about you, Karen Hallam—more than you might think."

"Stop it!" I told him. "Don't play games. I can't believe you're as callous as you seem."

His look lost none of its brightness, but he was suddenly in earnest. "Will you have dinner with me, Karen? It would please me very much. And I want to show you something of importance. Something you may find interesting. Something you ought to know."

I hesitated for a moment longer, his very earnestness persuading me. Whatever it was that Giff Caton was up to—and I didn't think it was the pleasure of spending an evening with me—I needed to discover what it was.

"All right," I said. "I don't feel very lively or gay, but I'll go along with the game for now, whatever it is. You needn't walk me back to the house. I'll hurry and be ready in half an hour."

For an instant triumph shone in his eyes and I winced, remembering Lori.

"Wear that watermelon pink you had on a few days ago," he said, and waved me on my path. "Run along now."

I didn't run as I followed the way back to Trevor's. I could look forward to an evening with Giff with nothing more than uneasy curiosity.

Nona, when I reached her, was not pleased with my plans. "Watch yourself with that one," she warned. "Lori and he were a pair made for trouble ever since they were young. Lori used to take the lead, but in that lazy way of his, Giff was often the one who thought up their pranks."

I patted her shoulder. "This isn't the start of a love affair," I said and hurried off to my room. The watermelon pink hung in my closet, pretty and frivolous. It didn't suit my mood. I wore the black silk suit I'd brought for David's funeral, brightening it with gold earrings and a yellow chrysanthemum from the garden pinned on my shoulder. When I went upstairs Giff was waiting for me and he raised an eyebrow at the way I'd dressed, but made no comment.

From the first he bent himself to being attentively good company, yet he couldn't hide the inner current that I had sensed earlier, and my uneasiness increased.

The Hotel Greencastle had been Vinnie Fromberg's last fling, built some ten years before, when he was in his late eighties. I had noticed its conspicuous place on a hill outside of town the few times I had been in Gatlinburg, but now Giff gave me something of its story.

"What Vinnie wanted was a local office for himself. Nothing he had used really suited him, so he built a hotel around the office he wanted. The town had a fit when he put that thing up there against the mountains, but he only laughed at those who objected. He painted it green, built on a couple of turrets and gave it its name. The whole tenth floor belongs to Fromberg Enterprises, and he had his own apartment adjoining his office. Of course at the very end, when he finally gave up, they took him back to the house on the island to die. That's where his heart always stayed, anyway."

"I'm sure this hotel isn't one of Trevor's creations?"

"Good lord no! Trevor would never go in for the splashy and spectacular. But it's been a success. Not so much for its outward appearance, but because guests can count on the luxury we give them inside. And the tremendous view."

"We?"

"Dad's at the helm, of course, and I'm errand boy, as usual. Management is delegated, but we keep an eye on things, and Dad's office is in the building too."

Giff's station wagon wound its way up the climbing road to the hotel, and when we reached it he used his own parking space. Through revolving doors we stepped into a huge central atrium, with eight or more floors circling around it before a ceiling closed it in for the business floors above. The open cages of elevators overlooked the space on one side. We went into the hotel dining room on the main floor, its spaces softly lighted, and the head-waiter seated us with a flourish in respect to Gifford

Caton. Our banquette curved about a round table, and the menu was impressively enormous in size. Giff suggested the local mountain trout, and I let him order for me.

But all the while that I looked and admired and listened, I waited for something that so far hadn't emerged. I still didn't know why I was here. Giff's earlier excitement had subsided a little, though I sensed that whatever it was that had so stirred him still lay ahead. Nothing was going to happen while we were eating our dinner, and I tried to relax. Now and then, I noticed, he looked at his watch.

"Have you an appointment?" I asked after the third time.

"Sorry. I didn't mean to be so obvious. Yes, in a sense I suppose you could say that we do have an appointment."

"Then why not tell me what and where?"

His eyes sparked with Lori's teasing impudence. "All in good time," he said.

I didn't like either his excitement or the faintly ominous postponement, but I knew that no urging would make him give me an answer until he was ready. All I could do was pretend that this was a social evening and try at least to enjoy the food.

The waiter boned our trout expertly. The biscuits were light and melted, buttery, in my mouth. The spinach was creamed and nutmeg flavored, and we had saffron rice instead of potatoes. At least I managed to eat, putting away from me whatever lay ahead in the evening. When the time came and I had to make decisions, I would make them, and I didn't mean to let Giff Caton lead me down any road I didn't want to take.

In spite of that eye he kept on the time, our dinner was long and leisurely. Nevertheless, I sensed that he was glad when it was over. As we walked into the atrium that formed the lobby, he turned toward the elevators.

"Wait," I said. "Where are we going?"

He smiled at me almost tenderly. "What a suspicious young thing you are. Don't you want to see Great-grandpa Vinnie's office—around which all this elegance is built?"

"I'll manage to live if I don't see it," I told him, and not until he gave me an odd look did I hear the echo of my own words. Living—and dying—were so close together in our minds just now.

"Come," he said. "The floor upstairs is well lighted and patrolled. And I'm really not the firebug they're looking for. Don't be so silly, Karen."

His words stung and his impatience had begun to show. I went ahead of him into the elevator. It was true that I couldn't see Giff in the role of arsonist, or as the murderer who had left David's body under those vines on the island. Nor could I see him harming Lori. Yet I was not altogether sure that he might not have hired someone else to do whatever his father wished.

The elevator was self-service and when Giff pushed a button the open cage started slowly upward. We could look down on the great lighted spaces below, with the lounging area of the lobby, where guests moved about, or stood before the recessed desk where business was transacted. Below us were hanging plants, wall sculptures and mirrors everywhere to give a sense of space and light.

The number 10 lighted above the door and the car drew to a gentle stop, even with the floor. When the door slid silently aside, Giff motioned me out. At once a uniformed guard came toward us, only to recognize Giff and let us through to a corridor that ran past office after office. Nothing on this floor seemed novel or particularly interesting. Except that I was seeing an office at night, when all the familiar movements of people, the voices and sounds of typewriters and machines were hushed. Instead, there was a heavy, blanketing silence. At least the floor wasn't dark. Lights burned overhead, some of the cubicles we passed were lighted and in more than one someone sat at a desk working late.

I glanced at my guide, still questioning why I was here.

"Wait," Giff said. "There's more to see. Vinnie's office is the heart of the building. We've left it alone—since one must respect a shrine. But Dad and I haven't fared too badly. Dad with reason, myself only in the role of heir apparent."

I glanced at him, hearing the faintly bitter note in his voice. But his smile was as open as ever, and if there was cynicism, we both let it pass.

He showed me his own luxurious suite first and I noted the deep-piled wall-to-wall, the enormous expanse of clean desk, several comfortable chairs and the lurid painting of a tiger lily on the wall.

"Maggie, of course," I said, walking over to look at it.

"Yes. I couldn't hurt her feelings by refusing to hang it, and it is a beauty. Though sometimes I get the feeling that it might sneak from its frame and take a bite out of me. I'm not at all sure it isn't carniverous."

"What makes her paint like that?" I asked idly, knowing that I already had some of the answers, but wondering what he, as her stepson, might say.

"All those squirmy things that go on inside her, of course," he answered readily. "I don't think she was all that much of a kook before she married Dad. Sometimes I wish *I* could paint. To let off steam the way she does."

"Is he a very difficult man, your father?"

"Difficult—and complex. Comes of all those years with Vinnie Fromberg, when Dad was held down. He could hardly breathe on his own in the early days. I can remember when I was a kid and the edicts used to come down from on high. Vinnie never accepted the fact that he was getting old, and he certainly wasn't senile. He never let go of an ounce of power until the end. So now I can't blame Dad for going whole hog on being the big tycoon. He's earned it. But he can't take opposition these days, any more than Vinnie could. That's why Trevor's Belle Isle project is giving him an ulcer. But it looks as though all we have to do is wait and let it fall apart on its own."

"Only it isn't falling apart on its own," I said sharply. "It's being helped along pretty expertly."

"How right you are! And wouldn't I like to know all the ins and outs of what's going on!"

"Are you sure you don't?" I asked him point-blank.

"Ouch! You and that tiger lily! Come along and I'll show you the next exhibit."

We went along the hall for a couple of doors. I was feeling more comfortable now, and less uneasy. I had a good pair of lungs, and people on the floor could hear me if anything went wrong. Besides, I couldn't see Giff actually using physical assault. He would be far more devious than that.

The door he flung open next showed the largest room I had yet seen. The carpeting was a deep, dark crimson, the paneling walnut. The room looked like a magnificent stage set, and in the center of it stood a vast polished desk with a red leather chair behind it. In the chair a man sat watching us.

Giff paused beside me in the doorway, and I was aware of his sudden hesitation. "Hello, Dad. Karen and I had dinner downstairs and I was just showing her a bit of the empire."

His manner and tone had changed, and I glanced at him in surprise. It was as though his father's presence had reduced him so that he was no longer the expansive and confident conductor of this tour. Was this why he often seemed more observer than participant?

Eric showed no annoyance, however. He left his desk and came to take my hand, conveying the impression that he had missed me since we'd last met (yesterday?), and that he was delighted to see me again. A charmer, indeed, as I'd thought before. Even Giff could take lessons from him.

"I'm glad my son has the sense to take you out to dinner, and I hope this is only the first time," he said. "How do you like our hotel and offices?"

I returned the flattery. "They're magnificent. I imagine you must have played quite a role in their creation."

He admitted readily that he'd had a managing hand in the entire project, although the initial plans were, of course, old Vinnie's.

"I brought Karen up here to show her Vinnie's office," Giff said. "We'll go along now. I didn't know you were working tonight."

"I don't suppose you did." Eric spoke mildly, but I sensed a sting of meaning for Giff, whom his father probably regarded as a playboy.

We made a somewhat hasty exit and by the time we were out in the corridor, with Eric's door closed behind us, I was aware that Giff was seething with suppressed rage.

"One of these days——" he began, and then cut off his own words in self-derision. "That day will never come because I'll never do one thing about him. I've been scared to death of him all my life. If I wanted to, I could destroy him with a flick of my fingers and he knows it. Yet that doesn't bother him in the least. Vinnie Fromberg was reasonably honest, considering that he belonged to a pirate generation. He'd never approve of the way Dad skates close to the brink in a good many of his ventures. I wonder if that's the way I'll operate if I ever step into Dad's shoes? But then, I'll never step into them, will I? The corporation will take over. I may have the name, but never the power. Dad will see to that."

His hand on my elbow was urging me down the corridor, and I held back. "Please—no more offices tonight, Giff. I'd like to go back to the house now."

He made an effort to throw off whatever feelings the encounter with his father had aroused, and once more he glanced quickly at his watch. "No, no, you can't go home yet. It's a very young evening. You can't expect me to give you up so soon. There's more to see after Vinnie's office. Something you won't want to miss."

Uneasiness stirred in me again, but there was no harm in seeing what further magnificence Vinnie Fromberg had arranged for himself. Then, when we returned to the elevator, I would insist on going home.

This time the office was near the end of the corridor. Giff reached in for the light switch and flung the door wide. I stood in the opening and stared in disbelief.

The room was tiny and almost bare. Against one wall stood a battered roll-top desk, with a swivel chair before it. A glass-doored bookcase stood in the corner, and there were two straight wooden chairs without arms. A smaller desk held an old-fashioned manual typewriter, and the obviously worn rug was a dingy brown and anything but wall-to-wall.

Giff laughed at my expression. "There you are—the shrine!"

"You mean he built this entire building—everything!— in order to install this?"

"He sure did. Got a big kick out of it."

"But he could have set this anywhere."

"No—because he wanted the two extremes. For himself he liked the plain and unadorned. This is a replica of the office he started with, and I suppose he enjoyed slapping visitors in the face with it. Then, for flaunting, he had all the luxury out there to show what had grown from this. To say nothing of owning Belle Isle, with that octagonal house eccentricity he built over there."

I remembered the Roman emperor tub of rose-garnet marble that I had seen at Vinnie's house. That, indeed, belonged to the opposite extreme from this humble office.

"Look over there on the wall," Giff said.

The calendar sported a nymph dipping her toes in a stream, advertising a well-known beverage, for which the ads had changed only a little in later years. The date went back a long while and the month was November.

"The month of Cecily's death," Giff mused. "He kept that calendar all those years. He used to enjoy bringing some mogul across the country to see him, showing off the outer offices, then plunking him down in one of those hard chairs, while he rolled down the top, put his feet on the desk and gave forth with edicts. I've seen him do it when I was a kid—while some poor guy in a gray flannel suit with his own posh office in some metropolis squirmed and fidgeted. He was quite a boy, old Vinnie."

I was beginning to like him myself, except when I thought of Cecily. On the wall behind the door were a few pictures—a partial record of the family dynasty. Cecily was there, and another beautiful woman who must have been his second wife. Eric as a young man looked out at the world with his same deliberate charm, and Giff and Lori were there as children. Even Maggie, with her sweater askew, smiled determinedly at a camera she probably hated to face.

"Okay—you've seen our Exhibit A," Giff said. "I won't bother to show you Vinnie's apartment next door. It's not as Spartan as this. Besides, it's time now for the curtain to go up. Come along, Karen."

"To go where? For what?" I asked, as he led me toward the elevators.

"You'll see." The sense of something electric was stirring in him again—that excitement which made me so uncomfortable.

At the elevator the door of the cage stood open and Giff waved me through and pushed a button on the panel. To my surprise the car went up, not down.

"We're going to the roof," he said in answer to my look.

That was when I dug in my heels. "No! I hate heights, Giff, and it will be too dark to see anything."

I didn't mind heights at all, except in this case. I simply didn't want to go with him up to the hotel roof. It seemed unknown and threatening territory, even though I could reason that my alarm was foolish. What was he going to do—throw me off? Certainly not when everyone knew I was with him! Nevertheless, in a way that had nothing to do with reason, I was apprehensive.

The car stopped and the door slid open before a small enclosure.

"It may be chilly out there," he said. "Karen, you're already shivering! Honey, I didn't mean to scare you. You know I'm about as harmless as they come. Even if you hadn't been invited especially, it's still a good idea to have *two* of us here for this meeting."

"M-m-meeting?" I chattered. "What do you mean—invited?"

"Yes, sweetie. She wanted you especially. I didn't tell you before because I didn't want you worrying. There's a lady coming to meet us up here on the roof. A sort of lady. Over the telephone she said her name was Gwen Bruen, and I think she might be someone interesting for us to meet."

Thirteen

I must have stopped shivering out of shock. I couldn't manage another question until we left the enclosed section before the elevators and stepped through a heavy door into whipping wind.

At first it seemed so dark outside that I could make out only shadowy outlines. The two castle turrets, one at either end of the roof, rose in black silhouette against a lighter, star-filled sky. In the center was a mass of machinery forming a dark mound and shielded by a metal screen. The rest of the enormous roof was open, free of obstacles, and we walked across it to the nearest parapet. No one seemed to be in sight.

I managed to recover my voice. "Tell me what this is all about."

"In good time. Come along, Karen, and enjoy the

view." His tone was light, airy, but I knew his excitement was growing and I trusted him less than ever.

The air up here was like the air on a mountaintop, and the wind blew across us, fresh and clear and bracing. As my eyes accustomed themselves I could see all those billions of stars that could never be glimpsed in New York, and among them a sliver of moon cruising the deep blue sky. The night was bright with starlight out here, but Giff turned me toward the neon reds and greens and yellows of the town, with its observation tower standing high and crowned with more light. I tried to relax and watch a scene that was far from static. Traffic moved solidly along the main road through town, with windows of houses shining here and there on the hills around. It was all quite beautiful, but my anxiety hadn't abated. What if Giff had made all this up about meeting someone named Gwen Bruen? What if this was some trap he hadn't yet revealed?

Nevertheless, when he drew me toward the farther end of the roof, there was nothing to do but go with him. From this aspect dark woods and hills closed us in, and the mountains themselves were black and unrelieved by any speckling of light.

"There's no one here," I said.

"Give her time." Giff was confident. "She sounded anxious enough to meet us, but of course I can't be sure she hasn't changed her mind by now."

"She called you on the phone?"

"Yes. This morning at the office."

"But why? Why you, and why me? What does she want?"

"Perhaps I seemed the most innocuous of the choices she could make. I always try to keep my low and feckless profile intact. When I tried to shunt her over to Dad, she wouldn't have anything to do with the idea. And the suggestion of meeting Trevor seemed to terrify her. So I was left. And you. She seemed to know a lot about all of us, but she wouldn't tell me on the phone what she wanted. She just asked me to bring you to meet her in some quiet spot where nobody would see us. So I thought of the Greencastle roof. The perfect place for a secret rendezvous, don't you think?"

"Why wouldn't she expect you to call the police, under the circumstances?"

"She seemed to believe I wouldn't."

"And she was right?"

He moved his hands expansively. "As you can see."

"Have you any idea what she wants?"

"I'm not sure, but she sounded as though she might be doing the woman-scorned bit. So it's possible we may get something out of her. She also sounded scared. However, she accepted my suggestion of a place, so I don't think she's frightened of me. She told me she'd be here at eight-thirty. Providing no one else came with us. It's a little past the time now. So let's walk around and enjoy while we're here."

I still wondered if this whole thing was a fabrication on Giff's part, but I moved with him along the roof toward the other turret. As we neared it a shadow separated from the mass and came toward us. She must have been watching all along, perhaps sizing us up and making sure we were alone.

"Mrs. Bruen?" Giff asked, as though we were meeting at a party.

She didn't answer, but came on, walking slowly. In the starlight her face looked white and set, her dark eyes fixed. Her shoulder-length hair, tied back with a scarf, looked dark and she wore slacks of some neutral color and a dark sweater, so that she blended with the background.

When she reached us she stopped before me. "You're Mrs. Hallam?"

I nodded. "Yes."

She began to speak in a rush. "I'm sorry about your husband. I don't think Joe meant what happened. But that's what started it all. And then there was that woman —Mr. Andrews' wife." The words came in a confused spate, as though she had to hurry, or perhaps not say them at all. Then she ceased abruptly, as though she had run out of all she had come to say.

"I don't understand—" I began, but Giff put a hand on my arm.

"I'm sure you have more you want to tell us, Mrs. Bruen. There's a bench over there. Let's go and sit down so you can talk comfortably, and we can listen."

He took her by the arm and she didn't resist. When we had seated ourselves on the workmen's bench, with Gwen Bruen between us, Giff spoke to her again, quietly.

"How did Hallam's death come about?"

"I only know what Joe told me." She glanced anxiously from side to side, as though she might discover someone listening. "I was in New York. I read about it in the papers. So I wrote to him down here—at an address where he got his letters general delivery. And I asked him to phone me."

"What town is that?" Giff asked.

She stopped staring around and gave him an irritable shake of her head. "I'm not telling you. Not yet, anyway."

I urged her on. "What happened to David?"

Her hesitation was longer this time, as though she wondered how much she dared tell us. But again, when she spoke, the words were blunt.

"David caught Joe over on the island. They were both big men, but maybe Joe was a little bigger. When they fought, Joe hit him with a rock. Harder than he meant, I guess. Joe had already set another house to catch fire, but then he had to get rid of—of the body. So he used some explosives he'd brought in and was saving for the right place. He was in demolition in the army, so he knew all about that kind of thing."

"Then Lori found out about him, didn't she? And she knew too much," Giff said softly.

The flood of words dried up. "I don't want to talk about her," she said grimly.

"Then talk about whatever you want," I said.

After a moment she went on. "Anyway, it doesn't matter now. All that's over with. But it's got to stop. Maybe Joe's gone a little crazy about fires. It used to be a job he'd do and then he'd get out fast. But he's changed. He wants to watch things burn!" She bent her head and covered her face with her hands.

"Go on." Again I urged her. "If you tell us enough, perhaps we can help you."

"Nobody can help me. But I'm not going to take anymore. When I came down here he said we were through and I should just go away."

Giff looked at me over her bent head. "How recently did you see Joe Bruen?"

"Yesterday," she said. "He—he was awful. I was scared of him."

"And now you want to tell us where he is so something can be done to stop him?" Giff said.

Her head came up fiercely. "No! I mean—not yet. I don't know. I'm all mixed up. I thought it would be easy. I thought it would be a way to get even with him. After that—that woman. The Andrews woman!"

So Lori had been playing with danger again—walking the high edge of the precipice. But the woman between us wasn't ready to talk the whole thing out as yet. Her own actions had begun to frighten her.

"Perhaps it isn't necessary to tell us all about Joe," I

said quietly. "Someone hired him, of course. If you just tell us who that person is—"

Giff stirred on the bench beyond her. "No, Karen. That isn't good enough. It's Joe we want. Go on, tell us the rest, Mrs. Bruen."

She was staring at me. "Yes, I'd like to tell you about who hired him. But not now. Not here. Maybe another time. If I could just see you alone."

I shook my head emphatically. "No. That isn't possible. You'd better tell us everything right now while you have the chance."

But we had pushed her too far, and she jumped up from her place between us and ran in the direction of the elevators. Giff was after her fleetly, his hand reaching for her arm, and when I joined them I took her other arm.

"Don't be afraid," I said. "No one's going to hurt *you*. You were right in coming to us. But you need to tell us everything or there's no way we can help."

She went limp between us, making no attempt to struggle or get away, and by the time we reached the lighted area opposite the elevators she seemed entirely unresisting.

Nevertheless, we waited, not pushing the button for the car at once. Now that there were lights overhead I could see her face more clearly. She had put on very little lipstick, but her eyes had been carefully lined and thickly shaded, and the lashes were long and false. She was pretty in a not too distinguished way, and her figure, even under the heavy sweater, was opulent.

"What sort of work do you do?" I asked her.

She was being cautious now, and she thought about that for a moment as though she feared some trap. "I used to be a go-go dancer. But Joe didn't like me to keep on after we were married. We didn't need the money, so I quit. Though sometimes it gets awfully boring—not working."

"Not lately, I imagine," Giff said.

Her expression was more startled than the remark seemed to call for, and she reached past him and pressed the button for the car.

"Look," she said. "I'll show you something. I'll show you just one thing."

Fumbling in her hurry, she opened her plastic handbag and took out an envelope. She didn't release it into our hands, but removed a wallet-sized picture and held it up for us to see.

"That's Joe," she told us. "It was taken just last year."

The man who looked out at us was some years older than Gwen. His mouth was hard and straight, his chin slightly weak, and his gray hair curled in a thick mass over his forehead. It was a face one might easily cast as the villain in any B movie.

"Well, that's some help," Giff said. "Though not much. Now we know what he looks like, at least."

"Your father already knows him," I pointed out.

Giff's look was scarcely approving, but he made no comment.

The elevator was taking its time, and Gwen Bruen had begun to fidget. It was clear that she wished herself elsewhere by this time.

"Where are you staying?" I asked her.

"You think I'm nuts—to tell you that? I'd like to talk to *you,* Mrs. Hallam. But when you're alone. That's the only way I'll do it. I only called Mr. Caton because I didn't think you'd come alone the first time to meet me. But maybe now—"

"No way," I said. "I wouldn't any time."

"That's too bad. That's really too bad. But maybe you'll change your mind."

"How can I if there's no way to reach you?"

"Oh, but I know how to reach you," she said. The elevator door slid smoothly open, and she stepped ahead of us into the waiting car.

I tried to catch Giff's eye on the way down, but he avoided my look, and his usually expressive face seemed blank and guarded. I wasn't sure that Giff would co-operate in turning Gwen Bruen over to the police. I suspected that he had his own secrets to guard—perhaps having to do with his father.

We walked through the atrium lobby, and out revolving doors to the paved strip in front of the Greencastle. Neither of us was holding her arm by that time, and without warning she darted away and ran across the driveway, disappearing into thick bushes that dropped down the hillside to the next level of road. I started after her, but Giff pulled me back.

"Let her go, Karen. It's no use. She won't tell us anything more now, and she'll have a car down there ready to go. We can't catch her on foot. Or in my car, by the time we get it out of the parking space."

I wasn't sure that he couldn't have captured her if he'd gone after her on foot, but I could also see that if we became aggressive we might frighten her off entirely. When we were in Giff's car he patted my arm reassuringly, his good nature reviving.

"Don't worry. She'll be heard from again. And when she is, let me know. Don't, under any circumstances, go off to meet her alone. We can't be sure how much of what she told us was the truth, or what her unsavory husband may be up to now."

I agreed readily enough, but I was still wondering about Giff. The excitement I had sensed in him earlier had disappeared—perhaps because he was no longer keyed up to meet an unknown adventure. We found little to talk about on the drive home, and when he dropped me off at

Trevor's I thanked him politely for the evening. He held my hand for a moment, his familiar, somewhat mocking expression back in place.

"Will you tell your father about tonight?" I asked.

He looked startled. "Certainly not. He'd find whatever we did wrong because he would have handled it better. Are you going to tell Trevor?"

"Yes, of course," I said.

His smile had a twist to it as he drove away. I went into the house, looking into one room after another. I could hear Nona playing her dulcimer, but I didn't seek her out in her own rooms. Trevor was the one I wanted to find.

The door of his office was open, and he was at his desk. When I paused in the doorway, he looked at me across the room, his eyes cool and uninviting, as I had seen them that afternoon.

"I'd like to talk with you," I said.

He stood up, gesturing me into the room, and I went to sit in an easy chair near his desk, feeling unutterably depressed. There was nothing about him to invite easy confidence, nothing to tell me he cared whether I stayed or went. The change in him had been growing worse in the last day or two, and he was a man I no longer knew.

I sat primly upright, my hands clasped in my lap. "I went out to dinner at the Greencastle tonight," I said. "With Giff."

"Yes—Nona told me. It's a pleasant dining room."

"Giff didn't take me there because it's pleasant. He'd had a phone call from a woman named Gwen Bruen."

That seemed to startle him. "Go on."

"Giff had agreed to bring me to meet this woman when she called him on the phone. He chose the roof of the hotel for our meeting."

Trevor flung down the pencil he was holding with a violence that bounced it off the desk. "My God! Why?"

"I think Giff likes to be whimsical. First he gave me the grand tour of the tenth floor and showed me Vinnie Fromberg's office. At eight-thirty we went up to the roof."

"I'll talk to Giff. He should never have taken you up there."

"Mrs. Bruen wanted to meet *me*. It was the only way she would come. I think she's feeling revengeful toward her husband. I think she'd like to turn him in, but is afraid to."

Trevor's first surprise had died a little, and now, strangely, he didn't seem particularly interested in what I was telling him.

"What else did you learn?" he asked.

"Very little. She wasn't ready to talk. Not with Giff there. Though she admitted that Joe caused David's death, and she showed us a picture of her husband."

"Much good that will do if we can't find him. You remember we have his fingerprints too. Did his wife have any suggestions?"

"No—though she wanted me to meet her somewhere alone."

"Which you mustn't do under any circumstances."

"Of course not. I told her so. When we came downstairs she ran away from us, and there was no chance of catching her."

"That wasn't being smart of Giff—to let her go."

"She surprised us. We never expected—"

"Giff wouldn't. Perhaps he didn't want to stop her. Anyway, it's a blind alley. She's not going to lead you to her husband, no matter what she says. It could be some sort of trap. Have nothing to do with it."

I wasn't sure of anything, but I didn't want to argue

with Trevor. Nor could I endure more of this cold indifference he was showing me.

"Anyway, now you know," I said, and left my chair to walk through the open doors onto the deck. He let me go outside alone and I stood at the rail looking toward the mountains.

We were even higher than the Greencastle here, but the lights of Gatlinburg were missing. The night and the stars, the dark mountains, were the same, but they gave no lift to my spirits. There was so much to weigh upon me now. David's futile death—since according to Gwen Bruen it could have been unintentional. And she hadn't wanted to talk about Lori, though I had sensed jealousy there. True, there had been no more fires since Lori had died, but that didn't mean there wouldn't be more. I couldn't believe that any of it was ended. Now Trevor had turned against me for some private reason—or else he was so lost in the darkness of his own mind that there was no longer room for any thought of me.

If it weren't for Chris, I would pack up and go home tomorrow, I thought. I must go soon, anyway, no matter what Nona said. The boy was improving and next week he would be going back to school, doing extra make-up work as well. I would miss him. Something warmer than friendship had grown between us. What it meant to him I couldn't be sure, but it had begun to fill a long-suppressed need in me. And that in itself was dangerous.

I didn't know that Trevor was near until I felt his arms come about me. Startled, I turned and looked up at him. I wanted to say, *Don't—don't hurt me anymore!* But I didn't speak because there was an enormous sadness in his eyes. He held me close for a moment, then kissed me gently.

"I'm sorry, Karen. I'm sorry for everything. I think it's

best if you go home very soon. You'll be better off away from whatever else is going to happen here."

I started to protest, but he released me and crossed the deck into the house. He had held me tenderly, he had kissed me—but he had walked away. I didn't understand. I couldn't understand anything!

There was no one else I wanted to talk to and I went down to my room and closed the door. When I turned on the light I saw the sheet of notepaper lying on the floor and picked it up. There were only a few words.

You're to call someone named Bert at this number tomorrow morning.

Nona

Chris must have brought this down to slip under my door. I didn't know who Bert was, but I had a strong feeling that when I called I would find Gwen Bruen behind the number.

During the night it began to rain—no small thunder shower that would quickly blow away, but a hard, steady downpour. Trevor had insulated well and the beating on the roof over my room was muted and distant. But even with the enclosed grotto outside, wind flung sheets of rain against the glass doors of my room, striking them with intermittent force. At any other time I might have loved the sound, might have fallen gently asleep to its accompaniment. Now, only torturing pictures went through my mind.

Visions of rain pounding down upon Belle Isle, stirring ashes and char to a black paste. Rain running like a waterfall down the tiered steps of Cecily's theater, falling on Vinnie Fromberg's octagonal house, beating its way through voracious green vines to flood a hidden cabin.

And most of all heavy green vines pressing down upon me, burying me as the man in Maggie's painting had been buried. This would be my nightmare for years to come.

It was a long while before I slept, only to awake early the next morning to the continued sound of storm outside. Up here on the mountain wind struck the house with enormous force, but it scarcely shuddered because Trevor had built solidly and well.

My guess about the number I was to call was right. After breakfast I phoned from the hall telephone upstairs. Bert, whoever he was, answered and went away. A moment later Gwen Bruen spoke in my ear.

"Have you changed your mind?" she asked. "Will you meet me?"

"Not if I have to come alone," I said.

"Then the fires will go on. And God knows what else. Do you want that to happen? A guard can't be put on every house, and there are ways to get in all around Belle Isle." She sounded indignant with me, and also a little frantic—even desperate. "You *have* to take a chance, Mrs. Hallam. I won't talk to anyone else."

"Why me?"

"Because you're concerned. Because of what I can tell you about your husband. You want to know, don't you? You don't want to go all the rest of your life wondering what he was into—you couldn't bear that. Besides, you're the only one who can help me. Any of the others would bring the police, and I'm not about to face that."

"How do you know I won't?"

"Because you've got sense enough to know that would lose you everything I can tell."

"Does Joe know you're doing this?"

"Of course not!" The truth rang in her voice and I

sensed that my first guess had been right. She wanted to
pay off her husband.

I played for time, to keep her talking. "Where do you
want to meet me?"

"Come to the house on the island. I'll meet you outside
at ten-thirty this morning."

Startled from me, my laughter had an hysterical ring.
"That's the last place I would think of going!"

"But what I have to show you is there. Telling won't
do. You have to *see*." Again conviction rang in her voice.
She believed in what she was saying.

"No," I said. "I won't come."

"At ten-thirty. Don't be late," she told me and hung
up.

I put down the receiver and turned around to find Nona
sitting in her wheelchair across the hall, watching me.
Obviously she had been listening.

"You'd better come and tell me," she said, and wheeled
back to her own living room.

Yes, I thought, I could tell Nona. She, at least, would
have Trevor's interest at heart, and perhaps she would
know what to do. I followed her into the cool spacious
room, where rain curtained the windowpanes in a moving
sheet of water. I sat again on the couch beside the dulcimer, and Nona wheeled her chair opposite me. This morning her graying hair hung in a long braid over one
shoulder, as it had the first time I'd seen her, and her
green eyes were alert and probing.

"Begin," she said.

I told her what had happened last night on the roof of
the Greencastle, putting in all the detail I could remember. She heard me out with no interruption, her look never
wavering from my face.

"You'll have to go, of course," she said when I finished.

I stared at her in astonishment and her smile was wry.

"Oh, not alone. We'll have to figure something out. I wish I could go with you, but I wouldn't be of much use. Trevor—"

"Trevor wouldn't hear of it. And I don't think he'd go himself. He really wasn't much interested in Mrs. Bruen. I don't want Giff. So who is there?"

Neither of us mentioned Eric, and Chris was too young.

"Maggie," Nona said. "She's sound enough in a crisis, and she'd jump at the chance."

"Two women? Into goodness only knows what trap? No thank you."

"That's a cliché. You want brains, not brawn, at a time like this. Poor little Lori didn't have either."

Already she was overriding my protest, wheeling her chair down the room to her own telephone. A moment later she had Maggie on the line. I listened, feeling that I was being catapulted into space by a force that couldn't be resisted.

"Maggie, hon," she was saying, "are you alone? . . . That's fine. Listen, sweetie, do you still have that automatic Eric gave you a while back? . . . Good. Get it out and load it. Karen is coming up to see you right away. It could be that something's in the wind to stop all the trouble at Belle Isle. . . . You'd like to help on that, wouldn't you?"

A moment later she hung up and turned back to me, her expression alive with excitement. I remembered her telling me once that she would do anything for Trevor and Chris. Even to sacrificing me?

"Run along now, Karen. Go over to Maggie's right away, and let her make the plans. The minute it's all over, you come back here. I'll want to know everything that happens." If I followed her directions I wasn't sure I would ever come back. Yet already I knew the catapult had been fired and I was the missile. But when I started reluctantly to the door, Nona held out her hand and I went to her.

"Listen to me, Karen. I don't know what's over on the island, but whatever it is, it has to be stopped. Until we find Joe Bruen, nothing can be ended. You'll be all right."

"How can you possibly say that?"

"Because I know. I really do know, Karen. No one is going to hurt you. Go and talk to this woman. That may be all that will happen. Just talk. I know you'll be fine."

Her voice was low and somehow compelling. As though hypnotized, I believed every word she was saying. It was as though she had given me some charm against evil that would get me through. Perhaps she was something of a magician in her own right.

"Go see Maggie," she finished.

I picked up my raincoat and went out to my car. This was no day for walking in the woods. The world ran with water, the mountains had vanished, the road shone with puddles and the trees were green satin, slashed through with the black emphasis of wet trunks.

Maggie stood under the overhang, waiting for me as I drove into the carport. She took me upstairs at once to the kitchen, where I had first sat beside her at a counter, drinking her good coffee. Now she plied me with more and asked me questions.

"Nona phoned," she said. "What is this all about?"

Once more I repeated everything, wondering how much she could be trusted, how much anyone could be trusted, including Nona. But Maggie, presented with a physical problem—something that required action—took hold with admirable confidence. Though even as I listened to her plans, I wondered if everything, including my own control over my life, was slipping away.

"We'll go in your car," she decided. "And we'll go well ahead of time. I'll stay on the floor in the back until we're sure there's no one around to see me. Then I'll find a place where I can be well out of sight and watch. It's nine-thirty now, so we'll leave in a few minutes."

I had a weird feeling of scenes repeating themselves. Once before, Trevor had said almost the same words to me—that he would follow us to the island and stay out of sight. But he hadn't been there when I needed him. Now, at least, I would have a bodyguard with me—if that was what Maggie was supposed to be.

She moved a dishtowel from the counter and I saw the deadly little gun it covered. "Don't worry, Karen. Eric taught me how to use this and I'm a pretty good shot."

I felt like saying, *What if it's Eric you find yourself facing?* But I didn't dare. By this time she was a missile too, and well on her way. But whose hand had fired the machine? Nona's? Or someone behind Nona?

At least Maggie was in her element and I was beginning to understand she was a born plotter and eagerly involved. Perhaps recklessly involved?

When we went out to my car she carried a blanket to spread on the floor in back, where she curled herself up comfortably.

"Okay," she said. "Let's get going."

I turned on the windshield wipers and drove down the mountain. There were slippery places where gravel had slid into mud, but I went carefully around the turns in low gear until we reached the highway.

My mind was anything but quiet on that drive to Belle Isle. I knew why I was doing this. It was because of Trevor. If he wouldn't believe in Gwen's involvement, wouldn't lift a finger in that direction himself—then I had to follow up this one lone lead. I hadn't wanted to go to the island with Chris that other time, yet what he'd had to show me had put us a great jump ahead in our realization of the facts. Now perhaps Gwen would give me another piece of the puzzle. And I had to admit that I felt a great deal safer with Maggie in the back seat than I'd have felt with Giff.

The guard let me through, and I drove slowly around the lake toward the island. There was still no building going on, no clearing of the places that had been burned, no repair. We drove past the ruin where David had died and I saw that one of the blackened trees was sprouting a little green out there in the rain. If only human beings could put out new shoots.

The lake waters were rough, lifting into small waves in the wind, the entire surface gray and roiled with rain.

"How is the causeway?" Maggie asked from her place on the car floor.

It was directly ahead now and running with shallow water. "We can get across," I said. But the water was flowing and frothy, buffeting the car, so that I could feel its impact as I drove.

"I've seen times when the island is cut off from the world," she said.

I didn't want to think about that. I had to be able to escape when the time came. Escape? But I mustn't try to think from what. Right now I could only move ahead toward what was already inevitable. The water was inches deep about the wheels, the force against the car increasing, but I could still see paving and avoid deep water on either side as I drove slowly across.

"Where shall I leave the car?" I asked over my shoulder.

Maggie sat up to peer out an edge of rain-swept glass on a rear door. "I can't see much back here. Go slowly and watch for a turnoff space among the trees on the right. Stop there and we'll decide what to do."

I found the spot where bushes had been cut back, and swung the car into a wet stand of weeds.

"Do you see anyone around?" Maggie asked.

We were close to the house now. It stood up ahead of us, dark and formidable, its octagonal sides streaming water. On this lee side of the storm the veranda looked reasonably dry, however, with the door to the house closed and no one in sight. Nor did any face look down at us from visible windows.

"I think we're here ahead of her," I said.

"Then I'll go with you to the house," Maggie decided, and swore at the rain as she got out of the car.

We ran for it together. Maggie kept her hand in the pocket of her coat where it sagged a little with the gun. A sense of unreality possessed me, and I fought against it. That way lay helpless drifting. Everything was real enough —including arson and death and Maggie's gun. I had better stay alert.

"If the door isn't open," I said as we ducked through the rain, "Chris showed me a way to get in at the back."

The door was unlocked, however, and I didn't know whether that made me feel relieved or frightened. We stepped into the foyer and Maggie looked around quickly.

"I haven't been here in years. Thank God for the pre-historic furniture."

She placed herself behind a huge carved chair with a worn leather back, well hidden from view, but still beside a window, where she could look out.

"I'll stay here, where I can see anyone going or coming, inside or out."

"And I'll wait on the porch," I told her. My memories of this house were anything but pleasant and its great mass overhead oppressed me.

Outside, the steps were wet, so I seated myself cross-legged on a dry patch of veranda against the wall to the right of the door. The lion's-head knocker watched me, as though old Vinnie's eye were upon me derisively. He wouldn't have approved of women taking action. Rain was coming down harder than ever, and the wind made a roaring sound through the trees as the storm grew in strength. I looked at my watch and found that we were only twenty minutes early, due to our slow trip down the mountain.

From the corner of my eye I caught movement, but it was only Commodore stepping around a corner of the veranda with a careful dignity that avoided puddles. "Come here," I said, and held out my hand. Perhaps he was glad of company for once, and he approached me with deliberation and allowed me to scratch the white ruff of fur around his neck. As he looked up at me with his one blue and one yellow eye, I examined his shoulder where the wound and fur had been cut away. It appeared to have healed nicely. Once more I remembered David's liking for cats and wondered if he had ever met Commodore. It was remarkable how clean he kept himself, no matter what his living conditions.

I too was glad of company for this little while. Maggie, kneeling inside by her window, seemed very far away.

Gwen was no more than five minutes late. I heard her small car bumping along the road, coming up the wet drive. She sat alone in the front seat, and for a moment after she had stopped the car she peered through the windshield, looking around. When she decided that I was alone, she got out and came scooting up the steps to the veranda out of the wet.

"Where did that cat come from?" she demanded.

"He lives here. He was Vinnie Fromberg's cat and he belongs here."

"Joe always hated cats," she said. "That must be the one he threw a stone at."

So that was how Commodore had come to be struck

with a rock, I thought, despising Joe Bruen even more. Commodore, however, was not my main concern now, and I scarcely noticed when he removed himself from me and went haughtily off around the veranda, still avoiding the patches of wet.

"We'd better hurry this along," I said, standing up. "Rain may make the causeway impassable. Do we go inside, or stay out here?"

"We can stay here for now. I like the air better outside."

"What is it you want to show me?"

"First we talk a little," she said, and dropped down on the veranda floor as I had done. Luckily, she was under Maggie's window where she could be clearly heard.

I didn't join her at once. "What if your husband shows up? Wouldn't it be better to be inside out of sight?"

"He won't. I know where he is." She smiled at me reassuringly and I saw her small pointed teeth. "Do sit down, Mrs. Hallam"—as though she offered a comfortable chair. "As I said, first we talk."

She had changed subtly since last night, I thought, returning to my cross-legged position with my back against the house wall. I could make out her features better by daylight—her rather sleazy prettiness, the shoulder-length hair that no longer seemed as dark as it had last night, the huge hazel eyes, again carefully made up. But it was her manner that had changed. She still seemed nervous and a little edgy, but no longer frightened. This morning she was far more matter-of-fact.

"I didn't want to talk in front of Giff Caton last night," she said. "I had to see you alone. Because I want to tell you a whole lot more about your husband than you seem to know. You can be pretty glad that you're out of that deal altogether. He was badly in debt, you know."

I nodded, startled. "I found that out. But I don't know how it happened, or how you know about it."

"It was blackmail, of course. He was paying out plenty for his own safety."

"I don't know what you're talking about."

"You are an innocent, aren't you? Remember that big fire in New York a while before he came down here? The Oriental import shop that burned? He made a pile out of that. All he had to do was report that he found no traces of arson and the fire was legitimate. The insurance company had to pay up. There was a split of that payment between your husband and the owner. Not the first time, as maybe you ought to know."

Her words made me feel ill. The one thing I had admired in David was his pride in his work. He knew all about fires, and he had hated the men who started them. Or so I'd believed. Yet if Gwen Bruen's words were true —and somehow they carried the sound of truth—then he had been corrupted for I didn't know how long. But I couldn't accept them without question.

"I don't see how David could have gotten away with anything like that," I told her. "A fire marshal's squad would look into those fires too."

"Joe was an expert. He wouldn't leave traces if he didn't want to."

"You mean that Joe Bruen set that import-store fire?"

She grinned at me impishly. "Sure. It was all worked out ahead of time. The owner took a whole night to get his most valuable merchandise out of the store and substituted cheap goods. When it was over no one could tell whether all that burned-out stuff was valuable or just cheap junk."

That small Buddha, I thought. Somehow it had escaped full damage, and someone had found it after the fire and mailed it to David with the note about money. A threat.

The whole thing was too awful, but I was beginning to believe in spite of myself.

I already knew the answer to my next question, but I had to ask it. "Did David know Joe Bruen in New York?"

"Of course. David recommended him for some of those jobs. Of course he knew him. Who do you think hired Joe to come down here to work on Belle Isle? It was David Hallam, naturally."

Fourteen

For a moment or two, sitting there on the cold veranda floor with the bare siding of the house pressing against my back, I felt as though I couldn't breathe. I felt as though the storm that pounded the island beyond the veranda's edge was pounding inside my head.

"You all right?" Gwen asked. "You look a bit woozy."

I made myself breathe long, deep breaths that would revive me. "Why are you telling me all this now?" I asked.

"I should think you'd see why. To get even with Joe. Because Joe was beginning to threaten David. And in the end Joe killed him."

"I—I don't understand any of this," I faltered. "Why would David send Joe down here?"

"You don't know anything, do you? Mr. Andrews, David's brother, came to see him in New York and told him about a fire some kid had set at Belle Isle. So then David got the idea of paying his brother off in a really big way. Maybe he was a little crazy when it came to hating his brother. And some of that was because of you."

"How do you know so much about David?"

She jumped to her feet and stretched widely. It was almost a gesture of triumph. "You know he played around, didn't you? Only he stuck with me pretty well for a long time. Until Lori Andrews came along!" Gwen paused, lost in her own petulant thoughts. "I don't know if I'm so sorry that she's dead. That they're both dead."

"Go on," I said. I had to hear it all.

"It was pretty funny when David's brother asked him to come down here to investigate. He had a real good time pretending to look into the Belle Isle fires, when all along he knew who was setting them and was paying to have them set. Or anyway he was supposed to pay, only it was falling off."

Her smile was a grimace as she went on.

"Joe had a showdown with him over here on the island. Right near that old cabin under the kudzu, where nobody ever came. Joe told me about it afterwards. David got nasty and Joe hit him with a big rock. He only meant to knock him out. But when he found he'd killed him he had to get rid of the body. I told you about all that. Only I fixed it up a little last night."

"So now you're trying to punish Joe for what he did? By talking?"

Her look hardened. "Why not? I got pretty sick of him in the years since we got married. David stuck with me for a while, but Joe never did."

"And Lori? What about Lori?"

Gwen Bruen's eyes brightened with vindictiveness. "She was always coming over to the island. She used to meet David here. It never mattered to her whose husband she played around with. When she ran into Joe after David died, she began to catch onto what was happening. At first it was all right and we didn't think she'd talk. But she liked to stir things up—that one. So Joe figured out how to get rid of her and make it look like an accident. That liquid glue she was using in the dressing room was just right for him. Only I hated that!" Genuine feeling seemed to mark her words. Then she spoiled it. "It could have been done some other way. Not fire. Not always fire!"

"But *you* wanted her dead too?"

Gwen was silent, staring off into the rain, seeming to listen to the noises of the storm. I wanted to keep her talking—for Maggie's benefit, as well as mine. In her desire to betray her husband, she was willing to tell everything and I sought for a question that would renew the flow of words.

"Do you know anything about who broke that skylight over my bed at Trevor's house?"

"Sure. That was Lori. Joe told her to do something that would scare you away. Because you were so bound on finding out about David's death. You were getting to be dangerous. It isn't good to be dangerous. Lori found that out."

Yes, I thought, it was the sort of thing Lori would do. She could easily have worn gloves to keep the char off her hands.

"There's something I still don't understand," I went on. "Why would Joe stay around after David was dead? Why wouldn't he leave as fast as he could when he knew there'd be no more pay coming in?"

Gwen moved to the edge of the veranda and held her hand out to rain that slashed across her palm. When she turned back to me she was smiling, her slightly uneven teeth giving her a look of piquancy.

"You don't get it, do you? Now the stakes are bigger

than ever! Now the pay is a whole lot better. Now he's getting out of it what he really wanted."

I thought of Maggie crouched behind her window just at my back. What was she thinking?

"You mean someone else is paying Joe now?"

"We don't need to go into all that."

"You'd better tell me," I said. "Why have you brought me here? What is this all about?"

"It was so easy." She seemed to be musing almost to herself. "He could hide in that cabin, where nobody ever looked. And when he wanted to he could get off the island to where he'd left his car in the woods. He could go to a town where nobody knew him and stay at a motel, if he wanted to, and move out the next day. He could bring back supplies to the cabin. Or I could bring them in, after I came down."

"But why am *I* here?" I pressed her.

"Because I know where Joe is," she said softly. "Maybe I'll even tell you. And there's still something I want to show you in this house. If you're going back to that man you're in love with—that Trevor Andrews—and you're going to tell him everything, you have to see this one thing more."

She moved toward the door, her hand on the knob, waiting for me to get up from the floor and come with her.

I didn't want to move. "Did Joe and David use this house too?"

"Sometimes. But Giff Caton was around, so they didn't come often. For a while Joe used to leave notes for David in one of the rooms."

"Yes. I found one of them." I didn't add that Trevor had sent it to New York and that Joe's fingerprints and identity were known through that note.

She was growing impatient. "Do come along. Don't forget about the causeway."

I felt an enormous reluctance to step inside the house again. I sensed spite and vindictiveness in Gwen Bruen toward her husband, but what her true goal was I still didn't know.

"Come on," she snapped. "We don't want to stay here all morning. I don't think we'd make good company for a house party, do you?"

I got up and followed her through the doorway and across the wedge-shaped foyer, thankful for Maggie, hiding behind her high-backed chair. Gwen went ahead of me into the huge room that circled the stairs, and I didn't dare glance behind to see what Maggie was doing.

Gwen darted from room to room around the outer rim, looking into one after another.

"I just want to make sure you didn't bring anyone else in here," she told me, but fortunately she didn't look again into the foyer we had passed through. My fear was growing. It wasn't possible to sort out and digest all the bits of information she had given me. My mind felt muddled with words that might or might not be true. I had no time for all that now—monstrous as it was. I could only focus upon whatever it might be that waited for me upstairs. No matter how afraid, I was here.

Gwen paused at the foot of the steps and nodded to me. "Wait here for a minute. I just want to make sure everything is ready up there. There's a room I want you to see. Now don't go running off, Mrs. Hallam. That's a bad storm out there and the causeway won't be easy to get across."

There was nothing to say. I no longer felt like a missile shot from a catapult. All the forces that had driven me seemed to have been used up, dissipated. I could only stand helpless and numb—waiting.

Gwen ran up the stairs lightly to the second floor. Above me she paused, and called a name softly.

"Joe?" she said. "Joe, are you there?"

So that was it? That was the trap. Yet I stayed where I was, listening.

There was no answer and she disappeared from the landing, following the circle of an upper corridor. I looked around for Maggie and saw her standing at the door of the foyer, watching me. When I turned she beckoned to me frantically.

"There's someone upstairs, Karen. I've heard footsteps. Don't go up there. We've got to leave now."

"But we have to know," I said. "We have to *know*."

Her look was a little wild. "I don't want to know. I'm leaving—right now. Come with me, Karen. While we can still get away."

"And while you still don't know the whole truth—is that it, Maggie?"

"I don't want to know!" she whispered.

"Then give me the gun and I'll stay," I told her.

"No! You aren't going to do any shooting."

"I have to stay. It's already too late to get away. Don't you know that, Maggie?"

"Not for me it isn't. Give me your car keys and let me go. Maybe you'll be all right. Nona told me that on the phone. She said she wouldn't let anyone hurt you."

"Nona wouldn't let—" I began, and then paused because I could hear Gwen's footsteps in the bare corridor above. She was approaching the stairs.

Maggie came to me quickly, and before I knew what she intended, she snatched my handbag from my arm and ran out the door of the house. After it banged shut, storm sounds hid her going. In my handbag were the keys to my car.

Gwen clung to the railing above me, looking down. Apparently she hadn't heard the door under the sounds of drumming rain. "You can come up now, Karen. Everything's ready. Now you'll know I've been telling you the truth about everything."

My mind said, *Run! Get away from the house. There's safety out in the storm.* But my feet walked toward the stairs and started me up. I climbed without any will of my own. Because I had to climb. Because something in me had to know.

Gwen waited for me and her excitement was a little like that which had driven Giff last night. She held out her hand and when I halted she bent to grasp mine and pulled me up the last steps, impatient with my slowness.

"Have you ever seen old Vinnie Fromberg's bedroom?" she asked. "It's like a room out of a museum. I want to show it to you. I want to show you what's in it."

Was this the way a man condemned to be shot might feel? I wondered. Was this the last mile—for me—that I was walking? What had Maggie meant—that Nona had said I wouldn't be harmed? I had no faith now in promises I didn't understand, nor any faith in my ability to escape from whatever fate awaited me in that room along the circular corridor.

The door was closed, and she tapped lightly before opening it. "I've brought her," she said.

There was no answer and she thrust the door wide, stepping back to push me into the room.

The draperies were long and dark and had been pulled across all but one of the nearly ceiling-high windows. There was no light except for gray storm light that fell through that one tall, open window. Rain pounded against the other side of the house, but nothing came in to dampen the rough clothes of the gray-haired man who stood before the window.

I had seen him before. I had seen that curly gray head and the rough green lumberjack shirt. It was the man I had glimpsed in the theater that day, watching Lori dance.

"Here she is!" Gwen announced triumphantly and he turned and looked at me.

He held Commodore in his arms and he stroked the white cat with tender affection as he came toward me gravely, limping just a little as he walked. He was David Hallam, my husband.

This was what I had been moving toward from the beginning. This was why I had come up those stairs. This was what I'd had to know.

A big armchair stood nearby and I found that my legs would actually move when I commanded them, so that I could take the few steps to the chair and sit down. I could only stare at him with the white cat purring in his arms, and that unfamiliar, but not at all incongruous, gray hairpiece on his head. He looked brown and fit, as well he might, but there was something different about his eyes, and I looked away because I couldn't bear to see what was there.

Behind me Gwen was doing a little jig of glee. "I did it, Davey!" she cried. "I told her everything—all the things you said she ought to know. And then I just put Joe's name in all the rest, instead of yours—switching everything around, the way you told me. She swallowed the whole thing!"

"That was fine, Gwen." He spoke as if to a child. "Now then—if you'll leave us alone for a little while. . . . Just go into the next room, Gwen, so I can talk to my wife. I haven't seen her for a long time, you know."

Gwen Bruen, however, had no intention of leaving him alone with me. She was quite ready to exert her own claim.

"Oh no you don't, Davey boy! I'll stay right here. There isn't anything you can say to her that I can't hear."

Davey boy! I knew by the look he gave her that her

words and voice grated. David had never liked to be called anything but David.

"All right," he told her. "Stay, if you like. Listen, if you like. But don't blame me if you don't care for all you hear."

She grunted rebelliously and seated herself upon a moth-eaten ottoman near the window. David let the cat go and drew another chair opposite mine. I met his look now, met the burning intensity in his eyes. Outwardly he seemed calm and in control, but his eyes were a little mad.

More than anything else, I felt stupefied. It was as though I had received a blow that had stunned me, so that I wasn't able to rally.

"Ask questions if you like, Karen." He was smiling. That beautiful, angelic smile that I remembered, which had nothing angelic behind it. I remembered my childish comment at Trevor's dinner table—about photographing good and evil. Now I knew that evil seldom looked like evil, and that a camera couldn't capture a mind gone wrong.

I shook my head. No questions occurred to me. My brain had turned into a cauliflower, and no one could think with a cauliflower.

"Then perhaps I'd better fill in for you," he went on. "Perhaps there are a few things Gwen left out. It was a good idea for me to come down here, you know. Joe was doing an expert job with the fires and I was paying him well. However, things were getting a little hot for me in New York. Don't mind the pun—it fits in nicely, don't you think?"

I tried to breathe deeply again, recover my ability to think, to act. David, who had hated all firebugs, had turned into an arsonist himself. And he was a murderer twice over. Yet he could sit there calmly, making small jokes. This was more terrifying than if he had ranted.

"I knew I'd have to get out of the country eventually, so I wrote you that letter after I came down here. I didn't know then how well things would work out, but I wanted to pave the way for my own disappearance—presumably by foul play. I had no idea that you'd take my supposed death so seriously, darling."

He nodded at me in bright approval and I closed my eyes as he went on in the same horribly conversational tone—as though what he said had no bearing on human life.

"There were those who were onto what I'd been doing now and then. They had proof on that fire in the import store, and they were demanding an exorbitant cut. Which I certainly wasn't going to pay. You thought I was strapped, didn't you, Karen? In debt. I was in debt, all right, but I was just putting everything away for what I knew was coming. I'm a very rich man, and I can live abroad very comfortably now."

I managed to look at him again. "The Buddha. They sent you the little Buddha from that fire?"

"Yes. I didn't like being warned that way. Though it made me laugh to think of how that fire fooled the authorities. But sending me that burned-out figure as a threat put too much pressure on and I knew I had to get away soon. First, though, I wanted to finish paying off my brother. He was always so clever, so successful in everything he did. Until now. He hasn't been able to stop the fires, though, has he? So the thing I wanted most is done, accomplished."

I asked a direct question. "You killed Joe Bruen, of course?"

Gwen burst in. "I told her he'd killed *you!* But I told her it was an accident. Like it really was when you hit Joe."

"Ah. But accident or not, he was dead. So the whole

thing opened up for me and I knew exactly what I could do. David Hallam would disappear into bones and ashes, and I would become Joe Bruen. With my little accomplice here, Joe's wife."

Gwen giggled and I could only think what a fool she was.

David smiled at her almost benignly. I knew him so well. I had seen him smile like that just before he hit me with the flat of his hand.

"You see," he went on, enjoying his own narration, "I'd already had Joe set that house up with an explosive, and plenty of accelerant besides. So I knew it would go up with a bang in a blaze of destruction. Joe never knew it was to be his own funeral pyre."

He looked at Gwen, and for the first time her delight in all that was happening faltered a little.

"Then you planned—? I mean, it wasn't an accident like you told me, when Joe died? You meant to do it all along?"

"Not really—it just grew as I got into it. He was getting too greedy. He had the nerve to threaten *me*. Besides, we wanted to be rid of him, didn't we?"

"I suppose so. He was getting suspicious about us. Sure—I can see now how it was."

She was trying to backtrack—a little too late. David had noted her hesitation. He had always been a loner. I had never amounted to anything more with him than a gesture against his brother. For David, women were to use.

"It was easy enough to work out," he went on. "I dressed him in my clothes and used the ones he kept in the cabin for me. Though I don't care much for his style. I hid the body there in the cabin under the kudzu until it was dark. Then I took it over to the house that was already set to blow. The guard was on his rounds on the other side of the lake when I set things off. There wasn't much left of him afterwards. Just enough to make them think it was me."

"There were teeth—" I began.

He looked pleased, as though I'd given him marks for cleverness, and he nodded at Gwen. "Teeth?" he said, questioning.

"Joe's teeth were rotten when he was a kid," she supplied. "He didn't have any left of his own."

"So I made a little substitution," David said gently. "Joe's teeth didn't have to go into the fire, and I left my own side bridge at the perimeter of where the damage was likely to be. So it wouldn't be destroyed altogether. Good identification, wasn't it?"

I shivered, my horror growing. "But two people saw his body. They saw him in that cabin, lying there dead— and they believed it was you. Did you know that?"

"Not at first. But it didn't matter. Joe and I were around the same build. I put that ring Lori gave me on his finger, and my good watch on his wrist. As well as giving him my belt with the fancy buckle. All rather a sacrifice. But I knew there'd be enough scraps to identify as mine. Then I left him in the cabin and went up to Trevor's and had a bang-up fight with him. I thought he might get picked up on suspicion of murder. That's one thing that's never worked out. I'd like to have seen Trevor blamed. But I couldn't have everything.

"That cabin was a real inspiration. Like Chris, I played there when I was a kid around here, and I remembered that it must be there under the kudzu. I showed it to Joe when I came down, as a place where he could hide. I can guess what must have happened there when Chris found Joe, and later the same day when Maggie found him too. That could have been bad. But with his head bashed in and all that blood, he didn't look very pretty, so I'd dropped my Stetson over his head. He was wearing my clothes and he was dead. I was lucky that neither of them wanted to look under the hat with all the blood around. They just beat it. Lori told me all this later, when she found out."

"And Lori?" I said. "What about Lori?"

His smile was rueful, almost regretful—and terribly chilling. I wondered why I'd ever thought that David resembled Trevor.

"She got a bit too reckless," he said. "For a while she was fun, but then she began to want too much."

Gwen snorted. "I told Karen about the liquid glue Lori brought down from the house, and the way you made everything look like another accident."

David nodded. "She used the business of fixing up Cecily's dressing room to get down here often to see me. It made Gwen a little restive though, didn't it?"

"It sure did. But you fixed all that."

Gwen was like a small, feral animal, I thought. She had no more conscience than Commodore would have about killing a mouse.

No one said anything for a little while, and David seemed perfectly comfortable waiting. The thought of what he might be waiting for terrified me. Outside the open window the storm still raged and the rush and roar of it filled the room as gusts increased their force. I wondered where Maggie was. Had she escaped across the causeway? Had she abandoned me entirely? Perhaps she would find Eric and Giff at home and know that she needn't be afraid anymore of her husband's involvement. But it didn't matter now. It was too late to help me. No one could get here in time.

"What are you going to do with *her?*" Gwen asked, nodding toward me.

"Just listen," David told her, his irritation showing.

He left his chair and came to draw me from mine. He held my two hands in his and I knew it would do me no good to struggle in their clasp. I knew very well how powerful he was.

"Will you come away with me now, Karen?" he asked. "This is what I've stayed around for. As I've told you, I'm a rich man, with a great deal of wealth abroad. I've always wanted you as my wife."

Gwen squealed her outrage. "Davey—you're crazy! You know she's in love with that brother of yours! She's always been—just like you said. Only he's in love with her now too. Lori told you that."

He paid no attention to her outburst, but held my hands tightly, while his gaze never left my face, its intensity frightening. "You'll come away with me, Karen? We'll have a good life together abroad. We'll—"

It was unbelievable that he could be so blind, so wrapped in his own conceit. But knowing him, I knew it was so, and that I had to stop his words.

"Because you want to take one more thing away from Trevor?" I cried. "That's it, isn't it? Our marriage was never anything else but your need to pay Trevor off for being all that you aren't."

"Maybe that's why I value you so highly, darling."

"What about me?" Gwen wailed.

He glanced at her coolly. "I have plans for you. Just relax and I'll get to you soon."

I could see the dawning of fear in her eyes. Much too late.

"Don't worry," I told her. "You can go with him, Gwen. Because I shan't."

He had dropped my hands and now he moved quickly, crossing to the bedroom door. Just as he reached it the door was pulled open and he stood staring at the small figure in yellow oilskins framed in the opening. In equal astonishment Chris stared back at David Hallam.

I heard my own voice before I even framed the words in my mind. "Run, Chris! Go for help! Run!"

But it was already too late. David reached out with a rough hand, jerked Chris into the room and locked the door. When he had pocketed the key he stepped back to regard his captive.

"How did you get here?" he asked, his tone deceptively pleasant and mild.

Chris still gaped at his uncle as though he beheld a ghost. Always, in his effort to stay far away from the man on the island, he must have been too far off to recognize him. To say nothing of the fact that the clothes and hairpiece, and Chris's own mind, would automatically have furnished him with a mistaken picture.

Somehow he found his voice in the face of David's question. "Aunt Nona said Karen was going to the island. But she wouldn't let me come. So I took my bike and rode down here anyway. I was scared that Karen might be over here alone."

He glanced at me, and I tried to smile an encouragement I didn't feel. It broke my heart that Chris had come here on my account. This made the entire situation more frightful than ever. It was dreadful to think of Trevor's son walking into David's hands. I knew how little the blood relationship between David and Chris would mean.

"Go on," David said to Chris.

"Well—I just rowed across to the beach. The water wasn't too rough in the lee of the island. You—you aren't dead, Uncle David."

"As you can see, I'm not," David said. "I'm sorry there's no time for explanations now, but I'm glad you're here, Chris. You can be useful." He swung back to me, and though his tone continued calm, I sensed deep rage in him. "I suspected you wouldn't come with me, Karen, so I've made other plans. You and Trevor both owe me something, don't you think? Would you like to see the arrangements I've made? You too, Chris. You'll fit into them nicely."

The boy tried to squirm away when David grasped him by the collar of his yellow coat, but he was helpless in his uncle's hands as he was marched across the room. I could see David's paranoia clearly now. It had always been there, I suppose, though I'd never wanted to admit it. Now it had increased to a dangerous state where the things he himself had done were making fantasy real.

In desperation I looked about the room for some means of escape. We had to get away—Chris and I. We had to get away—somehow!

The huge fourposter bed, where Vinnie must once have slept with his Cecily, dominated the room. There was nothing there to assist me. The rest of the furniture was large and dark, and nowhere offered me a weapon. There was not even a poker standing beside the fireplace. Nevertheless, I mustn't panic. I had to fight David—for both Chris's life and mine. Only once did I glance at Gwen Bruen, to see her huddled and pale—and of no use to me.

"What are you going to do with us?" I demanded.

"This way, please." He gestured rather grandly and went ahead across the room.

When he flung open a door on the far side and beckoned, I saw again the turn-of-the-century bathroom that Lori had shown me the day she'd brought me here. As David had said, his plans had been carefully laid. I could smell the fumes at once—probably of kerosene—and icy terror ran through me. David's madness had to do with fire—always with fire.

"Don't go into that bathroom," I warned Chris.

But the boy had no choice. Held as he was in his uncle's

grasp, he couldn't free himself, though he fought all the way. In the end, David cuffed him roughly and then picked him up under one arm and carried him into the bathroom. Quite calmly, as I watched through the door, he took a length of nylon cord from a pocket and started to bind the boy's wrists together behind his back, ignoring Chris's kicking and struggling.

When I saw what he intended, I rushed at David where he knelt on the floor, pushing him, beating at him with my fists, trying anything I could to keep him from tying Chris up. It was useless. He struck me a blow that sent me reeling against the wall.

I stumbled back into Vinnie's bedroom, searching frantically for any sort of weapon. There was nothing. Not even something I could improvise with. I couldn't lift one of those heavy chairs to fling at him. Futilely I threw myself against the stout hall door, as I had done in Cecily's room, and it scarcely rattled.

Gwen had dissolved into utter terror and when I went to stand before her I knew it would do no good to plead for her help. All her earlier cheekiness was gone, and she had her own fears to deal with.

"I don't like fire!" she wailed. "I never wanted him to use fire!"

I turned away, and when David came for me, I too fought him as Chris had done, and it did as little good. He was even stronger than I remembered.

What was it Nona had said? That when one was weak, one used brains instead of brawn? But I lacked even a tiny rock with which to improvise against Goliath.

From then on everything began to happen as though I moved in a terrible dream. I scarcely felt the pain of being brutally handled, the cutting of the cord he knotted about my wrists and ankles. I existed only in my mind, seeking, searching. In the end, thoroughly bound, I gave up the physical struggle and went limp.

Once we were both bound he carried us in turn to the huge tub of rose-garnet marble that was almost as deep and wide as a swimming pool, and dumped us bruisingly into it. A marble tomb brought here from far away to hold us, I thought in anguish. This was a purpose that old Vinnie Fromberg had never envisioned.

Beside me, Chris lay facedown on cold, rosy marble, and I spoke to him softly.

"We'll get out. We have to get out."

He managed to roll on his side and I saw that courage had at last forsaken him. He was a small and frightened boy, with tears rolling down his cheeks.

Making an effort, I got to my knees so that I could look about the room. David had crossed my feet when he bound my ankles, so I couldn't stand. Kneeling, I could see a second door to the hall, but I was sure that it too would be locked. Above it an open transom offered air, cutting the dreadful fumes a little. High in one corner was a single window, closed, with rain streaming down the pane.

David stood watching us speculatively, his expression one of eerie pleasure. He noted my roving eyes. "That door is locked and there's no way for you to reach the window or transom. Anyway, I'll close the transom now. Kerosene fumes don't explode as gasoline fumes will. That's not what I want." He was using a stick to close the high panel of the transom. *"This time* that's not what I want. Don't worry—the gases in the smoke will put you out before the fire reaches you. Perhaps in all that marble you'll never be burned at all."

He spoke with a dreadful enthusiasm, as though the only thought he held in his mind was of fire itself. A monstrous thing had happened to him—something that had sent him across the line of sane reasoning. That he was talking about our *lives* seemed to impress him only in the sense that it gave him power. Yet all the while he looked entirely normal—excited, perhaps, but quite pleasant and happy. I again thought derisively of my wish to discover whether evil might be photographed in a face. I knew better now.

Desperately, I tried to think, to find a way to stop the horror that he intended. What little light shone into the room came from that high-placed window, against which the rain was beating, and the room was dim and dusky. The walls were of old-fashioned wood paneling. The toilet bowl was covered by a four-legged wooden chair with a wicker back and hinged seat. The washstand was a marble pedestal, again of rose-garnet, and there were gold faucets for the running water that must have been a luxury when the house was built. The floor had once been tile, but much of the surface was missing or broken, to show rotting wood beneath. It was a room made for burning.

However, it was the large hamper of woven basket strips placed in the center of the floor that held my attention. It was over this that he had poured the accelerant. On thin wooden strips of the lid had been placed a nest of soaked rags, and as I watched he took three small candles from his pocket. Innocent pink candles that should have graced a birthday cake—and held them up for me to see. There was something quite terrible about the delight in his eyes.

"I found these in the pantry downstairs. They're more suitable than bigger candles that would burn too long. You'll have about twelve minutes after I light them. Time enough for me to get to Joe's car down behind the house. My car now. I'll take Gwen along, so you needn't look to her for help. It's a shame that it's raining, since I'd like to see the whole house burn. But at least the interior will go. It's old, dry tinder."

I heard Chris moan as he wriggled closer to me, where I knelt staring over the high rim of marble. If only my arms were free, so I could hold and comfort him—comfort myself.

How delicately David pinched the tiny candles in his fingers, smiling as he pressed them one by one into the bits of rag on top of the hamper, coaxing them to stand. The candles would burn down quickly, the rags would catch and the entire soaked hamper would go up in a whoosh of flame. And after that the rotting wood of the floor, the walls. . . .

Beside me in the tub Chris was very still, staring up at David as though hypnotized by his own terror. The most dreadful sound I had ever heard was the striking of a match from the book David held in his hands. And the most dreadful sight was David's face at that moment when he lighted the first candle. He was mad—completely fire-mad. The little pink candles, with their flames burning to a height almost as great as their length, might have been the face of a loved woman—the way he studied them. But this was a terrible, unholy love.

He spoke without moving his eyes from the flames. "It's too bad, Karen, that it all has to end this way. But you had your choice. And perhaps this is best after all. It will hurt Trevor more this way—losing both you and the boy. Perhaps I'll stay down there under that window until I can see the flames at the glass."

The door shut gently after him, so as not to disturb the candles with a rush of air, and the key turned in its lock from the outside. In the other room I heard him speak to Gwen, heard her cry out in panic as he must have grasped her arm. Then they both went away and a second door closed and was locked.

Still I knelt on hard marble, searching the room in my desperate need. Vinnie—or Cecily—had liked mirrors. I had noticed how many there were the first time I'd seen this room. Now in every reflecting depth glass flames burned. A flicker of memory returned to me. Lori murmuring about a glass flame. So she too had seen a candle in a mirror in that dressing room before everything turned to fire.

I stared at the real candles. Already the wicks were long and black, the pink wax growing shorter. Chris stirred at my side and I bent to nudge him with my shoulder.

"Try to think, Chris. If I could just find a way to get out of this tub—"

The sides were straight and steep and slippery, and there was no way for me to get to my feet with my ankles crossed. The rim was too high for me to sit on and swing my legs over anyway, and the steps, the handholds, were of no use in my bound condition. Yet I must get over the edge—somehow.

"Help me," I said to Chris. "See if you can boost me up."

"How?" he wailed. "How can I with my hands tied behind me?"

My head ached from the smell of kerosene. Gray light that fell through the single high window had been brightened by myriad flames burning in every mirror. And above the hamper the three little flames that were not made of glass burned on. The wax had only a little way to go. Perhaps two or three minutes. And perhaps the rags would catch even sooner.

Fifteen

"Help me!" I cried again to Chris. "Try to wriggle up on your knees and get under me. Boost me up."

But terror had stupefied him. He wasn't even crying now.

I bent toward him. "Chris, remember the kudzu. Remember how you helped me then. You didn't run off and leave me, even though you were scared of the man on the island. Now you've got to help me again."

My words seemed to reach through his frozen state and intelligence returned to his eyes. He began to get the idea. Struggling, squirming, he used his shoulders, his body, his knees to fight the slippery tub and wriggled under me. Once on his knees, he could lift with his haunches, even with his arms that were bound behind him. He was a sturdy boy, and strong, for all his slight build, and with

311

his help I managed to hold to the edge of the tub with my chin, fighting for some sort of purchase.

The flames still burned brightly, but the three black wicks had begun to bend a tiny fraction. And all their counterparts in the mirrors were bending too—as though in some ghastly ballet. I saw what would happen. In the final seconds they would lean gently over into the kerosene—and that would be the end of everything.

Then somehow I was on the wide ledge of the tub's rim, wriggling like a fish on dry land, rolling myself into the air. I missed the steps and landed facedown on the floor beside the tub. All the flames in the mirrors danced with the shock of my fall. Most of my bones must be broken, I was sure, but I began to fight myself to my knees. Once there I could move painfully over the broken floor.

I mustn't strike the hamper. I mustn't knock over what was left of the burning wicks. The fumes in my face made me sick and dizzy, but my chin rested on the hamper's edge. I must blow gently, or I might tip the flames right into the rags below. I lifted my head, puffed my cheeks and blew. The three tiny flames trembled and went out with a puff, leaving trails of gray smoke rising from blackened wicks. My birthday wish was granted!

"Chris, it's all right!" I cried and fell over on the floor on my side and lay there, weak and entirely drained. How we were to get out of our prison and what David might do when no flames appeared at the window still remained unanswerable problems. But for this little moment we were safe from immediate threat.

Chris called out to me excitedly. "Karen, someone's coming!"

I listened intently, and far away in the house there were sounds. Was David already returning?

We held our breath, listening. There was the sound of

feet running on bare floors, pounding up the stairs. I heard fists banging on the door of Vinnie's room, and a voice calling. Trevor's voice. I screamed to him in response, and so did Chris, shouting at the top of healthy young lungs.

"We're locked in the bathroom," I called. "But we're all right. Break in the hall door!" And Chris shouted, "Break it in, Dad!"

"I'll be back!" he called to us, and again I heard him running on the stairs.

Then Maggie's voice reached us from the hall. "He's gone to get some sort of tool, Karen. We'll get to you soon. It's all right now, Chris."

In moments Trevor was back with a small ax from the kitchen and he attacked the locked door furiously. The moment he could break through he came in to us, and saw at a glance the death trap David had set.

"Chris first," I told him.

He picked up his son in his arms and carried him into the hall, where I could hear Maggie crooning over the boy. Then he came back for me, bore me out to where the air was fresher and knelt beside me, working at my bonds, as Maggie loosened Chris's.

"David's alive," I told Trevor when I found I could speak. "He's out there now—getting away."

"I know he's alive," Trevor said. "I saw him here on the island two days ago. I had my binoculars and I saw his face, but I couldn't get near him. I couldn't tell you right away, knowing what might lie ahead for you. That's why your story about Gwen didn't impress me. I knew it wasn't Joe Bruen on the island. And this time David had to be stopped."

"How did you get here to the house?"

"Nona sent me. She told me you were coming over here with Maggie to meet Gwen Bruen and I must go after you.

She had a time finding me, or I'd have been here sooner. She knew I would never have let you come, but that I'd follow once I knew. How did you get here, Chris?"

Chris told his father, while I pondered. So that had been what Nona was promising—that I wouldn't be hurt, because she meant to send Trevor after us.

He went on. "I met Maggie driving your car and she flagged me down."

"I've been a fool," Maggie said. "I failed you hopelessly, Karen. I ran away because I thought—"

"I know," I said. "You've been afraid all along that Eric was mixed up in this."

When my ankles were free, Trevor held me for a moment, and then I went to work rubbing my wrists and ankles, getting the circulation started again, painfully.

"David may still be out there," I told Trevor. "He's got Gwen with him. He said he was going to watch for flames from where he could see the bathroom window. So he'll be on this side of the house and he probably never heard you come up the drive in the storm."

"Then I don't think he'll get far," Trevor said. "The causeway is flooded. We barely got across in my heavy car. But I'll go and look for him. Stay right here."

Maggie and I looked at each other for an instant, and then she tore after Trevor. I had difficulty moving because of the shooting pains in my legs as the numbness went away. Nevertheless I stumbled after them, and Chris came with me. In moments we stood at the rear veranda rail beside Trevor, while wind and rain slashed over us.

David was there—as he had said he would be. He sat in his car—Joe's car—with the windshield wipers going. Gwen crouched fearfully beside him and they were both looking up through the glass toward the window high above, waiting for flames that would never come. I sagged against the rail, feeling sick with reaction.

He saw us then—saw Chris and me, alive and free, and Trevor and Maggie with us. Rage twisted his face, but now he knew his own safety was at stake. He opened the far door and pushed Gwen out into the rain, where she fell to her knees, splattered with mud as David stepped on the gas and swung the wheel mightily. The car jerked its way onto the weed-grown driveway that circled the house, its wheels squealing and the engine roaring as he headed for the road off the island.

Maggie and Chris and I ran with Trevor to where he had parked his car near the front steps. He knew it was useless to try to leave us behind. We went bumping over the same road, though not at the same wild speed David was attempting. Here and there we glimpsed his car ahead, the space between us growing.

He had rolled down his windows in spite of the storm, the better to see out and watch the edge of the causeway. He was already halfway onto it by the time we reached its approach, and Trevor braked his car. Under water that poured over it, the road across was invisible, except for white rapids where the causeway had been. Arcs of water curved up behind David's car as he plowed ahead—full into the center of raging currents.

We couldn't see him through his rain-swept rear window, but we saw the smaller car hesitate, buffeted by wind and water, until it tilted a little to one side. Then, almost as if in slow motion, it slid sideways, hovered for a second —and tipped gently over into the lake. Water poured in the windows and it sank slowly from view, tumbling over on its side. We sat in silent shock, watching.

"Stay here," Trevor ordered. This time we obeyed. He got out, leaning into the wet slash of the wind as he walked to the edge of the swollen lake.

Out there in the water nothing happened. There was

only a gray mass of tossing waves to be seen, with no car top visible, nothing human breaking the surface.

"Why doesn't he get out?" Maggie murmured. "The windows were open."

I spoke the words softly. "He can't swim."

Trevor heard me as he returned. "He was always scared of water. But nobody could swim in what's out there now. And there's no possible way to bring him up without machinery."

In the front seat Chris clung to me and now there was nothing to keep me from putting my arms about him and holding him close.

We waited for a little while longer, and then Trevor drove back to the octagonal house, where Gwen Bruen sat on the steps, waiting for us helplessly.

By sunset the storm had cleared. Trevor and I stood on the upper deck of his house, looking out toward Belle Isle. There would be no more fires. It was all over now, except the aftermath. Perhaps Maggie, her fear for Eric behind her, would paint something less tortured in her canvases. Giff I didn't know about. His struggle with his father would probably go on. Eric himself had never really been touched or deeply aware of all that was happening. Certainly not of his wife's fears.

The day just past seemed confused and crowded in memory. When we could get over the causeway we drove to where Maggie had left my car. Then I'd come back to the house with Chris and Maggie, while Trevor went for the police, taking Gwen with him. In the afternoon David's car was brought up from the lake bottom, his body taken in charge by the police. The questions, the explanations, were endless, and they weren't over yet. Unexpectedly Gwen Bruen pulled herself together and helped more than anyone else. I could only hope that she would get off with a light sentence. Her mistake had lain in loving David—as that had been Lori's mistake too. And mine, for deceiving myself. There would be difficult days ahead for all of us, but we would face them together, Trevor and Chris and I.

For me, David had died weeks ago and had been buried. I had been able to grieve then for a life wastefully lost. Now I felt nothing but shock over what the man who had been my husband had done. Only in these sunset moments, standing at the rail on the deck of his house, with Trevor's arm about me, could I come to life a little.

"I'm going to finish Belle Isle," he promised and I heard new hope in his voice. "I want to take you down there soon—I want to show you my plans."

I would go with him gladly, but I would not soon forget all that had happened on the island. Nor, I knew very well, would he.

Chris had come to stand beside us, and he smiled at me with love. There was so much we had shared. So much more than we'd had time to absorb and fully understand. Yet I knew that this was the beginning of a family—the three of us. I loved them both, even as a new aching began in me, and sorrow for wasted lives. David, Joe Bruen, Lori. Even Gwen. We who were left must now fight our way toward peace and healing.

For me I could only hope that when enough time had passed I would be able to close my eyes on quiet darkness in which no glass flame would ever burn again. For a long time I would want no lighted tapers in the rooms of any house in which I happened to live.

I leaned closer to Trevor and his arm tightened about me, as mine tightened about Chris. Belle Isle was fading to a dark shadow out there beneath the mountains, with only a last glow of sunset shining on the lake.

Like the shining of *fire*.

ABOUT THE AUTHOR

Phyllis A. Whitney is America's most successful writer in the field of romantic suspense. Her many top-selling novels include *The Turquoise Mask, Spindrift, The Golden Unicorn* and, most recently, *The Stone Bull*. Born of American parents in Yokohama, Japan, Miss Whitney has always been involved in the world of books —as bookseller, librarian, reviewer, teacher of writing, and bestselling novelist. Recently she served as President of the Mystery Writers of America.

FREE
Fawcett Books Listing

There is Romance, Mystery, Suspense, and Adventure waiting for you inside the Fawcett Books Order Form. And it's yours to browse through and use to get all the books you've been wanting . . . but possibly couldn't find in your bookstore.

This easy-to-use order form is divided into categories and contains over 1500 titles by your favorite authors.

So don't delay—take advantage of this special opportunity to increase your reading pleasure.

Just send us your name and address and 35¢ (to help defray postage and handling costs).

how it happened, or how you know about it."

"It was blackmail, of course. He was paying out plenty for his own safety."